THE
VOYAGE of the
FORGOTTEN

The VOYAGE of the FORGOTTEN

NICK MARTELL

This edition first published in Great Britain in 2023 by Gollancz
an imprint of The Orion Publishing Group Ltd
Carmelite House, 50 Victoria Embankment
London EC4Y 0DZ

An Hachette UK Company

1 3 5 7 9 10 8 6 4 2

A CIP catalogue record for this book is
available from the British Library.

ISBN (MMP) 978 1 473 22571 8
ISBN (eBook) 978 1 473 22572 5
ISBN (audio) 978 1 409 18428 7

Printed in Great Britain by Clays Ltd, Elcograf S.p.A.

MIX
Paper from
responsible sources
FSC® C104740

www.gollancz.co.uk

For my friends who were alongside me all this time.
To those I grew up with and no longer talk to.
To those who have walked down highways with me and
who know how to tie water balloons too well.
To those who I swam with, did stupid stuff with,
played games against, and all the other stories I can't write down.
Thank you all for everything.

DRAMATIS PERSONAE

KINGMAN AND ROYALS:

Michael Kingman:
    Middle child of the Kingman family.
    Bonded Kingman to Serena Hollow.
    Known titles: King Killer, Dragonslayer,
    Apprentice Mercenary of Orbis Company.
    Nullify Fabricator.

Gwendolyn Kingman:
    Youngest member of the Kingman family.
    Bonded Kingman to Adreann Hollow.
    Last location unknown. Presumed endangered.

Lyonardo Cityborn:
    Oldest child of the Kingman family.
    Bonded to the deceased Davey Hollow.
    Husband of High Noble Kayleigh Ryder.
    Blood Fabricator.

Juliet Kingman:
    Head of the Kingman family.
    Widow of David Kingman.

David Kingman:
    Known as "the Kingman Who Murdered the Boy
      Prince."
    Deceased.

Davey Hollow:
    The murdered boy prince. Former heir to the Hollow
      throne.
    Bonded to Lyonardo Kingman.
    Deceased.

Serena Hollow:
    The Queen of Hollow.
    Bonded to Michael Kingman. Engaged to Jay Prince.
    Force Fabricator . . . Why is it so weird to write notes
      about myself?

Adreann Hollow: Second in line to the throne.

Known throughout Hollow as "the Corrupt Prince."

Bonded to Gwendolyn Kingman. Recently married.

Metal Fabricator.

Isaac Hollow: King of Hollow.

Bonded to David Kingman.

Deceased.

HIGH NOBLES OF HOLLOW:

Charles Domet: An immortal asshole.

Known as "the Lifeweaver."

Connected to the Wolven Kings?

Kayleigh Ryder: Firstborn of the Ryder family.

Wife of Lyonardo Cityborn.

Kyros Ryder: Third born of the Ryder family.

Known as "Kai." Blind.

Currently apprenticing at the Institute of
   Amalgamation.

Sound Fabricator.

Joey Ryder: Youngest child of the Ryder family.

Mute. Inheritor of the Fire Dragon's heart.

Danielle Margaux: A High Noble from Michael's childhood that he's
   forgotten.

Eldest of the Margaux family.

Known as "Dawn" and "the Girl in Red."

Deceased.

Sebastian Margaux: New heir to the Margaux High Noble family.

Current location unknown.

RAVENS AND MEMBERS OF SCALES:

Efyra Mason: Captain of the Ravens.

Mother of Chloe Mason.

Naomi Dexter:	Former member of the Executioner's Division of Scales.
	Wind Fabricator.
	Apprentice Raven.
Chloe Mason:	Two-feathered Raven.
	Daughter of Efyra Mason.
	Lightning Fabricator.
Karin Ryder:	Three-feathered Raven.
	Second child of the Ryder family.
Rowan Kerr:	Four-feathered Raven.
Michelle Cityborn:	Five-feathered Raven.
Hannah Hyann:	Six-feathered Raven.
Katherine Naverre:	Former High Noble. Deceased wife of Angelo Shade.
Angelo Shade:	Foster father to Michael, Gwen, and Lyon.
	Former Commander of the Watchers in Scales.
	Current location unknown.

ORBIS MERCENARY COMPANY:

Dark:	Recruiter for Orbis Company.
	Known as "The Black Death."
	Son of Angelo Shade and Katherine Naverre.
	Considered to be a "Worldbreaker"-level threat.
Tai:	Commander of Orbis Company.
Imani:	Second-in-command.
Alexis:	Gun Master.
	Sister of Zahra, Dark's deceased fiancée.
Beorn:	Poison Master.
Haru:	Weapons Master.
Cassia:	Sailing Master.
Gael:	Explosives Master.
Otto:	Magic Master.
Jade:	Memory Master.
Nonna:	History Master.

REGAL MERCENARY COMPANY AND CLIENTS:

Jay Prince: Current primary client of Regal Mercenary Company.

                            Merchant Prince of New Dracon City and former
                               Skeleton.

                            Highly suspected that "Prince" is not his real last name.

                            Engaged to Serena Hollow. Connected to Angelo
                               Shade.

Papa Noble: Leader of Regal Mercenary Company.

                            Known as "the Butcher of Vurano."

                            Real name is unknown. Rumored to be "Vako."

Liam Noble: Youngest child of Papa Noble.

                            One of the four commanders of Regal Company.

Ciara Noble: Second-oldest child of Papa Noble.

                            One of the four commanders of Regal Company.

IMMORTALS AND OTHER CATASTROPHIC THREATS:

The First Wolven King: No known information. Presumed alive and dangerous.

The Second Wolven King: No known information. Presumed alive and
                               dangerous.

The Third Wolven King: No known information. Presumed alive and
                               dangerous.

Rian Smoak: Dragon Historian for the Church of the Eternal
                               Flame.

                            Immortal. Smoke and Beast classification.

The Archmage: Author and Master Surgeon.

                            True Immortal.

Emelia Bryson: Former leader of the Hollow rebellion.

                            Known as "the Emperor."

                            A former sacrifice. True Immortal.

                            Connected to Angelo Shade.

OTHERS:

Symon Anderson:	Known as "the King of Stories."
	Former Recorder for the Hollow Archivists.
Treyvon Wiccard:	"Big Brother" of the East Side of Hollow.
	Light Fabricator.
Jamal Wiccard:	Younger brother of Trey Wiccard.
	Deceased.
Sirash:	Michael's con-artist accomplice and former Skeleton.
	Real name is "Omari Torda."
	Current location unknown.
Arjay:	Sirash's younger brother.
Jean Lorenzo:	Sirash's girlfriend.
	Student at the College of Music.

THE STORY SO FAR

Michael Kingman is . . . is a man who is trying his best. Arrogant at his worst but loving when the crowds are thin. Some call him an obnoxious child with delusions of grandeur. Others a king killer. But I've only known him as my Kingman. My shadow. The man who had sworn never to leave me, yet did before I understood how uncomfortable a throne is. And, I suppose, that's all our story has ever been. A Kingman and Hollow trying to remain apart yet together.

I wanted to kill him a few months ago. Back when he was the primary suspect in my father's death. After all, Michael was seen, blood splattered and holding the gun that killed my father. How could it not be him? But it wasn't—and that accusation stuck, because no one wanted to admit the truth. We saw each other hours before my father died. Michael told me he was searching for one of his friends and I believed him. My grief clouded my thoughts afterward, when I wanted revenge. I wanted him to feel a fraction of the pain I experienced. So I declared war on him. Found a plot for him and dug a grave he could be buried alive in. And yet the fool persisted, swearing he would prove he was innocent.

I ambushed him, and he didn't fight back even when he could, almost giving me permission to kill him if I wanted to. He outran my Ravens when I ordered them to kill him. He attacked a Waylayer trying to assassinate me while I was performing as Red. He played gun roulette with me—and then left me a blubbering fool when I thought he was about to commit suicide. And then he hunted down the Heartbreaker Serial Killer in a matter of days to save my life. For all he has claimed to be or will be . . . that an imbecile like him turned his lies into reality will never cease to amaze me.

His title of Dragonslayer became a reality. Will his title of King Killer as well? Because I know of one king he's got his sights on. Especially after he kidnapped Michael's sister.

But I'm getting ahead of myself. After he killed the Heartbreaker, he did the worst thing possible: revealed that he'd had feelings for me since we were children, right as I was prepared to become a Forgotten to save the city from the rebel invasion. Thinking that I was about to die . . . I admitted I felt the same. And then we found out a Merchant Prince by the name of Jay had routed the rebels with Regal Company's help. All he wanted in thanks was for my hand in marriage, so that together we could restore Hollow to its former glory.

I did what I had to, and I accepted his proposal. I became the proper queen and suppressed the emotional girl who believed her Kingman was the only person who ever truly understood her. And yet . . . in a moment of weakness . . . I found Michael and just for a moment we stopped fighting our feelings, and we acted on them instead.

Love unacted on is always hollow like childhood crushes. It only blossoms when two people commit to it. When he kissed me, we were nothing more than buds desperately trying to survive till spring . . . and now here we are. Lovers who will never know peace, pulled apart by duty but bound together by fate. We share the same heart. The same rhythm. But you already know all of this, don't you?

So now that I've told you my version . . . will you answer my questions?

What are the names of the Wolven Kings? And why are they important?

And why does Michael Kingman think us being together will shatter Tenere?

———

Serena Hollow stared down the monster that had stolen her face, eager to learn more. This hole she found herself in was cramped and dark, more akin to ancient ruins than the back of the pantry where she had found the hidden entrance. Mirrors surrounded her, reflecting her face back at her from all angles. Some of them seemed more judgmental than others. Some kind. Some sad. And some seemed like they were from another life, in which she had chosen a different path. Those were the ones that hurt the most to look at. But, thankfully for her sanity, she focused on the monster in front of her. The thing that had offered her knowledge in exchange for information.

It wore her face and replicated her body perfectly. Identical in every way. Talking to herself was strange, but . . . there were other forms this monster could've taken that would have been worse. Plenty of others. At least she was used to being angry at her own face. All the mirrors in Hollow Castle had been covered for a reason: she hated the sight of herself.

"I don't know if you've given me enough to exchange for one of the Wolven King's names," it said, pacing back and forth. "I'd need more. A memory of yours, perhaps."

"A memory? Can you take memories from me? Or do you just want to see one?"

"I can take them," it said softly. "I'm a . . . connoisseur of memories. The perfect observer. I take people's memories, trade them to others, and watch my collection over and over and over and over again." It stopped suddenly and its eyes turned catlike. "You have something I crave. A perfect treat. One I'd trade for whatever you want."

"Anything?"

"Anything," it confirmed. "And all I want are two small memories from your childhood. Give me them and I'll give you the name of the third Wolven King. It's the most elusive one."

"Which memories?"

It crept closer as if trying to avoid scaring off a wild animal. "The first is a small one. Truly paltry in the grand scheme of things." Its hand, which seemed smoother than skin should ever be, grazed her shoulder. Lightning seemed to jump from its fingertips to her clothes. "I need the moment you first kissed Michael Kingman."

"It was when we were children," she said. "It was nothing. A foolish game. Even if our parents scolded us as if we had committed treason. I wasn't allowed to see him for a week. And while I was locked away in my room writing verses of penance . . . he had to stand outside in the blistering heat holding a bucket of water over his head. Another day was added to his punishment every time he dropped the bucket." Serena gulped back the painful memories bubbling in the back of her throat. "He was out there for nearly two weeks."

"Then you shouldn't feel bad about forgetting—"

Serena slapped the monster's hand away. "Don't try to manipulate me. Tell me why you want it. Then I'll decide."

"I want it," the monster drawled. "Because I think it will break you. Leave you unable to put love above duty. Care to prove me wrong? Think you'll still love Michael Kingman as much as you do, without that moment? The first moment of defiance is usually the hardest. But it gives you faith that you could do it again without the world ending."

Serena had never considered herself a prideful person. Her sense of duty had always made the weight of the crown hard to ignore. And pride and duty mixed as badly as chocolate and pickled plums. Pride had eaten away at her father's confidence until he became a hollow shell who couldn't see beyond his own failures. But, for once, Serena did have pride. That her love would not be so easily extinguished. They had come so far. Fought so many obstacles. Found each other when they were broken and begun to repair their lives together. Could forgetting a single memory really destroy the foundation of their love?

Forgive me, Michael, she thought. *But this will not be the end of us. I know it.*

"Take it," she said dismissively. "What's the other memory?"

The monster slid next to her, one arm around her shoulders, with a smile that made Serena's stomach lurch. "The other memory is even less important. I want a single memory of your brother, Davey."

PART 1:

DENIAL

30 DAYS UNTIL THE FINAL DEATH OF MICHAEL KINGMAN

"My death has been set in stone. As has yours.
But, sadly for us, we plug our ears and shield our eyes
hoping we can defy an unwavering, undefeated hunter.
I suppose that is the ignorance of humanity. That we believe
we can change what has always been."

—A conversation between a master and their apprentice, overheard
hours before the destruction of Vurano by Regal Company

68

CHASING SUNSETS

"I love you, Serena. Always have, always will."

The Queen of Hollow's glass goblet slipped out of her hand and shattered on the balcony floor. That wasn't the reaction I had been expecting, but it was better than being slapped. Or so I told myself, if only to make myself feel better. Saying I love you and getting silence in return was perhaps the most humbling thing I had ever experienced.

If my sister had been with me, Gwen might have smacked some sense into my delusional head. There were very few rules the Kingman family were expected to obey without question. Not falling in love with the Royal we were bound to protect might have been higher on the list than not killing them. But, I suppose, I had always been a slow learner. Hollow didn't know me as Michael dumbass Kingman because of my sparkling personality and sound judgment.

I felt like a child in a costume, picking at my fancy clothes as Serena stared at me, green eyes wide and lower lip trembling. She was beautiful any way I looked at her. From the freckles over the bridge of her nose and her braided auburn hair to her long pale blue dress and the black cosmetics she wore around her eyes. I wished I could be beside her for forever and a day.

Trying to deny it for so long was, perhaps, the greatest lie I had ever told myself. Finally telling her the truth was my attempt at rectifying that mistake.

"Are you going to say anything?" I asked, holding my left wrist. "I know I probably should have told you sooner—"

"We've spent every night together since that night!" she shouted. And then lowered her voice, trying not to attract any of the other guests' attention. "Why would you choose now to tell me? We're at Adreann's wedding!"

"Look," I said. "It's bad timing. I'm aware. But I had to let you know how I—"

"You run away whenever I try to talk to you about our relationship. Literally. You dove into a lake rather than talk about your feelings—let alone have a conversation that wasn't about Angelo, saving Gwen, or our duty. And now you want to tell me you love me? And that you always have and always will? Were you always this much of a dumbass or did you take one too many hits from Dark recently?"

"I was struggling to understand my feelings," I explained. "After what happened in Hollow, I was . . . I didn't know what to do. We're Kingman and Hollow. There are precedents we must follow." And there was the whole warning from Angelo, that if I stayed with Serena she would die. That our love could shatter Tenere. "Yet . . ."

"And yet," she repeated, turning away from me so her elbows rested against the balcony's railing. "And yet. And yet. And yet."

All of Vargo, her mother's city, was in front of us. Unlike Hollow, which showed the impact of many generations on the city, Vargo was too uniform to look natural. It was as if every hundred years or so the city was razed to the ground and built anew in whatever direction the current ruler desired. The current theme was sprawling, tall, and built around a shimmering pink lake with a palace in the middle of it. Every building was perfectly symmetrical, the flat clean architecture easily replicated hundreds of times. Past the city itself was a port bigger than the rest of the city, with more twists and turns and docks than the Narrows in Hollow. We could hear sailors shouting.

"We should have had this conversation a month ago," she said, when the silence became unbearable. "Not now. Not here. I've already accepted my fate. It's too late to change it."

"Serena," I muttered.

She swept the broken glass over the railing with the side of her foot. The pieces fell into the water below us like glittering shooting stars. "Michael, I've been in love with you for as long as I can remember. But I was a child then . . . and now I'm a queen. I must do what is best for Hollow. Regardless of my feelings."

"Do you really think Jay Prince is what's best for Hollow? He's in league with Angelo Shade!"

"I'm aware," she said icily. "I'm not a fool, but they'll try to get the throne with or without me on it. Adreann wants it now more than ever. Marrying that rebel bitch has only deepened his hunger. At least this way I can stand in their way and keep them in sight. I would not have let the engagement get this far if I thought Hollow was in danger, but I have something they need that I can barter with if things become truly desperate. Or do you not trust my judgment?"

"I do, but—"

"But nothing. This is how it is. How it must be."

I didn't respond, a thousand schemes and plans running through my head to set her free. But when she gave me a lingering kiss on the cheek, it felt like a final goodbye rather than a lover's embrace.

"You'll always be my Kingman," she whispered with a forced smile.

She returned to the celebration before I could reply, disappearing into the crowds of masked partygoers. I closed my eyes, letting the wind blow against my face, and then unclenched the hand around my left wrist. Where my palm had been, there were two letters in black ink over irritated red skin: *Es*. It was Serena's noble nickname. A tattoo I had just recently got to match hers of mine. It was meant to be romantic. Instead it was pathetic. I wrapped it back up in a bandage to hide my shame, donned my mask, and went back inside. There was no rest for a Mercenary. Not even a heartbroken one.

This party was no more threatening than any of the ones I had been to in Hollow. All that differed were the asinine rules everyone was forced to follow. And in the Gold Coast, nothing was held in higher esteem than one's mask. They were strictly regulated to show class, age, profession, and marital status. There were ten creatures to represent the ten families that originally made up the Vargo Clan: the rat, the dog, the shark, the snake, the monkey, the spider, the wasp, the eel, the cow, and the dragon.

Servants wore wooden masks of varying intricacies, indicating their own hierarchy, while guests were given simple colored masks based on where they were from. Mercenaries wore daemon masks. Gnarly things with obnoxious sharp teeth and horns. That was the only thing that made sense in this twisted new dance I had been forced to participate in.

I patrolled the party, one hand on the sword hanging from my hip, keeping an eye on Jay Prince and the noble siblings of Regal Company. Dark and Alexis were doing the same, while Titus was stationed in the kitchen to make sure nothing was poisoned. Meanwhile dear, sweet Cassia was being selfish, as usual. Rather than use her renowned abilities to help us, she had decided to continue reading the map she had been obsessed with throughout our trip to Vargo. It was old and brittle and written in a strange language that reminded me of the strange script I had seen in the Royal Crypts, but I had been unable to get a good look at it. Even with all the noise and festivity around us, she was studying it in one corner of the room.

Most of the party was focused on Jay Prince and he was kept surrounded, most feigning excitement about having a Merchant Prince engaged to their clan leader's daughter. As if they hadn't fought with Hollow against New Dracon City during the Gunpowder War. Their memories were fickle tonight.

Someone clinked a knife against their glass and drew everyone's attention. Erica Hollow stood on an elevated platform with Serena by her side. Erica Vargo looked nothing like Serena or Adreann—having a bigger forehead, a thinner body, and a bright blond braid of hair that went down to her shoulder blades. But her penetrating green eyes were the same as her children's. She wore leather pauldrons over a simple black shirt and trousers, a golden cape behind her, and three strips of white war paint over her right eye. In Vargo, the leader's goal was not to dress to impress, as it was in Hollow. It was to remind everyone who was in charge. Survival of the strongest was not a belief here, it was a daily practice.

"Dearly beloved, we are gathered here today to celebrate my son's wedding," Erica said overly sweetly. "It is a historic event that will unify many countries and wipe away decades of bad blood. Love can build bridges, especially when hate is all that's usually seen."

People didn't clap in Vargo, snapping their fingers in agreement instead.

"Sadly for us, my son is already celebrating their union with his new wife." Erica twirled her finger around the rim of her glass. "But, thankfully, my daughter and soon-to-be son-in-law are here. Jay Prince, would you join us onstage?"

Jay adjusted his coat and walked toward Serena and Erica. His black hair was kept short, his ears would have made an elephant feel self-conscious, and half of his face was covered in bone tattoos. When he reached Serena, he bowed deeply and then kissed her hand. I gritted my teeth and tried to remind myself of my duty rather than my hopes.

"Hollow has its own wedding rituals . . . as does Vargo and New Dracon City," Erica stated, putting her hands on Serena's and Jay's shoulders. "We wish to honor them all, but as of right now, we are quite . . . overwhelmed finding a way to do so. Therefore it has been decided to extend the engagement period."

Murmurs went through the crowd as my heart soared. Maybe there was still a chance I could stop Serena from marrying Jay. I had spent some time trying to figure out his connection to Angelo Shade, but there was nothing tangible to act on. All I knew was that they trusted each other completely. Dark wouldn't or couldn't confirm anything else. He liked keeping secrets too much.

"How long?" a rat-masked man shouted from the crowd.

"Thirty days," Jay said. "We hoped we could have the preparations complete by the end of the month, but we were both woefully ignorant of Hollow's strict laws and regulations for royal weddings. Prince Adreann's wedding only made matters more complicated."

Serena took Jay's hand. "Just as we were ignorant of how many of the Merchant Princes and High Nobles would feel slighted if they were not given enough time to attend. Vargo, for all its size, isn't even able to house all of them at the present moment. But in thirty days it will be. Or so we hope. We have builders working day and night."

"Does that mean you will be married during the upcoming solar eclipse?" a snake mask called out.

"Yes," Jay said, raising their intertwined fingers. "The astronomers even say that it will last half a day, giving us plenty of time to complete the full ceremony. It will be an unparalleled omen, befitting our legendary union." He smiled lovingly at Serena. "The skies above will stop, and learn what true love is."

I nearly gagged as others around me cooed and swooned at the handsome man's words.

As Jay and Serena answered questions, I felt a tap on my shoulder. It was Chloe. The one-eyed woman had two peacock feathers woven into her hair. She wasn't in her normal plate mail, had a decorative spear across her back, and had shaved the sides of her head and cut her hair into a neatly maintained black streak. No longer was she the fragile girl who would blow away in the wind I had met at the Shrine of Patron Victoria. She had morphed into someone capable of standing next to the Queen of Hollow.

"Can I steal you for a moment, Michael?"

I nodded and followed Chloe out of the ballroom and into a servant's hallway. It was cramped, but people were still able to pass us with covered and sparse plates, full and empty wineglasses, and everything else needed for a party. It all smelt wonderful, but for some reason I kept remembering the smell from the rebel attack on the Militia Quarter. Serena's rejection must've sent my mind to unfit places.

"Serena told me what happened before she took the stage," Chloe declared without fanfare.

Because of course she did. Fan-fucking-tastic. I crossed my arms. "Are you here to be my shoulder to cry on or something?"

"No," she said. "I'm here to make sure you don't do anything stupid. Until they're wed, you are the most dangerous man in Hollow. You do one wrong thing, and we could have a massive war on our hands."

"Angelo Shade would be offended to hear that. He's been trying to bring down Hollow for a long time," I mumbled. When she raised an eyebrow at me, I sighed and continued, "What do you think I'm going to do? Kill Jay?"

Chloe stared at me. "I wouldn't put it past you."

"I'm not a monster."

"You are a Kingman who thinks his Royal is making a mistake. Your ancestors are famous for doing whatever it took to stop them in a similar situation."

I played with my father's ring, always amazed how such a small thing could bring me comfort. If my father hadn't given it to me before his execution, would I even be here? Or would I have fallen for Angelo's schemes and lies?

"I am not my ancestors. What do you want me to . . ." I trailed off, the smell of sulfur distracting me again. People were shouting and screaming from the party, and it had been a while since any servants had crossed paths with us. "Chloe, I think—"

She was already running toward the ballroom door, slamming into it with her shoulder. It didn't budge. Smoke was coming in through the slit at the bottom, pungent and grey. Gunpowder smoke or fire smoke—we could hear people frantically pounding on the other side.

Chloe electrified her arms, shot lightning at the hinges, and then rammed the door with her shoulder again. It fell back into the room, smoke clouding our vision as people ran past us. They were all screaming, some of them without their masks. We pushed past them all and into the ballroom proper. The servants were swinging swords and aiming guns at Erica, Serena, Jay, and the other Mercenaries in the room.

Black tendrils slithered over the ceiling, periodically yanking someone upward until they slammed against something hard with a sickening snap or crack. Dark, as always, was a conductor of death, using his magic to control the battle around us as Alexis used her flintlock pistols to stop anyone from getting close to him. The noble siblings, the commanders of Regal Company, cut through friend and foe alike trying to join Jay, Serena, and Erica, though they didn't need their help, easily pushing back anyone who got close with Serena's Fabrications and Jay's bare fists. The only one not doing something to help was Cassia. She didn't even look bothered by the smoke in the corner of the room, still examining her antique map.

"Who are we fighting?" I asked as I punched someone in the jaw, sending them to the floor.

Chloe threw a bolt of lightning at a man with a gun, blasting him away from Serena and the others. "Does it matter? Stop anyone who gets close to them!"

Easier said than done. For every three people I knocked down or away, at least one was a civilian. And since it was impossible to tell who was who at a simple glance, I didn't feel comfortable enough using the sword attached to my hip. I may have done questionable things in the past, but so far I had only killed people who were unmistakably evil.

"Enough!" Serena shouted. "I'm ending this."

Everyone bowed before her, forced to their knees as an invisible weight pushed down on us all. The world around us was shaking as her Fabrications rendered any opposition futile. She was a titan among us mortals.

I nullified my body as quickly as I could—the only other person in the room who wasn't on the ground. But then something happened. Serena blinked and everything stopped—the screaming and sobbing, the gunfire and clang of metal, the inhale and exhale of deep breaths. A silence that lingered in the depths of all our lungs. The world darkened around us as my skin prickled. All I could see was her, but something was wrong. It was like being in a dream, only to discover it was a nightmare all along.

Serena looked at me, visibly confused. Her confidence and poise disappeared in a moment. "Who—"

A bullet hit her, and I screamed as Serena fell.

SPILT INK

I embedded my sword into the man who shot Serena. He died with a whimper, transfixed on the floor with wide eyes, clawing at the ground as Dark, Alexis, and the noble siblings dealt with the fools still brave or stupid enough to fight. Anyone that wasn't part of the attack was gone before the blood stopped flowing through the cracks in the tile.

Serena was whisked away by Jay, Erica, and every Raven in the room before I had a chance to approach her. The noble siblings dragged off any surviving attackers as I sat on the elevated platform Serena had been on, wondering if the woman I loved would still be alive by dawn.

I was drinking from a half-empty bottle of wine when Dark found me. "I have a job for you."

I must have sounded sour and pungent. "What can I do for you, master sir?"

"Enough of this pity party you're having," Dark sneered. "Did *you* get shot?" He patted my chest with heavy hands. "No wounds? Didn't think so. So swallow your feelings and get to work. We're Mercenaries. We have a job to do."

"You were willing to commit genocide to avenge Zahra. I don't even get a few minutes to compose—?"

Dark eyes flashed red. "Oh, I'm sorry. Did I miss the announcement about your wedding? Or you requesting your final contract to get out of Orbis Company? Or any other slightly healthy aspect of your relationship that wasn't you pining after someone you could never be with?"

I nearly spat something vicious back at him. But instead I put the empty bottle down and rubbed my brow. Dark was a prick, but he was right. This wasn't helpful. And this wasn't me. I was not an observer. When I wanted something, regardless of what it was, I acted. And I can't believe I had forgotten that—if even for a moment.

"What do you need me to do?" I asked, my voice steady.

"That's better," Dark said. "I need you to find Titus. He was stationed in the kitchens but he didn't come out here when the fighting started and that's not like him. Assuming he's not dead, tell him I want him to know what happened to the real staff—our attackers were all impostors."

"Do we even know who attacked us?"

Dark shook his head. "They didn't say anything first, which makes me think they're not the Hollow rebel remnants. They've never turned down an opportunity to speak to a crowd before. Our best clue is the leader who began the assault. He got away—injured—but Alexis followed a trail of blood he left behind. Once you're done with Titus, help Alexis. We can't let that man fall into the hands of Regal Company."

"I'll get it done. What about her?" I nudged my head toward Cassia, who remained in the corner with her stupid map. There were bodies at her feet, and she just kicked them away. "Does she get a job? Or is she going to keep doing whatever she wants?"

"Do you need to know what I'm doing?" Dark asked. "Because I didn't tell you. Or do you just assume that I'm doing something important?"

I didn't respond, playing with my father's ring instead.

"Now you decide to shut up." Dark bared his teeth. "Listen. Cassia is a bitch. We all know that. But she doesn't do things unless they're important. She's as lazy as she is smart. It's better if you just let her be, or at the very least ignore her. Else you'll spend every mission you're on with her frustrated. Understand?"

"Perfectly." I kicked away the bottle of wine and it fell, wine mixing with the blood on the floor. "Where should we bring the leader once we find him?"

Dark looked around and said nothing. His eyes lingered on the noble siblings still in the room. "Alexis will know. Just make sure that asshole is still breathing when I get there."

"I'll need a weapon I'm familiar with to guarantee that."

"You have one." He gestured to the sword in my hand. "Or are you claiming you've forgotten how to wield it?"

I tossed the sword to the ground with a sharp clang. "Something like that. Give me a revolver."

Dark didn't laugh like I expected him to. "Why would I do that?"

"Because I'm better with it than I am with a sword. Or do I need to remind you what happened with the Heartbreaker?"

Without speaking, Dark undid the holster across his chest and handed it and the gun to me. This revolver had fewer marks on the bone grip handle than Dark's and the metal still gleamed even when it wasn't recently shined. Likely the result of having spent a decade in a box rather than being carried around by Dark and acquiring a second skin of blood and grime. It had been used to kill both Davey and Isaac Hollow, and in the time since Dark had acquired it I had affectionately nicknamed it Kingkiller. Kingmaker was the name of the other one. Dark hated both nicknames.

"How many bullets are in it?" I asked as I strapped the holster around my waist.

"Three. Try not to use them all. They're hard to get."

"Ever going to tell me where they come from?"

"Maybe in a decade," he said. "Call it leverage, in case you ever get ideas about putting a bullet or two in my head."

I laughed. "You really think I'd need more than one?"

"You really think I'd go down with only one?" His face was expressionless. "Now, get to work."

"Dark," I said as he began to walk away from me. "Is Serena going to survive?"

He didn't look back at me. "Jay Prince and Regal Company have more experience with gunshot wounds than I do. She's in capable hands." He hesitated. "I hope she survives, murdering hundreds of people to avenge her would be a waste of my time. Especially when dragons still plague this world."

"How many are still out there?"

Dark didn't respond, walking out of the room over bodies and through pools of blood without hesitation. No matter how far I fell, or what mistakes I made . . . at least I wasn't him. I still had my humanity.

Titus was in the kitchen, sprawled out on the ground drooling and snoring like a sleeping bear. There were half a dozen servants who had been stripped down to their underwear around him and left sprawled in a pile on top of each other. It was by far one of the weirdest scenes I had ever stumbled upon. Especially since Titus had been knocked out while eating, a greasy piece of chicken hanging out of his mouth as his fingers rested on the bone. At least he looked happy.

"I tried waking them up," Naomi said as she approached me from behind. "But nothing worked. Pretty sure they've been drugged."

I put my hand on her shoulder, giving it a squeeze. I would never have thought that the ambitious and cruel girl who had tried to set me up for treason would become a friend. But after everything we had gone through together, it was hard to be anything but close.

Naomi wasn't dressed like the other Ravens and lacked the peacock feathers tied into her hair—only joining them on a trial basis at Chloe's insistence. Ever since she had dropped her Blackberry habit, she smiled a lot more. Except for right now. Right now she was very angry, her electric blue eyes sharp and vibrant.

"How'd this happen?" I asked. "Titus is supposed to be one of the best at detecting poisons in food."

"Wasn't in the food," Naomi said. She held out her palm. There were little black seeds amidst scattered ash, cracked in two so the white centers were visible. "They're called Night's End. They're a common sleep aid, and practical joke, in Hollow. Nobles sometimes use them when they don't want to entertain guests any longer. Tossing a handful into the fire releases an oxide that puts people to sleep for an hour or so. The more they use, the stronger the effect. The antidote is commonly available, and so long as the poisoner took it, they wouldn't fall asleep themselves. It's much more effective than food, which not everyone eats. These ensure everyone gets knocked out."

"Sneaky."

"Hollow is the farthest east they grow," she added. "Someone would have had to import them specifically." She threw the seeds onto the ground and then wiped her hands clean on her trousers. "Could the Andels have been responsible for this attack? They have a grudge against Serena."

I shook my head. "My ma has been tracking the Andels since they ran away. Most of them sought refuge in the Thebian Empire, though Roberta Andel went to Goldano. Ma would have mentioned it if any of them was headed to the Gold Coast."

"Could other nobles still be working with the rebels? Even though the main army has been routed?"

"They still hold Naverre," I said. "And we know Emelia is still alive, no matter what they say. I have to help Alexis find the leader before anyone else does. Can you join us or do you have somewhere you need to be?"

"I don't. But . . ." Naomi gestured at the snoring pile of bodies. "Shouldn't we wake them up before moving on?"

I shook my head. "Night's End wears off in time. And they're safe enough here." After scribbling a quick message to Titus to explain what was going on whenever he woke up and covering up the naked staff with tablecloths, we went off in search of the person responsible for leading the attack against Serena.

—————

We found Alexis in one of the palace's main gardens, gun in one hand as her other rested on the bark of a tree that was too tall and branchless for me to easily climb. And yet the man we were chasing had found a way and was still in the tree, the leaves far above us were moving unnaturally, and his blood dripped down like a drizzle of rain. If we didn't get to him soon, he was in danger of passing out . . . and if he fell and it killed him, Dark would be annoyed.

"Up there?" I asked as I went to Alexis's side. Naomi went to guard the entrance to the garden to make sure no one could bother us. She might not be a Raven, but she had the influence and respect of one thanks to Chloe's support.

The Azilian Mercenary nodded, eyes transfixed on the top of the tree like a cat. She was as gangly and awkward as any other sixteen-year-old—but had stark white hair that rested above her shoulders, a nauseating sulfur and iron stink embedded into her skin, and more pistols strapped to her body than necessary.

"Any idea how to get him down?"

Alexis reached into a pocket and pulled out strips of salted meat, handing me one. It was hard and splintery, but I had learned to eat whenever I had the chance, so I wolfed it down without complaint. "Did Dark want him alive?"

I nodded, still chewing.

Alexis made a strange noise with her tongue. "Shame. I was thinking fire."

"Not sure if the Vargo clan would like us setting a fire in their palace right after they've been attacked."

"Likely not." Alexis paused as she glanced at the gun at my hip. "How good are you with that? We could shoot them."

"Only have three bullets," I said rather loudly. "Have you tried talking to them? Maybe they'll come down when they realize they're surrounded, and they're more likely to survive talking to us than to Regal Company. They'll probably skin them alive. After a lot of torture. I can't imagine Papa Noble would miss the chance to yank the nails off someone."

Without missing a beat, Alexis said, "Papa Noble likes boiling his victims alive in a large pot and then feeds the remains to the local wildlife. I've always wanted to see how he—"

Something landed in front of us with a thunderous crash. Birds in nearby trees cawed and flew away as the dust settled. It was a body—a young man covered in bruises and dirt but dressed in finer clothes than the party had warranted. There was a symbol on his lapel: a tight whirlpool. High Noble Margaux's insignia. Which meant this was . . .

"This is High Noble Sebastian Margaux," I said. "Are you sure he began the attack on Serena?"

Alexis nodded. "I don't make mistakes. Besides . . ." Alexis lifted his shirt to expose the gunshot wound on his side. Sebastian winced and groaned but did nothing to stop her. "Should I dig out the bullet? Or will you take my word that it'll match that revolver?"

I had learned enough in the past month on the road that there were better odds of me not being born a Kingman than of both Dark and Alexis making a mistake. Alexis was too starved for positive reinforcement from Dark. She would rather get hurt than let him down, unless it concerned her deceased sister whose memory and legacy she worshipped the way devouts did God. And Dark had become even more paranoid and tactical after what happened with the Heartbreaker. Sebastian Margaux was the traitor we were looking for.

"What should we do with him?" I asked.

Alexis didn't answer me, binding Sebastian's wrists and ankles with ropes she pulled out of her pockets. Then she gagged him so he couldn't do much besides grunt. After, she checked his wound, quickly determining that a bandage would do for now.

"We have to get information out of him, don't we?"

Alexis nodded as Dawn's stepbrother squirmed on the ground, snorting and shouting muffled things at me, finally finding renewed life. Could I really torture him after what had happened to Dawn? After she had died protecting me?

"Want me to get Titus?"

I gulped back the bile. "No. I'll do it. Tie him to that tree. I'll start whenever he's ready."

Sebastian's eyes went wide, and he struggled even more than before. As Alexis got him ready, I prepared myself—both mentally and physically. I made sure the revolver Dark had given me was loaded, sharpened a few sticks to fine points, and I had a spare vial of gunpowder . . . in case terrible things had to be done. Until I knew who Sebastian was working with, I would do what was necessary. No matter the toll on my sanity.

Maybe Dawn would understand. Wherever that door of light had taken her.

When Sebastian was prepared like a hog before the slaughter, I slid the gag out of his mouth so it rested around his neck. He tried to bite me, but Alexis grabbed his head and held it still. It wasn't the best way to start an interrogation or prove his innocence.

"Sebastian, do you know who I am?"

He spat in my face, which answered my question. As I wiped it away, I said, "I'm going to ask you a few questions. If you answer them truthfully, your odds of getting out of here unharmed will increase. Do you understand me?"

"Murderer," he hissed. "You killed my sister."

The words struck something primal in my heart, and I almost slammed his head against the tree. Instead, I bit down on my tongue so hard, it bled. I swished some water from a bladder into my mouth and spat until I couldn't taste iron anymore.

"I did not kill Dawn."

"Just because you didn't rip out her heart doesn't mean you weren't responsible. What happened in that throne room that you're hiding?"

I gritted my teeth. "I'm not the one being asked questions here—you are. Did you organize this attack?"

"Yes."

"Who helped you?"

"Remnants of the Hollow rebellion and friends in high places."

I clenched my fists. "Why did you do this?"

Sebastian laughed, and it caught me off guard. "I went in search of God when Dawn died. Tried to find meaning in my grief. I found you talking to God in an abandoned church instead." My eyes shot open, but he continued to laugh. "No one was supposed to overhear you, right? Well, I did. And your words helped me make some new friends."

"'New friends'?"

The madman laughed and laughed and laughed.

"Fine, don't tell me. But if you were angry at me, why attack Serena?"

"She was the only one they were concerned with! She could clip their wings so *easily*. The attack was a way to take her out of the fight. I was just the appetizer."

"Sebastian, what are—"

Alexis cut me off by drawing two of her guns. I held my own, turning to see the threat. One of the four noble siblings of Regal Company dragged Naomi into the garden with a dagger held to her neck. Another had a spear and net in their hands. The wind rustled the tree leaves as we all stood frozen in place. So much for getting Sebastian out of here without incident.

"Sorry to interrupt," said the Mercenary holding Naomi hostage. "But we'll be taking that pig from you now."

CARTOGRAPHY LESSONS

Naïvely, I had thought Dark was the worst Mercenary I would ever meet. That he was the rock bottom when it came to morality . . . killing or maiming anyone that delayed his revenge. He was even willing to commit genocide to do it. But I had been wrong. Dark was a monster . . . there was no doubt about that . . . but even he paled in comparison to the four noble siblings of Regal Company. Dark did what he had to. On the road to Vargo I had seen them do and say unspeakable things just for shits and giggles. And now they had a dagger to Naomi's throat. Potential Raven be damned, they'd murder her without a thought for the consequences. If there were any. Only Mercenaries could take other Mercenaries to court, and who would be stupid enough to challenge one of the biggest companies?

Sadly, only me.

"Let her go," I ordered, grip steady on the revolver.

Liam Noble, the Mercenary with the dagger, smiled, showing the gap where his front teeth should have been. He was muscular and tall, with Goldani skin and hair and violet eyes—the only trait common to all the siblings. Their father—astonishingly—was even worse than his children, and each of them had a different mother. At least two of them were some of the strongest Fabricators Dark had ever seen, even rivaling his skills.

"I don't have to be the bitch who says that's only happening once you hand him over, right?" Ciara said, gesturing at Sebastian. She was slender and snakelike, smooth muscles hidden in plain sight. Her hair was blacker than the sky above us and her eyes as wide as a cat's. There was no way to tell where her mother was from or if she was one of the Fabricators I had been warned about.

"Orbis Company has the right to detain him as we see fit," Alexis said.

"Do you really think we care about who's in the right here?" Liam countered. He licked his lips, which was a lot grosser an act than I remembered. "That pig attacked Jay's beloved. Now hand him over before we kill this woman."

"Did Jay give you these orders?" I asked.

"No. We're acting on our own." Ciara tilted her head to the side, twirling the spear in her hand. "Nice try."

So much for holding someone accountable if this all went to shit. Mercenaries could only be held accountable for whatever deplorable things we did by our leadership council. Jay could be, since he wasn't a Mercenary, but if he hadn't authorized this attack . . . that plan was useless.

Naomi kept scowling at her captors as the wind around us began to pick up, blowing the leaves off nearby trees and sending floating seeds through the air. Just out of sight, people were running around and shouting, but as the noises slowly got closer to us, we all wondered who would start this inevitable conflict.

Ciara did. She leapt from her spot like a cat, claws replaced by nearly invisible knives between her fingers. Like a fool, I aimed my gun at her, prepared to shoot . . . only for a branch from a nearby tree to wrap around my wrist and yank it back. The revolver flew out of my hand and skittered across the ground, out of reach, as Ciara landed on top of me, forcing me to the ground and trying to embed her knives in my chest. Only luck, and the fact Alexis was shooting away any branches that tried to ensnare me, prevented her from succeeding.

One of them was a Weaver. Thankfully for me, I had seen one before. As I struggled with Ciara, I concentrated the warmth over my body before *expelling* it outward. The branches stopped moving and the wind died down instantaneously. Both would now know I was a Nullify Fabricator—if they didn't already. But as Liam gave me a bloody sneer, I knew who the Wood Weaver was. Physical pain allowed Weaving, while memory loss allowed Fabricating. It was one of the few rules about magic in this world I was confident about.

"Ciara. Liam. Enough."

Ciara rolled off me, suddenly turning meek. Liam let Naomi go, shoving her away as a man approached us. He was thin and short, ribs likely visible beneath his shirt. His skin looked cracked, as if he had scales, and his teeth were inhumanly white. Much like Angelo Shade, there was no way to tell where he had been born, and if it weren't for his violet eyes, I wouldn't have been able to determine anything about him. But considering only two of the noble siblings had traveled with us to Vargo—the other two were back at their headquarters near New Dracon City—there was only one person this man could be: Papa Noble, the leader of Regal Company and known throughout the world as the Butcher of Vurano.

"Children," he said, waving off a stick of incense as he strolled into the moonlit garden. He reeked of jasmine and sandalwood. "Behind me. Now."

They did as they were told, scurrying away like rats as Papa Noble put his hands in his jacket pockets and blew out a plume of white steam. "I apologize for my children. They are so used to fighting, they sometimes forget there are other solutions."

I didn't respond, making sure Naomi and Sebastian were behind Alexis.

"That man," Papa Noble said as he pointed at Sebastian, "led the attack against Queen Serena Hollow, yes?"

Alexis spoke before I could. "We have reason to believe so."

"His name?"

After only a slight hesitation, she answered, "High Noble Sebastian Margaux."

Papa Noble let out a long sound of realization, still staring at the moons in the sky. "High Noble Sebastian Margaux . . . His stepfather is Antoine Margaux, his mother is Camille Margaux, and his sister was Danielle Margaux . . . who just recently died, yes?"

My eyes gave away the answer, and we all knew it.

"The Low Noble families directly under them are the Rerio family, the Fargo family, the Larr family, the Nero family, and the Maro family. Currently, they have thirty-seven servants working for them in their keep. Excluding the seventy-five house guards." He stopped to clear his throat. "High Noble Sebastian Margaux's closest friend is a Low Noble named Alexi Nero, who he sees rarely now he's been conscripted into Prince Adreann Noble's Throne Seekers. And I think that Alexi was just recently wed to a harpist named Felisi." Papa Noble finally looked at us with his violet eyes. "Sebastian missed the wedding. What a shame."

"Are you trying to intimidate us?" I croaked out.

"No, Michael Kingman . . . I am not." He took a deep breath. "I am telling you what I know about High Noble Sebastian Margaux . . . and who I will kill if he is not handed over."

My entire body froze at this casual threat. Luckily for me, Alexis replied, "Orbis Company has the right to hold and detain High Noble Sebastian Margaux while Queen Serena Hollow is in recovery. We were tasked with her protection, and if she dies, we are responsible to identify those who harmed her. Regal Company was only here to protect Jay Prince, and since he was not harmed, you have no right to take—"

"No right?" Papa Noble interrupted in barely more than a whisper. "Our client was emotionally harmed. For this, we demand satisfaction."

"Not before we get ours," I said, courage finally returning.

Papa Noble stared right through me as if I were an ant beneath his feet. No one, not Dark or Domet or even Jay Prince, had looked at me like that. It made me feel like an observer to history rather than someone who could dictate his own fate.

"So be it," the Mercenary said. "If Queen Serena dies, you may keep him. But if she doesn't . . . I expect him to be delivered to the theater we're using. Or I will be forced to come get him myself." He turned to Alexis. "Make sure Cassia is aware of what transpired here. I suspect she will be more . . . forthcoming with my—"

Bells rang out from all directions. Frantic. Manic. Overwhelming. A system meant to warn and protect, suddenly used like a weapon. They never stopped. Nor did they sound like a warning about an incoming piece of Celona. This was a new a signal for certain disaster that would scare even the firmest skeptic into looking at the skies.

"Is this . . . ?" I trailed off.

"No," Papa stated. "Not us."

"*Finally.* They're here. I was wondering when they'd show." Sebastian beamed from his place against the tree. "I'm not the only family you and Dark hurt, Michael. We banded together to take our revenge."

High Noble Margaux pointed upward, where six shadowy figures hovered above the city. Each was a different color, size, and shape. Some were twisty and long like a babbling brook, while others were fat and stout like a thick slab of iron. They blocked out the moon and stars with their wings, plunging us into near-perfect darkness. A perpetual gloom fit to become a culling field.

The beast in the middle of the group stared at me. His body was big enough to block out Celona and Tenere before he spread his veiny bat-like wings. He had muddled silvery-black scales layered over his body like armor, a mouth full of pointy teeth, a tail that swayed back and forth in the air like a serpent, two bright red eyes returning my gaze, and a jagged scar on his neck from where I had shot him. I hadn't seen Rian's true form back in Hollow but had dreamed of it in the many months since our last encounter. It didn't disappoint.

Alexis, Naomi, and the Noble siblings gaped at the sky. Only Papa Noble seemed unfazed. Like a playwright watching the tomatoes thrown after a bad performance.

The days of myths and legends were over. Replaced with the truth that we are small in the grand scheme of things. Insects struggling to avoid being crushed by those that tower over us. And yet, I *smiled*. The sight of them made me feel alive. I wasn't an embodiment of vengeance, but I needed a good excuse right now to forget my heartbreak.

"Fitting they came here, isn't it? We're at the end of the continent." He laughed some more. "And do you know what cartographers used to write at the edges of the map?" Sebastian asked. *"Here be dragons."*

65

THE VIEW FROM THE TOP

"Liam!" Papa Noble screamed. "Cover us!"

The six dragons fired on us in unison, beams of different elements coming out of their mouths that conjoined into a multicolored blast of destruction. Liam slid across the gardens, then slammed his hands against the ground. Roots from nearby trees and plants shot out of the ground, weaving together into a thick dome that covered all of us. Everything shook as the dragons' blast pummeled it, but Liam's wooden fort held strong. All he had to do was dislocate more and more of his fingers to keep it going.

"Michael! Alexis!" Papa shouted. "Do you know the law of conscription for Mercenaries?"

We nodded. It allowed high-ranking Mercenaries to command Mercenaries from other companies if a world-ending situation occurred. It hadn't been used since the devastation of Goldano a hundred years ago. But now it seemed appropriate.

"Then consider yourself a part of Regal Company until further notice.

Listen to me carefully." Papa Noble scowled, but then added, "This does not affect our agreement about Sebastian Margaux. He'll be your captive as we previously agreed. We've got bigger things to deal with right now than who has the greater right to kill him."

"Thank you," I said.

He gave me a curt nod. Not respectful, just affirmative. "Liam, how long can you hold our cover for?"

"As long as you need me to, Papa!" There was a sickening snap as he bent his pinky finger at a right angle. "These dragons don't scare me!"

"They should," Papa muttered. "Where are my Mercenaries? We should have some covering fire laid down on them by now. Those slackers better—"

Fifty cannons went off one by one around us. The dragons' combined beam stopped, and Liam's tree cover melted away as the vines grew limp and lifeless, leaving the noble sibling clutching his mangled hands. The dragons wove through the air above us, dodging and ducking and batting back several of the cannonballs with their tails. Palm trees were snapped in half as iron balls flew through them before colliding into nearby shrines, pavilions, and halls. Bits of the palace blew away, rocks toppling into the pink lake around it. It wasn't long before white smoke covered the scene as I listened, with Alexis, Naomi, and Sebastian, for the crescendo of cannon fire to cease.

Yet Papa Noble stood in the middle of the gardens, arms crossed, waiting.

"Again!" he commanded.

The fifty cannons fired again. Blasting iron balls through the sky at the dragons flying above us. But the plan was useless, the cannon fire didn't strike. Dragons played by different rules than us ordinary mortals.

"Anything that's not been nullified will go through them!" I shouted amidst the cannon fire. "They're Spellborn! Their bodies are made of their elements! Iron balls won't hurt them!"

"I'm aware of that!" he snapped back. Ciara was carrying her brother under a nearby awning. "I hate fighting dragons. They're all glorious cheaters. But this isn't going to end like it did in Goldani, Kureye! You hear me! I'm winning this time!" He cracked his knuckles. "Michael, can you nullify the area? Or is it too large for you?"

"Too big!" I hesitated, glanced at Naomi, who knew what I was thinking and shook her head, and then said to Papa Noble, "Can you get me closer?"

Papa Noble gave me a toothy smile and then whistled. Two Mercenaries who could have masqueraded as giants emerged from the smoke, stood next to Papa Noble, and then squatted down slightly so all three pairs of their hands were bundled together. Their muscles hardened; metal Fabricators. Thanks to them my launch would be well beyond normal limits. I might touch the clouds.

"I'm not catching you, Michael!" Naomi said to my left.

"Yes you will." I took a deep breath. "You always do."

Naomi grumbled something that was lost in the roar of various dragons overhead. It was funny when she tried to pretend we weren't the closest friend the other had.

I slapped my thighs, picked up my revolver, nullified my body, exhaled, and backed off through the gardens. Two dragons must've seen me through the smoke, as a concentrated beam of light blazed in front of me while multiple strikes of lightning hit, leaving craters of blackened grass and endless thunder booming around me. But then I was running, got a foot into their hands, and was launched skyward like a bullet out of a barrel. And, to my surprise, *dozens* of other Mercenaries joined my suicidal flight from various parts of the palace.

"Fly, my children! Whoever brings me a dragon's head will earn a place at my side!" Papa Noble shouted from the ground. "Kill the myths you grew up on! Show them we are the new nightmares of this world!"

I flew up through the smoke, everywhere, and then there was a moment when I was floating, no longer going upward but not yet falling. Dragons swam all around me, moving sluggishly as my mind slowed to comprehend what was happening. I was *way* above the palace and Vargo, able to see its beauty. The way the nearby hills sloped or how the streets almost resembled an endless snake from above. Even the stars seemed close enough to touch and claim. The Mercenaries in the skies with me were fighting with whatever they had—Fabricating, Weaving, crossbows and flintlock pistols, and hooks with long metal chains. Five of them boarded a long, skinny dragon that had lightning crackling over its body as if they were pirates raiding a merchant's ship. The sky was alight with hundreds of lights and sounds like a painting that had been haphazardly splattered with every color imaginable.

This was not how our fathers had waged war. With their tidy lines of shields and spears advancing cautiously, honorable duels between knights in plate, or even tactical nautical battles. This was chaos, a magical conflict of the kind that existed only during the Wolven Kings' reign. Mercenaries attacked with magic, gunpowder, and whatever else they could think of. Logic thrown aside for pure animalistic dominance. But to kill our myths, to take back our fate from the immortals who sought to dictate our future . . . us mortals had become something else. Were we daemons? No. We were nothing more than children who had dreamed of flying through the skies finally having the chance to do so.

Because there wasn't a body in the sky who wasn't having the time of their life.

Amidst the chaos, I slowly fell back down toward the ground. Assuming, of course, the three dragons below me didn't decide they needed an after-dinner snack of raw Kingman and delay my impending splatter.

"Kill the Kingman before he can nullify the area!" Rian roared as he bucked two Mercenaries off him.

I smiled, stretched my body out as wide as it could get to slow my fall—Wind Fabricators helped, from above and below—and then aimed for the stocky dragon that looked like it wore a suit of armor. It was slower than the others and would be perfect to land on. I twisted my body, rolling out of the way of the jaws of the dragons that tried to claim me. Then my nullified hands grabbed one of the metal dragon's spines. I held on firmly as it twisted and tried to shake me off, screaming like a madman as we flew further and further into the sky, breaking the cloud line . . . floating horizontal with the shattered moon and Tenere . . . before falling back down.

Where was Dark? He should have been here by—

Thousands of black tendrils shot up out of Vargo like flowers trying to entangle the sun. They impaled everyone equally. Some killing Mercenaries while others surrounded the dragons, binding and constraining them like iron chains. All except for the dazzling bright white dragon that shone brighter than a midday sun. It easily banished all the darkness that came close to it and its brethren, but Dark's black tendrils were returning faster than it could handle. Even the metal dragon I was riding had been caught, held in midair as it writhed and wiggled and was dragged back toward the others. I stood upright on its back, waited until I found my balance, and then jumped from one dragon to another until I reached Rian. The others were doing the same, hacking and slashing through whatever dragon or black tendril was closest to them.

"You shouldn't have come for me, Rian!" I shouted as I climbed up Rian's back. When I was between his two wings, I drew my revolver, pressed the barrel against his scaled skin, *expelled* my nullifying warmth into the immediate area, destroying Dark's tendrils, and then fired my revolver. The bullet tore through the dragon, Rian screaming as he fell out of the sky.

We landed in Vargo's bay, a deafening thunderous crash echoing around us. The nearby ships croaked and groaned as the waves we created on impact jostled them. In the water, Rian reverted to his human form as I reoriented myself. Thankfully, he had taken the brunt of the impact, but my head felt as if it would split in two.

I felt at peace for a heartbeat as I opened my eyes and saw the tranquillity around me. Everything was a bluish green down here, the sandy seabed felt smooth to the touch, and the sight of all the barnacles sticking to all ships was something I wouldn't have seen if I hadn't gotten better at swimming. I grabbed Rian's collar, kicked like a frog a few times until the water was shallow enough that my boots touched the bottom and I could walk to shore. Waves crashed down on me as I stumbled onto the nearby beach, spitting out sand and wishing my boots didn't squish and squeak with every step.

I slapped the man with the mismatched eyes awake. He was still wearing the black-and-flame–trimmed robes of the Church of the Eternal Flame and I couldn't help but laugh. One of his hands was over the spot where I had shot him and it took all his strength to keep his eyes open, let alone try to run away.

I put my boot on his chest, pushed down until he was wincing in pain, and then aimed the revolver. "Nice to see you again, Rian. Call off the other dragons. You've lost."

"What did you shoot me with?" he groaned. He tried to dig into his flesh to remove the bullet, but when his fingers touched it, he recoiled in pain as if it were aflame in his body. "Did you mine the crystal from the pillar the Heartbreaker was being held in? That's the only thing that could explain—"

"Call off the other dragons. I won't ask again."

My demand was pointless. Four dragons soared through the air above me past the iron gate of Vargo, retreating into the outer sea as more cannons fired. The entire bay had joined the battle to defend the city, each ship captain eager to become a dragonslayer and every civilian eager to insult and shame them as they fled. Some would want to follow them, to hunt the beasts down, but the iron gates that protected Vargo from the outer sea would stay closed since we were stuck in a flooding cycle rather than a high- or low-tide one.

"Congratulations, Michael," he said quietly. "You win. We thought all six of us could stop *him* . . . but we didn't think Regal Company would join the fight." He winced. "Do you even realize what you're doing by aiding the Black Death? If a few more of us die, *they* will return. And they will continue their war until this world is nothing but ash. The only reason we survived last time was because of a lovestruck fool."

"Are you referring to the Wolven Kings?" I emptied my boots of sand. "They're still alive but imprisoned somewhere, aren't they?"

THE VOYAGE OF THE FORGOTTEN   33

Rian sucked his teeth. "You already found one of their tombs with the Black Death's father, didn't you, Michael? His name was Alphonse. And he was missing, wasn't he?"

"Is that the Wolven King who has my sister? *Alphonse?*" I stared at him and wondered how I must've looked, that he was forced to stare at the ground rather than return my gaze. "Tell me about him."

"Do I look like a fool to you, Kingman?" Rian snarled. "That information is worth more than my own life." He closed his eyes gently. "Get it over with. Take my heart to the Black Death and doom the world further."

I hauled him to his feet. As much as I would have loved to taunt him further, we didn't have much time. Alexis landed in the water nearby— barely a splash as she slipped into the bay—and the lights were already beginning to grow closer. Dark would be here soon.

"I'm not going to give him your heart."

"What?" Rian said incredulous. "Do you plan to destroy it?"

I pulled him close, shoving the tip of my gun into his open wound. He squirmed. "Revenge? Oh, no. You're going to help me save my sister, stop a madman from bringing the dead back to life, and write my legacy. Not as a Kingman, or a king killer, or even Dragonslayer—but as a man who butchers immortals. If you choose not to help me, then I'll step into your mind and steal your memories."

"You have no idea how outmatched you are."

"Dark is my enemy. Angelo is my enemy. The Wolven Kings are my enemy." Pressure welled up in my chest. "I have always been weak in comparison. Surrounded by those who want to do my family harm. But I'm tired of letting them dictate my life." I stuck out my tongue, as if madness had laid roots in my mind. "The world needs a villain to reset it, so I am here to play the role with a smile and a bow."

64

DESPERATE PLEAS

The clan guards were efficient, blocking off and quarantining sections of Vargo that had taken the worst of the dragons' attack as Alexis and I finished tying Rian up. Their philosophy of unity, teamwork, and rallying together against a common foe was not how I'd been raised. Not in Hollow, where manipulation, lying, and self-preservation were taught to babes before they could walk. Our time was limited, each slap of the foot against stone or shout of celebration another warning that we had to hurry. Dark couldn't find us with Rian. If he did, any chance of defying him would be lost.

"How do you want to handle Rian?" Alexis asked as scared citizens began to emerge from the buildings. Any Mercenaries that fell from the sky were being received like conquering heroes. "I can see how long Cassia's crew will hold him, but if Dark comes searching—"

"I don't trust Cassia's crew not to rat me out to her, let alone Dark." I made sure Rian's gag was secure. "Hide him somewhere Dark will never look. You know him better than anyone else. And don't tell me where."

"Suppose I can do that." Alexis was impossible to read at the best of times. If it wasn't for our shared desires to stop Dark and honor Zahra, I wouldn't have trusted her. She hadn't initially reacted well to hearing what I had seen in the depths of Dark's heart and what he wanted to do—which was to be expected—but once she had calmed down, she had decided we had to stop Dark from bringing her sister back. Zahra wouldn't have wanted to return to life, and her wishes had to be followed, even if it meant hurting Dark in the process. "And what will you be doing while I do the hard part?"

"What I do best." I saw Cassia's blue-sash–wearing sailors coming toward us. Was that out of concern? Or something more sinister? They had spent plenty of time spying on me before. Even going as far as to stop me from sneaking into Serena's room. "Making sure all eyes are on me."

Alexis waved me off, expressionless. There was a crowd on the docks as I climbed up them, clothes still sticking to me. I was pounded on the back as I passed, people hollering *"Dragonslayer! Dragonslayer! Dragonslayer!"* A few merchants even slipped claxo, minor trinkets, or sun-dried fish bones into my hands. As if I were some god they had prayed to for intervention and had to offer sacrifices to now that the skies had calmed and their lives hadn't been snipped short. All I felt like was a terror in another's tongue that hadn't yet been translated. Clan guards and sailors tried to push past the horde to get closer to me, but I made my way through the crowd and ran in the opposite direction.

The easiest way to get out of the docks was to follow the leaves caught in the wind. Trees were planted only near the palace, so they fluttered toward the sea like a trail only the locals knew to follow. I hopped in and out of the long banana-shaped boats floating through the canals as if I was jumping between rocks, much to the annoyance of those transferring baskets of fruits, cages of cats, or whatever else sailors needed for their long sea trips. Cassia's crew lost sight of me as I jumped onto a residential balcony from a boat and then climbed the walls to the roof. Orbis Company could take me out of Hollow, but I'd always be a street rat who had grown up climbing buildings.

Yet, I couldn't hide. The chant *"Dragonslayer! Dragonslayer! Dragonslayer!"* followed me endlessly. If I hid behind a brick chimney, children would point at me with stars in their eyes. Families showered me in petals if I ducked under their balcony, and sailors raised their tankards as I passed. And so I was forced to run endlessly through the streets of Vargo. Who knew being mistaken for a hero could be so bothersome?

Stone statues plucked from the Sea of Statues lined the streets evenly spaced out like planted trees. Some represented warriors from all over the continent from the Thebian Empire's Berserkers to New Dracon City's Engineers, while others depicted everyday jobs like cooks and butlers. The prettiest ones were in the most crowded area, and those that were discolored, damaged, or uglier than Dark when he just awoke had been banished to dark alleys or run-down taverns. It was almost law—in that everyone did it—that every house and business had a statue within somewhere for luck. Sailors rubbed their arms before going to sea, lovers slapped their cheeks before attempting to court someone, and clan guards headbutted them before battle. It was a silly tradition created when a clan head did it once and it gave him unbridled confidence. A year later, his servants discovered it had just been brain damage when he had passed away with his face in a bowl of stew.

Truth be told, I hated this city. Hated the smooth honey-colored sandstone most of the buildings were made from, and how wind chimes that hung from the awnings rang out with each strong breeze. Serena had been destined to take her mother's place as clan leader when Davey ascended to king. But following his death she had to become Queen of Hollow instead. The thought of her loss had left me with bitter feelings that even time couldn't quell.

Clan guards ended up cornering me in a dead-end alley where the poor citizens had already begun to scavenge some of the debris from the fight.

"Dragonslayer Michael," the leader of the small group said between breaths. "You must come to Mercenary Dark at once. Please stop running from us."

I clicked my tongue, wondering if I had given Alexis enough time to smuggle Rian somewhere safe. "Why? What does he want from me?"

"Six dragons attacked Vargo," the leader stated. "Four escaped and you killed one, shooting it out of the sky and drowning it in the bay, but the last . . ." He glanced away. "Mercenary Dark has cornered it in a building."

"And he needs my help in defeating it?"

"No," another guard answered. "*We* need your help to ensure he doesn't destroy our city trying to kill it. He's already turned a block of houses into solid ice, freezing all those that were inside without care. We can't find any other members of Orbis Company. We don't know who else to turn to. Who else but another Mercenary stands a chance of stopping the Black Death?"

There was a part of Vargo known for its fantastic food. World-renowned for the way their ever-burning fires never went out. The bread stuck to the inside of the large clay ovens was crispy on the outside, fluffy on the inside, and loaves could be made by the hundreds to feed a starving crew before they went out to sea or once they returned. It was of such cultural importance in Vargo that the district had been called Lighthouse Lane. For the skies over it were always hazy, and it served as a beacon for wanderers, just like Kingman Keep did for many in Hollow.

Lighthouse Lane was gone. In a single unstoppable rampage from a man who knew no equal. Who couldn't even be held responsible for his primal uncaring actions. Every building had been frozen into a translucent sheen that was more akin to glass than water. Dozens of citizens had been caught in the battle, either reduced to a burning husk from a strike of lightning or a frozen statue with their last moment etched onto their faces for eternity.

A single man sat atop a pile of red-stained ice. No one else was near—even the guards were too scared to get close to the Black Death in case they became his next victims. The body of an Eternal Sister of the

Church of the Eternal Flame lay at his side, long black scarf fluttering absently in the sea breeze, a hole in her chest where her heart should have been. Dark kicked the body away from him, letting it fall soundlessly to the street as he hoisted the still-beating heart to his mouth. The wet crunch of his teeth sinking into a human heart was the first sound he let anyone hear. Lightning ran up and down his arms almost immediately as he added another power to his arsenal.

My Mercenary mentor seemed more comfortable on the Gold Coast than he ever had in Hollow. The sides of his head were shaved, while the rest of his hair was tied back, his clothes were dark colored but loose and flowing, his skin was sun-kissed, and a hatchet swung from his side. A holster for the other twin revolver was strapped across his chest. But more peculiar was that his eyes were no longer a cool grey like Angelo's. Rather, they had a thin red line in the middle of them. Would they become permanently red if he continued to eat dragon hearts? It wouldn't be much longer before I would never be able to stop him—assuming I still could right now. I was in a magical arms race with a genocidal terror.

"So, Dragonslayer," Dark mocked between mouthfuls. He picked at the stringy meat stuck between his teeth with his abnormally long nails. "Did you bring me another meal?"

CURTAINFALL

"Where's Rian?" Dark asked as he vaulted down from his frozen throne. He sucked the tips of his fingers to make sure he got all the dragon's blood beneath his nails. It was a crude gesture that made light of everything around us. A levity that didn't deserve to bloom in blood-soaked soil.

"Bottom of the bay. Shot went through his heart." I made sure my eyes didn't dwell too long on his. It was all a balancing act. Some thought more information was the best way to lie, but I always was an omission man. It gave them less to pull apart. "You can go retrieve his body if you want, but Dawn's been avenged and I don't care about fish food."

"Hmm." Dark approached me slowly as if waiting for his cue to join the waltz. He lifted my chin with the tip of his elongated nail and then softly said, "Li-ar."

"Prove it."

"I will. You can't hide anything from me, Michael. I know you better than anyone else." He withdrew his talon. My skin was irritated, on the verge of bleeding. "It doesn't have to be like this. We don't have to be in opposition. You could help me stop my father."

"And let you do the same?" I countered. "As if."

"You act as if I'm Angelo," Dark growled. "I'm not. My father is a monster. I am simply a man who has abandoned his humanity to hunt monsters." He paused. "Or would you claim that role yourself?"

"Do you really think anyone can tell the difference between the two?" I gestured to the destruction around us. The frozen bodies slowly melting into puddles. The houses reduced to ruins and rubble. The gawkers that were more frightened of him than moon-fall or dragons. Natural calamities had left less destruction in their wake.

"Wouldn't you do the same for yours?" Dark gestured toward the castle where Serena would be waiting for me. "At least I'm not a hypocrite."

"Do you even know the price to bring someone back to life?"

Dark chewed on his lip like a beast trying to gnaw itself out of a trap.

"The fact you won't tell me is proof enough that no one would approve of it."

"The cost is unimportant." He looked down at me. "It could take a chicken's life to bring someone back from the dead and you'd still fight my father tooth and nail to prevent it from happening."

"I'm nothing if not petty."

"'Imbecilic' is the word I would have chosen."

"Tell me what the price is," I said, pressing him. My fingers were twisted around the grip of the revolver. "Tell me and I'll decide if I'm with you and against your father right now. But if you don't, I'll fight you both."

"Fine. I'll tell you what I know." He crossed his arms. "But not here. It's better I show you rather than have you trust my words alone."

"Oh?" I asked, perking up. "Another trip through your memories?"

Dark sneered at me. "No. The palace."

I made sure we walked side by side rather than me watching his back as we left Lighthouse Lane. I wasn't his dog anymore and wouldn't let him forget that.

————————

It was a door. The super-important thing he had to show me was a door. An unremarkable wooden door that looked so ordinary, I could have passed it a dozen times without noticing. It was at the back of a small shrine in the palace meant to accommodate any faith in need of a place of prayer. There was a faceless statue in one corner, while an eternal flame burned in the other. In between them was the door. The only unique thing was that it had hinges but lacked a lock, and yet when I pulled on it, trying to get it to open, it didn't so much as budge.

Dark laughed at my attempt as he sat on a nearby pew. "You can't open it, Michael. That's the point."

"The point of what?"

"What Angelo and I are trying to do," he said. "There are seven doors like that one in the world. All near places of religious significance. If legends and rumors and myths are to be believed . . . those doors lead to whatever lies beyond life."

"Seriously?" I stopped trying to open it. "That sounds ridiculous."

"It is. To a point." Dark rose, walked over to the door, and ran his fingers down the polished grain. "But it's the only chance us monsters have at being redeemed. And is it so ridiculous to believe there might be a door to the afterlife?"

I tossed the idea around, but it was too bitter for me to swallow. "What proof do you have?"

"Legends, rumors, and myths, primarily." Dark turned his back to me and the door. "But you don't have to believe me. Ask your beloved, Serena." When I looked confused, he clarified, "Her song 'The Angels of Naverre' speaks of a lockless door that angels emerge from to judge the citizens as the city falls. They take those who are worthy with them and leave those who are not to suffer." He grinned at me over his shoulder. "That sounds like a door to the afterlife, doesn't it? And I'm inclined to think she didn't just make it up—"

"I get it. I get it," I interrupted. "So you and Angelo are trying to open these doors. How?"

"It's a multistep process that involves old magic. The first step is to get the lock to appear. And to do that, you need to speak the three Wolven Kings' names in front of one of these lockless doors."

"Why?"

Dark shrugged. "No idea. It's just what legends say."

"Do you have all three of them?"

"No," he muttered. "Only the first two. And only because I got one from a Skeleton by chance before I understood how valuable they were. But that was a long time ago." He rubbed his brow. "Angelo has the same two. The one we're missing is harder to find than a Weaver able to manipulate time."

Did Dark know the same one I did? Alphonse? Or did he have the other two? No, if Dark and Angelo had the same information, then he knew about Alphonse. Angelo had been there when I had discovered it. I asked a different question. "What about the key to open the lock?"

"From what I understand . . . there are seven options."

"Which one is Angelo attempting? Which one are you?"

"Angelo's key involves you and your family to some degree. I don't know the details, but it's why he kept you alive when others would have crushed your skull beneath their heels for trying to show how smart you are."

"Li-ar," I echoed, speaking it into existence as if it were suddenly heavy and whole in my hand. "Tell me the truth. Whatever it is."

"So be it." Dark met my eyes, grey and red into amber. Everything around us turned into whirling darkness. "Angelo is going to open the door using the Hollow method, which requires a Kingman to kill a Hollow or a Hollow to kill a Kingman. He's going to get either you or Serena to kill the other. That's been his plan ever since he adopted you and your siblings . . . like a butcher preparing his pigs for slaughter."

All the lines in the tile and walls seemed sharper and bolder. I couldn't look away from this new clarity if I wanted to. But I held my tongue and waited for Dark to elaborate.

"The smartest thing Serena ever did was take Lyon's family name from him," Dark continued. "It makes him exempt from the conditions to open the door. Likewise your sister's servitude to a Wolven King—though I couldn't tell you why." Dark stepped toward me. "So you're the only Kingman who can die for this plan to work. You can try to kill Adreann or have Serena take away your last name, as she did with Lyon . . . but the ramifications of either would be worse. Especially if Angelo isn't ready to open the door when you do it."

"Why?" I asked, forcing my voice to be stronger than a fading whisper.

Dark went to the ever-burning cannister and waved his hand over the flame, daring it to try to burn his skin. "Because then he'll shatter Tenere, and it'll be all your fault."

"What?"

"Let me tell you how this story ends," Dark said. "You, me, Angelo, and Serena are going to return to this room for Serena's wedding to Jay Prince. On that day, you or Serena will kill the other and force the door to open or Angelo will shatter Tenere and use the backdoor method instead—think of it as taking a crowbar to a lock. Either way, you are out of time and out of options to change this fate, written for you without your consent."

"Fate is bullshit," I spat. "It's an echo from the dead trying to dictate which path we take in life. It beats us down with complacency while telling us everything was better before we were born. I refuse to accept I can't stop Angelo's plan. If I have to, I'll break the world and rewrite fate with a miracle."

"It's cute you think you still have a chance." Dark turned back to me. "But do what you must with the fleeting days of life you have left. Rebel, run away, kill and try to claw your way to freedom . . . you'll still find yourself on a darkened stage with the curtains drawn and nothing waiting for you but deafening silence." His eyes seemed kinder for a singular moment. "Neither of us are good people, but are you monstrous enough to let Angelo shatter Tenere and doom humanity just to be with Serena?"

I had no answer, and Dark knew I didn't, so he pounced on my hesitation with a sickly sweet smile and a smooth voice that carried nothing but lies.

"But I'm here to offer you a happy ending. I'm going to kill all the dragons in existence. It's the Gold Coast method of opening the lockless doors. All I need is the name of the last Wolven King. Bring it to me . . . and I really hope you do . . . and I'll kill Angelo. Then you and your family and loved ones will be safe. Isn't that what's most important to you? Their safety?"

He was manipulating me. I didn't know how I knew, but *I knew*. Dark wouldn't have saved me unless he had a use for me, and—considering how hesitant he had been to reveal the truth about dragons—there was no chance that he needed me to help him kill them. Because if he truly wanted to stop his father from bringing Katherine back from the dead, he would have wiped me and my family out by now. Did he think I'd believe his lie? Or was this just another trick . . . or was I being too paranoid?

I was spared from a reply as guards, servants, and clan members entered the shrine, haggard and lost. Most of the guards had their armor half off, revealing the slick gleam of sweat on their bodies and the stink of battle. Dark put his hand on my shoulder and squeezed hard. "Think about it, Michael. If you don't want to help me kill the dragons—fine. Just bring me the final name of the Wolven King. We could do so much together. It would be a shame to be enemies, wouldn't it?"

I held my tongue and pried his hand off me.

"I see," he snapped. "I'm going to help the others clean up. Make sure our company is still alive. Don't worry, we'll see this place again in due time. Remember that you are mortal. Remember that you will die. Remember your death. Do you want it to have meaning, or not?"

Dark left me there, mind reeling, trying and failing to figure out what I could do to stop Angelo and Dark from trying to kill Serena or me. Assuming the entire story wasn't just another lie to hide the truth. But as I stood there . . . I realized it didn't matter. None of it mattered. All that mattered was my friends and family.

I had to get Serena out of here. Hollow be damned. Ancestors be damned. We'd find Gwen on our own. We had been slaves to our legacies and ancestors for too long. It was time to dictate our own fates . . . it was time we ended the Kingman and Hollow families for good.

BROKEN BOTTLES
AND BROKEN DREAMS

My head was pounding when I woke and lifted it off the table where I had fallen asleep. A piece of someone's shirt was stuck to my right cheek and my sight was hazy. Titus was nearby, lying across four chairs lined up in a row with a stuffed boar's head on his bare chest. Alexis was curled up on another table, snoring peacefully amidst the destruction surrounding us. All the tables and chairs not currently in use were broken, discarded clothes hung from the wooden rafters, all the bottles were smashed, and most of the walls had burn marks from a game Titus had called Seven Fires. The fact the tavern was still standing after twelve rounds of it was nothing short of miraculous.

The city had celebrated its survival until dawn. Orbis Company—never to be outdone—had joined in. Which, according to Alexis, included me. She knew I couldn't be trusted alone—I'd cause a diplomatic incident with Regal Company demanding to see Serena. Only the information that she was alive—something I verified myself from a large tree near her bedroom window—had made me relent and join in. Alexis had tried to play it off as wanting to drink with friends after a long day. Which I might have believed if she hadn't brought Titus to join our festivities. Titus did not drink for fun. Titus drank to win. And if no games were being played when Titus started drinking, then he started some. Hence the twelve rounds of Seven Fires that had left this poor tavern looking as if it had been attacked by dragons.

I nullified my body, hoping that it might make some of the pain go away. The moment I tried to stand, I staggered and tripped, and then emptied the contents of my stomach onto the floor. It was more colorful than I'd expected, and just like that, I had learned another thing about my Fabrications—they couldn't nullify poison.

Alexis's eyes fluttered open as I continued to retch. "Ugh, what's that smell?"

"My bad decisions." I wiped my mouth and then tore the piece of shirt off my cheek. "What did you make me drink last night?"

"Scaro. It's spiced wine with a few drops of Thebian rattlesnake poison," she said. "You seemed to be enjoying it until the tenth cup." Her expression grew grim. "Then you started crying over the Hollow Queen."

"Did I say anything embarrassing?"

"Does you admitting you like it when the Hollow Queen strokes your hair count?"

"Yes," I admitted. "Speaking of Serena, I need to go and check on her."

"They still won't let you see her." Alexis uncurled so her legs hung over the table. She rubbed the sleep out of her eyes and then said, "But I'll come with you."

I stood up straight, trying not to topple over again. "What should we do about . . ." I gestured to the wreckage around us. ". . . all of this?"

"Leave it to Titus to handle." She went to her feet. "Orbis Company has a history of destroying taverns."

"You'd think I would have heard about that sooner," I said. "Along with Cassia's impeccable kindness, Titus's inability to cook fish, and the fact that one of its members is a dragon."

"You're wrong," she said, hands behind her back as she strolled over to the exit.

"About?"

"One of our members being a dragon." She opened the door and sunlight poured in, blinding me. The pounding in my head intensified and I would have nullified the sun if I could. "Two of them are. Dark just doesn't know about it." And then she stepped outside and left me stuttering with my jaw on the floor.

I ran after her, shouting and leaping over broken furniture—or attempting to and landing face-first on the ground instead. Picking myself up was like wading through honey, and by the time I was outside, shielding my eyes from the sun, Alexis was gone. I headed after her, toward the palace, shoving through crowds of tourists headed to the safe tropical islands and bored kids looking for things to trip. I quickly became their favorite target.

A vendor with a wooden cart took pity on me when I was sick again, offering a drink that smelt like liquid garbage with lumps of dough filled with tongue-numbing spice to ease my pain. I had to hold my nose to drink it and nearly threw it back up, but it did the trick and within a few heartbeats the pain in my head was gone. I gave the man a Hollow moon—apologizing that I didn't have any claxo—and chased after Alexis again.

I caught up to her at the palace gates, seeing the foxy grin on her face. "Feeling better?"

"I hate you," I said, catching my breath, ignoring the saluting guards and their muttered "Dragonslayer." Hollow forms of flattery never impressed me. "Care to explain what you meant by 'two'?"

We walked through the gardens. Most of the decorations from Adreann's wedding were still up, tattered and decaying like autumn leaves. The servants who had been bustling and running around yesterday were hidden away as if the palace was in mourning for all the lives lost last night. From what I had learned, even the provisional number was in the hundreds.

"I thought it was self-explanatory," Alexis said. "Dark isn't the only dragon in Orbis Company."

"Who's the other?"

"Otto. The blind man you met during your advancement ceremony. He yelled at you for having memory issues at such a young age," she said without hesitation. "He's the wind dragon."

"How do you know that?"

"We were on a job together in the Iliar mountain range. We were supposed to ambush a group of Thebian students from crossing. It was decided the best way would be to close the path off with explosives. It was my job to set them off once the group was in place. And I did, but . . ." She exhaled. "I miscalculated something. The explosion was bigger than I intended, and I fell into a ravine. He caught me. With wings sprouting out of his back."

"Did you see him last night?"

Alexis shook her head. "Otto doesn't talk to his family anymore and hasn't in centuries. Didn't say what happened. Only that he'd never willingly see them again."

"Why are you telling me this?"

She shrugged. "We're partners, aren't we? What's the point in keeping secrets?"

Wow. So that's what it was like to *actually* trust people. Both Dark and I could learn a lot from her. "And why haven't you told Dark?"

"Because Otto saved my life. How could I repay him with his own death?"

"But what'll Dark do when he finds out you've been lying to him?"

Alexis stopped in place, lifted her boot, and then sneered at the canape she had stepped in. "What makes you think I'd get any special treatment? In Dark's mind, there's only him and Zahra and those who prevent them from being reunited." She wiped her heel on the manicured lawn. "We all deserve the same fate."

"Nothing is going to stop him from committing genocide, is it?"

"No," she said quietly.

"We'll stop him. I promise."

She gave me a sad smile. "Don't make promises you can't keep, Michael."

We were halfway through the gardens when I spotted Chloe repeatedly punching a tree. She was dressed casually in a simple shirt and trousers, and weaponless. Shards of bark littered the ground, and despite the fact her fist was already bleeding, she kept hitting it as if in a trance.

Alexis waved goodbye as I jogged over to Chloe, grabbed her shoulder, and spun her around. "Chloe? What are you doing? Wear some gloves if you're going to do that."

"Michael?" she said, as if unable to tell it was me, and she struggled to collect herself. "Sorry, Michael. It's been a rough night."

"How is she?"

"Primarily sore, weakened from blood loss, and exhausted. Thanks to Jay we were able to get her injuries treated quickly, which speeded a lot of the long-term recovery." Chloe paused. "I imagine she'll be back to . . . she'll have recovered in a week or so."

The words should have comforted me, yet a tension permeated my body as if it were a string that had been tightened too much. "So why were you punching that tree?"

"To relieve some stress."

"Why?"

Chloe stared into my eyes, and the longer she did, the more uneasy I felt. It was as if she were wearing someone else's skin. Something was wrong.

"Chloe," I said, voice wavering. "Tell me, please."

She crossed her arms, one of her hands covering her mouth. "I don't want to tell you like this. I was going to find a better way—a better place—to break the news to you." Chloe took a deep breath. "We think . . . we think . . . she was extremely emotional when she used her Fabrications to fend off the attack. It's the only way to explain—"

My heart fell into my stomach, my face felt hotter than fire, my fists were clenched tight enough to draw blood from my palms. Everything around me was spinning. "Serena's become a Forgotten, hasn't she?"

THE WOLF'S CAPTIVE

Gwendolyn Kingman was far from home.

She had always wanted to travel. To see the Night Market in New Dracon City and the exquisite Military Academy in the Thebian Empire. Frankly, she would have gone anywhere that wasn't Hollow, given the opportunity. She didn't want to be stuck behind those towering walls in the city where she had been born until she died. And now she was in Eham, the capital of the pirates that harassed the Sea of Statues. Years ago she would have been thrilled, but now, as she sat in a flimsy wooden seat twiddling her thumbs, she longed to be back home. Her family had no idea where she was or why she had left so suddenly. And now the memory of her brother diving to try and save her before she was taken by her employer was seared into her memory, as black as the brand on the back of her left hand.

One day Gwen would return to Hollow and explain everything, but first she had to repay her debt. If she was lucky, she'd only be thirty when she was free.

"Gwendolyn?" A quartermaster was approaching Gwen. She was a

bespectacled Ehamian woman with a flair for brightly colored clothes
and large jewelry. "The Children of the Sky will see you now."

Gwen muttered thanks, took a deep breath, and then entered the
amphitheater. The hierarchy of Eham was built around the bounties the
Palmer Archipelago navy put out for the pirates that terrorized them.
Those with the largest bounties were in charge not just of maintaining
the peace in Eham but also deciding who they would ally with or declare
war on. Some of the members of the council had been on it for decades
if not centuries, changing names and identities whenever their longevity
became suspicious. She was here to speak to two of those members now.
Along with others from other parts of the continent. Her employer had
left her very specific instructions and she would follow them perfectly.

The Children of the Sky were gathered around a glass tank in the
ground filled with sharks that were fighting over the bits of meat they
were tossing in through holes in the glass. Gwen didn't recognize any
of them. Not that she could've. All had spent multiple lifetimes erasing
their presence from the world, leaving only crumbs of their desires and
identities behind. Because the Children of the Sky was the proper, formal
name for the dragons that dwelled in this world. Ironic, then, that she
would be the first mortal to be in their presence and know their identities. The sister of the man they called the Dragonslayer.

The closest to her were the twins: Wood and Steel. Opposites of each
other, in that the man was fat and stout while the woman was thin and
tall. Both were muscular, with bright blond hair and thin eyes, were covered in traditional pirate tattoos and jewelry, and were either pirate captains or elite captains in the Palmer Archipelago navy. Gwen suspected
the latter, only because it was easier to hide in order than it was in chaos.
Pirates prided themselves on destroying the earlier generations, while
governments tried to maintain balance for as long as they could.

Next was Water. She wore a loose white gown that always looked as if
it was fluttering in the wind, had black hair down to her lower back and
skin as pale as moonlight. Gwen's employer had said never to accept anything offered by her and to avoid cliffs or beaches with her. Those who

visited them had a habit of disappearing. Water had at her side an Azilian woman called Clover with bright red hair who clung to her gown like a child. Rumors said she was being considered for a position in the new generation of dragons. Out of everyone here, she would be trickiest to force to submit to her master's wishes. Youth had a habit of making rebels that refused to bow to tradition, but if Gwen was going to succeed here, she would have to outsmart the fledgling dragon. Or kill her.

She hoped it wouldn't come to that.

Finally, there was the Light Dragon. His face was obscured behind a mirror mask that seemed to consume all warmth in the immediate area. A long black cloak covered his body, gently swaying in an absent breeze. He was less of a man and more of an enigma. A question mark made sentient.

Gwen stood on a glass panel with the sharks swimming beneath her, her hands crossed neatly in front of her, and waited for one of the dragons to acknowledge her.

"Has the First come to taunt us while we lick our wounds?" Light asked as he wove strands of light together as if he were knitting a hat. The other dragons didn't look at Gwen, more interested in feeding the sharks below.

"My employer wishes to convey that your plan was rash. You should have accepted his help when it was offered. The Black Death would be ash by now if you had." She swallowed her fear and made her next words perfectly clear. "Don't make the same mistake again."

Water glanced at Gwen. "So thoughtful and wise, and yet he doesn't come himself. Is he still scared of us, after we nearly killed him at Thousand Craters?"

"Doubtful," Gwen said to Water. And then to Light: "Will you reconsider his offer to join him? Or should I return when two more of you are dead and gone, and desperation has set in?"

Wood and Steel glared absently at her. Like dolls on a shelf waiting for their moment to come alive. Light began to hum as Water approached Gwen, and the air grew colder with every step she took.

"Girl," Water said, baring her sharp teeth. Rumors said she had spent a lifetime sucking marrow out of bones. "Do not treat us like fools. We have killed kings, crumbled empires, and had more songs written about us than stars in the sky. We are eternal. The Black Death is just a thorn in our side we have not yet plucked. But we will. And after we kill him, we will restore our family to its proper size. Candidates are already being evaluated."

"As hopeful as that sounds, it won't matter once the Second returns. The time of peace is over. The war to end all wars has begun again. And you all must join a side, or die."

"Say you're right and the war is beginning again," Light drawled. "Why would we not join the Third's?"

"Because the Third has decided not to participate. He prefers to stay imprisoned, as he has for a millennium. Confinement has warped his mind. Made him fear the greater world. Nothing remains of the man you once fought for."

Water put her face directly in front of Gwen's. Her breath was sickly sweet like Hollow Blackberries, which made her heart ache for home. "Who says the First is any better? He lost once, so why should we trust him to lead us?"

"My name is Gwendolyn Kingman."

Light snorted. "Merciless sea, he ensnared a Kingman? He must love that irony. How did he do that, girl?"

"I made a deal with him when I was young," Gwen said. "I offered my life to accomplish something that was far beyond my grasp." Gwen swallowed her next words, the musty feeling of blood under her fingernails returning after ten years. The uncomfortable feeling of holding a deadweight in her small arms. The shadow of her employer blocking out the lantern light and the sweet words he'd spoken to her. She gulped and pushed those memories to the back of her mind. The decision was in the past. There was no point in dwelling on it. "Do you have other pointless questions?"

"I've got one," Clover said, speaking for the first time. "Why should my masters submit to a man who remains in the shadows? That is not our way. I will not serve a man who will not face me himself. Can you prove you are worth listening to?"

"It seems we're at an impasse already," Light stated. "Do you know what that means, inheritor?"

Gwen had been warned it might come to this. Out of all the beast immortals that served the Wolven Kings, the fliers were the most rebellious. But they would submit soon enough. As the swimmers and half the titans had. She only wished it didn't have to end in more death. The last beast immortal she had recruited had cost the lives of a village, and the memories of the bodies turned faceless and strewn from palm trees haunted her dreams in a way the Kingman Keep riots never had.

"What do I need to do?" Gwen asked, emotionless.

Light reached into his mouth and yanked out a golden tooth. He wiped it clean on his shirt and then dropped it into the tank below. A few of the sharks circled it until it hit the bottom, hidden by kelp, and became lodged within a pile of slimy round rocks. Without a word, Clover stripped down to bare coverings. Steel handed her a bone dagger with dozens of notches in the handle. She put the blade between her teeth and then began to stretch.

Gwen did the same as Light said, "First to retrieve my tooth will be victorious. If Clover wins, we will not submit to the True Heir. If the Kingman does, we will. Fair?"

"Fair," Gwen and Clover said together.

Wood handed Gwen a rusted dagger. It wouldn't be sharp enough to cut through sand, but she'd make do. It was better than nothing. Gwen tore off one of her sleeves and then wrapped it around her hand and its hilt so she wouldn't lose grip of it. She approached one of the many holes in the glass. Clover was already wiggling her toes over the edge of one. The young woman was eager to prove herself in front of the dragons. Maybe this was her final test to earn her place among them. In that way, Clover reminded her of Michael. Pride was something Gwen had never cared for, nor desired.

"On my count. Three . . . Two . . . One . . . Dive!"

Gwen held her nose as she dove into the water, white bubbles rising around her. The sharks circled her at once, forgoing the other distur-bance in the water, and Clover swam downward quickly, with deft skill. Gwen descended slower, feet-first, letting the air out of her body. Her goal was not to get to the tooth first. Just to stop Clover from emerging with it.

Her bare feet touched the bottom, sinking into the mud as if it were trying to swallow her whole. Clover was nearby, searching the stones for the tooth as Gwen made her way toward her, knife in hand, and the sharks circled above. None of them would strike until there was blood in the water.

Gwen slashed at Clover's arm, but the fledgling dragon twirled away and then struck back with a kick. It knocked what little air Gwen still had out of her, and she flew back until she collided with a glass wall. She bit on her tongue from the impact and then watched in surprise as wispy red tendrils left her mouth and ascended toward the surface.

The sharks attacked in an instant, shooting toward her like bullets. She was able to punch the first in the nose, deterring it from biting her, but the second was too close behind to stop as it bit into her forearm. Before it could rip and tear, she stabbed it in the eye with her rusted knife. It unlatched from her and she was able to push it away. The other sharks cannibalized it, preferring the easy meal than the harder one Gwen offered.

Clover had already retrieved the tooth and was halfway back to the surface. Gwen did what she had to. She wasn't a Fabricator. She didn't have the abilities to nullify magic like Michael or control blood like Lyon . . . but she was no longer a non-Fabricator either. Her employer had gifted her a power to defend herself whenever they weren't together. Its cost was high, but it was better than failing. Each time she failed, an-other year was added to her debt.

Gwen reached into her mouth and pulled out a small black ball that glistened like a pearl. She hesitated for a moment, but then did what she had to. She flicked it at Clover. The ball hit the pirate in the thigh and ripped away everything below the knee in a single moment, both legs consumed by the black ball. Blood gushed from the wounds and Clover screamed wordlessly, bubbles replacing her cries. She dropped the tooth as pain shuddered through her.

And for the second time that day, the sharks feasted on easy prey.

Gwen grabbed the tooth from the bottom and then swam for the surface, the victor. Her first breath of air tasted better than sweet bread. Hushed mumbles surrounded her as she pulled herself up and over the lip. She collapsed onto her back, arm still throbbing with pain, but she gritted her teeth and held up her prize.

"She's an Insatiable. No one approach her!" Light ordered. At his command, the other dragons backed away. "You've proven yourself. We'll listen to the First's request. But if we are truly joining him . . . we will require more."

"Demand whatever you want. My master will get it done," she said, forcing herself to stand. Winners did not lie on the floor. "But be quick. We sail to war on the first of the new moons."

"So soon?" Water inquired.

Gwen held her bitten arm, shivering from the pain. "Yes. My master seeks to deal a decisive blow to the second Wolven King before he can return to full power."

———

Gwen stitched the bite marks closed as she rested against a lighthouse that overlooked the black sand beaches of Eham. The moons were beginning to show in the sky, easing her nerves. Because even if she was far from home . . . at least she and her family all saw the same sky. It was the only thing they still shared.

She stabbed the needle through her skin again, wincing every time. Once thread crisscrossed over the bite marks in her bicep and held them closed, she tossed the needle and thread aside and took a gulp of wine she had been gifted after the meeting. It was meant to be a sign of good-will between the two parties, but it barely eased the pain in her arm. Let alone the pain in her heart.

Rocks fell from the sky next to her and a tear appeared soon after. Her employer stepped through the gate between two places without any words. He was faceless as always and dressed extravagantly to make up for it. A leopard pelt hung over his shoulders and framed his bare chest, his open-toed sandals glittered in the waning light, a bronze sash was wrapped around his waist, and he had donned metal gauntlets. No matter where he went, he made sure he looked the part of a conqueror. The Wolven King hovered over her like a concerned parent. "Do you need me to heal your wounds?"

Gwen shook her head. "I'd prefer the natural way."

"So mortal." Her employer walked over to the edge of the cliff, staring at the prison that housed his younger brother. "Did the meeting go well?"

Gwen took another drink of wine. "I had to kill Clover."

"A shame. But many more will die if my brothers return. We are doing what is necessary. Nothing more."

"You sound like Michael," Gwen admitted. "Funny, isn't it?"

"The Lifeweaver's immortal killer?" her employer clarified. Gwen nodded, and the immortal sighed dramatically. "Do you ever regret it? Trading your life for his?"

"Never," Gwen said quickly. "I got ten more years with him. And even though they weren't perfect . . . I'd do it again in a heartbeat."

"I wonder what it's like to love your siblings." The Wolven King went back through the tear. From the other side, he said, "I'll speak to the Children of the Sky and see what other demands they have before fully committing to our cause. Don't do anything stupid until we're ready. If you ruin what I've planned . . ."

"I won't," she promised.

The tear snapped closed with a deep growl, and Gwen was left alone with her wound, a half-full bottle of wine, and a view of an approaching armada. Thousands of Mercenaries were gathering on Eham for a war council. Some of them would join her and her employer's fight, while others would oppose them and side with the second Wolven King. War would engulf the world, and all Gwen could do was wait and see who would emerge victorious from the ashes.

61

A TOWN DIVIDED

Becoming a Forgotten was a fear for every Fabricator. We all thought that we'd be different . . . that our loved ones would be different . . . but we all knew in our hearts it was always a question of when, not if. Serena was the first person I knew to become a Forgotten, and I doubted she would be the last. But hers might be the one that hurt me the most.

It was midday when Chloe brought me to Serena, distracting the guards and sneaking me into her room. I had refused to believe her unless I saw it with my own eyes, as if denying the truth would spare me the pain. Standing outside Serena's room, I felt like a secret admirer trying to win her heart in the dead of night. Her window was open and caged birds sang within. Like a true thief, I pushed the window up and then tumbled into the room as gracefully as I could.

And found Serena restrained to a chair, wiggling and presumably cursing behind her gag. Half of her face was still covered in blood and dirt, and she was as modest as she could be only wearing trousers, a black silk slip over her breasts, and bandages wherever the bullet had pierced her. Upon seeing me, she wriggled harder and I saw hope in her eyes.

"What did they do to you?" I asked. "Does Chloe—"

Black tendrils ripped my hands away from her. A sturdier one wrapped around my neck like a snake and squeezed just enough to distract me. My body was already spreading nullifying warmth over it as my Mercenary mentor stepped from the shadows.

"Michael," Dark said, keeping his distance. "Get away from her if you value your life."

"Calm down, you'll only—"

Serena screamed—despite the gag—and rocked back and forth in her chair as we were forced to the ground by her Fabrications. Everything was shaking around us as dust fluttered down to the ground from the ceiling.

"Michael! Nullify! Now!"

I exhaled and let my warmth *repel* out of me and into the room. The weight on my shoulders disappeared, though Serena continued to struggle. As if she didn't know what she had done.

"This isn't happening," I muttered. "She can't be a Forgotten."

Dark ushered to a nearby table. He must have expected me, having already poured generous measures of rum, and there were enough small delicacies to feed a large family. I wasn't hungry, but I picked at the food after downing all the rum in a single gulp. For the first time in my life, the burn in my throat didn't make me feel better.

"Chloe said the two of you talked before the attack. And I'm telling you not to blame yourself. Whatever you may think . . . it's not your fault," Dark said, swishing his rum in its glass. "We like to think it's reasonable, that the stronger and more emotional the Fabrication, the more likely someone will become a Forgotten. But it's random."

"If I hadn't talked to her, she might have been calmer. She might have . . ." My words were hollow and tears began to well in my eyes. "Send me into her memories. I have to see it for myself."

"Michael . . ."

"Dark. Please." I looked away from him in shame. "Don't make me beg."

Dark nodded solemnly as he rose. We walked over to Serena together and he put a hand on her shoulder and then mine. "Don't linger in there too long. It'll only bring pain."

I mumbled something affirmative The blinding rainbow light came out of his hands moments later, destroying everything around us, and sent me into memories of the woman I loved. I landed gracefully in a city torn in two. One side had been aquamarine before it was splattered with blood and ash, while the other side had been white and flowery before fire ravaged it. Both sides of the city had ended up decimated, with faceless versions of Serena everywhere. It was impossible to take a step without tripping over the dead. A red river ran through the carnage—the only living thing left in the wake of utter destruction. If this was meant to be a representation of Serena's mind . . . then she truly was a Forgotten. Nothing of the woman I loved remained, but I went in search of a door that might take me to the depths of her heart all the same. Because maybe even if she didn't remember me, she might . . .

The path to her heart was obvious. I spotted a spiraled red-and-blue door, covered in chains and held by a padlock without a keyhole. I would have to figure out what would unlock it, just as I had in Dark's mind. But Serena was a Forgotten, what could she possibly be in denial about? Or was it something she had avoided before this happened?

I started with the obvious.

"Serena loved Michael Kingman but knew they couldn't be together." The chains stayed intact.

"Serena didn't love Michael Kingman?" I asked hesitantly.

The door remained chained.

"That's a relief at least," I muttered. "Serena was incredibly lonely. No matter who was at her side."

Nothing changed.

There were no memory bubbles for me to rely on: I was going to have to do this without any help. But I knew Serena better than anyone. Even if she currently was a Forgotten. So I sat on the ground in front of the door making statement after statement, trying to guess what Serena had locked behind this stupid door. It wasn't a denial, as Dark's had been, and it didn't seem to be some hidden secret either. So what was it?

I was on the verge of pulling myself out of this place when I decided to try one last statement.

"Serena wanted to accept Michael's proposition of running away with him."

The chains and locks melted away and the door swung slightly open. With a heavy heart, I went through the door to see what lay at the core of Serena's desires, even knowing it would cause me nothing but pain. But I had learned why she had rejected me at the party when she clearly didn't want to. Had she truly decided duty was more important than love? And if she had, could I go against her wishes and say anything to the reborn Serena about our relationship?

I entered a pristine dining room with a long table covered in Serena's favorite foods, from ruby seeds and potato and bacon stew to lemon-drop cakes and white wine. Each seat was occupied by middle-aged men and women while children ran around the table like buzzing flies. I recognized each of them instantaneously. After all, how could I not recognize my siblings and the other Royals?

Davey Hollow sat at the head of the table with a simple crown on his head. He was taller than he ever had been in reality, and the circular birthmark on his temple that had stuck out like a rash as a child had become a statement of his identity and confidence. There was a woman at his side who he stole kisses from when no one else was looking. He had a massive smile on his face, and I had to fight back tears knowing this was nothing but a soothing illusion.

Gwen, Adreann, Lyon, Kayleigh, and four children with bright blond hair and the Kingman amber eyes were at the table, all as happy as Davey. More surprising than all of us getting along was that Lyon and Kayleigh's children wore the colors both of the Ryder and Kingman families. Each had been allowed to choose whether to embrace my family's messed-up legacy. It seemed an impossible luxury to be allowed to choose.

And then there was Serena. No crown or jewelry adorned her, and a red mask lay on the table in front of her. The one she wore as the singer Red. So at the very core of her desires she was the leader of neither Hollow nor Vargo but a singer free to choose where she went, what she sang, and what she did with her life.

"Tragic, isn't it? All Serena desires is to be among her family, and it's the one thing she can never have," a familiar voice said from behind.

I didn't turn to face the man. I did everything to keep *him* out of my sight. Maybe if I didn't look at him, he'd leave. "Go away. Don't talk to me."

He stood in my shadow. "Now isn't the time to be childish, Michael. We need to talk about this."

"No, we don't," I barked. "Why would I want to talk to you of all the people here? The fact you're Serena's idealized version makes it even more terrifying."

"Why?"

I clenched my fists as my pain in the ass stepped into view, but I covered my eyes with my hand like a child trying to wish away the monsters that scared him.

"Seriously? Face me, Michael. Are you a Kingman or a coward?"

"Fine," I growled as I opened my eyes. "Hello, Ike."

Serena's idealized version of myself stood in front of me. Age had come for him in a way I never thought it would. Our once-messy brown hair was cut short and streaked with grey like strokes from a paintbrush. He didn't wear military clothes or even our family's colors, opting for simple dark clothing that covered many of our silvered scars. His hands were callused, the crown brand on his neck was gone, and rather than tattoos of lost loved ones or military allegiances he had a singular tattoo of Serena's name on his left wrist. He was the man I had always wanted to be, rather than the imitation I was, and it hurt in so many ways to look at him.

"Ah, smart. I'm Ike, while you're Michael, so you can keep us both straight in your mind," my older self said as a finger tapped his cheek. "I'm surprised you didn't try to avoid me for longer."

"I like to think I've grown. But you know us, we must always make a show of our true feelings. Even if we give in to logic eventually."

Ike gestured to the others at the table. "Do you want to meet the rest?"

I shook my head. "You'll give me enough of a headache."

"Fair," Ike said. "If you're here, you've come searching for answers to something about Serena. What is it you want? To know if you've a chance at ending happily ever after . . . ?"

"She's become a Forgotten."

"That's . . ." He almost choked on his words. ". . . not what I was hoping to hear."

"It makes sense," I said, staring at the happy table in front of me. "At least seeing this lets me see what could have been."

"Bowing to fate so soon? How pathetic."

Those weren't my words, coming from Ike's mouth. It sounded like Dark. But why would Serena have me act and speak like that? Did she think I was going to turn out as monstrous as he did? No, there was another reason. I just didn't see it yet.

"Are you two married?" I asked.

Ike nodded. "We married once Davey took the throne, after King Isaac passed away from old age. We were together in secret for a long time before that, but Serena was only willing to make it public once the succession had gone through without issues. After that she abdicated and became a singer, she always wanted to be, and I stayed by her side wherever she went."

"How adorable," I drawled. "Serena chose the throne over me. Even though she didn't want to."

"Have you asked yourself why she did that?"

"Out of duty," I said. "She probably didn't trust Adreann with complete power."

"That doesn't sound like the Serena I know." Ike crossed his arms.

"And, you know, I'm just a mental manifestation of Serena's desires, so I may not be completely right, but I'm definitely closer than you are."

Why was I such an ass?

"Why else would Serena turn me down?" I asked.

"Maybe she was scared."

"Scared." I chuckled. "That doesn't sound like the Serena *I* know."

"Then maybe you don't understand her as well as you think you do. Serena has always been self-conscious. Like you, she always feels eyes watching her, waiting for her to mess up." Ike looked at me, ashamed. "Maybe you don't deserve her love."

His words struck me, sharp pain resonating through my heart. "Shut up, old man."

"Make me, you disgrace."

"With pleasure."

Ike reached for his hip and then swept his hand across his body as a sword materialized in it. The longsword had a red-dyed blade and a bone pommel with a topaz in the hilt. As a child, I had always hoped to own exactly that blade when I became a master swordsman. It was like watching a dream become reality. Serena's ideal version of myself took his stance with both hands on the pommel, raised so it was level with his eyes. If he was a master of the Kingman style, then he planned to win this fight in a single blow.

"Come on, then," Ike taunted. "Try and kill what you could never be."

"As if," I countered. "Why would I bother—"

Ike lunged and time slowed around us. My body overruled my mind, leaping back, right before the sword sliced me in two. The tip caught my shirt—sliced it open. I skipped backwards, willing a sword into my hand, but as I stood to fight myself . . . it felt awkward in my hands, a lumpy mess rather than an extension of my arm.

"You can't run away from this fight, Michael," Ike said, creeping closer. "Fight me! Prove you are worthy of being at her side!"

I tossed my sword to the side.

Ike sneered at me. "Seriously? Fight me! Why are you such a cow—"

I unholstered guns instead and watched as the twin revolvers—Kingkiller and Kingmaker—formed in my hands. The sword wasn't my weapon anymore, guns were. I had felt the weight of the world on my shoulders for so long, constantly doubting my actions and what I wanted . . . but here . . . against him . . . there was no more denying my truth. I was a Mercenary who fought with guns, not an honorable fool who dueled with integrity.

"Brilliant." My idealistic self smiled, then took his stance again. "Show me why Serena would choose you when you're a pale imitation of the man you could have been."

I shot widely, missing by a large distance, and let the white smoke cloud both of us. Then I charged Ike. The glint of his sword gave away his strike amidst the haze, allowing me to dodge his downward strike with a sidestep. I elbowed him in the side, throwing his careful balance off, and sent him tumbling to the side. But Ike was a master swordsman. He rolled and came back to his feet and his stance. His breath was barely strained, and his eyes were focused. I took aim again, and we circled each other.

"Do you think I could deflect a bullet with my sword?" Ike crept closer. "I bet I can."

I ignored him. Age or experience wouldn't make our quips any less asinine. So I focused on the battle. I had no idea how many bullets these revolvers held, but I had to assume each were filled. How fast could I shoot them? Would I be quick enough to hit him? And if I ran out of bullets, could I create more?

"I know you're lost in my amber eyes, but could we please get the show started?" Ike quipped.

I shot, but Ike was faster, dodging to the side before launching himself toward me. He lunged, blade extended to stab me, but I leapt forward, taking the sword through my chest. Pain overwhelmed everything except my determination, and before Ike could pull his sword free, I shot him in the face. He couldn't dodge something *that* close. And he didn't, a bright red circle blooming where his left eye once was.

We tumbled to the ground in opposite directions, both injured and dying. I shuddered, trying to keep my sanity intact. For a place that I wasn't supposed to be able to interact with . . . this felt as bad as or worse than any injury I had suffered in reality.

"I should have expected that," Ike groaned, living when the injury should have killed him. "We always were the self-sacrificing type, why not more so here, where consequences are meaningless?" The world around us disintegrated, fluttering upward like flickering silver fireflies. "I'm proud of you."

"Why? This is a stalemate."

"And?" he asked, looking at me. "You stalemated with *me*. Think about that for a moment."

"What are you—"

Wait. Ike was right. I had tied with him. Me! A fuckup trying to be a hero. Did that maybe mean . . . did that mean that one day I might be able to surpass him? That although we had taken different paths, mine might be just as valid as his? I could never be like my ancestors, but could I be something just as respectable?

"You did well, Michael." Ike rose to his feet and then tumbled back down so we faced each other on the floor. Every move was a struggle, and his body was disappearing along with everything else. "It's going to be hard from now on. It's going to be hard for you, with Serena's memories lost. But you'll be there for her, won't you?"

"Always," I said without hesitation.

"Good. That makes me happy." He exhaled a wispy golden breath into his hand until it formed into a small ball of light. It reminded me of what Angelo had left behind for me back in Hollow. Ike pressed it against my head until it took root in my mind just like a Darkness Fabrication. "You'll need that memory. Not now, but later. Don't forget about it. It's Serena's parting gift to you." He smiled. "She loved you very much."

"I don't understand. What did you just give me?"

"There's no time to explain. Find the names, Michael." Most of his body was gone and now his head began to disappear. "Find the names of the three Wolven Kings. It's the only way to avoid shattering Tenere and—"

He never finished his sentence, every trace of him gone. As was the sword in my chest and the pain of the injury. Only a desert of whiteness remained. Every trace of Serena was gone. When I returned, she wouldn't remember me, or her family, or anything. She was a blank slate now, ready to become something brand-new.

It wasn't death, but it might as well have been.

60

THE CROWNLESS QUEEN

My eyes snapped open, and I took a deep breath as I returned to reality. Dark was hovering over me while Serena was slumped over in her seat. It must've taken a lot out of her.

"Satisfied?" Dark asked.

"I don't know if that's the right word," I said, still reeling. "Can I talk to her?"

"If anyone should break the news to her, it should be her Kingman."

Dark undid Serena's gag and found she was faking her exhaustion as she tried to bite off his fingers as thanks. She spat at us both like a wild animal.

"Let me go!" she screamed. "Why are you two holding me like this? Who are you?"

Dark retreated to a corner of the room while I set a chair in front of her, took the deepest breath of my life, and then sat. "Do you recognize me at all?"

She tilted her head, still sneering. "Not in the slightest."

I rubbed my eyes, pretending it wasn't Serena in front of me. That I was fine. That I didn't want to scream until my throat was raw, or let tears fall freely. Instead, I closed off my heart and wore the mask I had in the decade after my father's execution. "Do you know what a Fabricator is?"

"No."

I gave the explanation Serena hadn't asked for. "A Fabricator is someone who can create a magical effect. Each specialization is different. Some can produce fire. Others can turn their body to metal." I turned my hand in front of me. "You can put pressure on people. Literally."

"How?"

"It's different for every person. One of my friends imagines making things brighter, and he can create light. I feel a warmth spreading over my body that allows me to—"

Serena wore a sly smile as a familiar weight tried to force me to my knees.

I met her eyes, my body nullified, as I shook my head. "That won't work on me, so don't bother trying. I'm the one person who will always stand by you, whether or not you remember that."

The weight disappeared. Serena relaxed in her seat, even if it was just a little. "For someone I don't remember, you seem to know me pretty well. Care to spread the wealth?"

"I will, but before I do . . . tell me what you remember about yourself."

"Why?"

"Because every time someone uses Fabrications, they lose memories. Sometimes, in special circumstances, they lose everything and become a Forgotten. So tell me, what do you remember?"

Her hesitation told me everything.

I wanted to pick up my chair and throw it against the wall and scream. And scream. And scream. But that wouldn't help, so I swallowed my emotions and went back to work.

"You are Serena Hollow," I said quietly. "Queen of a kingdom currently engaged in a civil war and about to marry a man named Jay Prince, a Merchant Prince of New Dracon City. We are in your mother's palace. Your father, Isaac, and your younger brother, Davey, are dead, but you still have a younger brother, Adreann."

Serena was crying now, overwhelmed by a lifetime of emotions that struck her without the context or control of memory. All things considered, she handled it better than I would have. In barely a whisper, she asked, "And who are you?"

"My name is Mi—"

"Mikel," she interrupted. "Is your name Mikel? For some reason I remember that name."

I stared at her, and Dark crept closer in shock. She had pronounced it wrong, but that was *my* name. Why did she remember my name? I had just seen her heart's desires wiped out. Nothing of the Serena I loved should have remained.

"Do you know who I am?" I asked softly.

Serena opened her mouth, about to speak, but was cut off by the ringing bells signaling that a piece of Celona was falling toward Vargo. Dark went to the window, watched as the red-tailed piece of rock whizzed over the city, and then hit the water just past the iron gate. It kicked up a huge wave, but none of the water endangered Vargo. Dark muttered about the watchers getting worse about giving timely warnings as we turned back to Serena. At least that might be the only piece of Celona we'd have to deal with this week.

Yet, when we asked her the question again, she shook her head. "No. Not really. I just recognize your name. But I don't know why." She hesitated. "Who are you?"

For the first time in my life, I considered the consequences of my words. If I told the truth, she might view me as a protector and a shield as she relearned everything. It would be a more formal relationship, one that didn't spit in the eyes of our ancestors with every kiss we shared. But it was not the one I wanted. There would be no quiet moments where I ran my hands through her hair before she slept. There would be no playful giggles and quiet moments that the world would never be privy to.

But if I told her about our relationship, I would be taking advantage of her. How could she not fall in love with the one person who would never leave her side? But . . . if we were truly bound by fate . . . wouldn't she choose me again, no matter the circumstances?

I have always been weak, but in that moment I was stronger than I had any right to be.

"I am Michael Kingman. I am a Mercenary. I was born in Hollow on the isle, where the buildings are so tightly packed together on the southern edge you can knock on your neighbor's windows without having to extend your arm. Our company has been tasked with your protection." I gently twisted my wrist around so *Es* was visible. "This was your noble nickname. When we were young, we developed feelings for each other. Es and Ike—our parents said we were two parts of a whole. Hate and circumstance drove us apart, but just recently it brought us together again." My heart wouldn't stop thumping in my chest. "But what we were doesn't matter anymore. We're at the beginning again. I'll support whatever you want to do or be, and cheer you on whenever you pursue what you love." I chuckled awkwardly. "So maybe this is arrogant of me . . ." I gulped. "But . . . I'm going to make you fall in love with me again. Because I am yours. Forever."

Serena clammed up. Thousands of thoughts were dancing through her mind. What-ifs and what-had-beens leading the way. And then, quietly, she asked, "Assuming you aren't lying to me . . . what happens now?"

Dark put his hand on my shoulder. "That's where I come in. We're debating options but they all depend on you. It's your life, and we can't stop you if you choose to walk away."

That was news to me. Would they really let Serena walk away?

"What are my options?"

"We'll explain in due time," Dark said. "For now, I need your word that you'll stay here. We need to keep up appearances or we'll be feasting on an extra-watery shit stew. Understood?"

She lifted an eyebrow. "Where am I going to go? I don't remember anything."

"Fair," Dark agreed. To me, he said, "I'm going to get Chloe. Stay with her, but remember she's not the queen you knew. She may be . . . unpredictable."

Dark left the room, and it was just me and the girl I loved.

"Are you going to untie me?" Serena asked.

"Do you promise to stay here until Dark returns?"

She rolled her eyes, and it caught me off guard. The Serena I knew had never done that. "I'm a woman without memories in a city I know nothing about. At least let me be comfortable."

I took a knife off the table and cut the knots. The rope tumbled to the ground as she rubbed her red wrists. On her left wrist was my noble nickname clear as day: *Ike*. Rather than stare at it, I went to the wardrobe and tossed her a long-sleeved shirt.

"So," Serena said, pulling it on and sitting more comfortably in her chair, one foot on the seat and the other stretched out. It wasn't very royal. "Care to educate me? You said this is my mother's palace. In Hollow?"

"No. In Vargo," I said. "On the Gold Coast, east of Hollow. Rather than being ruled by a single dynasty, the Vargo clan is made up of several families. When one rises to prominence, someone from that family is usually elected to clan leader."

"And that's my mother?"

I nodded, carefully keeping my distance.

"Tell me more about Vargo. Does it have good food? Drink?"

"It's on the water. The fresh fish is divine, even if all the cooks make everything too sweet." I blinked a few times to clear my thoughts. "Don't drink scaro. It's pretty much poison."

Serena seemed to deflate in her seat. Who knew what was going through her mind? What could it possibly be like to wake up without any memories?

"I'm sorry. I'd show you around if I could. But it's better we stay here."

Serena rose from her seat and approached me, every step as intricate and planned as if it were a rehearsed dance. She reached for me—as a friendly gesture—but I backed away at the last second, leaving her confused. "Why don't you want me to touch you?"

A blush was creeping up my face. "I'm just a little nervous if you're too close I'll fall into old—"

Serena grabbed the back of my head, brought me close, and kissed me. My mind went blank, focusing on the softness of her lips and the sharpness of her nails on the back of my head. When she pulled away, my eyes were still closed, and I could feel the heat of her breath against my face.

"You weren't lying," she observed. "You *really* are in love with me."

And then Serena pushed me away. Hard. I scrambled backwards, off-balance, before landing on my back in confusion. She was already halfway out the window but stopped to smile at me. "Give me some time to have fun, alright? I promise I'll be back by dusk. But I want to know what's out there."

Serena was out of sight by the time I reached the window. I slammed my fists against the window frame. If she hadn't been a Forgotten, I would never have underestimated her ability to read me. To know me better than I knew myself. I wouldn't make that same mistake again.

"Michael."

An excuse for what had just happened was halfway out of my mouth before I saw who it was: Serena's mother.

"Serena just went out that window, didn't she?" She scratched at her neck. "Maybe we should talk."

59

UNLOVED

Erica made me help her clean the silver cutlery that had been tarnished in last night's attack. We were alone in the kitchen, most of the staff were recovering from being poisoned, knocked out, and then attacked by dragons. As I wiped down a spoon I realized that however little Erica Vargo looked like Serena or Adreann, her green eyes still seemed to be able to stare right through me, just like her children's. They were highlighted by a black cosmetic.

"How long has it been, Michael?" she said softly. "A decade or so?"

"Something like that."

"And still a decade too soon. You look just like your father." Erica picked up a knife, held it up to the light, and frowned. There were water marks all over it. "What do you want, Michael?"

I must have looked confused.

"What do you want? I know what you've done in Hollow . . . Serena has told me you and your father aren't responsible for Isaac's and Davey's deaths." She dipped the knife into a shallow pan of water, took it out, and started polishing it with a cloth. "Adreann disagrees, but Serena was very insistent. It's left me wondering: What do you want in life? What do you hope to accomplish before you die?"

I had no answer for her.

Erica set the knife down on the table and reached for a whetstone. "I ask because Isaac's death has freed me from Hollow Court and the Endless Waltz I endured for seventeen years. I have no boat in the race and trust that Serena is strong enough to dance on her own without her mother's help. I cannot get in the way of what she perceives as her duty . . . not even to save her from my own fate. She refuses to listen to me. I was a . . . a terrible mother." She began to sharpen the knife in long, slow strokes. "Which brings us to you. I can't stop her, but you might be able to."

"I don't understand."

"Then let me be clear. Convince Serena to end her engagement and abdicate. Take your family far away, and then let Adreann burn Hollow to the ground."

"What? Are you mad? Why would I—"

Erica pointed the newly sharpened knife at me. "Hollow has been cursed ever since Celona was shattered. It cannot be saved. It cannot be prosperous. It cannot be anything but a cemetery, and a moon-fall target. Good men and women have tried to change its fate, and all have failed. Isaac and your father are only the most recent casualties, but the curse of Hollow always wins. Nothing can be sustained there so long as Celona is shattered. I don't want my daughter to be another casualty."

"My family—"

"Your family was only ever a temporary solution. Eventually that foolish ideology will falter . . . if it hasn't already. You cannot save Hollow, but Adreann can: by destroying it. Let it be reborn from the ashes."

"You're insane," I said with a laugh. "Adreann is your son and—"

"Never call that thing my son," Erica growled. "I may have birthed him, but that monster is not mine. He was conceived in hate, carried in hate, and born evil. The day that monster dies, I will cry for happiness and thank the world for rectifying my greatest mistake."

How was I supposed to respond to that? I hated Adreann as much as everyone else, but . . . had anyone ever loved him? Had he been raised alone and hated his entire life? Had violence and sex been the only things that made him feel alive?

I steeled my will to focus on the conversation in front of me.

"You want me to convince Serena to leave Hollow so Adreann can destroy it? Why would she ever agree to that? And why would you want me to do that? You don't even sound convinced that my family is innocent."

"I've never met a guilty man whose loved ones thought he wasn't a paragon of justice," Erica said. "Davey and Isaac are both dead. But Serena isn't. And you are the only person who can convince her to abandon the throne. Or do you not know what's written on her skin?"

It was hard to forget my noble nickname on her left wrist. That spot was normally reserved for memory tattoos, which meant she had been in love with me for a very, very long time. Even if we had both been in denial about it for the past decade.

"Kingman and Hollow can't be together," I whispered. "It's the first rule we're taught. If I broke it, my ancestors would be ashamed of me." And we might shatter Tenere, but who cared about a minor world-ending threat like that?

Erica tilted her head. "Since when have you listened to the rules? Especially ones set by long-dead assholes more concerned with the status quo than helping Hollow prosper?"

"Because I can feel their eyes on me in the darkness," I blurted. "Like a thousand spirits swimming around me whispering lies, shouting madness, and telling me to act as if I deserved to have been born. Even now, having created my own legacy, I live in fear I'll never make them proud. That I will embarrass them and the precedent they set. Because for everything I am, have been, or could be . . . I still think it is my duty to martyr myself for the good of others. Old age isn't something I expect to experience."

Silence.

"Think on it," Erica said, swapping the sharpened knife for a dull spoon. "Besides, I imagine it'll take you time to convince Serena to leave. I'm not sure what she'll be like as a Forgotten, but I can't imagine it'll be well behaved."

"You know?"

The former Queen of Hollow nodded. "I knew the moment it happened. I had her in my arms after she was shot . . . She was like a newborn babe wondering who the stranger holding her was." She cleared her throat. "I may have been a terrible mother, but I don't think I'm so bad that being there didn't offer some comfort."

I put down the cutlery I was shining. "I don't know how to help her."

"Do you know what Serena has been doing in the decade since your father's execution?" Erica asked. "Or do you just know the exaggerated stories of the Two-Faced Queen?"

"Just the stories," I said, "I think."

Erica chuckled. "To be fair, the stories *are* entertaining. And she knew they would be. She thought that if everyone was focused on the idea that she was training with this secret organization or that secret organization, the citizens would be content with her absence. And they were. To a degree."

"Wait, so you're saying she didn't train with the Evokers or the Berserkers?"

"She trained with the Evokers a little. Enough to learn about how they conducted investigations." Erica picked up another piece of cutlery. "But the Berserkers? I don't know how anyone believed that lie. The Thebians would sooner let in a New Dracon City Engineer than let a Hollow—a Royal nonetheless—train with them at their military academy." She gave me a flat look. "Or have you forgotten your studies?"

The crown on my throat throbbed as I thought of the age before I was a branded outcast. "Just a little. If Serena wasn't with the Berserkers, where was she?"

"Being Red for a time. She's always loved to sing . . . And she did visit me. She wanted to know why I left Hollow, and I told her the truth. No matter how painful it was to hear." Erica made a weird noise with her tongue and lips. "And, ironically, she did what you were supposed to do . . . what you will have to do, now that she's a Forgotten."

I motioned for her to continue.

Erica leaned back in her seat. "Be there for her. Watch over her. Let her make mistakes and find her own way in this world. There will be times when she wavers, or when you'll want to strangle her for making a stupid decision . . . but you did the same, so you'll understand." She smiled. "Or did you really think it was luck that none of the low nobles you conned ever came after you? Because they tried to. Until Serena intervened."

I rubbed my face, trying to hide my disappointment in myself. There were so many people who had helped me without my knowing. When I should have been helping them. I felt like such a failure. Just this once, I hoped I could repay a fraction of what had been done for me.

"Do you have any idea what might catch her attention in Vargo?" I asked. "I have no idea where she went."

"Try to look at the world as a child," she answered. "Forgotten know nothing, so everything is exciting. Think about Hollow, what would catch your attention if you weren't so jaded?"

"The castle and the gardens," I said quickly. "They're amazing. Besides Kingman Keep, it's the only place in Hollow where you can see—" and I stopped, suddenly knowing where she had gone. "The boats. Serena always talked about the boats in Vargo as a child. She called them fat turtles and always told me made-up stories about how she had been allowed to captain one past the gate to the new world. And even from the palace, you can see them in the docks."

Erica lazily rested a hand against her cheek. "What are the odds she might be in awe of the same thing twice?"

"High," I said. "I'm sorry to leave, but I have to find her. Before someone else does."

"It's fine," Erica said, going back to her polishing. "But, Michael, I have a favor to ask of you if you happen to run into Chloe. Tell her . . . tell her that I said thank you for always being at Serena's side."

"Wouldn't it be better coming from you directly?"

"I doubt she'll think it's sincere if it comes from me," Erica said quietly. "Her mother and I have never seen eye to eye. And because of that . . . I imagine Chloe thinks I hate her as I do Efyra . . . which is the farthest thing from the truth." She hesitated. "I've never thought children should pay for the crimes of their parents. Not even when it concerned you and your siblings."

I didn't know what to say, so I muttered a pathetic thank-you and ran away before I embarrassed myself further. I was nearly mindless as I left the palace and went down to the docks looking for the biggest boat I could see. But as I ran, part of me wondered if I would ever be more than a fool focused on revenge and protecting those I cared about. After everything—the good and the bad, the extreme and the meek, the struggle between being the man I wanted to be and the man I was—I was still no closer to being at peace. It still felt like I was running on borrowed time, an invisible sand dial suspended over my head, only a few grains left to fall before the death I was owed was granted.

If given the chance, could I forgive and forget those who had wronged me and make the most of what was left with family and friends? Or would I forever be seeking revenge? I had no answers to my thoughts, and I had other things to worry about when I reached the docks.

The boats in the bay reminded me of the models some of the nobles built and displayed. They looked pristine, but beneath all the symbols, metals, and paint that adorned the vessels I wondered how many were rotting from the inside out. How many would snap or collapse at the slightest resistance, and how many were designed to make the tourists feel safe while on board rather than actually survive the greater sea beyond the safe area?

Cassia's ship caught my eye among the dozens of others. A beautiful imperfection among the others. It wasn't the largest, but it easily overshadowed many of the others around it with its style and elegance. It was made of a varnished red wood that shone in the limited light of the fireworks and moonlight, had three masts and a bowsprit that had been sharpened to a fine point. The figurehead was a muscular bare-chested man with long hair, a trumpet in his left hand and a compass in the other. The *Freedioso*.

But there was no way Serena was getting on there. There were too many armed guards patrolling and I doubted a Forgotten—even one as skilled as she was—could sneak onto it just because it was cool. But where had she gone from here? What had been the next thing to capture her—

I froze in place, a familiar voice reaching my ears. It called to me like a long-lost lover, a pleasant lullaby easing the weight on my shoulders. I followed the music like a hound trailing a scent until I came across an unpleasant tavern. It looked like one of the few things that had lasted for more than a hundred years without being torn down. A broken sign hung above the doorway: *Honest Drinks*.

Pushing the door open, the music overwhelmed me, a distraction from how run-down the place looked. Everything was either chipped or broken or in mid-disintegration. The liquor bottles had been left open and fruit flies buzzed around them, as thick as mist. But the music was almost as beautiful as the singer.

Serena had drawn a crowd of sailors around her. She stood on a table with her eyes closed and hand over her chest, singing "The Sailors' Sorry Serenade" as skillfully as she had any other song. I had come in at the end, as she hit the last note, and then the silence lasted just a moment before the thunderous applause only drunks could give began.

Serena opened her eyes and smiled wider than I had seen since we were children. Then she saw me in the back of the bar and that happiness shattered, replaced with a painted-on smile that would come off with the lightest of rain. She tried to get down and maybe make a break for the nearest exit, but one of the sailors pushed her back onto the table as others hollered for an encore.

"It's been fun," Serena said, keeping her eyes on me. "But I really should be going."

"Encore! Encore! Encore!"

"I don't know any other songs! I couldn't if I wanted to."

"You must know 'The Rabble-Rouser's Riot'!" the bartender shouted.

"Or what about 'The Minuet of Memories'?" another voice added in.

Others began to pitch their own songs as Serena stood on the table, rubbing her left wrist. So even as a Forgotten she still had that comforting habit. Even if she didn't know what it meant. What else of the Serena I knew was still there?

"Fine!" she shouted, holding up her hands and silencing everyone. "I have a song stuck in my head. I'll sing that. Just remember you asked for it if it's no good, alright?"

There were no protests, so I settled in against the wall, already knowing what song she was remembering. It was "The Angels of Naverre" and, just like the first time, I was ruined the moment she hit the first note. And yet, as I listened to the mesmerizing tale of Lyra and the fall of Naverre—without all the emotions that I had felt during the Endless Waltz—I was struck with the sudden feeling that something was missing. The words were the same, the song was sung the same way, but there was no pain in her voice. It was like watching a bird repeat the tune without understanding the message. There was no weakness, no suffering, and no love. Just a song.

Others in the bar weren't underwhelmed. They hadn't heard it before, so they marveled at the imitation. I felt like a traitor as she finished the song—everyone else so raucous—and I could barely clap when a few months ago a simple song had stolen my heart and left me flushed.

Serena descended from her stage, pushed through the sailors, and went to the bar. She brought over two dirty glasses filled with an amber liquid. The smell burned any hair I had in my nose when I took a whiff of it.

"What is this?" I asked, still recoiling from the smell.

"Scaro."

"Scaro?" A pause. "I'll pass. I drank too much of it last night."

Serena shrugged and tossed hers back, then drank the one she'd brought for me. She covered her mouth, shuddered, and then put the empty glasses down on the nearest surface.

"Are you here to drag me back to the palace?" She burped and then hit her chest, still looking pained from the drink. "Because I'd prefer not to go yet."

"We'll return eventually. Did you have fun singing to all these people?"

"Kind of. For some reason, it wasn't as fun as I hoped," she admitted. "I know nothing, so everything should be an adventure, something new to discover with every turn, but . . . but it's kind of lonely. Especially with everyone staring at me. Are they always going to do that?"

"In Hollow and on the Gold Coast they will. If you head out to sea, you might escape it. Or you could try your luck to the west. But you'll find that wherever you go, someone will always recognize you."

Serena rubbed her temple as she sighed. "That sounds like a nuisance. Is being queen better than spending my life running away from those responsibilities?"

"It's a lot of work," I said. "You have to be a symbol, always doing what the country needs even if it's not what you want. You never get a day off and you'll be lucky to have a few close friends to make the rough days easier. And if you're anything like your ancestors . . . well, then you'll be dead before you're fifty."

"How old am I now?"

"Nineteen."

"Was there a celebration?"

"Not really. There were gifts, but you were still grieving after your father's suicide."

She put her forehead against my chest. Shivers went through my body, and I nearly bit down on my tongue, hoping she would move. She didn't. "It all sounds so lonely. If you were in my position, would you want to return to that life? Or would you chase something new?"

I didn't reply, which gave her the answer she wanted anyway. We sat together, talking and sharing stories. This was her last chance at freedom, and it was the last private hour I might steal with her. We clung to the fleeting moment, knowing nothing would be the same when we returned to our ordinary lives.

NEW ROUTINES

Dark and Chloe were waiting for us when we returned a little before dusk. They were in the middle of an argument and, surprise surprise, they both wanted me flogged or in chains or dead or whatever. At this point, I was more surprised when people didn't want to kill me.

"—when I get my hands on him I'll wring his neck," Dark declared with accompanying hand motions. "Michael had one job, and he fucked it up. What a blithering imbecile."

"I prefer 'moonstruck fool,'" I said as we climbed in through the window. Serena came in behind me, stifling a yawn. "Sorry we left. Things got—"

Dark lunged for my neck, but Serena grabbed his hand before he could follow through. She stared him down as everything in the room slightly shook, invisible forces pressing down on it. "It was my fault," she said. "I ran away from him. Wanted to find out what was out there. If he hadn't found me, I'd be long gone. So give him a break, alright?"

Dark exhaled through his nose but relented. He cracked his knuckles in quick succession before finding a place to sit down. Chloe took his place, examining Serena. Showing a lot of restraint, Serena never questioned why this unknown woman was searching her body for injuries. Chloe found nothing and was about to give Serena a hug but stopped when Serena tensed up.

"Well," Chloe said, awkwardly trying to recover by backing away from us. "Serena is fine. And we should be grateful for that. But please don't do that again. Even though we're in Vargo, we must be careful. Who knows what others are planning."

Serena sat down like a defiant child. "It would be great to know who these others are before you fearmonger me into being scared of everything and anything."

"I'm sorry, Your Majesty," Chloe said with a slight bow. "This is—"

"Serena. That's my name, isn't it?"

"It is, but there are certain formalities—"

Serena raised her hand to cut Chloe off. "Right now I'm Serena. I haven't agreed to be anything or anyone else yet. So—and I say this politely—fuck your formalities. Treat me like a person, not a symbol your country desperately needs, and maybe we'll get along and I'll listen to your concerns. Understand?"

I wouldn't have blamed her if Chloe broke down then and there. But she stayed tall and strong, her eyes clear and dry, and did her duty. "I apologize, Serena. Forgive me. This adjustment is as hard for us as it is for you, and I have forgotten that. It won't happen again." She took a breath. "What circumstances of your life are you aware of?"

"Most of the basics," she answered. "Older brother was murdered, father committed suicide, younger brother is an asshole, and my mother hates me. And I'm engaged to someone named Jay Prince, a Merchant Prince from New Dracon City."

"And you know who he is?" Chloe asked, nudging her head at me.

"Michael Kingman," Serena said without hesitation.

"Were you told about the Kingman family and their relation to your own?"

Serena shook her head.

Chloe avoided looking at me. "The Kingman and Hollow families are intertwined. Each Hollow is assigned a member of the Kingman family who acts as their trusted confidant. They are our ancestors' solution to a seemingly impossible problem: Who can the Royals trust without hesitation? Who will be with them no matter what?"

"Ah." She turned to me. "So is that why I fell in love with you? Were you the only person I felt carefree around?"

I shrugged. "Part of the reason, but not the whole."

Dark rolled his eyes. Chloe was fidgety, unable to stand still. Probably because Serena was openly talking about things she shouldn't have been. It didn't take a genius to realize her talking about being in love with someone who wasn't her fiancé was a big mistake.

"Did Michael tell you the details surrounding your brother's and father's deaths?" Dark snickered. "Or did he conveniently leave those parts out?"

"I don't—"

"I was blamed for killing your father before it was determined the King committed suicide," I interrupted. "My father was blamed for killing your older brother. That's why some call me a traitor's son and a king killer."

Serena stared me down. There was no malice in her eyes, only curiosity. "You make no sense to me. You're a bundle of contradictions masquerading as a man. You say you're my protector, and yet you're also the most likely cause of my death. Which is true? One? Both? Neither?" She bit her lower lip. "What else aren't you telling me? Either by omission or purposefully."

"Plenty, but it's not malicious. I just don't want to overwhelm you."

"I'm not some delicate thing. Even in this state, I can handle the truth. No matter how harsh it is."

Dark slapped his thighs. "Yes, well, as lovely as this cute back-and-forth is, can we get on with what we're here for? Should I bring it up or do you want to, Raven?"

"I'll do it," Chloe said. "You will need to make a decision about whether you're willing to be Hollow's Queen or want out, but we have a third option."

"And that is . . . ?"

Dark crossed his arms. "To cure your Forgotten condition."

I snorted. Loudly. And then began to laugh, much to the confusion of Serena and the anger of the other two people in the room. "Very funny. Forgotten can't be cured. I know! I tried every cure out there on my mother. And she didn't recover, because—"

"You didn't try all of them," Dark interrupted. "And the one we're suggesting is the only one that has a chance of working. Michael, you've heard of the Reborn Titan, correct?"

I nodded, and let my foolish Mercenary mentor speak without any more snide remarks.

Dark pulled out a map from his pocket. It was fairly new, some of the ink having blurred recently. There were islands with names I had never heard of before—the Sleeping Isles, Maiden's Rest, the Sea Wall, and the Illuminated Path—and others I had. Eham, the pirate capital of the world, was at the very edge. Gwen had always wanted to travel there someday. Suddenly, even if I thought Dark's plan was ridiculous, I wanted to hear it out. If only to find out how to get there.

"We're here," Dark said, pointing to Vargo. "The Reborn Titan is over here. If we could pass through the abyss, it would be a day's voyage at most once we reach the Palmer Archipelago, but since we can't . . . we would have to go past Eham." He cleared his throat. "It's hard to say if it's actually a titan . . . or a statue of one. But it's by far the biggest thing I've ever come across. It blacks out the sun in the region, its hands are bigger than some buildings, and without a doubt it is unnatural. Something old, magical, and dangerous."

Was I seriously about to find out titans were real? Worse—when things inevitably went to shit, how was I supposed to kill a titan?

"And at the top of the titan, directly in the middle of its forehead, is a tree with pitch-black leaves and heart-shaped fruits. That fruit might restore Serena's memories."

"What makes you believe that? Just because this titan statue is some kind of weird magic?"

"I brought the titan to the surface. And I've eaten from that tree. Since then . . . I stopped losing memories when I use Fabrications."

That was a complete and utter lie. I had experienced Dark's memories firsthand thanks to Nonna and knew there were holes in them. Dark had no idea he had lost any memories, getting defensive when I asked for clarification on a point while he was explaining his life story to me. This fruit wouldn't heal Serena, and I was the only person who knew that for certain. Was it better for them to believe in a lie or to let the truth eradicate any lingering hope?

"My thought is that it may be able to restore Serena's memories, rather than simply prevent her from losing any more in the future," Chloe said. "It's a long shot, but . . ."

"But we don't have any other option," I finished.

They both nodded, but it was Chloe who spoke. "If it doesn't work, Serena can decide what she wants to do. Marry Jay Prince and govern Hollow, or walk away."

"If I walk away," Serena began, "what happens?"

"Honestly?" Chloe rubbed her brow. "Your younger brother taking the throne and letting Hollow fall into ruin may be the best-case scenario. Jay Prince may respond with anger and attack Hollow, or he may not. We have no idea what to predict if you step away. But we'll deal with that if we must."

Serena fell back on her bed, ruining some of the fine silk with sweat and dirt. "Is there anything else I need to know? Or can I get some sleep and continue this conversation later? My head hurts. Think I drank too much."

"We can continue later. We still must determine the best way for us to embark on a long voyage without insulting Jay Prince or giving him an idea what we're planning. But there is a reception tomorrow you'll have to attend. Please try not to reveal what happened to you."

Serena waved Chloe off like a child with a loud yawn. She began to pull her clothes off and throw them to the floor without care. Chloe was pushing Dark and me out the door as fast as she could, but before we were gone completely, Serena said, "Chloe. Leave my Kingman with me. I want him here while I sleep."

"Serena," Chloe said, with the most insincere smile I had ever seen. "Michael is a Mercenary, not one of your Ravens. He's not allowed in your room unaccompanied. It would prompt a lot of ques—"

"Is he not my birthright? Mine to do with what I wish? My shadow turned sentient? Or have I misunderstood the relationship between Kingman and Hollow?" She was already under her covers, a bundle of blankets in the vague shape of a woman. "Besides, Orbis Company is tasked with my protection and my fiancé is in league with Mercenaries. Would anyone be confused to find a Mercenary protecting me from other Mercenaries?"

Dark was having too much fun, and Chloe had to push him out of the room before Serena heard him laughing. "As you wish, Serena. But please do lock the door behind me."

Serena was already snoring, sprawled out on the bed like a cat in the sun. Her left arm was gripping a pillow as her right leg dangled over the edge of the bed. I left the room with Chloe, who was somewhere between wanting to break someone's nose and crying her eyes out. In the end, she put her hand over her mouth and screamed until a servant turned a corner, saw us, and then wisely decided to return the way they had come.

"That could have gone worse," Dark said. "She at least seems interested in going to the titan and eating the heart fruits."

"It's a week's journey there. Assuming nothing goes wrong . . . which it will," Chloe said, pacing back and forth. "I haven't even told her mother yet. How am I supposed to tell Erica her daughter's a Forgotten?"

"She already knows," I said. "She saw it at once. I doubt she'll tell anyone else, though. Erica's main interest was in helping Serena get away from—"

Dark looked down at me. "Why are you being so supportive? A few days ago you were throwing a tantrum at the very thought of her marrying Jay Prince, and now you're being kind and caring and agreeing to our, honestly, insane plan that has only a fraction of a chance to succeed." His eyes flashed red. "What are you after?"

"I just want to see Serena return to normal," I said, meeting his eyes. "Why are *you* being so helpful? Telling Chloe about the fruit is mighty generous of you. When you raised the titan from the sea, did you forget something? Do you have some other reason to return there?"

The shadows were flickering around him. Above us, black tendrils squirmed like worms in the mud after a heavy rain. Was Dark really going to try and intimidate me in front of Chloe? I knew his secrets. I knew his pain and why he fought. I knew who his father was and why we both wanted him dead. Whether Dark realized it or not—besides maybe Alexis—I was the closest thing he had to a confidant. And if he couldn't trust me, who could he?

"We'll talk later," Dark said to me. And then to Chloe: "Discuss traveling to the titan with whoever you need to. It'll cost you to hire Orbis Company for the voyage, but it's worth the price. We all know you couldn't get there without us."

As Dark left us, Chloe's fury grew until she slammed an open palm against the wall multiple times in a row. Then she took a breath and steadied herself . . . and the Raven she had trained to be returned.

"Michael," she said, "why are you the only person who Serena trusts right now?"

"Maybe it's because I'm showing her all of me. No restraint."

"Michael Kingman telling the truth. How novel." She whistled. "I'll let the maids and guards know you'll be guarding Serena's door until further notice. Someone will bring you a chair. When do you want someone to relieve you?"

"Whenever," I said, sitting against the door. "I don't sleep much

anymore, so it's not the end of the world if I'm here until she wakes up."
Before Chloe could walk away, I added, "Oh, Chloe, Erica wanted me to
pass a message to you."

The one-eyed Raven froze in place. She didn't look at me as she muttered, "What?"

"She told me to say 'Thank you for always being at Serena's side.'"

Chloe was breathing rapidly and shallowly. "Did she say anything
else?"

I hesitated, wondering if I should try to comfort her. "Just that she
doesn't hate you. That anything between her and Efyra is their business,
not yours."

"I don't believe a word of that," she said, voice fluctuating. "Not after
what she . . . I'll send someone to help you watch the door."

Chloe stormed off before any more words could be said. I had no
idea what I had done or what message I had just carried for the former
Queen of Hollow. Was there something I was missing here? Despite my
ignorance, I tried to make the most of my time, penning a response to my
friends in the lantern-lit hallway—the entire palace occupied with other
things, even the birds and mice—wondering how my mother, Gwen,
Lyon, Rock, Kai, and Trey were doing.

I missed them all so much.

PART 2:

ANGER

28 DAYS UNTIL THE FINAL DEATH OF MICHAEL KINGMAN

"Do we scream at the flowers that grow toward the sun?
Or the children that scrape their knees? Then why must we fault
the unwavering hunter for eventually capturing us?
Death is not malevolent, just apathetic."

—The Archmage of Hollow scolding his apprentice, Green

57

SHOTS IN THE DARK

Sometime in the middle of the night, Karin Ryder, the new four-feathered Raven, relieved me of my duties. I didn't want to leave, but I had to take advantage of a quiet palace and the assumption that I had gone to bed. I had my own plans. I'd scoped out the library a few days before, so I knew the most unobtrusive route. The library wasn't restricted, but there were so many Mercenaries staying in the palace and I didn't want to give any of them a clue as to what I was looking for. Some cards were important to play close to the chest.

The library had a dark stained-glass roof that illuminated the place in the day and made the shadows fester in the nooks and crannies at night. It was a long room with stacks of bookshelves down the walls and large tables in the center of the room. Everything smelt like old paper, pressed flowers, and unsolved mysteries. I was reminded of home and long days spent underground in the Hollow library, trying to decipher the life of an immortal man.

I didn't know how long I had, so I went to work immediately. The shelves weren't as carefully arranged as the ones in the Hollow, but the books I was looking for would be the thickest, and that was enough to avoid getting lost in most pirate tales of long-lost treasure and the harrowing journeys they went on. I pulled out two books—*Known Pirate Captains* and *Famous Ships in the After Shattering Era*—and brought them to the nearest table. I started with the first one. It was the most likely to contain information about Angelo. No matter how badly he had wanted to erase himself from history before arriving in Hollow, I knew there were traces left behind. A Hollow High Noble wouldn't have been able to disappear as easily as a Mercenary.

The book was organized in alphabetical order by most renowned nickname, and the catalogue detailed the name of their ship, estimated number of crew, flag description, and greatest accomplishments. The *a*'s were devoid of any mention of an Angelo, and the *s*'s had so many variations of "shade," "shadow," or "shimmering darkness," it was impossible to use that to find Angelo. So I went down the names of the ships, hoping for a name to jump out at me. Halfway through, one of them did—the *Lady Katherine*. It belonged to a free captain who went by the name of Nolgea—a very poor anagram for Angelo—who had a crew of about a dozen, waved a red flag, and had sailed to the edge of the known sea, where a wall of water stretched horizontally as far as the eye could see. No raids had been conducted under his flag, and he seemed unremarkable in every single way. If it hadn't been for the ship's name, I would have missed his entry entirely.

As I ran my thumb over the pristine ink, I tapped a finger against my temple. The last time Angelo had been seen in Hollow before his return was during the Day of Crowning, and for Angelo to have named his ship after his wife implied they had met before he went to the Gold Coast, not while he was there, as I had assumed. So where did they meet? Had Angelo gone somewhere else first? And why had Dark's mother been there, too? High Nobles couldn't move as freely as Mercenaries—her travel would have had to have been approved by her asshole father. So where could they have met?

I closed the book and tried to rub the sleepiness from my eyes. With every answer I found, three more questions sprouted up. Which, to be fair, was expected. I was trying to solve mysteries that had remained unsolved for a millennium. If the answers were easy to find, others would have found them by now. Was there anything else in this library that might be—

"Hello, Michael." Wheels screeched against the smooth tile. "We really need to stop meeting in libraries."

Symon Anderson, the self-proclaimed King of Stories and former Recorder for the Hollow Archives, rolled himself into the room on a wheeled chair. His nonfunctional legs were covered with a blanket, and the man who had once prided himself on the red robes of the Hollow Archivists now wore common clothes like everyone else. He had been forced to vacate his position after he had refused to accept a demotion while he recovered from his injuries. History was no longer his to control.

Without thinking, I left my chair and ran over to embrace him. He shouted profanities at me and tried to push me away but relented in time, returning my hug. We separated once my apologies made him angry and, rather than fight further, we sat down at the table together. This was the first time I had seen him since I had found his body outside of Kingman Keep, bloodied and with bones jutting out of his legs. The fall from the top tower hadn't killed him but had left him crippled from the waist down.

"How are you doing?" I asked.

"Fine," Symon mumbled. "Get me that book, will you? The one with the red-and-gold spine. No, not that one. The one below it."

I handed him what he wanted and he rested it on his lap, gently running his hand over the cover as if it were a cat. "Never apologize again for what happened to me. I was outplayed," Symon said, avoiding my eyes. "I should have realized who Gwen's employer was sooner. I just didn't expect it to be someone like *that*." He looked up at me. "But that doesn't matter anymore. How are we going to get revenge?"

"Is that why you left the Archivists? For revenge?"

"Yes," he said without hesitation. "But don't mistake me. My hatred of your family remains. And I will destroy your legacy once the Wolven Kings have been taken care of. But I can't do it alone." He hesitated. "If the records are to be believed, it was the Kingman and Hollow families who dethroned the Wolven Kings. I have a feeling you may be the only ones who can do it again."

"What makes you say that?" I asked, arms crossed.

"A hunch," Symon said. "Something about how the Wolven King talked about your family made me suspicious. He seemed to enjoy holding Gwen hostage. And he said I was right to believe that your family shattered Celona."

"He said what?" A pause. "Was he lying?"

Symon shook his head. "He firmly believes the Kingman family shattered Celona." He pursed his lips and his eyebrows furrowed. "What aren't you telling me?"

I told Symon what I had learned from Angelo about immortal killers, Gwen working for a Wolven King, and how Serena and I would shatter Tenere if we remained together. Rather than record whatever I said, he sat staring intently at the wall behind me as he tapped his index finger against his cheek.

"Do you think he's telling the truth?" Symon asked. "That your romance might shatter another moon?"

"I don't know. I was hoping you might. After all, you're the one who initially said my family was responsible for shattering Celona. What evidence supported that?"

"There was only a single line in the old scrolls," Symon replied. "It said, 'Those bound together created the new night sky we see.'"

"That's it?" I said with a chuckle. "You wrote a two-hundred-page examination of my family's position in society based on that single line?"

"My apologies. I should have written a thousand."

I hid a smile. It was good to see that Symon was still his normal ass-hole self. "If we assume my family did shatter Celona, then it must have been by the First Kingman, right? The moon was shattered before Adrian overthrew the Wolven Kings."

"Correct," Symon said. "But that's all we know. The First Kingman is barely mentioned in the records. We don't know their gender, their name, or even if they were a Fabricator. So whatever they did . . . I don't know how we'd figure it out."

I rubbed my eyes, sleep trying to claim me after a long day. "Could we find the answer through Adrian the Liberator? Angelo said it took a Hollow and a Kingman to shatter the moon. We might be able to find something there."

"History has been cauterized around him," Symon explained. "If Adrian did anything questionable—let alone bad—Archivists would have erased it by now. Countries need their founders to be perfect . . . and shattering a moon definitely isn't heroic."

I leaned back in my seat, hands behind my head, and put my feet on the table. "That's another dead end, then." I ran my tongue along the back of my teeth. "Wait. What about the sparkling pieces of Celona? Chloe said their messages could hold the answer to who or what shattered Celona."

"That's the theory. But . . ." He lost, or maybe changed, his next words, picking at his nails instead. "There are seven pieces in total. One is in Hollow, one in the Thebian Empire, one in Azil, one in New Dracon City, one in Eham, one in the Gold Coast, and one on the Skeleton Coast. We have neither the time nor the resources to find them all." Symon tore off a long, jagged piece of his nail, cursed when he saw blood, and then pressed it against his blanket to avoid staining the book on his lap. "We need to find our answers faster than that."

"I captured Rian the Smoke Dragon."

"You did what?" he shouted. And then, quieter, added, "How? Where is he?"

"No idea," I said. "I had someone hide him from me. But they'll tell me whenever I ask."

"Is that a precaution against the Black Death?"

I nodded. "But if I could get into his memories, we might learn what shattered Celona. Or learn more about the Wolven Kings. He claims to have known them but won't tell me anything."

"You'd need Illusion Fabrications for that," Symon said.

"Therein lies the problem." I played with my father's ring. "But Dark has them. Copied them from a Mercenary in Orbis Company when we were in Hollow."

Symon was skeptical. "And therein lies the problem."

"You wouldn't happen to know any other Illusion Fabricators, would you? I know they're rare, but—"

"Just steal the memories yourself."

I paused. "I'm prepared to eat his heart if I have to, but—"

"I'm not telling you to eat his heart," Symon drawled. "I'm telling you to steal them. The way you stole powers in the Church of the Wanderer to catch lightning."

I stopped lazing about and leaned forward. "What are you talking about?"

"I'm in league with an imbecile," he muttered. "But fine. Let me explain how *your* powers work to you." Symon couldn't help but smile. "A nullification specialization lets you cancel out magic in a given area and stops other magic from hitting you when you nullify your body." I nodded. "Well, think of it more broadly. When you nullify yourself, you're preventing magic from hitting you by stopping the contact of magic and your body. So what happens to the magic if it never hits something?"

"Uh, it remains where it was?"

"Yes. And if you could hold said magic, what could you do with it?"

Lightning might as well have struck me in that moment. "I could redirect it." I nearly fell out of my seat. "That's what I did in the Church of the Wanderer! I *redirected* lightning!"

Symon smiled broadly. "And what's to say you can't do it with other types of magic, too?"

"Nothing," I said breathlessly. "And Dark promised to show me how he raised the Titan soon. Which gives me an opportunity."

"But you'll need practice. If our only chance of getting information out of Rian is by going through his memories, you can't mess up stealing Dark's Illusion Fabrications."

I put my hand over my heart and feigned surprise. "Are you offering to help me practice? That's so kind."

Symon conjured a ball of light in his right hand and chucked it at me. Instincts kicked in before logic—story of my life—and I ducked, the ball of light smashing against the far wall like a firework exploding in the sky. The light dissipated into nothing as I popped my head back up. Two more balls were in his hands, and if he'd been wearing brighter colors, I would have assumed he was an Azilian circus performer.

"Try to catch it this time."

Symon threw another at me. I nullified my hand and tried to pluck it out of the sky like I had the lightning, but I misjudged where it was, and it whipped past . . . and collided with my face. It felt like a heavy stone and knocked me back, forcing me to scramble to remain seated. I patted my face to see if I was bleeding, but my hand came back clean.

"Hits pretty hard, doesn't it?" Symon mocked.

"You're enjoying this too much."

"Absolutely I am."

Symon chucked another one. This time I was a little more prepared, my fingertips brushing against the light as I curled them inward, slowing it down and putting it under my control until I was able to catch it. It pulsated in my palm like a beating heart. I tossed it up and down, wondering whether it would disappear after a few moments. It didn't. So what else could I do with it?

Symon and I kept practicing until I had enough bruises to form a constellation on my chest, neck, and face and a stack of balls of light at my side. Finished, I smothered them all into nothing with a nullified hand and then dropped my head onto the table, sweating profusely. My head was pounding, and my vision felt hazy. I didn't normally feel so tired after using Fabrications, I was usually just concerned about the cost, but this time was different. It felt more physical than mental. And that thought reminded me of something: Weaving.

"How much do you know about the magic the Thebians use?" I asked, lifting my head again.

"Weaving? Not much. The Thebians are pretty secretive about it, and the High Nobles that use it rather than Fabrications are even more so." Symon adjusted his blanket. "I tried to pry some information about it out of High Noble Sebastian Margaux. But he was surprisingly adept at holding on to his secrets."

"Dawn's brother was a Weaver?" I asked.

"He's a Stone Weaver. I figured it out when he punched a wall in anger and the wall *moved* around his fist. It was jaw-dropping. He'd just lost a duel during the Summer Festival to High Noble Elliot Castlen."

Since Sebastian was currently under Orbis Company's protection . . . maybe I could convince him to teach me what he knew. It would be one more tool to use against Dark, Angelo, and the Wolven Kings, and I needed anything that might give me an edge. But Sebastian hated me. And I didn't have anything to trade for his knowledge, not when all he would want was his freedom. And yet . . . I needed to pay Regal Company a visit. There had to be something I could offer to prevent them from brutally murdering Sebastian.

"I think I'm going to get some rest while I can," I said, stretching and getting to my feet. "Do you need help to get back?"

Symon shook his head. "I never slept much. Less so now. Just pass down some books from the top shelves. One of us has to solve these mysteries."

I didn't argue with Symon. While I would never admit it to his face, Symon saw history in a way I never could. Rather than people and places and events, he saw the patterns in events, easily able to decipher what happened based on limited information. If there was any man who might be able to determine who the Wolven Kings were and why my family might have shattered Celona, it was Symon. It was personal for him.

Once Symon had a stack of thick books on the table in front of him, I left the library in search of somewhere to sleep. Symon bid me good night and remained in the candlelit room. I knew without a doubt he would still be there in the morning. Archivists were dedicated beyond compare once they had prey in sight.

56

A BUTCHER'S PRIDE

Alexis once told me the only way to get information about Regal Company was to get it from them directly, unless I wanted to incur their wrath. So, when the sun had just barely emerged, that's what I went to do. It was a fool's plan, but straightforwardness had helped me before. There was a time for lies and misdirection, and this wasn't one of them.

Regal Company had taken control of a run-down theater near the docks. It had fallen into disrepair once sailors had decided chucking fish at the performers was more entertaining than the story itself. While only their senior members were staying there—two of their brigades either camping outside the city walls or in the numerous ships they had under their control—I was more nervous about meeting them than I cared to admit. I didn't have any leverage to protect myself, so I'd have to watch my tongue.

There were two Mercenaries guarding the entrance, flipping knives and arguing about whether the Goldani Fate Selection had happened by now. Apparently one of them had a cousin by marriage who was an

Unfortunate and hoped to improve their social standing and move out of the canyon where the unlucky resided. Their conversation stopped when they spotted the crown brand on my neck and the everlasting flame of Orbis Company on my inner bicep. My reputation preceded me once again.

"I need to see Papa Noble," I demanded, trying my best to imitate Dark. "Now."

"Why?"

"That's for his ears only."

"You'll have to demand a blood binding," the other spoke now. "If you're not willing to, then scram."

A blood binding was an oath only Mercenaries could swear, during times of peace, to talk to another company. It guaranteed they were there to talk—not for war. Any injury to either party would be met with retaliation by every Mercenary company on the continent. Only one company had ever broken it in recorded history, and they, their families, and their friends had been wiped out in half a day. It wasn't an oath anyone could break and live. Unlike Hollow blood oaths. But what was with everyone placing such importance on someone's blood?

"I'll expect Papa to declare it once our talk begins," I said.

"We can't guarantee that. It's his decision."

"I'll guarantee it," Liam Noble said from within the theater. He gave me a playful punch in the shoulder. Most of his fingers were still splinted and bound. "Will that suffice? Or do you need my father to swear the oath, too?"

I told Liam that his oath would be enough, and we entered their temporary headquarters together. The auditorium had been replaced with a sparring circle that was currently filled by two dueling Mercenaries, short sword and net versus a battle-ax. The Mercenary with the battle-ax set the net aflame with Fabrications, swept their opponent's leg, and then smashed them down with the butt of their blade. He won with a blade to the throat. Blood dirtied the sand as the other Mercenary died with a whimper. Some Mercenaries clapped lazily from the stands while others started removing the body. Ciara Noble was on the stage with a large stick, tapping it in a steady rhythm as she instructed two more to begin a duel with practice swords rather than sharpened steel. The next duel was fought with much less severity.

"Why did those two fight to the death?" I asked. "Over a blood dispute or something?"

Liam shook his head. "It's for glory and wealth. In Regal Company, we believe in the philosophy that the conqueror keeps. So if you beat your opponent in a death duel, you get what they have: position, wealth, rank, and troops—all of it."

"So that makes you and your siblings the strongest, since you lead the four brigades."

"Without a doubt. We're challenged constantly, and we have yet to lose." He pulled down his eyelid and exposed his purple eye. "We have to earn these. Unlike you Kingman."

"You're not wrong. My eyes are an inheritance," I agreed. "They're a curse. One that has taken my confidence, my family members, and those I love. And it will continue to take everything from me until nothing but shameful pride and legacies remain." I smiled at him. "Some friendly advice: I'd run from yours sooner rather than later."

My words flustered Liam for a heartbeat, but the jolly Mercenary returned in a flash. "Why don't we join the circle and dance, then? Let's find out whose legacy is superior."

"I think I'll—"

"Liam!" Ciara shouted. All eyes turned to us. "Is that who I think it is?"

"It is, dear sister!" Liam threw an arm around my shoulders. "He's come here under a blood binding to speak to Father."

"The utter gall." She tossed her stick to the side. "I love it." Ciara hopped down from her pedestal, ordered another to supervise the fighting pit, and came over. She linked arms with me and showed such a sweet smile I felt as if I had swallowed a dozen lemon pastries. "Don't mind me. I just want to make sure you don't lose your way to Father."

She dragged me to him, with occasional pauses to show off different aspects of their facility and company. Neither was secretive about the number of troops they had nearby nor cared if I wanted to flip through their archives of past jobs and accomplishments. Liam even offered me a chronicle of his greatest moments, waving it in front of my face as if it were a leg of chicken. It was a trap, and I wanted to give in to it . . . but I turned their offer down. Whatever information they were prepared to sell me, I didn't need.

Papa Noble was in the backmost room, standing over a table with a map of the Sea of Statues. Gear-shaped figurines used to denote opposing armies were approaching the island of Eham, while dozens of figures with little hats had been placed on the island itself. Other figures were spread out more erratically. There was a flame figure on Fire Island, a bone skull on the City of Orphans, a lantern on Vargo, and a handle holding a torch on Vargo surrounded by dozens of crowns. Four dragon-shaped pieces were at the side of the table, yet to be placed. Papa Noble twirled a wolf-head piece in his hand, tentatively trying to place it near Eham, but quickly picked it back up, visibly frustrated.

"What do you prefer I call you?" Papa Noble asked, still looking at the map. "Michael? Kingman? Mercenary Kingman? Dragonslayer? King Killer? Worldbreaker? It's rare for someone so young to have so many names."

"Worldbreaker? Who calls me Worldbreaker?"

"A man who had faith in your abilities long before you entered the Endless Waltz."

Only two men fit that description: Angelo and Domet.

"As much as I like titles, I like my name more. It's the only thing I've earned."

"Admirable." Papa Noble clicked his tongue. "Liam, is Michael here under a blood binding?"

Liam nodded. "He is, Father. I authorized it."

"Thank you." He shooed his children out of the room, and they went obediently. The leader of Regal Company had yet to look up from his map. "Let me ask you a question. Why would one of the biggest Mercenary Companies on the continent congregate all their forces on an island where personal freedom is not a gift but a fundamental right?"

"Are you talking about those gears going to Eham?"

"Yes. Those represent Machina Company. You know of them?"

"I do." I had met a few of them informally during the King's birthday. They had fed me turkey legs and too much wine. Lovely people. "I'm assuming by your tone that they're not invading Eham but are there for another reason—one you can't determine." I crossed my arms, glancing around the room again. There was nothing extraordinary in it, like a military barracks that could be abandoned at any time. And yet Papa Noble was clutching that wolf-head figure as if it were more valuable than gold. "Who does the wolf-head piece represent?"

"A Wolven King."

My heart thumped in my ears and my face paled. "Is Machina Company joining them?"

"Potentially. No Mercenary Companies except Void Company have any ties to the Wolven Kings that I've been able to discover, but . . ." He placed the wolf-head figure on Eham. "Who knows what can happen in a millennium."

"Do you know what the Wolven King wants?"

"No," Papa Noble said. "But I know someone who might."

I rubbed my brow. "And let me guess—you want me to get the information for you? That's why you're talking to me." I put my hands on my hips. "Who knows what they want?"

"Angelo Shade."

I hesitated. "Aren't you working with him and Jay Prince already?"

"Client is king, not god." Papa Noble reached under the table, procured a tall piece of wood, and began to carve it with a knife drawn from his side. Each shave was careful, as if he was trying to expose what was hiding within the wood rather than creating something. "Let me be clear. I will not betray Jay Prince so long as he continues to pay us for our services. But I worry what the active Wolven King is up to, and I need to protect my company from what may come."

"So you want to make a deal."

"Yes," he said. "One that may benefit us equally."

"If you wanted to make a deal with me, why wait for me? What if I never came?"

"Then you weren't worth the time. I expect those I work with to be courageous—not opportunistic."

This was a trap, like all deals with power-hungry men. But I wanted to hear him out to understand what else was going on with the Wolven King. My sister was one of their captives and I would do whatever it took to bring her back home. "What do you have in mind?"

"Jay Prince is meeting with Angelo Shade later today," Papa Noble began. "I'll tell you where so you can interrupt their meeting, or eavesdrop on it. In exchange, you'll share any information you learn about the Wolven Kings who are amassing troops, and give me Sebastian Margaux."

"What?" I spat. "You still want Sebastian Margaux? Didn't you swear—"

"I have *every* right," he growled. "High Noble Sebastian Margaux embarrassed my company and attacked someone we were protecting. Because of his actions I lost thirty apprentices to the dragons. Be thankful they weren't full-fledged Mercenaries, or I would be asking for much more." A pause. "I will have vengeance. You can gain something from it or not, as you choose."

Truth be told, the choice was simple. Everyone feared Regal Company would attack Cassia's ship to reclaim Sebastian, so giving him up would ease tensions and probably earn me some goodwill with Cassia. But I couldn't let Sebastian die. I didn't like him or what he had done to Serena, but I couldn't let Dawn's brother die. Not when my life was her gift—and one I hadn't deserved.

"I'll bring him to you," I said. "You can have him while I'm away dealing with Angelo. But when I return, he walks out of here alive with me. Understood?"

"Fine." Papa Noble pulled a small journal from his pocket and laid it open to reveal a picture of a man, his anatomy labeled. Each part had a numerical value from zero to a hundred. The heart had the highest value, while a fingernail had the lowest. "I require fifty points of pain to be satisfied. You may help me decide what I'll take."

"No wonder Regal Company are called the butchers of Vurano."

"This is a standard system for Mercenaries," Papa Noble replied. "Orbis Company does the same. Why put such emotion into something that can be solved rationally?"

I didn't have the time to argue. Business was business, and I had to go and get Sebastian before Papa Noble would give me Angelo and Jay's location. I pulled the journal closer as my stomach churned in disgust with my own actions. "If I select an arm . . . will you cripple it, or remove it?"

"We'll put a tourniquet above the chosen section, drain it of blood, and then remove it with cleavers and bone saws. The body tries to escape into unconsciousness, so we're careful to pump them full of drugs to make sure they feel it." He nicked his thumb while carving but kept going as if blood wasn't staining the wood. "We take no pleasure in it. But it is necessary."

Another day, another level of brutality I uncovered. What a fool I had been to think Domet was the worst person I'd ever work with. "What is this twenty-point option connected to his head?"

"We shave his head and then carve Regal Company's symbol deep enough that it won't fade away when it heals."

I gulped. "Is there anything you insist on?"

"Either an arm up to the elbow, or all of his fingers."

Each finger was worth three points, so eight of them would make up only twenty-four. I'd still need twenty-six more. Meanwhile an arm up to the elbow was thirty-five. Economically . . . fuck . . . economically it was better to sacrifice one of Sebastian's arms than all his fingers.

"I'll let you take an arm, but I want to choose which one after I drop him off."

"I'll agree to that. What else?"

Fifteen more points. Whatever difference I had clung to that separated me and Dark was long gone. "Brand him."

Papa Noble stopped carving and arched an eyebrow at me. "You would have him branded with our symbol rather than beating or skinning him, or losing an ear or a few toes?"

"If I let you take more from him, he might lose himself . . . but if he's branded—then he'll never lose his hatred of you." My own brand throbbed on my neck. "If you're going to do this, I'm going to make sure he comes for you afterwards."

Papa Noble smiled broadly. "Creating an enemy for your enemy is a formidable strategy. We'll see if your plan works, because I will do everything in my power to drain High Noble Sebastian of his will to live." He put the piece he had been carving down on Vargo. It was a broken crown. No subtlety there. "Now bring me High Noble Sebastian Margaux."

BURNT SKIN

In Vargo, thanks to the constant flow of pirates pillaging and raiding the Sea of Statues, the locals had developed games to entertain those stuck on shore leave. The most popular game was fruit slingshot, where sailors honed their aim by shooting at targets floating in the bay. According to Alexis, Cassia, Dark, and Titus played it every morning. Today was supposedly no different.

I pushed my way through the crowds to get to the dock, but before I could take a step onto the sun-soaked wooden boards, Titus grabbed my shoulder.

He said nothing but pointed to Alexis and Cassia as they stood in front of a giant slingshot with a basket of fruit at their side. Both had cloths wrapped around their foreheads to keep their hair out of their faces. Alexis chose a mango, loaded it into the pouch, and pulled back the contraption. She carefully moved to the left and right like a crab, one eye open as she took aim at the fruit-splattered targets off the shore. All of them were obnoxious colors with black numbers. The point values increased the further away they were from the shore.

Alexis fired and crowds held their breath as the mango soared through the air and smacked into the 70-point target to the jumping, stamping, roaring celebration of those around us. Cassia kept her sights on the targets. She took a small watermelon in her hands, twirled it slightly, and then fitted it in the pouch. Unlike Alexis, who had waited and aimed, Cassia yanked it back and let it go. It followed an identical arc to Alexis's shot and hit the 70-point target in exactly the same place. The crowd blew in applause as Cassia grinned wickedly at Alexis.

"How did she do that?" I muttered to no one in particular.

"Cassia has a perfect memory," Titus explained. "It doesn't matter what it is—music, maps, or movements—if she sees it, she can replicate it perfectly. We joke about it, but many Mercenaries who've fought her think it's the equivalent of dueling with their shadow."

"No one has a perfect memory," I said.

"Then Cassia's memory is the closest we'll ever see. It helps she's not a Fabricator. She doesn't lose memories like you or Dark do."

I hesitated. My memory wasn't perfect—I had no delusions about that—but it was still hard to come to terms with losing memories every time I used magic. Who knew what I had already given up? Part of me wished it was clearer. That the memories at risk would appear in front of me, right before I used magic, so I could decide if I could give them up. But they didn't. Or I couldn't remember it, at least. When it came to Fabrications, I was like a child grasping at clouds. It was dumb luck that I had survived the Endless Waltz.

"I need to speak to Cassia when she's done," I stated.

"Is it vital?" Titus asked. "Cassia needs time to gloat after she wins."

"I want permission to give High Noble Sebastian Margaux to Regal Company."

Titus recoiled away from me. "What did they offer you for that?"

"Information I can't get otherwise." That didn't satisfy him, so I added, "It could help me find my sister and stop Dark's father."

"I'm not going to say don't do it," Titus said. "But are you sure you're in the right headspace to negotiate with Regal Company? They're about as cutthroat as they come, and I don't want you making bad choices because of the attack on the Hollow Queen."

"My feelings for Serena won't cloud my judgment."

Titus squeezed my shoulder. "If you truly think that . . . then you need to think again. You went through something that changes people forever. The woman you loved is gone, whether you want to admit it or not." He gave me a weird side hug. "Take the time you need to mourn."

Grieving was a waste of time. I needed to act. My sister was still missing, Angelo was still trying to bring someone back from the dead, and Dark was ready to destroy the world to get what he wanted. They had to be stopped. Even if, of all the lies I told, that one was the only one I couldn't convince myself to believe. Like Dark, I'd give anything to walk away from all this, if I could do it with Serena.

Titus left me to chitchat with some of the local fishermen about the proper way to cook rockfish. Apparently it was a hotly debated topic. The Goldanis thought it was best served cold, while those from New Dracon City only served it blackened. I waited for Cassia, who caught sight of me as two blue-sashed sailors were congratulating her. Whatever she said alarmed one of them, and she walked over as Dark and Alexis started to play fruit slingshot.

"Hello, Michael. What do you want?" she asked with her arms crossed.

I motioned for us to go to somewhere more private and we stepped into a secluded alleyway that smelt like cinnamon and fish guts. I told Cassia what I wanted to do, bluntly, hoping the truth might soften the blow.

"Weren't you the one who fought the hardest for us to *protect* High Noble Sebastian Margaux? Why the sudden change?"

I rested one leg against the wall. "I underestimated Regal Company. They're going to have their vengeance on Sebastian no matter what happens to Serena. They're prideful like that."

Something softened in her visage. "Regal Company is known for getting what they want whether it's justified or not." She looked to the side. "Have you already met with Papa Noble?"

I nodded. "He wanted fifty points of vengeance."

Cassia made an exasperated sound. "It could be worse. Usually their minimum is seventy." She paused. "What do you get out of this deal?"

"Information."

"About?"

I didn't like Cassia, but now wasn't the time to lie. "My sister has been taken by a Wolven King, and Papa Noble knows something about them. I'm trading Sebastian for information that might help me save her. I have to be prepared to face them."

"Is that it?"

"No," I admitted. "He'll also tell me when and where Angelo Shade and Jay Prince will meet today."

"Ah," she said, dragging the word longer than was standard. "That's worth the guilt."

"I hope so."

She began to walk away as a figure casting an elongated shadow appeared at the end of the alleyway. "My quartermaster will release him to you when you ask. Tell her: *Whales on the starboard*." Cassia passed Dark as she left the alley. My skin felt colder with his arrival, and the sun seemed to have vanished. "Good luck, Michael. You'll need it."

My Mercenary mentor stared me down with red eyes. "Something I need to know?"

"No," I stated. "But you still have something to show me."

"You want to see how I raised the titan?" he asked, one hand on the hatchet at his side. His features looked elongated, the whites of his eyes grew bigger, his tongue grew long and snakelike, and I could've sworn I saw black wings on the walls. "Are you sure?"

"You weren't a Spellborn when you raised the titan, so whatever you did . . . it was as an ordinary boring mortal." I stepped toward him. "How scary could it be?"

"You'll see." Dark clasped me on the shoulder and rainbow light flooded out of his hand. I put my own nullified hand over his, grasping at the light, and the city of Vargo melted around us like candle wax dripping to the floor. I had hold of something long and slimy—I hoped it was Dark's Illusion Fabrications—and stuffed it into the uncorked vial in my pocket. No time to examine it now, with Dark's deranged smile keeping me company until we plunged into the cold deep water of his memory. We broke the surface together.

A titan's head with a black-leafed tree sprouting from the forehead towered over us. It wore a curved mask of steel that had rusted from the gentle lap of salt water. There were black voids where its eyes should have been, mesmerizing to stare into. The skin beneath the mask was crusted with mud, making sure it was impossible to tell if it had ever been flesh, fur, or just the stone it appeared to be. There were handholds carved into it, and we climbed up silently.

There was nothing up here but rocks and grass and the tree in the middle of the titan's forehead. The roots were thick and sprawling and the onyx leaves let no sunlight pass. Four heart-shaped fruits hung from the branches, dangling like lanterns from the limbs. Davis, the younger version of Dark, was standing under it, tentatively reaching for one of them. His ribs showed underneath his burnt red skin, his lips were chapped and cracked, and his hair had lightened from pitch-black to a dark brown, thanks to the constant sunlight. It was another glimpse into the human Dark had been before he became the terror standing next to me.

"You came here after you were exiled from Vargo, right?" I asked, hoping the question might get him to open up. If my previous adventures had taught me anything, it was that having more information was always better. Even if I didn't understand the greater context immediately.

"Correct," Dark said, arms crossed. "The Vargo clan couldn't touch me once they discovered I was a Mercenary. It was supposed to be a five-year sentence, but it was lessened once Orbis Company was tasked to protect the Hollow Queen."

"What did you do, that they tried to punish a Mercenary?"

"I killed a dozen or so people who were trying to overthrow Erica. She was forced to make a show of force to reprimand me."

"How'd you do it without magic?"

"My reputation as the Black Death was in place long before I became a Spellborn. And while some of it was exaggerated—I only sank one Palmer battleship, not however many they claim—I'm good at finding the cracks in people. Be it a combat weakness or personal one." A pause. "And then I exploit it."

"What's my weakness?" I asked.

"Your family, your legacy, and Serena Hollow."

Bold of him to claim that when I had already lost two of the three. "Why did you come here when you left Vargo? Were you just chasing mysteries?"

"I left Vargo on a raft. I didn't really choose where I was going." Dark stood side by side with his previous self as Davis picked the fruit. "Arriving here was a fortunate accident."

"It's a long way to float."

"Not when you're debating whether your life is worth living." He paused. "Eventually I decided it was. I imagine the world would have been happier if I hadn't."

Davis bit into the heart-shaped fruit and black juice spilled down his chin. He devoured it, spitting out the rock-like pit, and then kept eating fruits as if it was the only thing that would keep him alive.

"I hadn't eaten in a week," Dark said. "Truth be told, the fruit doesn't taste very good. It's not unlike slimy seaweed. But in that moment, it was divine."

I walked around the tree. It all looked so manicured for something that was supposed to be remote. Nothing seemed special or out of place or looked as if it could be a special mechanism. So I asked Dark how he had raised the titan.

He rapped his knuckles against the tree, a metal hollow sound ringing out around us. I was about to ask what that meant when Davis made the same discovery. He touched the bark and felt metal rather than wood. Suddenly, more skeptical of the fruits he had eaten without thinking, he pulled at a branch with one foot planted against the tree as support, and tumbled away when it popped open. I watched him reapproach it cautiously. A human spine traveled down the center of the metal tree with a weathered brown note attached to it. It read: SWGLSQWUQXDQYWEE.

Why was the weird lettering from the Royal crypt here? What connection did this place have to Hollow?

"I still don't know what that note means," Dark said as his younger version examined what he had found. "I suspect it's a dead language."

I glanced at the note again without alerting Dark that I had seen it before. I knew only one word—Alphonse—which translated into GVHRQXJE, but I would decipher as much as I could. Code breaking was new to me—my style of thieving had always been more hit-and-run—but Angelo could do it, and anything he could do, I could, too. So I committed the letters to memory, to puzzle over when I was away from Dark.

Davis pulled on the spine in the tree as if it were a chain and . . . nothing happened.

"I would have been disappointed if it was that simple," I said.

Dark pointed to the bone hand sticking out of the ground. Another bone hand shot out of the ground, gripped the grass, and then pulled the rest of its body out. It was a grey-and-white skeleton, identical to a surgeon's diagram except for its golden tongue, pearly smile, the rubies in its eye sockets, and the fleshy heart that hit the rib cage with every beat.

With a raised hand and bright white smile, it said, "Hi!"

Davis bonked his head on one of the tree limbs, cursed, spun around, and then dove behind the tree to hide from the skeleton. I had to put a closed fist in front of my mouth to avoid laughing. Dark was muttering unpleasant things at Davis as if he were me.

"You well there?" the skeleton asked, creeping toward Davis. "You're a little sunburnt, but you look fit and healthy. Are you a Forgotten? No other reason to come here and eat those."

"What are you?" Davis asked, keeping the tree between them.

"Oh. My apologies." The skeleton bowed deeply. "I'm a skeleton. I can't tell you my real name because it's this whole thing. I promised a friend I wouldn't, and I don't want to go back on my word despite it being rather silly." He waved his bone fingers around dramatically. "You can call me Skelly."

"You're a Skeleton? Like the slaves from the Gold Coast?"

"The Gold Coast? I've never heard of it— What year is this?"

"Fourteen thirty-two A.S."

"'A.S.'?"

"After the Shattering," Davis explained. He pointed to the outline of Celona that lingered in the daytime. "That one."

"Well, slap me silly and throw me in mud—they left me behind!" Skelly kicked at the ground. It did little to disturb anything. "Those ungrateful heart eaters. I can't believe they did that. Did they think I died or . . . ?" He stared at the water splashing against the side of the titan's face. "Maybe they had more reason to leave me than I care to admit."

Davis blinked rapidly. "Are you and the titan connected somehow?"

"We're one and the same, boy. Do you know what a Spellborn is?"

Davis shook his head, and I felt my face pale.

Skelly shrugged. "It's not important, but I'm one of them. There are three classifications of us—walking, swimming, and flying. I'm of the walking variety. All you really need to know is: Avoid anyone who claims to be Spellborn. They're nothing but trouble."

I was furious as Dark smirked next to me. There were *three* different kinds of Spellborn and Dark had kept that information from me? The insufferable prick. He must've been loving this. Once again I looked like a moonstruck fool. Thankfully for him, I wanted to hear this conversation more than I wanted to rant at him.

"I only know about Fabricators, Weavers, and Patchworkers," Davis said. I blinked. I was unfamiliar with Patchworkers. What did they do? Where were they from? More questions for another time.

"I'm surprised Patchworkers are still around. They're strong. I would have expected the Insatiables to wipe them out in the millennium I've been asleep." Skelly ran his fingers up and down his rib cage as if it were a washboard. "Not surprised Fabricators and Weavers are still around. They're like cockroaches." He looked up. "Are you one?"

Davis shook his head. "I'm nothing."

"Do you want to be something?" Skelly reached through his bones and pulled out his fleshy heart. "You'll get my powers if you eat this."

"No, thanks," Davis said without hesitation. "I'm a magicless human and I'd like to remain so. It keeps me sharp."

"How humane." Skelly put his heart back in place. "Then would you care to help me regain some of my strength in return for an invaluable piece of information?"

"I'd rather have a way home."

"Can't help there," Skelly said. "But I promise you my reward will be worth the mild inconvenience."

Davis hesitated, then said, "What do you need me to do?"

Skelly's demeanor changed from excited to forceful and focused. He snapped off one of his rib bones, bit it with his pearl teeth until one end was sharp and pointy, and then handed it to Davis. "Stab yourself."

Davis twirled the bone knife. "How will this help you?"

"I'm weak," Skelly said, gesturing to himself. "I need power. Think of me like a parched plant, only rather than water you're giving me blood."

"This conversation reeks of motives left unspoken." Davis tapped the bone knife against his thigh. "I want more than you're offering me."

"You don't even know the value of what I've offered."

"And that's the problem." He pointed the bone at Skelly. "Give me something of—"

"Zarack," Skelly interrupted. The name overtook everything around them like an endless void, sucking in all the noise. And yet it lingered in the air like a note that had rung flat, making sure we knew it was unnatural. "That's my King's name. Do you understand the ramifications of what I said?"

"Which one?" Davis breathed.

"The second."

"Tell me about them," Davis snapped, eyes flinty. He stabbed himself in the thigh with the bone. "And I mean *everything*."

Skelly tilted his head back with his arms extended as the titan's head rumbled below them, slowly rising. Red dots shimmered around him before latching onto his bones like leeches. All four of us rose higher and higher into the air as more of the titan was exposed. But before it was raised completely, Dark clenched his fists and everything around us went pitch-black.

"Is Zarack"—I spat the Wolven King's name out and the earth shook beneath my feet—"the Wolven King who has my sister? Is that why you showed me this? To gloat?"

"Zarack doesn't have Gwen," Dark said. "He's still imprisoned."

"So Alphonse does."

Dark side-eyed me. "How do you know that name?"

So it was the third name that he didn't have. That was good to know. "Luck. I knew it for a long time before I understood its meaning. But the more interesting question is: How do you know it? You learned the second's name from Skelly, but where did the first's come from?"

"You saw me learn it," Dark countered.

"What are you—" I cursed loudly. "The church with the faceless man. That's where you got the second's name, wasn't it? That's who you met there!"

"We're done here." Dark waved his hands and we reappeared in the Vargo alleyway. "We'll talk to Chloe about returning to the titan for the memory fruit. It's our best chance to—"

"Just tell me the truth. Why do you want to return to the titan?"

Dark stuck his hand in his pockets and stared at me, unflinching.

I played with my father's ring, trying to focus. What could he want with the titan? It wasn't for Serena. There was something there he couldn't find anywhere else. Maybe a piece of information from Skelly? But what information could he crave so badly? What could it be . . . ? He wanted the third Wolven King's name. That was it.

"You think you can learn the third name there, don't you?"

"Skelly is the only person I can think of who may have it," Dark admitted.

"So the memory fruit is a lie then," I muttered, trying to hold back tears.

"You heard him, didn't you? He said: 'Are you a Forgotten or something? No other reason for you to come here and eat those.'" Dark turned his back to me. "Why would he have said that if the fruits couldn't restore the Forgotten's memories?"

I held my tongue.

"This is a win for both of us, Michael," Dark said, ever so sweetly. "Help me get the third's name and we can both have our loved ones back. And isn't that what you want? Isn't it worth it, to have Serena back?"

Curses ran through my mind, and I swallowed them like bitter medicine.

Dark turned to leave. "I knew you'd understand."

He left, and I stood in the alleyway long enough to be certain he wasn't waiting for me, working at deciphering that strange string of letters. I knew Alphonse—*GVHRQXJE*. Most of the letters from the note— *SWGLSQWUQXDQYWEE*—were different. I couldn't do much until I found more of this strange script.

Until then, I had a hostage to hand over and a meeting to interrupt.

54

THE WEIGHT OF A MAN

Cassia's quartermaster—a lovely Ehamian woman with a knack for telling the dirtiest jokes imaginable—had Sebastian blindfolded, bound with rusted chains, and gagged with torn cloth down his throat by the time I arrived. She gave me his restraints as she told me a joke about a bee and a naked man, but before she hit the punch line, her expression grew grim and she said, "Whatever happens to him is on you now."

Not even the end of the joke could make the feeling of the weight of a man's life in my hands go away . . . and so we walked toward Regal Company's makeshift headquarters in relative silence. Not that Sebastian had any choice in the matter. But even I couldn't lead him to the void without a chance to experience the grass and sun one last time, so I removed everything except his restraints and let him have a moment on a bench in a small park filled with wildflowers and dried-up water grass beside a canal.

Sebastian didn't fight or try to run. Instead he leaned back in his seat, kicked off his boots, and dug his toes into the dirt. In a small voice, he asked, "How is it going to happen? Ax like in Hollow?"

I shook my head. "I'm turning you over to Regal Company. They're going to torture you for what you did to Serena, Sebastian."

"Delightful," he cooed. "Just torture? Or will I die, too?"

"You'll live."

"But will I enjoy it? Or will they leave me a husk who prays for the afterlife?"

"They're going to take one of your arms and brand you with their symbol."

"That's it?" Sebastian asked, nearing laughter. "And here I thought almost killing the Hollow Queen would bring more dire consequences."

"There would have been if they had to take you. But since we're giving you up—"

"Oh, *you're* giving me up?" he interrupted, scooting away from me. "That's good to know. How's it feel to be on the other end of the executioner's block?"

"Sebastian . . ."

"I remember what it was like during your execution. I was with Dawn and our parents forbade us from going near the Isle, so we listened to the execution from the balcony instead." He closed his eyes, bathing in the sunlight like an outstretched cat. "She *cried* when she thought you died. And then hollered like a boy in knight training when it was clear you didn't." A pause. "She deserved better."

"She did."

"And you let her die." Sebastian moved something around in his mouth. "Once Regal Company is done with me, will you tell me what you think happened to her?"

"Yes," I said, hauling Sebastian back to his feet. "I promise I will."

"Are your lies always so sweet?"

I chose not to respond, and we walked in silence to our destination. Liam Noble was waiting outside, a big smile on his face as he rocked back and forth on his heels. "Honorary guest!" He gripped Sebastian's shoulders. "We are going to have so much fun today!"

"Remember our deal," I warned.

"Of course," Liam said. "Did you decide which hand it'll be?"

I faced Sebastian. "Which is your dominant hand?"

He waved his right, so I told Liam to take the other.

"How kind," the Mercenary said. Two others took Sebastian away into the theater. Laughter echoed from inside as the Mercenaries prepared for the show.

"And the information I was promised?"

"Church of the Eternal Flame." Liam pointed to the cliffs that hung over the water. "Walk of Flame. All the way at the end. And hurry—they're meeting at midday. Best find a place to hide before they get there."

And then Liam went into the theater, locked the door behind him with a clank, and left me out in the blistering sun, sweaty and annoyed. But there was no time, so I went off to reunite with my former foster father.

According to who one asked, the very notion of evil was a fable passed around by the simpleminded. A falsehood created by those in power to distract the common people from their daily injustices in favor of rallying them all together against the truly irredeemable. I became one of these evils when I was named King Killer. But I was nothing more than an obnoxious kid who thought the world owed me. Evil was not so easy to see. The Heartbreaker was one of the few things I could call evil. They had committed brutal murders for entertainment and bloodlust.

Angelo Shade was not evil. He was just a man who wanted to bring his wife back from the dead. By whatever means necessary. Punishing the Hollow High Nobles was just a prelude that kept his hunger at bay. And I had to remind myself of that as I went to spy on his meeting with Jay Prince.

As in Hollow, the Church of the Eternal Flame was easy to find. It glittered in the midday sun, and there were plenty of gold-plated signs pointing the way. The church was nestled on a small cliff overlooking the bay and a permanent cloud of smoke lingered over it. As if a firestorm was about to descend on it from the skies.

Because there were no services today, only a few monks were wandering the grounds. Some were tending to the ever-burning cannisters of fire neatly organized to light the path to the main cathedral, while others tended the foliage, swept the paths, or performed other menial tasks. None of them stopped me as I went to the main prayer area, careful not to draw too much attention to myself. There was a massive fire pit burning at the opposite end of the church, and lingering in this space even for a few moments made me sweat profusely. A few people lingered in the pews, muttering nonsensical things to themselves with their heads back and eyes closed, as if they were lost in another world.

"Hello," a monk said as she approached me. Her black flame-trimmed robes fluttered at her heels as she walked, and I wondered how she could stand the heat. "Can I help you?"

I shook my head. "I'm just looking for a quiet place to repent."

"May I suggest the Walk of Flame? It's the perfect secluded place to reconnect with what you value."

"That sounds lovely. Can you show me the way?"

The monk did so with a smile. I was led down a set of stairs and then into a side room with piles of loose-fitting white robes that were mandatory to wear in the Walk of Flame. I stripped, put my clothes away in a closed wicker basket, grabbed a gown, and then made my way into the chamber of isolation. Steam greeted me like a slap to the face and burned my throat as I inhaled. The basement was lined with coffins and the heat dried the bodies until most of their remains were fit to be transferred to the valley of devouts down in the Gold Coast. I had a feeling Katherine's coffin would be here somewhere, so I pushed through the steam with watering eyes, searching for it.

I found it at the end of a corridor, perched upright against the last indentation. There would be nowhere to hide when they arrived. Unless . . .

I grabbed the edges of the coffin, opened it gently—dried-up flowers pouring out—and saw Katherine Naverre. Her body was wrapped in brown cloth and the yellow dress she wore was little more than threads, but there was plenty of room in the coffin for two people if necessary. Angelo must've wanted her to lie in luxury in death as she had in life. I kicked away the flowers that had tumbled out, picked a few up . . . and then shut myself in the coffin with Katherine. Her cloth-wrapped skull touched my nose as sweat dripped down my face and made my breathing labored and short. I was sweating profusely by the time Jay and Angelo arrived, tongue uncomfortable in my mouth.

"—could have chosen somewhere else to meet," Jay whined as his voice crept closer to Katherine's coffin. The Mercenary coughed harshly on the steam. "I hate this place."

"That's the point. Everyone does, except the monks," Angelo explained.

I could only identify my former foster by his voice, but it was more than enough. Every aspect of Angelo was seared into my memory like the brand was onto my skin. He couldn't disappear as long as I lived.

"I saw another set of clothes in the changing room before we entered," Jay stated quietly. "Are we free to talk openly?"

"Yes," Angelo said. "Just be careful. And feed the brazier. Make sure no one can see us unless they come close."

I heard Jay pour water over the hot coals, and they hissed as more steam filled the corridor. Even if I wasn't inside a coffin, I doubted I would be able to see them anymore.

"Have you been well, Father?" Jay asked. "I know the accommodations aren't the best, but it was hard to find somewhere Mother's coffin wouldn't raise too many questions."

Father? Mother? What was Jay talking about? Angelo's only child was Dark.

"It's fine," Angelo said tentatively. "If only she weren't confined in such a dark place." He paused. "Have you found what I asked you to yet?"

"I haven't. It's harder than I thought it would be." Jay chewed loudly on something. "Are you sure it's out there? Just because the first two were doesn't mean the third is. It would make sense if it weren't. Especially with his connection to High Noble Char—"

Angelo shushed him. "No details."

"Sorry, Father." He shifted on the wooden bench. "Why can't we talk somewhere else?"

"Because it'll make you weak. I taught you to speak without giving clear answers as a child, remember? Treat this as another lesson." A pause. "You've grown complacent."

"Complacent?" Jay snarled. "How dare you! I conned one of those Merchant Princes out of his seat on the New Dracon council while you were busy playing a prideful soldier in Hollow! I'm the youngest to hold the position since Merchant Prince Galero." He huffed. "How dare you call me complacent."

"It took you eight years when my plan only called for five. So, yes, I call that complacent."

"Says the man that took seven years to become a commander in Scales."

"Only because Bryan Dexter was suspicious of me. I had to lay low until he became obsessed with something else."

"Luck?" Jay laughed. "Or planning?"

"He was a good man." Someone poured more water on the coals and the accompanying hiss was sharper this time. "I sympathize with men who do whatever it takes for those they love. But . . . they are easily manipulated."

"Love is a double-edged sword," Jay said. "I was once jealous of your connection with Katherine. That you would go so far to bring her back. But now . . . I don't know if I want that. It's why I keep Ciara at a distance. My ambitions cannot afford to be held back by another person."

"The ultimate goal is to have someone who uplifts you and supports your goals—no matter how outrageous they may be. Most don't find that, though." He sighed. "Blaming another for one's personal failures is a cowardly way of living."

"What did you want to be before you met Katherine?" Jay asked tentatively. "You never told me."

"You'd insult me if you knew."

"I would never."

"I'm not talking about you."

"Father, I don't under—"

"He's in the coffin."

It opened suddenly—the steam clouding my vision—and I tumbled out. Jay Prince glared at me with his fists clenched. He had torn off half of his gown at the knees and then draped the cloth around his neck like an animal's pelt. Angelo looked the same as always. Tidy appearance and neatly trimmed black hair, sharp angles in his face, fit and trim. The only difference was that he wasn't wearing his rings.

"If you knew I was here the entire time, you should have said something," I said, picking myself up off the ground. "Don't you enjoy our conversations?"

"I do," Angelo said as he wiped away some sweat. "But how else would I get you to listen to us? You tell me, Michael—was any of that the truth? Or were they lies created just for you?"

"You don't matter." I pointed at Jay with a sly smile. "You didn't know I was here. You told the truth. So, who's going to explain 'Father' to me?"

"Why would I explain anything?" Jay asked, turned on his heel, and left.

"He'll be back with a weapon. We should savor what time we have," Angelo said. "Jay isn't like you, Michael. He leaves when there's nothing to be gained from a conversation. You could learn a thing or two from him."

He was right. It had been foolish to think Jay would've answered my questions. But Angelo seemed more than content to talk. Did I take the bait and risk being manipulated, or follow Jay's example and leave? Getting here had cost so much . . . so I wasn't leaving quite so soon.

"Why did Jay Prince call you 'Father'?"

"Because I adopted him. Oh, don't look so surprised, Michael. It was before you and your siblings or Dark. Back when Katherine was having trouble conceiving." Angelo closed his eyes, as if dreaming of better days. "Jay resents Dark. He feels he stole his place in the family. I probably should have shown him he would always be family, but . . . I never was that good a father. Shade men never are."

"Did you even try to break the cycle? Or did you just give up when it got too difficult?"

There was a crack in his pristine mask for a heartbeat. A scowl when he would normally have laughed at me. He stared into the coals and softly said, "Have you ever heard how the iron gate that guards Vargo came to be?"

"No."

"Centuries ago a fisherman lived in the village that one day would become Vargo. But the bay in which his ancestors had settled was slowly drying up. The fish were dying out. So he looked upon the massive stone wall that protected his village from the chaotic ocean and decided he had to create a path in it, so his village would survive past his generation." Angelo shook his head, disdain on his face. "So every day he woke up at daybreak, fed his family, and spent the rest of the day chiseling away at a mountain. He worked on it every day for twelve years. And, miraculously, his plan succeeded. He created a crack in the foundation that allowed fish to travel from one side to the other. His village hailed him as a *hero*."

I motioned for him to continue.

"His village was destroyed a week later when a rogue wave crashed against the wall that he had undermined. Only the man survived." He raised a finger. "But here's the thing. His friends were dead. His family was dead. But he *refused* to let their deaths be meaningless. And so he came up with another plan. He would build an iron wall within the new opening that could be opened without risk to the village." Angelo paused for dramatics. "It took him twenty-two years. He died a week after its completion. And it was another two years before people risked resettling on the site of the destroyed village."

"And?"

"So here's my question, Michael: Does failure make us strong or weak? If you had asked me when Katherine was alive, and Dark was a babe in her arms . . . I would have said it made us weak. That my failure to beat your father on the Day of Crowning scarred me for life." He dug his nails into his skin. "But now I think differently. The strong only fail until they get what they desire, while the weak succeed throughout their lives, until one failure sends them into a spiral they never recover from. Those prodigies and geniuses we hold so high are paper-winged fools." He smiled at me. "It's why I always thought you had so much potential. You fail at everything."

"Conquering failure isn't the lesson I would have taken from that story."

"Oh?"

"A man looked beyond himself to create something others would benefit from even though he had nothing to gain." I scratched at my crown brand. "That's a true legacy."

"We'll agree to disagree."

I stayed silent, hoping it would get him to continue talking.

"Are you going to ask me the obvious question? Or do you enjoy ignorance?"

Knowledge was power, so I swallowed my pride and asked, "How does me being with Serena risk shattering Tenere?"

"The act itself can't shatter Tenere," Angelo explained. "It's what you'd do to protect her that could." He examined his nails, picking at a fleck of dirt underneath his thumb. "You, me, and Dark are all fools for love. But do those we've devoted ourselves to love their fools? Or was our time together just a passing dream? That distinction will make us villains, heroes, or tragic fools left out in the cold."

"Which do you think you are?"

"The fool left out in the cold," he admitted. "Katherine was out of my league in so many ways. I doubt she waited for me."

What did he mean by that?

Angelo chuckled. "Ah, yes, I doubt you really understand what happens when we die. You never were one for religion. So focused on the legacy you left behind that you never paid attention to what lay after life. I'd learn more about that if I were you. Haven't you ever wondered why so many immortals stay close to the churches?"

I was about to reply when Jay Prince—fully dressed in the tight leather armor widely loved in New Dracon City—skittered to a stop in front of us, sword in one hand and a flintlock pistol in the other. He tossed trousers to Angelo and aimed the gun at me.

"This meeting is over," the former Skeleton said, making sure he was between me and Angelo. "Get lost before I—"

"Shoot me," I taunted. I rose, grabbed the barrel of the gun, and then held it against my bare chest. "Shoot me. C'mon, Jay. *Do it.* You know you want to."

Jay's hand didn't shake, but he didn't pull the trigger either. He glanced at Angelo, who shook his head. While the Skeleton was distracted, I kicked Jay in the knee and then twisted the gun out of his hand. I aimed it at Angelo, who tried not to yawn as Jay recovered from my hit.

Everything slowed around me, giving me time to think. Was the gun loaded or was it a bluff? If it was loaded and I didn't try to kill or at least harm Angelo, I'd never hear the end of it. But if the gun wasn't loaded—which would explain why Jay hadn't shot me—I'd make a fool of myself if I pulled the trigger. I doubted Angelo would take the bullet either way. Jay seemed like the self-sacrificing type. And if I shot Jay, even by accident, Regal Company would come after me. What could I do that would protect— Oh, I had an idea . . .

"Are you going to kill me, Michael?" Angelo asked, entertained. "Think of the consequences—"

I turned away from him and fired at Jay as Angelo lunged for me, screaming for me to stop. There was a bang, and a cloud of sulfurous white smoke flooded out of the gun, overpowering the scent of the coals. Blood ran through the grooves in the tile until it reached my toes. I waved away the smoke, trying to see if I had killed Jay. He should've understood us lovestruck fools have no limits. I would do anything to protect Serena, including murder. Did he think none of what he and Dark stood for had rubbed off on me?

Angelo was holding Jay Prince in his arms, trying to stanch the wound in his chest. I had missed his heart, but the bullet was likely lodged somewhere nearby. It would be difficult for any surgeon to extract. Wonderful.

"Why did you shoot him?" Angelo hissed at me. "Do you realize what you've done? You shot Regal Company's client! Do you think they'll take this laying down?"

I flipped the flintlock in my hand, ready to use the butt of it like a club in case Angelo rushed me. "No, I fully expect them to come for me."

"Then why . . ." Angelo's eyes went wide. "You're going to use their pride against them."

I smiled broadly. "Tell me, oh, dear foster father, who wins in a fight . . . Regal Company or a Wolven King?"

"They won't fight a Wolven King, they're not stupid. Why would they? . . . You're thinking of Gwen." Jay was clawing at Angelo's arms, desperate to live. "If they can't find you . . . they'll go after your family. And if Gwen's the closest—"

"So they'll go after her. The Wolven King will be forced to retaliate. So tell me, who wins?"

"I can't stop this," Angelo muttered. "Regal Company won't believe it's a trap. They'll come after you to maintain their honor. This will ruin everything I've planned." He looked at Jay and then at me. "You outplayed me."

I bowed deeply. "How does it feel? Terrible, I'm—"

Angelo put his hands around Jay's neck and crushed the life out of him as the Merchant Prince thrashed in his lap. He was too weak to do anything but whimper, and tears streamed down his face before his eyes glazed over and he went unnaturally still. And then Angelo cradled Jay's body in his arms, sung him a lullaby as he swept his hand over Jay's bloodstained visage, and lowered him to the floor. Bruises were already darkening around his neck.

I couldn't even curse and question what Angelo had just done, just stare as I backed away. Just when I thought I had him, he did something so outrageous and unexpected, I couldn't have planned for it in a thousand years.

Angelo rose to his feet and slicked his hair back with Jay's blood. "He deserved a better death than that. But it was the only way to continue the plan. Regal Company can't go to war against the Wolven King if they don't know who the murderer is. I won't reveal the truth, and who would believe *I* killed him?" He put his bloody hand over his left eye and cackled.

I started backing away from Angelo. "How could you *do* that?"

Angelo ran his hand down his face, leaving a bloody trail to the base of his neck. His eyes were dark, his smile deranged, and his normally tidy appearance was wild and uncontrolled. "Do I look like the sort of man who would give up so easily? I have been planning to bring Katherine back for decades. *You* will not ruin my plan." Angelo stepped over Jay's body. "Nothing will."

"But Jay is dead. Serena can't marry him now. Wasn't the whole point of the rebellion to get them together?"

"It was," Angelo admitted. "But I have a backup plan."

"Adreann and Emelia."

Angelo nodded. "Aren't lines of succession wonderful?"

I stepped toward him with the butt of the gun raised. "I won't let you hurt her."

"Serena was too valuable to remove from the stage," Angelo said. "But all I have to do now is force a vote of no confidence to get Adreann on the throne. After all, Serena is a Forgotten. Do you think the High Nobles will let her be queen in that condition?"

My hands were shaking. I wanted to charge Angelo, to end it here and now, but in this deranged state . . . I doubted I would be able to overpower him. I had to retreat . . . and fight another day.

"I'll stop you."

"No, you won't, Michael." He gestured toward Jay's body. "Not when I'm willing to go this far. You will never be able to beat me, not while you draw breath. I will always beat you. Just as I did your father and that useless Hollow King."

I clenched my teeth, swallowed my pride, and ran away. I barely stopped to put on my trousers in the changing room, sprinting away with my shirt wrapped around my neck. I had made a move that should have stopped Angelo in his tracks. Yet all it did was make him stronger. He was too far gone to stop with anything but death.

The Shade men were monsters who would maim, torture, and murder to get what they wanted—and I had to start treating them as such. Only monsters could stop monsters.

Oh, my poor humanity.

53

SKIPPING STONES

Liam was smoking fireleaf outside the ruined theater when I returned. He was wearing a blood-splattered butcher's apron and looked content, relaxed, and blissfully unaware that his client had just been strangled. He'd have no more peace until the murderer was discovered. And so long as Angelo refused to tell them it was me . . . I would be forced to tell them myself. And then they'd come for me without hesitation. Without mercy. Until I was nothing but bones and memories. I'd have to pick the perfect moment to reveal what had happened. Sending Regal Company after the Wolven King was the best plan I had come up with. It turned Gwen into bait, but sometimes there had to be a riot in jail for prisoners to escape. Now I just had to figure out how to make it all work.

"Where's Sebastian?" I asked.

He blew smoke into my face. It smelt like dry wood and chilies. "He'll be out soon. We finished a while ago, but we're still stitching him up."

"I thought you'd just hand him back however you left him."

"Sadly not," Liam said. "Papa finds that the mental state of those we hurt is far worse if we heal them after maiming them."

It brought back bad memories of how the Ravens had treated me when I turned myself in for killing King Isaac. Those gentle touches after brutal beatings had left me unable to look most of the Ravens in the eye anymore. Their compassion, having taken such glee in my pain, was almost worse than what they had done to me physically. My body had recovered. My mind hadn't. Some scars never went away, and it was better to push them to the back of one's mind than dwell on them. It wasn't the healthiest thing to do, but it was the only way for me to survive.

"Did you enjoy seeing Angelo again?" Liam asked.

This was going to be an awkward conversation as we waited for Sebastian, but there was no point in staying silent. Who knew what I could get out of Liam if we talked? Especially while he was smoking fireleaf. It was a potent medicine used to relieve pain, which often left its users loose-lipped.

"It's always a fun time," I muttered, hands in my pockets as I glanced around the area.

Liam snorted. "His keeping his dead wife's body in a coffin that he carries around is wild, isn't it? First time I saw it I was dumbfounded." He took another pull from his fireleaf. "Did he give you the whole talk about why she's wearing that yellow dress?"

"It wasn't just her favorite?"

"No, no, no. She was wearing it when he first saw her in New Dracon City. She was the flash of color in his boring grey world. So melodramatic." He exhaled rings of smoke. "Some days I wonder if . . . never mind. I can't speak about things like that." Another inhale. "Not sober at least. Someone would have my neck."

"I know more about him than you'd suspect."

"Really?" he asked, voice fluctuating. "Care to prove it?"

And the fish was on the line. Now to reel it in. "What do you have in mind?"

"Tell me something I don't know about Angelo Shade and I'll—" He put his fist over his mouth and burped. "—and I'll tell you *anything* you want to know about him."

I drummed my fingers against my thigh. "That deal seems one-sided. What do you get out of this? Especially since it puts you in a dangerous position."

"Has Orbis taught you nothing?" One last inhale of the fireleaf, and then he tossed it aside. "Information is power. It's the difference between those who rise and those who fall. Angelo Shade is dangerous. Even to Regal Company. This is me getting an ace up my sleeve."

"Fine," I said, leaning against the wall. "Let's play. I'll start with something easy . . . Angelo has a son."

Liam looked unamused. "You'll have to be more specific."

I opened my mouth to respond, hesitating at his words. That was an odd way to refute my claim and may have given away more than he thought it did. Was he alluding to Jay? Not as if that mattered anymore. "Angelo has a biological son named Davis. He also goes by the name of Dark in Orbis Company."

"I'm aware of the Black Death. Anything else? Because this is a very poor way to start. Best foot forward, Michael."

"Angelo's wife's name is Katherine Naverre, a former High Noble of Hollow."

Liam yawned dramatically as he closed his eyes. "Yes, yes. Try again."

"His biological father was a man named Vance Shade, the Darkness Dragon. Vance was murdered by Dark after the Heartbreaker Serial Killer incident in Hollow three-ish years ago."

"Wrong," Liam snapped. "Vance wasn't Angelo's biological father. He was adopted. Are you even trying, Michael? Because this is embarrassing."

Angelo was adopted? I'd have to get back to that. I was running out of specifics. But I had one last thing to try. Something I didn't understand the full meaning of, but Liam might. "Angelo was searching for a key in Hollow. He thought it was hidden in King Adrian the Liberator's tomb, but it wasn't. Only a Wolven King's empty tomb was."

That got Liam's attention. "He's been searching Hollow for the key? And you're telling me he found a Wolven King's tomb? You're *sure*?"

"Yes," I lied, and nothing more.

Liam stared at me, running his tongue over his teeth. "You're lying."

I returned his stare and ever so slowly repeated from memory, "*GVHRQXJE.*"

"You know the King Script? We must—"

Ciara burst out of the theater carrying Sebastian over her shoulders. Regal Company's symbol of four crossed daggers had been branded onto his neck in the same spot mine was. His left arm had been cut away below the elbow. Blood was leaking through the bandages and his eyes were hazy, but when he saw me, he fought to his feet. He made it three steps before falling into my arms.

"Papa expects you to keep your end of the bargain, Michael," Ciara said. "You know what will happen if you don't, don't you?"

I waved the Mercenaries away. Liam was displeased, questions sitting on the tip of his tongue, but he relented when Ciara told him to. Whatever this King Script was, he'd ask me about it again later, and I could demand my answer.

I carried Sebastian away from Regal Company toward the docks, stopping only for a cream that would ease the pain and speed the healing of his brand. It was the same kind I had used for mine and I showed him how to apply it, doing it myself as he faded in and out of consciousness. He wasn't grateful, but then, I hadn't been when Lyon had done this for me. We were cut from the same cloth. A mirror version of my younger self.

"Where are you taking me?" Sebastian mumbled as we reached the docks. Passengers were queuing up for some of the massive ships to nearby ports: other cities of the Gold Coast clans, the Skeleton Coast, Eham, and the tranquil islands in safe zones. Sailors loaded the luggage of the wealthy, letting those of lesser status do it themselves. "Back to my cell in that ship?"

"No." I set Sebastian down on a bench near four stone statues. "I'm giving you an out."

He stared at me, waiting.

I rummaged through my pockets until I had enough suns to pay for my mother's room in the asylum for a year. Mercenary work paid well. I handed it all to him. "This will buy you passage wherever you want to go. Pick somewhere, and never return to Vargo or Hollow."

"Exile?" he spat.

"It's the best way for you to reclaim your life," I said. My tongue felt uncomfortable in my mouth. "You forfeited your life in Hollow when you tried to kill Serena. I won't let you support Adreann any longer. So you're going to leave and never come back."

"You think I wanted to support that asshole?" Sebastian laughed, then grabbed his arm and gritted his teeth. "Adreann was always a prick. I was a part of his Throne Seekers only because I couldn't stand in Hollow Court alone. He made me feel safe. Even if I hated him."

"You *chose* to stand by his side and you—"

"I've never had anything!" Sebastian screamed at me. "My mother was High Noble Camille Margaux's mistress turned wife after Dawn's mother was killed under mysterious circumstances. I was ostracized from noble society the day I was born! I didn't even have the advantages of being a Fabricator, all I had was my sister's love. So don't make me out to be a villain because I tried to survive a corrupt society where names and legacies determine who you are before you know yourself."

"Necessity doesn't free you from the consequences. Trust me— I know that better than anyone else. I've been a whiny, immature brat for most of my life. I could try to excuse myself, that my mind was locked at the maturity of a ten-year-old by Darkness Fabrications for a decade, but I won't. Accept the consequences and move on. That's all you can do."

Sebastian deflated in his seat. "How foolish of me to think you'd have compassion."

"What do you think this is?" I snapped. "I'm giving you a chance at a life where you're free of Hollow and those painful legacies. Take it."

"And if I want revenge?"

"Then I won't save your life twice."

Sebastian lowered his head, put his hand over his fresh brand, and slapped it repeatedly.

"What are you—"

The four stone statues rumbled to life around me. Only one was armed, and it lunged with its spear with all the skill of a master. I leapt out of the way, but it still sliced down the length of my forearm, drawing blood. The other three statues leapt on me like back-alley thugs. Stone hit harder than flesh and bone, so I gathered the warmth in my chest and nullified the area before they broke through my guard.

They stopped mid-strike, towering over me and blocking out the sun. My entire body screamed at me as I rolled out of their circle, gasping for breath and hoping nothing was broken. My arms felt swollen and bruised, and Sebastian was looking at me with a small smile on his face as onlookers gawked. A group of sailors had come to help, and I pushed through them . . . but by the time I reached the bench, Sebastian was already gone. There were three ships still loading passengers nearby: one to Eham, one to the city where the Eternal Flame's grand cathedral was located, and another to the coastal city of Medceli.

Hopefully, he had boarded one of the ships and given up his desire for revenge. I didn't want to have to kill him to protect Serena. Dawn wouldn't forgive me for that. Had love made me a monster? Or had I always been like this . . . and I'd only now found the drive to do whatever was needed?

A TASTE OF GOLD

"—then he got beaten up by a group of statues!" Titus held up my left arm to show off the yellow-and-purple bruises. "I told you letting this kid into Orbis Company would be worth it! Who else gives us this kind of entertainment?"

Cassia was doubled over with laughter. Alexis was more restrained, at least having the decency to cover her mouth as she laughed to save my pride. If only a little.

All three of them had showed up as the sailors were trying to decide what to do with the statues that had come to life. It was unthinkable, akin to the trees that lined the streets turning sentient. The stone statues were nothing more than pretty decorations in Vargo and suddenly these people had been forced to see them differently. Like anything, in the wrong hands these statues could be deadly weapons . . . or they all thought it was an elaborate prank. It was hard to tell. The sailors were taking it seriously but no one else was.

Cassia was wiping tears from her eyes as she said, "I'm assuming High Noble Sebastian is gone, then? Any idea if he's still in Vargo?"

"I gave him enough money to go wherever he wanted." I watched the last of the nearby ships prepare to leave. "Maybe he left."

"Until we have proof, let's assume he's still around," Alexis said. Her eyes narrowed at me. "What aren't you telling us?"

I looked around. "Not here."

"How important?" Cassia asked quietly.

"Very. But Dark can't know."

"Titus."

"On it," the large Mercenary said as he went to deal with the sailors and the statues. If Dark came looking, Titus would be able to distract him.

The three of us walked along the canals, weaving between groups of people my age who were sharing bottles of wine and regaling each other with ever more exaggerated stories. Debating whether the abyss in the Sea of Statues was human designed or a godly punishment. A prison for daemons or an empty abnormality. It was a peaceful life I had always been jealous of, but as I strode past them . . . I didn't want that anymore. I wanted to be right where I was. Regardless of all the pain, bruises, arguments, and headaches.

Cassia brought us to a man-made pond with stone floors and sides. It was filled with fish daily, to feed those who couldn't afford food on their own. The only requirement was they had to catch it. The Gold Coast didn't like the word "free." Everything had to be earned and charity was so looked down upon here that the churches had developed positions below their Initiates, called the Bonded, whose sole job was to visit and water the plants once a day. For their work, they were given the necessities and once they could afford those on their own, they gave a tithe to the Church of the Eternal Flame as thanks and renounced their positions. It seemed so foreign to me as a concept. Why not accept help when it was needed? Was pride that important to people? Or was it more to do with their clan system? That even the weakest member had to contribute to the greater whole?

There were only two other people in the area. A child trying to catch a fish with his bare hands and an elderly man slumped on a bench.

"What happened?" Cassia asked. "This had better be important, or I'll—"

"Jay Prince is dead," I interrupted.

Cassia blinked at me, opened her mouth, pursed her lips, and then looked away, brows furrowed. Alexis was the one who responded. "How do you know that?"

I told them what had happened, explaining that I planned to manipulate Regal Company into pursuing Gwen and the Wolven King for me. Neither interrupted, nor did they scold me. Both were too shocked that Jay Prince was dead to do anything but wear their fear on their faces like a Vargo mask.

"And you're sure he's dead?" Cassia pressed. "Could it have been a trick or an illusion?"

"If it was, I can't explain how. I know how death looks and that was it."

Cassia put her hands behind her head. "I need a moment to think. I'll be back," and she went over to the boy with a big smile and offered to help him catch a fish. He lit up as Cassia took off the giant emerald ring on her finger, removed the gemstone from it, bit into it, and then tossed it into the water. Lightning rippled through a section of water no bigger than a hand, and a fish floated to the surface heartbeats later. The boy dove after it and then held it over his head as if it were more valuable than gold.

"What was that?" I blinked away astonishment. "Please tell me that's not *another* form of magic."

Alexis didn't respond.

"Alexis?"

"Hmm? Oh. Yes, it's called Alchemy. Now, do you suppose—"

"Where does it originate from?" I demanded. "How does it affect substance and what's the cost?"

The Azilian Mercenary was caught off guard by my questioning. "It's from New Dracon City. And from what I understand, it allows them to store things for later. Like lightning, fire, sound, and ice. Imagine them like little elemental bombs disguised as gems." She tapped a finger against her chin. "The cost? Not sure. You'd have to ask Cassia."

The ramifications of such magic were boundless. Anyone could use Alchemy, to fight battles, or the gems could be repurposed as technology, advancing things enormously. There was always so much I didn't know. "Do you know how many countries have their own forms of magic?"

A gentle gust of wind stole the answer from her lips, carrying it up and away. The Archmage had told me I wouldn't be able to learn that answer, but I had tried anyway. I could be a persistent fool. Why had I forgotten that, of all things? And what did it have to do with the mystery I had tasked Kai with solving?

Cassia returned once the boy had left. "If Jay is—"

"What's the cost of your magic?"

"Seriously? Now?"

"Just tell me."

"Emotional instability. Some people stop feeling joyful, or sad, or angry. But it varies from person to person. Satisfied?"

I nodded. Creation and memories. Manipulation and pain. Alchemy and emotional instability. And then there were Spellborn, Patchworkers, Abyss Walkers, and Insatiables that I still didn't know the cost of. Still, magic was becoming clearer in my mind. Piece by piece.

Cassia crossed her arms. "If Jay is dead, then we need to prepare. Regal Company will interrogate the entire city to find his murderer. Assuming they don't just burn it all down."

"What are the odds of that?"

"Fifty-fifty," Alexis said. "Maybe more, depending on how the body is found. The more humiliating it is, the more likely they'll turn to violence." She faced me. "Do you think Angelo will desecrate the body?"

"No. He was Angelo's adopted son. He was so upset he had to kill him." I paused, realizing how strange a sentence that was. "Besides,

Angelo wanted to avoid a war. I wouldn't be surprised if he tried to hide the death for a while."

"Papa Noble won't go more than a few days without seeing his client."

"So where do you hide a body? And how do you unveil it?" Cassia paced. "Should we search for the body ourselves, or is the risk of being found with it too great?" She checked her own pulse. "Can you be traced back to it at all, Michael?"

"Not if I don't want to be."

Cassia plucked a purple gem from one of her earrings and swallowed it whole. Her body shook as it slid down her throat, and then a blissful expression spread over her face. Did purple gems contain a drug of some sort?

"*That's* better," she whistled once she was still again. To me, she said, "It's crystallized opium. It helps calm me. Without it I can suffer intense bouts of shaking and panic if I'm overwhelmed by something unexpected."

"And here I thought you were infallible."

"Order keeps me calm. Sadly, not even I am perfect," she said with a fleeting smile. "Since we have some semblance of control at the moment, I think we should wait to see what happens. And get Titus's opinion before we make a decision. We'll have to hope Michael's hypothesis is correct and that Angelo won't try to frame him for the murder."

"If I'm wrong?"

She patted my shoulder. "Then I'll kill you myself."

How delightful. We talked for a bit longer as the sun began to descend in the sky, but there were signs of an incoming storm, and Cassia couldn't bear the uncertainty. She left to find Titus. She was still an ass, but reliability and sympathy were one powerful drug.

"Thank you for telling us what happened," Alexis said. "I'm glad you did."

I shrugged. "Sometimes trust has to be given freely."

"Very true." A pause. "And we should talk about the dragon we're hiding from Dark."

"Does he suspect anything?"

"Almost definitely," Alexis admitted. "We should act before he gets suspicious."

"Tonight?"

"Tonight," she confirmed. "I'll find you, after everyone else is asleep."

She left with a smile and I remained by the pond. Rain began to fall gently, and a peal of thunder boomed far away. I let the rain wash away my pain and ease some of my bruises as I took a moment to gather up the courage for what was to come.

THE WOLF'S CAPTIVE

The waves erased the sandcastle Gwen had been building, just as her employer stepped through another pathway and onto the beaches of Eham. He was mid-sentence as his feet crushed what little hadn't been destroyed by the water. "—and I have an assignment for you, Gwendolyn. One that requires perfection."

Gwen sat back on the sand, stifled a yawn, and let the dying sun warm her aching bones. This was the first time in a week she had a moment to herself. So of course her employer would interrupt her solitude. He always did this when she was in Hollow, too. Out of the hundreds of times she had tried to read by the river, she only succeeded once. And that had only been because he was spying on Michael and Domet. "Does it concern the Machina Mercenaries? Because I tried to warn you—"

"It's about the Smoke Dragon."

Gwen sat up, suddenly very awake. "Scorcher Rian Smoak?"

Her employer waved his hands. "Is that the name he's going by now? So ugly. But yes, him." He stared at the shattered moon, which was just beginning to show in the dusk sky. "The dragons have made their demands. They want Rian freed. Your next assignment will be in Vargo. From there we'll finish negotiating a deal, and potentially add another titan to our ranks."

"How?"

"Rian and Skarlo, the lost titan, were friends despite serving different kings. My hope is that they might rekindle their friendship and that Skarlo will help me destroy my younger brother. I cannot afford to let pride guide me. I need as many dragons, titans, and behemoths as possible if we're going to stand a chance."

Gwen deflated. "Who has Rian under captivity?"

The Wolven King made a sickening noise. "It doesn't matter."

"Of course it does. How could it—" She stopped, eyes growing wide. "Celona's Mercy. It's Michael, isn't it? He's holding Rian captive!"

"Yes." The king sounded grudging and Gwen couldn't contain her laughter.

"I told you he would mess up your plans! You should have let me stay with my family. He's coming for you."

"And if he does . . ." The Wolven King snapped his fingers, creating a slice in the sea so the sandy bottom was visible. Fish flopped on the ground, struggling to survive. Both sides crashed down a few heartbeats later. ". . . I will crush him."

"Michael is going to bring down the heavens and end your stupid war once and for all."

"Why do you have so much faith in such a whiny, pathetic child?"

"Because," Gwen said, "Michael isn't the smartest or the strongest . . . and he's always comparing himself to our unattainable ancestors." Gwen smiled at the Wolven King. "But he's a monster who devours those around him, stealing their skills and logic and intelligence. Do you really think you can stop someone who has never ever felt complacent?"

"What a unique way to describe a parasite," her employer said. "You have your task. Any attempt to contact your brother or the Hollow Queen will be met with severe consequences. Avoid the Black Death if you can." He plucked a memory from her mind, one of her mother, merry and cooking in Kingman Keep. He let it blossom for a moment, and then returned it to her mind. "I'll send her to Celona to die if you do anything to jeopardize my plan."

"I understand." Gwen brought her knees to her chest. "I don't know why you still threaten me or my family. I've never disobeyed your orders."

"But you did try to save that Archivist. That was an act of defiance."

"It was mercy," she whispered. "He didn't deserve to go like that."

"Life is unfair." The Wolven King ripped open a tear to Vargo. A shrine with a faceless statue, a small ever-burning cannister, and a lock-less door were beyond. "Go. And be quick."

Gwen got to her feet, brushing off the sand. "Can you tell me any-thing more about where Rian is imprisoned? He'll be hard to find if I can't interact with Michael."

"The Azilian Mercenary of Orbis Company will be your best bet to find him."

"That's it?"

"My help will come when you need it most," her employer said, star-ing at the faint outline of the shattered Celona in the sky. "Watch the skies. They will give you the distraction you need. I just need to goad it into attacking Vargo."

Gwen perked up. "'It'? Are you talking about Celona? Are you imply-ing you can control moon-fall?"

Her employer pointed at the pathway he had created for her, looking displeased. "If you want answers, prove you deserve them. Do this and maybe I'll tell you."

Gwen muttered a sarcastic affirmation and then stepped through the tear to Vargo. Her skin felt as if it was being pulled in all directions in the moment before she felt the cold tile stone beneath her bare feet. The tear snapped closed as she cursed her own stupidity at leaving her boots behind. But there was no time to wallow in it. She had to find Rian before Michael found her, and she had no doubt that Michael would be stupid enough to stumble upon her at the wrong moment. He was lucky like that.

Before Gwen left the small shrine, she spat on the faceless statue. She wasn't normally one to disgrace religious symbols, but she made an exception for *him*. After all, if it wasn't for him, she wouldn't be a wolf's captive. If only Michael and Davey hadn't left that night, looking for . . . But she pushed those thoughts away, knowing that focusing on the past would only make things worse. She could reflect on it but not live in it. And right now, when time was limited, she had to search the palace for the Azilian Mercenary of Orbis Company.

———

Gwen found the Azilian in one of the more remote gardens, knitting a blue scarf under a persimmon tree. The wind from the sea would pick a few leaves off every so often, showering her in the only kind of rain that didn't chill the bones. Gwen stayed in the shadows, watching the Azilian, until she was sure no one was around and then approached with a flint-lock pistol she had stolen from a guard who was currently locked up in a storeroom. She didn't want to kill anyone, just threaten, and yet if she was forced to—

"I know you're there," the Mercenary said calmly. She didn't turn to face Gwen, just continued knitting as if there wasn't a gun aimed at her head. "What do you want?"

"Where's Rian?" Gwen asked in a deep voice. It wouldn't disguise the fact she was a woman, but it wouldn't allow Alexis to identify her as the missing Kingman, either.

Alexis hesitated over her next stitch. "Did Dark send you?"

"No. Now tell me where he is." Gwen cocked the gun. "Don't make me kill you."

"Tell me who sent you." Alexis set her incomplete scarf down, hands flat out on the stone bench. "My partner will throw a tantrum if Rian escapes and I can't tell him anything."

"Why do you think I won't kill him?" Gwen countered.

Alexis chuckled. "Call it a hunch."

"Too bad." Gwen bit her lip. She wanted to give the Mercenary a fake name to relay to Michael, but she couldn't take the risk. Not with her employer. He had killed for lesser infractions. A slip of the tongue had cost one of her childhood friends their eyes. Ever since then she had avoided getting close to people. So they couldn't be harmed to control her. "Are you going to tell me where he is, or do I have to pull the trigger?"

"One," the Mercenary said softly.

Gwen took a step forward. "What?"

"You should have brought more than one gun."

The Azilian flipped onto her feet, drawing two guns from her chest holsters. She fired one as Gwen dove behind the tree and the other as she scrambled out of the Mercenary's range. She shot wildly over her shoulder, forcing the Azilian to kick over the stone bench as cover. But as Gwen attempted to tear open packets of gunpowder and iron balls, the Mercenary had two fresh pistols in her hands and fired again. One of the bullets struck Gwen through the hand and sent her to the ground screaming profanities. Blood stained the grass, and her vision grew hazy as the white smoke settled over their fight. The Azilian hopped over the bench with a thud and crept toward her.

Gwen tore her sleeve, wrapped her hand as best she could, and then pressed her back against the tree trunk. Her vials of powder were smashed around her. She had no option but to rely on the abilities her employer had given her. She hadn't earned them like Weavers did nor been born with them as Fabricators were, and it made her sick whenever she used them . . . but she had to. She reached into her mouth, let a black ball form in the back of her throat, and then yanked it out like a rotten tooth.

Every ball she created decreased her life span. In some ways it was an easier cost than memory loss to comprehend. But in another way . . . it was a lot worse. She didn't know how many days or months or years each ball cost her . . . only that it cost her something. And she had no idea how long she would have lived, if she had never become an Insatiable. Would she even live long enough to repay her debt?

"Surrender now and I'll let *you* live," the Mercenary mocked as she got closer to the tree.

"I'm sorry," Gwen muttered. She twisted around the trunk and then threw the black ball. It stopped right in front of the Mercenary, expanding to the size of another person as a sharp whistle pierced the air. The black vortex consumed everything around it, falling leaves and flintlock pistols disintegrating into it as if they were clay. The Mercenary abandoned her yarn, needles, and then the stone bench as they were all eaten. She only narrowly escaped it herself, losing a boot in the process. Only once there was nothing else to destroy within its radius did the ball crush in on itself and disappear.

The Mercenary poked her head up from her hiding place, only to find Gwen aiming a flintlock pistol at her head. It wasn't loaded, but—as she learned from an imbecile—perception could win the fight before it ever began.

"Where is he?" Gwen demanded.

"You're an Insatiable." The Azilian flopped onto her back, hands making her pure white hair messy. "I didn't think there were any of you left. Who created you? Did you really sell your heart to a daemon like the legends say?"

Gwen ignored the questions. Her employer wouldn't like her giving away his secrets. "Don't make me ask again."

"Shoot me," the Mercenary taunted. "Then my allies will kill yours."

"No, they—"

"Hey! What are you doing?"

Her brother's voice cut through her like a cold breeze. Michael was on the other side of the gardens with Serena. He ordered the Queen to remain under the closed pathway—and was obviously ignored, because the two of them sprinted toward Gwen. They were faster than they had any right to be, shouting as if Gwen were the villain here. As if she were in league with Angelo Shade. And while she wasn't . . . maybe she did deserve their hatred.

Gwen did what she had to—she ran, tossing the gun aside and

throwing up her hood so Michael wouldn't see her face, or her eyes. If he saw them, he would ask too many questions, and she had too many answers that would end in heartbreak. He couldn't see her again until she was free. Not before.

Michael did the honorable thing, asking Serena to look after the Azilian while he continued the chase. But Gwen was smarter, using her years of experience to slip away from him. He had only ever caught sight of her once—in the Shattered Stones while she had been on a mission—and she had lost him in the twisty confines of the palace. Now she hid in the shadow of a corridor as Michael caught his breath, hands behind his head, frustration clear on his face.

"Dammit," Michael cursed, staring down the hallways frantically. "Who was that? And how did I lose them?"

Gwen watched as he searched for her, for longer than she'd expected. He almost found her, hiding in the shadows of the scaffolding, but the darkness played tricks on his sight and he stopped, confused and scratching at the back of his neck. Then, with one last grunt and a dying curse, he went back to Serena and the Azilian Mercenary.

Gwen hopped down from her spot, still nursing the hole in her hand and hoping the blood didn't leave a visible trail. But the shadows swarmed her before she could take a single step. Darkness roped around her neck and under her armpits and hoisted her back up. She hung weightlessly, squirming to free herself as a man emerged from a crack in the wall like smoke escaping a furnace.

It was the Black Death. He clicked his tongue and then smiled at her, his teeth all points and fangs. Even his eyes seemed to be permanently red now. The beast immortal was losing more of his humanity with every passing day and with every heart he feasted on. If he wasn't stopped soon, he might become stronger than her employer. A new nightmare for a new generation.

"Dear, sweet Gwendolyn," he sang. "Did you really think you'd be the only one following Michael?"

51

BRED IN CAPTIVITY

"I can't believe I lost sight of them," I muttered as I returned to the gardens. "I can't do anything right."

Serena was helping Alexis up, skirting a fresh crater in the ground. It wasn't scorched, like the aftereffect of an explosion, just . . . empty. As if everything had disappeared. Even the sounds of nature had stopped. What had happened here? Who had been bold enough to attack a Mercenary in the clan leader's palace?

"She escaped?" Alexis asked as Serena helped her up.

"She did," I said, hands on my hips. "Did you get a good look at her? Maybe we can have Dark or the Vargo family put out a bounty for her capture."

"I don't think that would be wise. It was a woman pretending to be a man, about as tall as Serena, tanned and with dark brown eyes."

"Not much to go on there . . . Anything special about them?"

"They were an Insatiable."

I knew that title for a magic user from the Archmage. But I knew they could destroy substance, in contrast to a Fabricator's ability to create and a Weaver's ability to manipulate. I asked Alexis the logical question: Where were they from and what was their casting cost?

"I don't know where they come from. I'm surprised there are any left. Dark told me they were extinct," she said through gritted teeth. She pulled up her shirt slightly to see long, thin cuts down her ribs. She touched them gingerly, winced, and then put her shirt back down. "They pay with their life span. Their body slowly deteriorates whenever they create one of those void balls they like to throw around."

I gestured to the crater in the garden. "That was a void ball?"

Alexis nodded. "They're easily the most dangerous type of magic user out there. One of those balls could kill dozens, destroy fortifications, and wipe out supplies. They'd be unstoppable." She looked up at me. "I don't even think your Nullification Fabrications could stop one of those."

That was concerning. That was *really* fucking concerning. I could even the odds against any other magic user—Spellborn included. I didn't need to run into one that I couldn't. Maybe I could redirect them, like I could other magic? But given that the ball destroyed everything in a radius . . . I'd likely lose my hand trying. Brilliant.

"How many kinds of magic users are there in the world?" Serena asked quietly.

Alexis told her, but she might as well have spoken in a foreign language. That was still one of the biggest gaps in my knowledge—and I was unable to figure out when I had lost the memory or why it was so important. I was relying on Kai to solve that mystery for me. Hopefully, he was doing well at the Institute of Amalgamation.

"Michael," Alexis said, interrupting my thoughts. "We need to talk now. Our business? That's what my attacker was after."

My face paled. Serena was glancing between us, not understanding. "Are you sure?"

She nodded. "They asked about him by name. They knew what we did."

"Dark?"

"No. He'd do it himself if he knew."

I put my hands behind my head and inhaled deeply. Serena looked incredulous. "Are you going to explain what's going on?"

Alexis looked to me for approval. It was our secret, but my decision to include another in it. We knew the dangers of going up against Dark, but Serena didn't. And though I didn't want to lie to her, she couldn't know about this. She had enough to deal with as a Forgotten.

"It's just Mercenary business," I lied with a smile.

Serena opened her mouth to object—to call me a liar—but at the last moment, she glanced away. She didn't have the confidence yet. Would she ever find it again?

"I'll find my Ravens," she said with a huff, turning on her heel away from us. "Don't worry—I won't bother you anymore."

Serena stomped on a few flowers on her way out of the gardens. It was childish, but it was also funny. Alexis was too preoccupied with watching for her attacker to care about the Queen's theatrics. "What are the odds my attacker will follow us to Rian if we go right now?"

"High." I looked around, but aside from the crater, not a single leaf looked out of place. If Alexis's attacker was nearby, they were doing a remarkable job hiding. Or, perhaps, had they moved on to an easier target? "We could try to set a trap."

"We don't have time."

"Then we don't have much choice." I motioned to the exit. "Let's go deal with Rian."

"Are you sure that's wise? We'd lead them straight to him."

"Of course it isn't," I said. "But we're Mercenaries. We don't live in fear of those who lurk in the darkness. We are the things which go bump in the night."

Alexis had hidden Rian in the sewers below Vargo. They were little more than damp, half-flooded passageways where questionable things floated on murky green water. Any metal down here was rusted and crumbly and the stones were covered in slimy goop. Rian was chained to a brick wall with rusty manacles around his wrists, ankles, and neck. The gunshot wound in his shoulder was festering, greenish white pus oozing from it. Dirty water was nipping at his ankles, covering them whenever a surge of muck came down the tunnels. A drop of it in my mouth was enough to make me gag and pray for something strong enough to burn the taste away.

Rian cackled like an overdramatic asylum inmate when he saw us. "Just because I can't die unless my mind or heart are destroyed doesn't mean you should leave me for so long without food." His stomach grumbled. "It's mean."

"Would you rather I kill you?"

"That depends on the tides. When this place floods . . ." Rian shuddered as he stuck out his tongue. ". . . I won't bore you with the mundane details. Let's just say I can tell when it's after supper." He paused. "Are you here to eat my heart, or just to talk?"

Alexis glanced at me, letting Rian know I was in control of this situation. How nice of her. "I'm going to give you an ultimatum: Tell me the names of all three Wolven Kings, or die."

He relaxed. "Death it is."

"So be it."

I jammed my finger into his wound and pressed down as he screamed, and screamed, and eventually passed out from the pain, becoming a deadweight hanging from his chains. I wiped my hand on my pants and then steadied my breathing. Doing things like this made me feel like a shadow of my former self . . . yet it was necessary. Or maybe that was just another lie I told myself, trying to feel like a hero rather than the villain I truly was.

"Was it not worth trying to talk to him again?" Alexis asked.

I shook my head. "He thinks the Wolven Kings are the worst beings in this world. There's nothing we could say to get him to help. That pathetic piece of torture was just to satisfy him that we're serious. Torture never works. They just lie or make something up to make the pain stop." I looked at the imprisoned dragon, a voice in the back of my mind telling me I was no better than Dark. We were just different shades of the same desperation . . . fools for love who ignored reason for vengeance. "Besides, it's better he's not awake for this. I don't want him to see me coming."

"So you got it?"

I nodded, reaching into my pocket and uncorking the Illusion Fabrication I had stolen from Dark. I dumped the wispy rainbow mist into my hand, muttered that I'd be back once I had more information, and then slammed my hand into Rian's face and watched the world melt away as I descended into his memories.

It was time to learn the third Wolven King's name.

THE IMMORTAL
PLAYGROUND

I didn't know what to expect as I descended into Rian's memories. Dark's mind was represented by a sea of darkness that only he was able to control, and Serena's was a city divided into two distinct halves, ravaged by war. My mind was a plane of light that had become a weirdly perfect cathedral once I regained my memories. What was Rian's going to be like?

I landed in a derelict field full of scrap that had been turned into a play area for children. There were rope swings tied to convenient branches protruding out over the forest clearing and piles of bricks and metal that had been turned into climbing frames. It was a child's paradise, unlike the streets in Hollow most of us grew up on. Eleven children were playing around the area.

A boy with bright red hair was kicking dirt at a crying child while another tried to tend their wounds as they apologized for the bully. Fraternal twins splashed into puddles with vigor and threw mud balls at each other, screaming that they'd sink the other's ship first. A blind boy jumped through the trees as if guided by the wind as a young girl followed his every movement. A child who blended in with the light stood atop the highest structure surveying the area as if it were their kingdom as they twirled a wooden knife. A girl with a charming smile flirted with a boy too preoccupied with a book on military warfare to pay her any attention. And a genderless child played in the dirt alone, building and destroying structures like the tide.

"Who are you?" a child behind me asked.

I turned to face a dark-skinned boy with old eyes and a shaved head. His hands were in his pockets, and he looked like he could entrap an adult with a thousand questions.

"I'm Michael," I said quickly. "Who are you?"

"The others call me Null. It's not my real name, but I don't have access to that information." Null looked me up and down. "You're not like the rest of us . . . yet I feel comfortable with you. Why are you here?"

Null spoke like an adult trapped in a child's body. "I'm looking for a weird door. It's probably covered in locks and chains. Have you seen anything like that?"

"Are you trying to steal Smoke's memories?" I took a step back, but Null continued. "I'll help you. I just want to know the truth."

I relaxed a little. "I am. How are you so conscious of what's going on? I've never encountered a memory that can see me, not outside a person's core."

"Smoke stole some of my memories during our last encounter," Null said. "Physically the only thing he's noticed is that one of his eyes is now the same color as mine. But inside his head I've gained some sort of consciousness despite not being alive. Tragic, isn't it?"

Null's situation reminded me of Zahra in Dark's mind. Alive yet not. "How did he steal your memories?"

A shrug. "No idea. Only the real me would know that." Null made a clicking noise with his tongue. "Are you a Nullify Fabricator or a Weaver?

Either would explain why I trust you. Research has proved that those of the same specialization are drawn to each other."

"How did you—" The puzzles clicked into place in my head. "Wait, Null as in Nullify? Are you the Nullify Dragon?"

The boy nodded and then gestured to the children around us. "And these are my siblings. All thirteen of us, minus Smoke."

I looked around the play area again, suddenly able to see the similarities between these children and the dragons I had already encountered. The girl mimicking the tree-swinging boy was Mocking Bird. The bully and the girl acting as the nurse were Louis and Anna Valenti. The flirting girl was the Eternal Sister Dark had killed, and the child swinging through the trees was Otto, a Mercenary in Orbis Company. And the boy reading alone was Vance Shade. So who were the others? Had I met them and I just didn't realize?

"Have we met in the real world?" Null asked.

"No," I said softly. "But I know of you. They call you Idris Ardel."

The boy swished the name around in his mouth as if trying to capture its flavor. "That doesn't feel completely right. It's not a true name, but I like it more than Null. Call me Idris from now on."

"Alright. So where's the door?"

"Come with me," Idris said as he walked into the forest. I followed, taking one last look at each child, committing their actions and traits to memory. We were beneath the thick tree canopies when Idris said, "If you're aware that I'm a dragon, does that mean you've met one of my siblings before?"

"I've met a few of them. Fire, Sound, Shadow, Wind, Lightning, and Darkness."

Idris whistled. "Impressive. By accident, or willingly?"

"A little of both."

"Are they dead?"

"Fire, Sound, Ice, Darkness, Lightning, and Shadow are. But there's a new fire dragon."

"I hope they end up better than the previous one," Idris said with venom dripping off his tongue. "I'll never forgive Darkness for bringing Fire into our family. He was an utter disgrace to all we were trying to accomplish."

"Isn't a depraved man like him the best kind of soldier?" I asked.

"Not when we were fighting for equality. He made us nothing but rebels with a bloody cause, rather than visionaries trying to create a utopia." Idris spat. "Some days I think we deserved the fate we got. Everyone thinks living forever would be wonderful, but all it means is we hold grudges for longer. Hate is easy and sustaining, and love is oh so hard."

Few words rang truer. "If this is Rian's representation of you, then I would love to meet the real you. You were the first to investigate my father's death and believe it wasn't as clear-cut as it appeared. Without you, I wouldn't have been strong enough to investigate myself."

"I've always believed in upholding ideals rather than giving in to despair and ugly desires." Idris watched a bird fly from a tree. "Tell me . . . do you have any idea how the real me is doing?"

I shook my head. "You disappeared ten years ago. Not even the immortals know where you are."

"I wonder if I'm dead," he muttered. "I can't imagine myself dying quietly." Idris hesitated. "If you ever get the chance, go to the Wanderer's tomb. It's located in the Azilian Rain Forest. If I'm anywhere—I'm there."

"The Wanderer doesn't have a tomb."

"Not a public one. But everyone dies somewhere."

I repeated the location to be sure I'd remember it. Idris stopped in front of a tree that was unlike any of the others around it. It was fat and stout, and its branches twisted inward. There was a faint outline of a door on the trunk, covered in chains and locks.

"So this leads to Rian's core," I said out loud. I pulled at the chains, and they were firm despite my touch. "The information I need will definitely be in there, but I have no idea what unlocks it. I barely know anything about Rian."

"And you won't learn anything while you stay in this idealistic version of his memories." Idris leaned against the door. "You know getting out of here will be tricky . . . if not impossible."

"Can't I cut through his mind with my Nullification Fabrications?"

"Maybe with most people, but not Smoke. You don't think he's developed precautions against our specialization? Trying that will only alert him that you don't belong, and he'll send my siblings after you. It's dangerous, but unless you take drastic measures, you'll remain here." Idris reached into his chest and pulled out a translucent white ball. A painting moved within it like the memory bubbles had in Dark's mind. "But with this . . . well, you'll be able to get the information you want and more."

I took the ball from him and twirled it. Despite his size, his words and actions were unmistakably mature. Was there a reason he had retained his maturity in Rian's mind while the others hadn't? "That's an extracted memory, right?"

Idris nodded. "Have you never seen one before?"

"I have, though I don't know how to view them in reality."

Idris paced in front of me, hand to his chin. "I'm not sure how they're viewed in reality either, which is . . . strange. I should know. Could Rian have hidden that knowledge?"

"I don't know. But if I can use this, I'll descend into Rian's memories?"

"No. That ball represents *my* memories."

"What?" I asked, laughing awkwardly at the confusion. "*Your* memories? How is that possible?"

"Rian stole my real memories of our time together before the Wolven Kings fell. It's why I'm a little more . . . active than my siblings, in here. In this dream realm, if you eat this ball while our minds are interlocked, you'll take them from Rian and be able to relive them yourself."

"There will be consequences, won't there?" I hesitated, my tongue starting to tingle.

"There are risks to everything," he answered.

I waited for him to say more, but he didn't. Staring at me instead. Unblinking. Unwavering. Eyes were the only part of someone that couldn't deceive. That was why I took note of them so much. Small movements gave his true desires away. He was a hunter waiting to let an arrow fly once the deer was in his sight. Everything about him was calculated. A dancer's grace and an old man's wisdom hidden in the body of a child. Knowledge had been left unshared. Purposely. If I wanted what he was hiding, I'd have to expose it. What could be the ramifications of taking another's memories in my mind? What could—

"Your memories will bleed into mine and I'll get them mixed up. Assuming your memories don't erase mine." My head was aching, trying to comprehend all the possible ramifications. "If only your memories were in my mind, would I still be me? Or would I be you?"

Idris blinked at me.

"I wonder if you're still alive out there, or if this is your attempt to get free," I muttered, arms crossed. "I'd be a fool to take your deal."

"I guess you don't really care about the truth, then. What happened in the Wolven King War will remain a mystery."

I refused to let others manipulate me based on my insecurities anymore. Pride was a disease, and I had no intention of making a rash decision in case I could be perceived as weak or insecure. But . . . he *could* be right. Rian's memories were the only possible place to find the third Wolven King's name without going to the titan. Was the risk of taking Rian's memories worth the knowledge I'd gain?

It didn't feel right.

"I'll find the truth on my own." I tossed the ball back to Idris, who caught it deftly. "Taking shortcuts will only harm me in the long run."

"If that's your decision . . . then so be it. I hope you don't regret it." He stopped leaning on the tree. "I'll give you some advice, though . . . You've met a decent number of my siblings and have an idea what to expect, but not all of them. Water is fluid in everything, so don't bother making them take a firm stance. Light is fiercely competitive, especially with his rivals. If possible, Wood and Metal are best avoided and . . . Are you listening to me?"

I was, but my gaze was focused on the locked door within the tree trunk. Who was Rian truly? What did he regret and what did he desire above all else? "I'll see you again once I've figured out what Rian desires most in the world."

I nullified my hands and tore open a crack in the air. It flooded everything nearby in light. I tumbled through it, Idris shouting good luck before it was all blackness and nothing.

POISONOUS TONGUES

According to Archivists, one can become impervious to poison by ingesting small doses of it until their body builds up a tolerance. This is, of course, a simplification. There are dozens of poisons and dozens of side effects they can have on the body. Some paralyze. Some make the blood burn. Some cause loss of breath or taste or sight or hearing. Some cause madness or hallucinations. And some peel the skin off in nice, uniform layers until the victim tries to tear themselves apart to get a little relief.

Most poisons came from plants or insects.

So imagine my *fear* when I realized I was floating on a moving, ticking, and scratching ocean of bugs that crawled around, under, and over me. Insects with hundreds of legs scurried across my forehead while scorpions pinched my inner thighs and threatened me with their stingers. Flies landed around my eyes and blurred my vision as worms wiggled between my shirt and skin, slithering across my chest with nowhere to go but up to my mouth or down to my crotch. Both were sickening.

I was in darkness aside from a pinpoint of light from above. Idris waved down with half his body over the lip of the hole, and a look of concern. "I tried to warn you!" he screamed. "I told you Rian was different! He laid traps!"

"How bad is it?" I said through gritted teeth, trying to prevent a beetle from shuffling down my throat.

"There's enough poison down there to kill you a hundred different ways."

I had assumed so, but knowing more about my predicament didn't exactly comfort me.

"Can I die in someone's memories?"

"It's possible," Idris warned. "You're in someone's mind, so in here the pain will feel real. And if your mind believes it's real and there's enough of it . . ." He trailed off, looking away.

What a shit show. My pride had made me ignore his warning and think the nullification would work, because it had in the past. I should have considered it more carefully. Stupid Michael fucking Kingman. When would I learn?

"How do I get out of here?" I shouted up.

"You don't," Rian declared from nowhere.

A plume of smoke began to issue from the ceiling, covering everything. I couldn't see my hand in front of my face, let alone Rian, Idris, or the bugs surrounding me, now frozen in place. A dragon of smoke circled above me like a vulture over its next meal. Balls of twisting grey smoke fell from it, exploded, and then wove between the still bugs. I stayed perfectly silent as the plume of smoke washed over me. And then once everyone was covered, the smoke twirled back up. The Rian I was more familiar with appeared in front of me on a platform of smoke as the bugs began to move again, crawling over my body.

"You shouldn't have underestimated me," he said, displeased. "This is my mind, and I am not as weak here as I am in reality."

I wanted to make a rude gesture at him, but the bugs made that difficult. So I tried something different: overconfidence. "Rian. I'll ask you again. Tell me what I need to know, and I'll free you. We don't have to be enemies."

"Do you really think I'll believe that? I killed your friend. You'll tear out my heart and give it to the Mercenary as soon as I give you what you want." Rian's body was dissipating, smoke tendrils coming off him. "But I will not go quietly. If you want my memories—come and get them. I have fended off worse than you."

The bugs swallowed me, sucking me down. They crawled over my clothes and skin with their thousands of legs. I had to close my eyes and mouth and risk their bites just to put my hands over my ears to prevent them from burrowing into me. It worked, but a few bugs with diamond eyes sunk their fangs into me and sent bolts of pain throughout my body. Then more bugs bit me. And more and more and more until I was compulsively shaking and squirming and longing for it to end until I couldn't bear it, feeling the bugs slip under the flimsy barrier of my skin and begin to wiggle against the muscle and fat. My skin lifted and lowered whenever the small invaders moved, slowly headed toward my heart.

I had no choice but to nullify everything. Maybe I would be expelled from Rian's memories. I didn't know if I'd ever have a chance to return . . . but the risk of dying was too great. I'd find another way to—

My body stopped sinking downward and the bugs slithered off me like water dripping to the floor. I cautiously opened my eyes and saw Idris standing in front of me with an arm extended. "I can't protect you for long, but I can buy us a moment to talk."

I hauled myself to my feet with his help. The floor crawled and clicked endlessly under my boots. "Let me guess—you're going to offer me a deal."

"I am, and you're going to accept it." Idris crossed his arms. "Rian has locked you out of his memories, but if you inherit mine . . . then you can learn what happened in the Wolven King War. Even learn the Third Wolven King's name. If you search hard enough."

"I wonder . . . ," I said, massaging the places the bugs had bitten me.

"Is all this just a trap to make me desperate enough to take your memories?"

Another expressionless blink. And yet . . . Idris wasn't disappointed that I had been caught by Rian. He was forcing me to accept his help if I wanted the information.

Well . . . I guess there was only one option, then. To protect Serena . . . to protect Gwen, my mother, and all my friends . . . I'd risk Idris trying to take over my memories if he wanted. Maybe I wouldn't be Michael Kingman or Michael Orbis or Michael the Dragonslayer. But—no matter what—I would always be Michael. Besides, did he really think I wasn't stubborn enough to stop him? Who did he think I was? A normal person? I was nothing short of a moonstruck imbecile.

"How do we do this?"

Idris smiled wickedly, pulling that shimmering white ball from his chest. He tossed it to me, and I caught it awkwardly. Not one of my smoothest moments.

"Once you have my memories, we'll use your own mind to relive them," Idris explained. "It'll take time for you to adjust, so we may have to go somewhat chronologically through my life. Thankfully, Rian and my lives overlap quite often. It's why he didn't want me running around with certain memories."

"Thankfully," I repeated, eyeing the ball of memories in my hand. Hopefully it wouldn't be foul, but I was expecting something hard and tasteless. Maybe even metallic. "If you try to take over my mind, I'll devour your memories until no trace of you remains. Is that clear?"

"Perfectly." Idris grinned at me, exposing a mouth full of fangs and reminding me that he was a dragon, just like all those I opposed. "Are you ready?"

I put the ball in between my molars and then chomped down on it. It was about as pleasant as rhubarb pie and went down as easily as shards of glass. My head felt like it was pounding, people punching me in the face over and over again until I was on my knees screaming for the pain to stop. It was worse than the bug bites. The warmth in my body was going wild, falling and rising without any way to control it. It took everything I had to concentrate it in my chest before expelling it outward, hoping the pain would stop.

The world disappeared as a lingering laughter filled my ears.

INTERLUDE

THE WOLF'S CAPTIVE

Dark brought Gwen to a dingy wooden stand that served brown noodles soaked in either fat, oil, or whatever made the food smell faintly spicy. Dark slid two claxo to the cook, owner, entrepreneur extraordinaire, and received two bowls. Gwen didn't have to take a bite to know that nothing in that bowl was going to be crisp, but food was food and she had never been one to turn it down before. All growing up on the king's diet had ever done was make her angry when the pain grew too severe.

"Eat up," Dark said. He picked up the bowl and began to shovel food into his mouth with a wooden stick that had been cleaned so often it was smoother than river stones.

"Why are you feeding me?" Gwen asked, taking a fork with only one prong from the random jar of utensils. "Shouldn't we be following Michael?"

"Calm yourself," Dark said between mouthfuls. He pointed his chin toward a metal grate near one of the canals. "They're down there." He slurped some of the brown broth. "But we need to talk before we run into him again. Let's avoid unnecessary violence or sudden betrayals in which I'm forced to stab anyone." He paused. "I hate getting blood on my clothes. It never comes out right. Even on black."

"What if they get away?"

"They won't," Dark said. "Michael is likely in Rian's memories right now and it'll be some time before he goes anywhere."

"What? How?"

"How is that possible or how do I know?" Dark continued to eat. "The answer to both is: I'm everywhere. Nothing gets past me. But enough about Michael. The kid gives me enough of a headache when I'm talking to him, let alone about him."

Gwen hesitated and then began to eat. The noodles were soggy, and the broth was slightly sour, but it filled her body with a pleasant warmth. "What do you want, Dark?"

"Which one are you working for?" Dark asked. "Alphonse or Zarack or the third?"

"Alphonse," she admitted. One of her employer's few rules was that she could say his name in conversation so long as she didn't say it first. "Do you want something from him?"

"I'd love the third's name, but I doubt he'll give it to me. I punched him last time we met. The faceless prick should have killed me when he had the chance." Dark finished his bowl and then ordered another. It arrived quickly, cold, and with the oil and water in the broth separated. "I'm assuming you're bound to him?"

Gwen nodded.

"Do you know how you were bound? Death? Life?"

Gwen put her bowl down, pulled back her long sleeves, and revealed the tattoo of a metal link chain that wrapped around her forearm, shoulder, and upper chest before stopping right over her heart. Her family had always assumed she had worn looser clothes to hide her crown brand from the world, but in reality she had been hiding this tattoo. It was the ultimate mark of shame, binding her to another and constantly reminding her she wasn't free. She might not even be free in death. An eternal servant. The first and second liked to pretend they were different, but both had a hard time letting go.

"Ah." Dark signaled for her to pull up her sleeve. She did so without delay. "That's some constrictive magic. What do the links represent?"

"Either years of my life or tasks accomplished." Gwen ate slowly and surely. "For every task I complete, one of the links disappears. And every time I fail . . . another gets added. There were only five to begin with but . . . let's just say a seven-year-old isn't the best spy you can find."

"How many now?"

"Twelve."

"My condolences." He stacked his empty bowl on top of his previous one and asked for another. The more he ordered, the worse they looked. "You realize he's never going to let you go?"

Gwen slurped the soup, recoiled from the strong fish taste, and tried to ignore Dark's question. Some things didn't become real until they were spoken aloud, and this truth was one of them. So she lied: "I'll be free one day."

"Oh, those pretty lies we tell ourselves," Dark muttered. Then, louder: "Abandon the Wolven King. Transfer your chains to me."

"What?" Gwen nearly coughed her meal back up. "It doesn't work like that. I can't—"

"No, you can," Dark interrupted. "I'm telling you to. Your fate with the Wolven King has already been foretold. But . . . with me . . ." His eyes flashed fully red. "Maybe you can pull off a miracle."

"Why do you care about me?" Gwen asked. The truth struck her like a lightning bolt. "Oh, it's not about *me*, is it? It's about taking me *away* from the Wolven Kings."

"A little bit of both. Say what you will about Angelo, but he always had a backup plan and thought ahead. I'm doing the same."

"Isn't your endgame to be reunited with Zahra? This seems . . ." Gwen paused to collect her thoughts. "Say you're reunited with Zahra . . .

Angelo won't be with Katherine, so he'll continue his quest. This war between our families isn't going to end soon, is it?"

"No, it's not. Either we succeed or die. There are no other options. And desperation will make both of us more dangerous than we currently are. We've both turned away from the Wolven Kings for now, but . . . do you think that will last if we see the other with their beloved? Or worse—Michael actually stops us?"

Just the thought of Dark or Angelo working with her employer was enough to make her crave something stronger tasting than bad soup. The Wolven Kings were walking calamities on their own, but with a member of the Shade family . . . Gwen suspected the world might end.

"And my joining you? How does that stop you allying with a Wolven King?"

Dark cracked his neck, hit his chest until he burped, and then said, "Do you know what one of the core beliefs of being a Mercenary is?"

Gwen shook her head.

"The first belief is that we are the nightmares of this world. That nothing will stop us from accomplishing our goals. Not even death itself. The second belief is that we have no need of our memories, for the world will remember us even if we don't." Dark stacked the last bowl. "The third and final belief is that you keep what you conquer."

Gwen stacked her bowl onto Dark's. The sloshy remnants collected at the bottom like tea leaves. "You plan to kill a Wolven King and take their place if you can't bring Zahra back."

"Correct." Dark stood, flicked another claxo to the owner, and then began walking toward the sewers. "Let me know when you're ready to join me. I promise it'll be worth the hassle."

There was nothing to say, so Gwen followed Dark. Shadows seemed to twist around him like swirling darkness, but Dark was better than her employer . . . wasn't he? The answers didn't come easily as they went below the city and walked alongside shallow pools of murky water with more surprises in it than the mystery cake they served at the end of the Summer Festival in Hollow. When Gwen was nine, she had bitten into a slice and found something hard and white. She spat it out before she could learn whether it was a tooth or not.

They heard a woman's voice in the distance, gradually growing louder and more frantic until they stumbled upon their target. The Azilian Mercenary was crouched over Michael's body. He was passed out on the floor, stiffer than if he were encased in ice. Rian the Smoke Dragon was hanging from manacles on the nearby wall, head slumped as if he were sleeping for all eternity. The Azilian Mercenary snapped to attention at the sight of Gwen and Dark together.

"Dark?" she asked. "What are you doing . . . Wait. She's the one who tried to kill me in the gardens!"

"This is Gwendolyn Kingman, Michael's younger sister. Don't worry about her. She'll behave." Dark strolled over to look at Michael. "How long has the imbecile been out for?"

The Azilian Mercenary didn't reply.

Dark yawned. "Doesn't matter." His eyes fell on Rian. "I'm disappointed, Alexis. I expected Michael to try something like this, but not you. You knew I would find out about him eventually. Do you want to explain yourself?"

The Azilian Mercenary stayed silent.

"Then we'll talk about this later." Dark's right hand turned sharp and scaly. "Want to know something interesting, Gwendolyn? People can go into others' memories and mess around, but even I don't know what'll happen if Rian dies while Michael's still in there. There's a chance his mind will die along with Rian."

"Dark!" Alexis screamed. "Stop it! This isn't right!"

"Unfortunately"—he had the tips of his nails over Rian's heart—"Michael had his chance to join me. If he dies, he dies. I've had enough of his nonsense."

"Wait, Dark!" Gwen said frantically. "Let him live. I'll join you! Whatever you—"

Light blasted out of Michael's chest, blinding everyone in the immediate area. A sharp squealing sound echoed off the walls and back at them like a boomerang. As the light died away, Michael rose from the ground, rubbing the back of his neck.

"So much for getting rid of Michael." Dark stepped away from Rian. "You imbecile. I knew what you were doing. I'm smarter than—"

"Shut up, asshole. My head hurts," Michael growled. His voice was lower than normal, more primal and foolish.

"Dark," Gwen said, creeping away from everyone. "I don't know who that is, but that's *not* my brother."

"What did you say—" Dark cut himself off, hand slowly going to his side to draw his hatchet. "What did that imbecile do?"

The impostor smiled at them all. Amber had been replaced with a tweeker's . . . no, that wasn't the correct terminology anymore. Michael's eyes were now red, like those who had a dragon's heart and abilities. "He made the wrong deal." The man wearing Michael's face straightened and then bowed deeply. "My name is Idris. Pleasure to meet you all."

THE WOLF'S CAPTIVE

"What did you do to my brother?" Gwen screamed, face hot. Her mind was racing: Was Michael gone for good, or was he just indisposed?

Idris was examining the backs of his new hands, admiring them. "We made a deal. He needed information about the Wolven Kings and took my memories to do so." He paused, meeting their eyes. "It was his risk to take, that my memories could take over his mind."

"So he's not dead," Alexis breathed, guns aimed at Idris.

"No, he's not." Idris tapped the side of his head. "But the longer I'm out here and he's in there, the more control I'll have in the long run. Eventually he'll be nothing more than a whisper in the back of my mind."

"Doubtful," Gwen stated, relaxing her posture. "Knowing my brother."

"Perhaps," Idris admitted. "But how long will it take?"

"Long enough." Dark put away his hatchet and stuck his hands in his pockets. "Where's the real you? The Nullify Dragon?" He looked him up and down. "Or is this all that remains?"

Idris sniffed him. "You stink like my family and yet I don't recognize you." Suddenly he understood. "Who did you kill?"

Dark met his eyes. "Does it matter?"

"Idris!" Rian screamed, squirming from his prison. Gwen hadn't seen him wake but it was likely around the same time Idris emerged. "He's killed half our family! Stop him before he kills us all and takes our hearts!"

"I'd advise against trying to stop me," Dark said sweetly. "You don't have a dragon's heart, so you're not my enemy. But if you want to stop me from claiming Smoke's heart . . ." He leaned in and whispered something in Idris's ear that made him laugh rather than cower.

Dark didn't like that.

"You're hundreds of years too young to threaten me, boy," Idris said with Michael's voice and face. If anything, to Dark, that made it a thousand times worse. And yet Alexis and Gwen couldn't help but stifle their initial laughter. Neither was used to seeing Michael act that way toward Dark and likely never would.

"Who do you—"

Dark jumped back as Idris drew a shimmering silver sword from nowhere and struck horizontally at him. But he was too slow and the blade sliced him in half, separating his torso from his legs. Both ends hit different sides of the narrow tunnel. Alexis was the next to die, killed before she had a chance to cry for help or fire one of her guns. Gwen was last, whimpering as Michael's face smiled at her and then he crushed her head against the wall—

And then she blinked, gasping for air, with a hand over her rapidly beating heart. Idris hadn't moved, but Dark had. The Mercenary skidded backwards, drawing his weapons as he did. Armor that Gwen didn't recognize as any nation's current style began to materialize on Idris's body. Circular metal pauldrons covered his shoulders as greaves etched with gold lettering and flowers grew out of his body. Flowing chain mail followed. And then the crown brand on his neck changed into a crying wolf head. The Third Wolven King's personal symbol.

Idris was not a Wolven King. He didn't dominate all those around him like her employer did. Instead, bloodlust and a killing intent radiated from him like steam from a warm body in the cold. A man killed sloppily. A monster killed expertly. Idris was the apex predator among the dragons, assassinating others in their minds without ever moving from his place. Alexis was on her knees next to Gwen, muttering nonsense and in shock that her body was still whole.

Dark was the first to recover, spitting out a slew of curses. "He has Weaving knowledge along with Michael's Nullification abilities! Alexis, don't get close to him! But you may do as you wish, Wolfen Captive."

"How is this possible?" Gwen countered. "I've never seen anything like it."

"He's combining his Weaving and Fabricator abilities," Dark said. "Fabricating allows him to create what he needs and then he weaves it into armor and weapons. It's a common enough, if lied about, skill. Half the Fabrication teachers out there are Weaving masters in disguise. It's why the nobility is so strong: they're using two kinds of magic without realizing it."

Gwen was flabbergasted, but Alexis was unfazed and Idris was amused. "Is that how it's done nowadays? Limit who knows how magic works to control how many people can oppose you? Interesting tactic." He looked at Gwen. "Branded girl, you stink of the Wolven Kings. Which one are you working for?"

"The first."

"What did he send you here to do?"

"To find Rian and take him to the Reborn Titan."

"How delightful." Idris swung his sword and cut the rusted metal chains that held Rian, freeing him. "We'll be coming with you. Mercenaries, will you attempt to stop us?"

"How does he know we're Mercenaries?" Alexis whispered.

Dark didn't answer her. "I've eaten the hearts of more than half your family, do you really think you can stand against me?"

Idris snapped his fingers and dozens of translucent spears came out of the walls, floor, and ceiling, skewering Dark. The Black Death *screamed* in pain. Gwen had never thought she'd hear that sound, and it felt stronger than the Queen's Force Fabrications. It made the tunnels shake. Alexis cowered like a cat beside her as Idris hauled Rian to his feet and walked over to the infamous Mercenary he had taken out with a single attack.

"He's not dead," Idris said nonchalantly. "Just indisposed. Once all the spears are pulled out of him, he'll be fine. But the effects of nullifying his body to such a degree may make it impossible to use magic for a few days."

Dark's eyes were burning red as he struggled to pull the spears out of himself, screaming as if his flesh burned whenever he grabbed hold of one. "I'm going to kill you. I'm going to kill the *real* you. I'm going to make you regret—"

"Yes. Yes. I'm *so* scared. Don't struggle too much or the effects will last longer," Idris interrupted, patting Dark's head as if he were a puppy.

"We should kill him. He's grown too strong for his own good," Rian said, spitting into Dark's face. "And he wouldn't spare us if the positions were reversed."

"There's no justice in killing someone so weak," Idris said, walking away with a confident stroll. "Our family knew what they were getting into when they chose to become dragons. Our deaths were always going to be bloody. And if the Mercenary doesn't take this lesson to heart . . . I and my real self will kill him next time."

Rian's hand lingered over Dark's heart but he shook his head and followed his superior. "As you say, Idris."

"Come, Wolven Captive. Our time here is fleeting."

Alexis scrambled to pull the spears out of Dark as Idris and Rian left the tunnels. Gwen followed, half because she was bound to accomplish her mission and half because she had to keep her brother's body in sight. Michael would return soon . . . wouldn't he?

48

HOLLOW GROUNDS

Two moons were in the sky. Two *whole* moons. Celona wasn't shattered.

My jaw hung open as I lay on a lakeshore staring at the dusk sky, taking in the sight. Where or when was I? Was I in Idris's memories? How did Idris have a memory of Celona being whole? After seeing the painting of Domet with the shattered moon I had assumed . . . ah, that was my mistake. All I knew for certain was that Domet had lived during a time when the moon had been shattered. Who was I to say that he hadn't seen it whole before he became immortal?

"Null!" a man called out as he ran toward me. It was a younger version of Rian. He wore spectacles, was more skin than muscle, and wore what was clearly his only fancy set of clothes. His shoes were scuffed and covered in dried mud. He was a peasant trying to appear noble. "What are you doing out here? We're going to be late!"

"Late?" I said as I pushed myself up. "What for?"

Rian huffed at me. "The selection trials, remember?" He put the back of his hand against my forehead. "Are you feeling ill? Or did you get into another fight with your parents? You aren't normally so forgetful."

"No, I . . . I'm fine. It's just been a long week." I hesitated, wondering if I should ask what the selection trials were or just figure them out on the way. Not wanting to expose myself as an impostor, I said, "Let's go. We shouldn't be late."

Rian helped me up and we left the lake, his lantern lighting the dirt paths. Only a square segment of the sky was visible, as if the rest of it was blocked away by some ceiling I couldn't make out in the darkness. There were also thick walls taller than mountains off in the distance that seemed to contain this area. All the circular houses were made from mud bricks that seemed fit to collapse at any moment. Something felt off about it all, but I couldn't determine what. Even though I didn't know where we were going or where we were, my feet knew the paths. It all felt so familiar, whether thanks to Idris's memories or my own.

Rian didn't give me much time to ponder, skipping around like a child. "This is so exciting, isn't it? What if we're selected and we actually help end the war? It might not be a big deal for you, since you're the son of a duke, but me? This could make me *someone*. Rather than just the kid people ask to transcribe things for them when they're desperate."

Were the selection trials picking candidates to become dragons? The real Rian had mentioned they were part of ending the war. But if that was the case . . . had I been transported back in time to the Wolven Kings' era? Was the first Kingman around here somewhere? Was King Adrian? Was Domet?

"Do you know what these selection trials might—"

Bells went off in the distance and those around us screamed, dropped what they were carrying, and dove for cover. It didn't matter if it was underneath a tree, at the bottom of a ditch, or into the nearby lake. They threw themselves off the main road. Before I could ask what was happening, Rian pushed me against a mud house and then shielded me with his body.

There was an earthshaking roar, a blast of white smoke in the segment of the sky that was visible, and then when it cleared . . . the road was aflame. Lush green trees were transformed into thin brittle grey twigs struggling to stand straight, grass was ash, and anything left behind on the road was now a lumpy black remnant. The smell reminded me of the Militia Quarter during the rebels' attack. Anyone hit by the flames had been reduced to ash before they could scream. But just as quickly as the attack had come, normality returned.

Rian brushed the ash and dirt off his clothes as I stamped out a stubborn flame. "That was a close one," he said. "Their attacks are getting more frequent."

"How much longer do you think we can last?"

"Less than a year." His eyes were stern and hard. Something rumbled far off in the distance, eerily like the rumble I had heard in Dark's mind. Was it a signal telling me to lay low or risk letting the mind's owner know where I was? "The army is struggling to hold the lines, never mind push into enemy territory. Unless we find an edge. But that's why this selection process is so important. It's our only chance to overwhelm the others."

I glanced at the moon. "What if they try something desperate?"

"They won't have the chance," Rian stated. "We'll win before they understand what's happening."

I stopped pressing him, letting him speak freely about whatever caught his mind. Most of the town looked as if it had been constructed in a hurry out of desperation as we made our way to a plaza. There was already a crowd around a masked man in plate-mail armor with a wolf head etched into his chest. He spoke from a wooden crate, and with a passion that could consume everything around him if given the opportunity to grow. Rian and I pushed our way to the front to hear him better.

"—and this is our single chance to win the war!" he screamed. "Can I guarantee it? No! But what else can we do? We have abandoned the city above and now hide like rats below it. Do you not all miss the sun? The stars? Are you content with the sliver of the sky we get a day!" The man gestured to the hole in the ceiling. "I want to walk on grass again! Who else misses the feeling of the sun on their skin?"

There were a few murmurs, but they were drowned out by those who disagreed. The armored man was pelted with balls of mud from the most vocal dissenters. They splattered against him with soft thuds. He ignored them and kept speaking. "I know I have betrayed your trust before, but I—"

"You still wear their symbol! You're one of them!" an elderly woman called out from the crowd. "Why would we trust anything you had to say? All those who were fit to wage war were already taken! All that remains are the old, young, broken, useless, or protected. Don't guilt us into a fight we can't win."

"She's right!" another said. "Why should we trust you when you won't even show your face!"

Most of the crowd—Rian included—agreed with the protestors. A few people spat at him and then turned to leave when the armored man took his helmet off. I was shocked to see Charles Domet. Or, at least, the younger version of him I had seen in that underground painting with Emelia. My heart should have been pounding, but I felt calmer than ever before, wondering if I'd finally begin to unravel who Domet was and why he so wanted to die.

"As some of you know . . . my name is Xavier of Wolvenguard," Domet said. "I was born in a farming village five days from here. My parents died from a sickness when I was young that the surgeons described simply as apathy. Leaving me to take care of my younger sister. And so we traveled here and sought a better life. It took us years of hard work, but eventually we both passed the palace selection trials and joined the ranks of the Wolven knights."

Was this the truth . . . or was it another of Domet's lies?

"From there, I lost sight of my humble origins. I lived in the palace, dined with royals, trained with the knights, and thought myself above those who dug the earth, planted food, or cared for animals." Domet saw a few members of the crowd prepared to throw more mud balls at him.

"But I was wrong. I'm not special. I'm a man who was so blinded by opulence, he lost sight of what truly matters."

"What happened to your sister?" I called, the words emerging without thought, as if spoken by another. Was this Idris's influence on me?

Domet was startled, and Rian mouthed polite but creatively rude things at me for my sudden outburst, as if I had insulted his mentor. When I had initially met Rian, he had claimed they were friends. Had that been the truth?

"My sister is dead," Domet said. "She was murdered by the Wolven Kings she served at Wolvenguard."

"Wait," Rian whispered to no one in particular. "Was Xavier's sister Lady Javi of Wolvenguard? They found her body surrounded by flowers. Her death was one of the catalysts of the war!"

I asked Domet as much, and the crowd was silent as they waited for an answer.

"Yes," Domet admitted. "My sister was Lady Javi of Wolvenguard. But the second question is a little more complicated . . . Her death was a factor in the division between the three brothers, but not the breaking point."

"Then what was?" a random voice asked. "Who started this war you want us to finish?"

"I did," he said matter-of-factly. "I killed the third brother and—"

"Liar." It was my voice—not Idris's. "That's one of your biggest regrets, isn't it? That you let him live when you should have killed him."

Everything froze around me. Domet's head did a complete rotation, defying logic and sanity and resilience of bones. And then familiar words came out of Domet's mouth as the memory reasserted itself.

"Yes," Domet admitted. "My sister was Lady Javi of Wolvenguard. But the second question is a little more complicated . . . Her death was a factor in the division between the three brothers, but not the breaking point."

"Then what was?" a random voice asked. "Who started this war you want us to finish?"

"I did," he said matter-of-factly. "I killed the third brother and—"

The memory continued, but different words came out of my mouth. "The third brother lives. Why would you lie and say you killed him?"

"Because I abandoned him, which might as well have been a killing blow," Domet said, voice light and fleeting. "When we abandon those closest to us, can it be considered anything other than death? For us and them?"

It sounded like an omission passed off as a truth . . . And why did it sound more personal than anything he had ever talked about before? What was I missing? The crowds didn't give me enough time to think, growing more bloodthirsty the longer Domet stood in front of them. They saw him as a symbol of all they hated, a curse upon their lives, and nothing could sway most of them to his cause. Only the young seemed to listen, and even then it was hard to tell if it was because they thought he was right or if it was out of pity.

"If any of you want to help me end this"—Domet pointed to the square cut out of the ceiling that revealed the night sky—"then leave this hollow and join me in the city above tomorrow night."

I had to suppress my laughter. How hadn't I realized it sooner? I was back in Hollow, in the underground area where the lake and dragon prison had been. All the architecture I had seen there was the same as this . . . but if this area was called the hollow . . . what was the city above us called? And how had my city been born?

"What's the cost?" Rian bellowed from the crowd.

"Your humanity. You will become monsters, but the war will end." The crowd fell silent in a heartbeat; his words seemed dramatic but true. His eyes didn't hold an inkling of dishonesty. Domet continued, like a storyteller reaching their finale: "I'm sorry for what I was complicit in. That I didn't stop them when I had the chance. And I'm sorry this is the only way to change the world."

Domet stepped off his platform, trudging away with his head down in shame. No one followed him, though quiet murmurs spread through the crowd like a sickness. And then they began to disperse until only the memory of the bloodthirst remained. I wanted to follow Domet, but the boundaries of Idris's memory held me in place.

Rian nudged me in the side to break my focus. "What do you think he meant by becoming monsters?"

Idris said, "There's only one way to find out."

"I guess that means we're going," Rian replied. "We should—"

The landscape around me shattered, Rian disappearing into smoke, and I found myself in a colorless void that stretched for an eternity. The only things out of place were Idris and a black door supported by nothing but an empty frame. The Nullify Dragon gave me a soft smile, no canine teeth showing.

"Exciting, isn't it?"

"How does Domet relate to the Third Wolven King?" I asked, walking toward the door.

"A man is only himself before he gains power. This is what we were all like before we became dragons. Innocent youths who wanted to change the world. Now only jaded adults remain." He looked away, distraught. "You have to know what we were willing to sacrifice."

It made no sense to me, and yet I didn't argue. "Show me what happened next."

The door opened and sucked me inward, the air distorting around it. And so I continued to dive into the past, hoping the third's name was somewhere in Idris's memories. What would I learn next about Rian, Idris, Domet, and the Wolven Kings?

A TRANSACTION OF FLESH

"I'm sorry."

Domet plunged a blade into a man's chest, right above the heart. Parts of his body had begun to change, half of it covered in blue-white scales. The victim's eyes were pure red orbs, half his teeth were falling out, and his nails had grown so suddenly that they curled inward, touching his own wrist. Domet lowered the man as he squirmed and coughed up blood, desperately clawing for air. Nothing humanlike remained once he touched the dirt. The fifteen onlookers that circled them were silent as Domet extracted the blade, muttered another apology, and waved his hand over the body. It wasted away into ash and dirt within a few heartbeats.

What was going on here? A river rushed past the tip of the land on both sides as fifteen people surrounded Charles Domet. Was he mortal here? Or had he already become immortal?

"I warned you all that not everybody would be receptive to the process. But I apologize that you all had to see that," Domet said quietly. "Who wants to try next?"

Rian, Vance, Anna, Luis, and the older versions of the children I had seen in the playground made up the circle. But the two outsiders were the ones that caught my eye. One was faceless, their features so smooth and clean that I couldn't determine if they were male, female, or identified as neither. Were they forgotten on purpose, or by accident?

The other was a small man with dirt underneath his nails, narrow eyes, and an utterly bland face. He was so plain and ordinary that I skipped over him twice. Was he just another victim here, or did the face not match his importance?

"How do we know this ritual works?" Luis bellowed. Anna flinched at his side but steeled herself quickly. "Because right now all I see is an executioner surrounded by fools."

Domet wiped the blade clean on a cloth he had lodged between his armor and the clothes beneath. He did it methodically, making sure no blood remained. "Do you think I want more death on my hands? I've killed more in my lifetime than you could in a thousand."

Luis smiled, showing his canine teeth. "I doubt that."

"Knight Xavier isn't exaggerating," the faceless one said, arms crossed. "I served under him and saw what he was capable of at the Sword Graveyard. Hundreds died thanks to his blade."

"Most of those I imagine were women and children. That helps increase the kill count. If you're so brave, then why don't you volunteer next?" Luis asked. The faceless one looked away from him as the ordinary man whispered, "Coward."

"I'll do it," a man said as he approached Domet. He was scarily skinny, covered in purple and yellow bruises, his hair was thin and falling out, and he had long scratches along his wrist. Tweekers were more put-together than this man was. "If I die, I die."

"You shouldn't devalue your life." Domet knelt, opened the trunk near him, and showed off the thirteen hearts that had been carefully placed inside it. Each heart was a different shade from the typical muddy red. "Pick one."

"Are they different?"

"Each will give you different abilities," Domet said. "Choose which-ever appeals to you most."

The thin man picked up a whitish-grey heart that already had a bite taken out of it. "I might as well take another's discard." He looked at the spot where the man Domet had killed had been. "How will I know if it worked?"

"You won't get a blade in your heart," Luis said.

The thin man side-eyed Domet. "If this works, make sure he doesn't get an ability better than mine."

Domet nodded. As the silence became deafening, the thin man took a bite out of the heart in his hands. Every bite was a strain, a fight against sensibility that he should be eating a human's heart. But the man ate and ate, forcing it all down his throat until he sucked on his fingers to get rid of the blood that lingered on his skin. He burped, held his fist over his mouth, and then waited. A flower of ice blossomed from his neck and then spread across the rest of his body until he was covered from head to toe.

"Another death," Luis said. "This is all a—"

The ice on the thin man melted away until a puddle formed at his feet. He twisted a ball of ice in his hand, admiring it with childish glee. Then he stomped his foot, and a thin pointy spear of ice came up from the ground and stopped right before it pierced the underside of Luis's chin. The future Heartbreaker didn't so much as flinch, breaking off the tip instead and walking it over his knuckles.

"What is this?" the thin man asked. "I thought this kind of power was reserved for gods."

"The gods are dead and I've stolen their powers. Only we remain." Domet faced all those around him. "Will the rest of you join me in my quest to destroy the Wolven Kings? It will cost you your humanity, but . . ." He trailed off, the young man acting as if he had already lived a thousand years. ". . . but I promise it'll be worth the sacrifice."

Luis stepped forward, claimed a bright red heart from the trunk, and then began to feast. His body burst into flames, but it went out in a blink, leaving only his arms engulfed from fingertip to elbow. "My body finally matches my mind. This is wonderful." He snapped his fingers at Anna. "My love, come and join me."

Her eyes went wide. "But . . . but I thought I wouldn't have to. You said I was just keeping you company. I don't want to—"

Luis held out a grey heart to her. "Join me."

The Heartbreaker's wife tentatively did as she was instructed, taking the heart in both hands. Just holding it made her gag, blood dripping through her fingers and to the dirt below. "Must I?"

"Yes." Luis took the heart from her. "I'll help. Open wide. And chew slowly, so the stringy meat doesn't get stuck in your throat."

I couldn't watch what happened next. It was a sick display of power, and I wanted no part of it. Especially since I knew how each of their stories ended. I waited until it was eerily quiet, and then an ear-popping shout came from Anna, making everyone clutch their heads. Luis cared for Anna as she shook on the ground, as he gently reminded her over and over how much he loved her and how this was the best thing for them.

"Who's next?" Domet asked.

The twins volunteered. One ended up covered in metal while the other looked like their skin had turned to bark. Following them, a woman and an androgynous person gained the powers of lightning and water respectively. Neither looked happy and they bickered about wanting the other's abilities until Domet politely told them to leave the circle. Vance, Mockingbird, Rian, and I—serving in Idris's place—would take four of the remaining hearts. Which left the ordinary man, the faceless man, and the boy who spat at the ground whenever someone left the circle to take the next two hearts: light and wind. Which of them wouldn't join the ranks of the dragons, and, more importantly: Why not?

"Are we sure there's no other way to stop the war?" the ordinary man asked of no one in particular. "Why must we lose our humanity?"

"Grow a backbone, Adrian," the spitting man snapped. "Do what is necessary for once in your life rather than what's easy."

Wait. Did he say *Adrian*? As in *my* Adrian? Adrian the Liberator?

The future king of Hollow? And if that was Adrian . . . did that mean the faceless man was . . . ?

If my father was my hero, then the First Kingman was everything I aspired to be. A perfect representation of what my family was supposed to stand for. They had overthrown tyrants, installed a system of government that had remained in place for a thousand years, and given birth to a legacy that none could replicate. I was so close to them, and unable to ask a single question. It made tears form in the corners of my eyes. I wanted them to be proud of me—to give merit and purpose to a life that seemed too overwhelming to shoulder—but that validation would never come. Especially not here.

"It's not a matter of doing what is easy, Kureye, but what is right." The First Kingman gestured to the box of hearts. "And that is not humane. There must be another way."

"There is," Domet said casually. Those who had eaten hearts went wide-eyed. "But the cost is even higher. If you want to end this war, then we need warriors who can fight the Wolven Kings. We can make a few elite forces or give everyone the ability to use magic."

Both Adrian and the First Kingman reacted the same—jubilation mixed with relief—but Adrian spoke first. "Then why are we doing this? Why not give everyone the ability to use magic?"

"Because the price to do so is unsurmountable," Domet said. "It costs one individual their humanity to manipulate, create, and transform a specialization. But to give magic to everyone?" He tapped a finger on his chin. "Do you believe in an afterlife?"

"Which variation of it?" the First Kingman asked.

"Any of them."

"Like most, I believe the goddess will judge me against the weight of my bad deeds. If the good outweighs the bad, I will reunite with those I love in the realm of my ancestors. If not . . . if not, I will descend into the realm of monsters and fight in the eternal war until my debt has been paid. And then I will enter the void and know peace."

Nothing my ancestors said had made sense to me. Most people, now, believed in a singular genderless God. And a realm of monsters where people fought an eternal war if they weren't good enough? I knew of nothing like that. Beliefs changing in a thousand years wasn't unexpected, but for them to disappear without a trace? It made me suspicious. Especially given what Dark had told me about the lockless door being a path to the afterlife.

"Would you give up your afterlife to give the world access to magic? Would you dethrone the goddess?" Domet hesitated. "Would you kill her?"

My face paled. Oh, no. Was I about to witness . . .

"Yes," my ancestor declared. "Without hesitation. Whatever it takes."

And so the war between my family and God began beneath two whole moons surrounded by immortals. Bearing witness to it was not a gift, but a curse. I had always believed the First Kingman was the best of us, but now doubt crept into my heart and a new terrifying thought crossed my mind . . . Could we be villains the world had turned into heroes only because we were victorious?

"That's blasphemy!" Rian shouted. "How dare you?" He turned to Domet. "And *you*, do you realize what you just insinuated? That the goddess could be held to mortal standards? She cannot be dragged by our poisonous whims."

"One of the greatest lies ever told is that those above us cannot be like us," Domet said. "But that is not true. Our gods are just reflections of our own desires for perfection. They are not better. If anything, they are worse because they are unable to grow."

"No." Rian threw his hands up in anger. "I won't listen to this heresy any longer. Do what you all believe is necessary, but I won't—"

My body moved on its own and grabbed Rian's shoulder. "Stop. We have to do this. For all those who cannot."

Rian was silent for a few heartbeats, thinking as he gazed around the circle to see who would become his forced family and those who would always oppose him. It was clearly not an easy decision to make, and yet as he strode toward the box of hearts, plucking out a sickly grey one, he reminded me of a conquering hero. That feeling was short-lived as he bit into the heart, thick white liquid dripping down his chin and lips. He tore into it like an animal, ripping and tearing the muscle until it was soft enough to swallow. Smoke tendrils wafted from his body as he swallowed the last bite, making sure nothing was wasted.

My ancestor and the future King of Hollow turned their backs to the circle and walked away, silent. Domet shouted after them, "If you wish to take another path, find the third brother. He is fighting his brothers alone. And though I refuse to aid him, perhaps you can do what I cannot."

They left without a word of affirmation, and I desperately wanted to follow, but I had to remain in Idris's footsteps. The bright white heart tasted stringy and foul, and it slithered down my throat like slimy algae. When the last morsel was gone, a burst of warmth blew from my chest and canceled out all the other dragons' magic. The memory fizzled out, Domet's soft smile the last thing I saw as the darkness swallowed me whole.

Idris was waiting for me again, next to a grey door in the nothingness between memories.

"Can I meet my ancestor?" I asked, trying to hide my desperate plea. "You must've met them at some—"

"Other than during battles, we never spoke. They went their way, and I went mine," Idris said. "I'm sorry. You'll find no answers here." He hesitated. "But you will see what they did."

I asked the question I didn't want to but had to. "Did they shatter Celona?"

"Yes," he answered. "Do you want to ask more, or is the truth too—"

"They killed the god, goddess, or whatever was in charge back then and gave magic to the world, didn't they? Maybe that's what shattered Celona or maybe it was something else, but it changed everything. Was it their punishment to be erased from history?"

Idris didn't reply.

"Can't answer, can you? So I must be right about something."

Idris put his index fingers against the sides of his mouth and then pulled his skin upward, revealing that his mouth had been stitched closed.

Whatever limitations kept the truth from being revealed affected people even in memories. How terrifying.

"And so the fool goes on in search of the truth."

I stepped through the door, into the next memory, and was stabbed in the stomach before my feet touched the other side. I fell to my knees, clutching at the blade, but the unknown soldier held it firmly in place. All I could do was struggle. Echoes of war surrounded me as my face hit hot sand, burning against it. My eyelids closed, pain abandoned me, and I died.

HOW TO DIE

But here's the thing about death—I was *good* at it.

I had almost died so many times that when the familiar darkness swallowed me, trying to force me down, I knew how to counter it. I took a breath—full of pain—and returned to the battlefield as my murderer stood over me, shocked as I pulled the blade out of my chest. My blood mixed with the sand, forming wet clumps. I impaled the soldier on his own sword, and then forced him to the ground, holding him with one foot on his chest until he was still. His death was nothing more than a long-ago memory, and yet it felt as real as if I had done it with my own two hands. A wave of soldiers rushed past me and clashed with opposing forces. A plume of smoke hit the ground next to me and Rian appeared in his human form, arms crossed.

"That soldier nearly got the best of you," Rian said.

Idris's voice came out of my mouth as the wound in my chest healed. "He caught me off guard. Nothing more."

I was in control again, brushing the dirt and dust off my clothes as I gazed upon the battlefield. I didn't recognize it . . . but one day I would: the Desert of a Thousand Craters. It was located between the Thebian Empire and New Dracon City on the wrong side of the Iliar mountain range. If history was to be believed, it was where the Wolven Kings had fought their bloodiest battle. Both moons were still in the sky, so Celona hadn't been shattered yet. Would it happen during this battle, or another?

"Domet wants us to clear a path to the heart of the battle," Rian explained. "The brothers are already there, slapping each other like children." Rian made a sucking noise with his mouth. "He's planning on ending the war here."

"He's said that for the last five battles," I said with Idris's voice. "And every time, whenever we get close to the brothers, they scatter. Domet scares them more than each other."

"It's because his issue with them goes beyond politics, morals, or the well-being of this world. That man *made* a fourth faction to fight them after his sister's death. That's not sane. Especially when he would have been the right-hand man to anyone he joined."

"Sometimes we act for our own sanity, not according to what others want or say," I said, uncertain if I was leaking out of Idris or if those were his words. "That choice separates the fools from the wise."

"Are you calling me a fool, Idris?" Domet asked, appearing behind us. He was in the same armor he'd worn in the hollow below the broken city. Only now translucent red worms seemed to be crawling out of his skin like a sentient rash. "Because I won't disagree with you, but you should watch your tongue in public. Others may not be as self-aware as I am."

I remained silent, taking in the battlefield as Rian apologized to Domet. It seemed even here—surrounded by those he called family—Idris was always an outsider.

The battlefield was something out of a mythical story that seemed too bizarre to belong in the world I knew. Two towering titans of stone, flesh, and bone lumbered across the desert, swatting at flying dragons. The first titan walked on four legs like a feral dog with curved horns, patches of brownish green moss that could be mistaken for fur, and huge shards of bone sticking out of its back. It was bigger than any building I had ever seen and made the Iliar mountain range in the distance look small.

The second titan was completely different. A massive six-legged bone spider with shiny metal fangs that dripped poison onto the poor soldiers below. Just one touch of it burned away any surface: bone, metal, or someone's face. The smart soldiers avoided the spider, but others clung to the titan's heels as though proximity would offer some kind of safety.

Just beyond the titans, an isolated storm raged over an oasis. Dark clouds and walls of heavy rain made little of the area visible. But there was no doubt in my head that the Wolven Kings were fighting under it. And yet . . . it was still three armies, two titans, and an entire life away. Could I get there without dying? And if I could, how was I supposed to get the Third Wolven King's name from one of them? Being lucky enough to overhear it was the only solution that wouldn't end in total disaster.

"The others will keep the titans preoccupied," Domet said dryly. "Are you going to use your dragon form, Idris? Or do you still consider yourself above it?"

"I have pledged my life to end this war," I said. "And I will do it my way. If we lose our humanity in search of lofty ideals, we are no better than the Wolven Kings."

"Noble to a fault." Domet crossed his arms. "But I knew what I was getting into when I invited you to become a dragon. Your parents were the shining example of righteousness that the King of Kings liked to ramble on about." He was too fidgety to be as understanding as his words sounded. "How do you expect to get through the army? Will you at least use your Fabrications and Weaving abilities?"

"Yes," I snapped. "Watch me carve a path through the hordes!"

Rian looked at me, concerned, but took off into the air with a plume of smoke. I knew Domet well enough to understand when to press for more information and when not to and—to no one's surprise—I was about to be a thorn in the memory version of his ass when two soldiers swarmed us. Idris's body was stronger and faster than my own, so I was able to duck and weave through their lunges before separating hands from arms and heads from torsos with a sword.

Domet shook his head as their bodies hit the sand, and muttered, "May there be peace in death for you all." And then to me, "Get on with it, Idris. You're not scared of them, are you?"

Never. And like a fool I charged into the battle and, inadvertently, to my death.

The battle was designed to kill me. All the weapons were either made from the magic crystal or were coated in a thin, translucent layer of it. I was killed six steps after leaving Domet's side, half a dozen arrows impaling me in the face. Idris's Spellborn abilities did nothing to save me, and the pain made me scream. But before I could fall to the floor, everything stopped, and I took a breath—and then the war seemed to reset, and I was back at Domet's side again.

"Get on with it, Idris. You're not scared of them, are you?" Domet mocked.

I stared at the immortal man, blinking rapidly, and wondered whether something was wrong with this memory or maybe—worse—wrong with me. Turns out both were correct. I went a different way, easily dodging the arrows that had killed me before, only to run into five spearmen with a one-eyed wolf sigil on their armor. I cut down the first two that lunged at me but took the third's spear to the side. The fourth was to my back and the fifth was to my chest. They skewered me like a pig over an open flame.

And back to the beginning I went.

"Get on with it, Idris. You're not scared of them, are you?"

But before I could rush off again or fully understand what had happened, Idris appeared in front of me. He looked carefully optimistic as everything stopped around us. "I'm sorry, Michael. But this is where we part ways."

"What's happening here?" I asked. "I died and yet—"

"And yet you lived," Idris answered. "This is my memory of the

Battle of Desert of a Thousand Craters. It was the bloodiest battle in the Wolven King War. The real me tore through the battlefield to get to that oasis and confront the Wolven Kings. Sadly, you will not be able to do the same."

"Why not? Just tell me how to . . . but you're not going to, are you? You're going to trap me in this memory . . . in this endless battle, aren't you?"

Idris nodded. "I've taken over your body. There's nothing you can do to stop me."

"Doubtful," I countered. "Seems to me all I have to do is get to that oasis and see how the memory ends rather than die on this battlefield."

"That's easier said than done. Everyone here wants to kill you. *I* nearly died hundreds of times when this battle happened. And I was a master of Nullification Fabricating and Weaving. You don't even understand the full extent of your abilities, much less mine." His face grew grim. "You don't stand a chance in a thousand lifetimes."

"My persistence outmatches my intelligence." I kicked at the sand. "I'll get to that oasis, finish this memory, and take back my body."

"You'll go mad long before you reach the end." Idris began to dissolve away. "Goodbye, Michael. I'll look after your friends and family if I can. I'm sorry it had to be like this."

A strong gust of wind blew the rest of him away and the battle resumed.

"Get on with it, Idris. You're not scared of them, are you?"

Idris had underestimated me. And no matter what I had to do— I *would* return to reality.

But first, I stabbed Domet in the stomach with my sword, just for the pleasure of doing it. The immortal aged me a thousand years with a snap of his fingers and I returned to his side before I really understood what had happened. His voice was already bothering me. It felt as if his prickly-thorned tongue was pressed against my ear.

"Get on with it, Idris. You're not scared of them, are you?"

Feeling a little bit better, I took Idris's dagger off my hip and carved the number three on the back of my right hand, cracked my neck, and then charged into the swarm of soldiers. How many deaths would I suffer here before I reached my goal? Dozens? Hundreds? Thousands?

Or would madness claim me long before that?

DIE FOR ME

My next six deaths weren't worth mentioning. I was stabbed with anything and everything from swords, spears, pointy bits of armor, and even two sewing needles that felt rusted beyond belief when they pierced my eyes and then were yanked out, red flakes lost along the way. It was like blinking out fire.

Or I died by magic. Lightning Fabricators struck me down when I tried to rush them. Ice Fabricators froze me before shattering me with the butts of their weapons. Some Earth Weavers sucked me into the ground and crushed me to death in the dirt. The pain stopped bothering me after a bit. His voice when the cycle began again never did.

"Get on with it, Idris. You're not scared of them, are you?"

Five more deaths, each just as horrific as the last, and I was no closer to my goal. I started to laugh manically whenever I returned to Domet's side and heard that awful sentence again. But each death brought me a *little* bit closer to the center. So I did the only thing I could.

I used it as an opportunity to hone my Fabricator abilities.

I'd never had time to learn how to use my Fabrications, patchworking my abilities together through observation, and experimenting at the cost of my memories. But here I could use magic without losing my memories. It was a perfect opportunity to train.

I made it just a body length this time. An Ice Weaver impaled me with three spears as I tried to catch a Lightning Fabricator's attack. My blood dripped onto the ice and froze instantaneously as my heavy eyes closed. The battle continued around my death.

"Get on with it, Idris. You're not scared of them, are you?"

I carved the next number on my hand and charged the battle again. One step further than the previous cycle. Until a Metal Fabricator fell out of the sky and onto me, crushing my bones and paralyzing me from the waist down. A soldier put me out of my misery with a sword to the neck. I saved his life in my next five lives as thanks.

After the first hundred deaths, my mind began to bleed into the battlefield. Buildings from Hollow—falling apart and ruinous—sprouted out of the sand as if uncovered after a harsh storm. Kingman Keep was followed by Hollow Castle and all the other High Noble Keeps. And then the green-and-white–striped house from my nightmares. I avoided that place as if it were a plague that would consume me if given the chance. Without knowing how or why . . . I was confident the door to my desires was in that building. But I had no intention of seeing it.

Some things deserved to remain hidden. Or so the beautiful lie went.

It took a hundred deaths to learn to redirect lightning and fire with perfect efficiency. Ice took another fifty. I wasted a hundred and fifty deaths trying to figure out if I could redirect wind. I couldn't, but I could mitigate being pushed or pulled around at the Fabricator's or Weaver's whims. By the time I'd died four hundred times, I had trouble remembering my loved ones' faces and names. So, I abandoned them. We would meet again, and when we did . . . I would ask for their forgiveness. But in the meantime I turned my hatred into a source of strength, pushing forward no matter what.

"Forward," I said as I severed a soldier's arm at the elbow with a dull sword.

"Forward," I said as a Blood Fabricator made bodies explode around me, bloody bone shrapnel flying everywhere.

"Forward," I said as I made a Fire Fabricator set themselves on fire.

"Forward," I said as Light Fabricators blinded me as their allies swarmed me with axes.

"Forward," I said as I caught lightning, watching my enemies flee in terror at the sight.

"Forward," I said as Wind Weavers and Fabricators dropped rocks on me from above.

"Forward," I choked as Metal Weavers tightened their nooses around my neck.

"Forward," I pleaded as I was stabbed over and over again until I was holier than those who pledged their life to God.

"Forward," I whispered as I reached out for the sky, wondering if I would ever experience peace again.

There was no answer, and so I returned to the war and died . . . and died . . . and died.

For a hundred deaths in the early thousands, I wandered the battlefield naked with a bottle of wine like a madman. The sight of me drove many away and I killed those who chose to stop and fight. In that span, I learned how to beat Metal and Wood Fabricators with my bare hands. The trick was to nullify a small part of my body so they only fought with their own flesh. My sanity didn't recover until the numbers I carved onto my body were scars in my mind rather than on my flesh. And even then, it took me a hundred more deaths until I remembered my goal.

I died five hundred times to Darkness Fabricators and Weavers and grew no closer to stopping them than I was at the beginning. Those with a Light specialization were the same. Something about how their magic twisted and hid made it impossible to redirect it back at them. And so I resigned myself to nullifying the area and fighting without magic whenever

I ran into them. Each one was practice for . . . whoever my Mercenary mentor had been. And for every time I fought and died against one, I fought them another three or four times until that loss was a fluke rather than a pattern.

I didn't even realize I had made it to the center of the battle—titans walking around me and creating minor earthquakes whenever their hooves hit the ground—since I was in the process of taking on a Blood Fabricator who had wrecked half a division of soldiers. I cut his throat with his own hardened blood, then stood in front of the wall of rain in disbelief.

I had died so many times . . . yet finally reached my goal. Domet approached me from behind carefully, likely wondering if cutting through so many soldiers had left me with any shred of humanity. Truth be told . . . I didn't know if I was mad or simply thought I was mad, to cope with what I had done. How many times had I died? The number on the back of my hand was hard to make out with all the blood covering my body.

"You did well, Idris," Domet said. His hand hovered over my shoulder, but then he shook it and returned it to his sword hilt. "Do you need a moment to collect yourself?"

"No," I said, tasting metal in my mouth. "Let's get on with it."

We passed through the wall of rain together to confront the Wolven Kings in silence. But rather than a crowd waiting for me inside . . . there was only one person. A conglomeration of shadows made human, twisting and contorting and sucking in all the light around us. It was leaning over the edge of a pool of clear water, gently creating ripples as it ran its fingers over the surface. The two whole moons hung directly above, as if framing them.

At the sound of my entrance, it rose and turned to me. The sounds of the battle were gone, replaced by a gentle breeze blowing through the large leaves hanging over the water. "You're not supposed to be here."

"Yet I am." I whipped my sword through the air, sending droplets of sweat and blood and whatever black bile the titans ran on to the sand below. "Which Wolven King are you?"

"None of them." It stepped closer. "And you misunderstand me. Idris is supposed to be here. *You* are not, Michael Kingman."

I nearly choked. "What did you just say?"

"Mi-chael. King-man," it drawled. "The middle child of—" My father's name was carried away by the wind. "—brother to Lyonardo Cityborn and Gwendolyn of the Wolves. By divine luck or modern stupidity . . . you are the last of us. My final descendant. And here we are— the first and the last—meeting inside a dragon's memories."

"The First Kingman," I whispered. And then louder said, "Seriously? But how are you talking to me like this? Are your memories—"

"Shut up," they snapped. "There's no layers of memories or anything. The rules apply differently to me. Every version of me that ever was— except for a few stolen by that asshole immortal fool—can be viewed simultaneously by my consciousness. Consider it one of the benefits when you break the natural order of things." They thumbed toward the broken moon. "Or did you assume a Wolven King was responsible for that? No, it was me. I shattered Celona and stopped the Wolven Kings from taking control of the world."

The First Kingman shattered Celona. That revelation should have shattered me. Broken my persona or my sense of self. Confirmed my worst fear—that the Kingman family truly were the villains of history— but I felt my mouth twitching upward, slowly turning into a broader smile.

I asked what so many had wondered for so long. "How?"

Perfectly white teeth returned my smile from the shadows. "Let me show you. The true shattering doesn't happen here . . . but I'll still show you how I did it." It jammed its right hand toward Celona as if grasping it in its palm. "I had to steal from the goddess to get this power. Experimented a little as well, to get the right combination." Celona pulsated like a beating heart in rhythm with my own. "After that, it just takes a little force and a little manipulation of its orbit." That smile vanished. "And the resolve to change the world."

Celona shattered into seven major pieces as a cloud of dust and stone and anything else that had ever resided in it exploded outward. Moon-fall fell toward us, covering the sky with thousands of streaks of white. The world shook around us and I fell to one knee, an unseen pressure forcing me down. And yet the First Kingman remained standing. A true titan of unknown proportions.

My heart was racing with excitement. Fear had no place here. Not when I had been chasing the First Kingman for so long. To finally be in their presence felt like a gift.

The First Kingman returned their focus to me. "You did well to get here. But you can't move forward as you are. You fought with rage to cross that battlefield. And if we are to meet again . . . then I need a protector. Not an embodiment of vengeance. That was my way, but it will not be my descendant's."

"Why not?" I asked, struggling to stand.

They crossed the small distance between us and then placed their hand under my chin, lifting it so they could stare into my eyes. Their hands were hard and callused, their face a shadow. "Because one day you will have to kill me. And if you are the last . . . you must live. For both our sakes."

"No!" The force pressing down on me was nothing in comparison to the weight I had carried on my shoulders all my life. I pushed myself up with the tips of my fingers, defying my ancestor's will. "I'm fine with being a villain. With breaking the world to reset it, but I *refuse* to let you dictate me any longer."

I wobbled to my feet as the force grew heavier and heavier. I stuck my hand out as if grabbing the pieces of the newly broken moon. "You've had a say in every part of my life from my birth to my death. I've inherited your eyes, your hopes, your regrets, and even your will. No more. You want me to stop you? Fine. But on my terms."

Pride welled in my chest as I stood straight, face-to-face with my ancestor. "I'm going to reunite Celona. Maybe not today. Or tomorrow. Or in a decade or a century. But one day I will fix your mistakes. I swear it not on our family, our legacy, or any of that other nonsense but on my ego." I smiled painfully. "I have inherited your legacy. I am the worst Kingman that ever will be. I'm going to destroy you, end our family, and free us from our amber-eyed curse."

"You truly are mine," it said. Its smile was soft, almost approving. "I'm going to send you back to the beginning now, with a few changes just in case your body remembers the path. When you reach the oasis again, you'll find Idris. Remember that this is *your* mind. You are in control of every aspect of it. Use that to defeat him."

The ground began to swallow me whole, and no matter how hard I struggled to resist or nullify my body, I sank down. "The third name. I need the Third Wolven King's name. Give me that and I'll find you before you know it."

"I can't. I'm sorry. I can only leave you with one thing, and it's better you will remember how our meeting felt. I hope it will be enough to shape your path forward. Hate is temporary, but love is forever." My ancestor backed away. The shadows around their face started to disappear, revealing their bright amber eyes, and I saw the First Kingman had been a woman. Knowing that felt like a secret only we shared. "May we meet again, Michael."

Sand filled my mouth. All I could spit out were half-formed curses and muted garbles. I slipped through the darkness, falling endlessly as bubbles of my memories painted onto them flew out of my body and away. I kept my mind focused on the First Kingman. The scar across the bridge of her small nose. The deep-set bags beneath her amber eyes. Their thin lips and short eyelashes. Their pained smile. Their . . .

Remember not the madness . . .

Remember not the pain . . .

Remember the measure of a life . . .

Remember the purpose of death . . . it is not to be feared. Embrace it.

Return to the beginning.

The battle raged on as if none of my deaths had happened. Domet was by my side.

"Get on with it, Idris. You're not scared of them, are you?"

I took Idris's dagger off my hip, carved the number three on the back of my right hand, cracked my neck, and then charged into the swarm of soldiers. How many deaths would I suffer here before I reached my goal? Dozens? Hundreds? Thousands?

It didn't matter. Madness be damned. I would never give up.

I'd see my family again.

44

DIE FOR THEM

My next six deaths weren't worth mentioning. I was stabbed with anything and everything from swords, spears, pointy bits of armor, and even two sewing needles that felt rusted beyond belief when they pierced my eyes and then were yanked out, red flakes lost along the way. It was like blinking out fire.

Or I died by magic. Lightning Fabricators struck me down when I tried to rush them. Ice Fabricators froze me before shattering me with the butts of their weapons. Some Earth Weavers sucked me into the ground and crushed me to death in the dirt. The pain stopped bothering me after a bit. His voice when the cycle began again never did.

"Get on with it, Idris. You're not scared of them, are you?"

Five more deaths, each just as horrific as the last, and I was no closer to my goal. I started to laugh manically whenever I returned to Domet's side and heard that awful sentence again. But each death brought me a *little* bit closer to the center. So I did the only thing I could.

I used it as an opportunity to hone my Fabricator abilities.

I'd never had time to learn how to use my Fabrications, patchworking my abilities together through observation, and experimenting at the cost of my memories. But here I could use magic without losing my memories. It was a perfect opportunity to train.

I made it just a body length this time. An Ice Weaver impaled me with three spears as I tried to catch a Lightning Fabricator's attack. My blood dripped onto the ice and froze instantaneously as my heavy eyes closed. The battle continued around my death.

"Get on with it, Idris. You're not scared of them, are you?"

I carved the next number on my hand and charged the battle again. One step further than the previous cycle. Until a Metal Fabricator fell out of the sky and onto me, crushing my bones and paralyzing me from the waist down. A soldier put me out of my misery with a sword to the neck. I saved his life in my next five lives as thanks.

After the first hundred deaths, my mind began to bleed into the battlefield. Buildings from Hollow—falling apart and ruinous—sprouted out of the sand as if uncovered after a harsh storm. Kingman Keep was followed by Hollow Castle and all the other High Noble Keeps. And then the green-and-white–striped house from my nightmares. I avoided that place as if it were a plague that would consume me if given the chance. Without knowing how or why . . . I was confident the door to my desires was in that building. But I had no intention of seeing it.

Some things deserved to remain hidden. Or so the beautiful lie went.

It took a hundred deaths to learn to redirect lightning and fire with perfect efficiency. Ice took another fifty. I wasted a hundred and fifty deaths trying to figure out if I could redirect wind. I couldn't, but I could mitigate being pushed or pulled around at the Fabricator's or Weaver's whims. By the time I'd died four hundred times, I had trouble remembering my loved ones' faces and names. So, along with the number on the back of my hand, I started every cycle by carving their names on my arms and chanted their names as a prayer as I fought. Their love and forgiveness were the only divine intervention that mattered to me.

"Gwen," I said as I severed a soldier's arm at the elbow with a dull sword.

"Lyon," I said as a Blood Fabricator made four bodies explode in bone shrapnel.

"Kai," I said as I caused a Fire Fabricator to set themselves on fire.

"Trey," I said as Light Fabricators blinded me while their allies swarmed me with axes.

"Chloe," I said as I caught lightning, watching my enemies flee in terror.

"Naomi," I said as Wind Weavers and Fabricators dropped rocks on me from above.

"Dawn," I choked as Metal Weavers tightened their nooses around my neck.

"Ma," I said as arrows blocked out the sun and rained down on me.

"Serena," I pleaded as I was stabbed over and over again until I was holier than those who pledged their life to God.

"Serena," I whispered as I reached out for the sky, wondering if I would ever experience love or peace again.

An answer would never come, and so I returned to the war and died . . . and died . . . and died.

For a hundred deaths in the early thousands, I wandered the battlefield searching for any clues about the Wolven Kings. All the soldiers wore patches that separated them into three groups: a wolf head with its eyes sewn shut, a wolf head bearing its fangs, and a crying wolf head. But their insignia was all I could learn of them. Instead, I tried to save as many of my comrades as I could to learn about Idris . . . but it was a labor of uselessness. But after so much death . . . I felt as if I had to try and hold on to my humanity somehow.

In that span, I learned how to beat Metal and Wood Fabricators with my bare hands. The trick was to nullify a small part of my body so they only fought with their own flesh. My ability to kill didn't recover until the names I carved onto my body became scars in my mind, and even then it took me a hundred more deaths to advance toward my goal again.

I died five hundred times to Darkness Fabricators and Weavers and grew no closer to stopping them than I was at the beginning. Those with a Light specialization were the same. Something about how their magic twisted and hid made it impossible to redirect it back at them. And so I resigned myself to nullifying the area and fighting without magic whenever I ran into them. Each one was practice for . . . whoever my Mercenary mentor had been. And for every time I fought and died against one, I fought them another three or four times until that loss was a fluke rather than a pattern.

I didn't even realize I had made it to the center of the battle—titans walking around me and creating minor earthquakes whenever their hooves hit the ground—since I was in the process of taking on a Blood Fabricator who had wrecked half a division of soldiers. I cut his throat with his own hardened blood, then stood in front of the wall of rain in disbelief.

I had died so many times . . . yet finally reached my goal. Domet approached me from behind carefully, likely wondering if cutting through so many soldiers had left me with any shred of humanity. Truth be told . . . I didn't know if I was mad or simply thought I was mad, to cope with what I had done. How many times had I died? The number on the back of my hand was hard to make out with all the blood covering my body.

"You did well, Idris," Domet said. His hand hovered over my shoulder, but then he shook it and returned it to his sword hilt. "Do you need a moment to collect yourself?"

"No," I said, tasting metal in my mouth. "I'm ready to go home."

We passed through the wall of rain together to confront the Wolven Kings in silence. But rather than enter the oasis . . . I went somewhere else. Somewhere *wrong*.

Idris awaited me in a strange room made from a patchwork of glyph-carved sandstone. Multicolored light shone in through the stained-glass windows and there was a tall basin of water in the direct center of the room. Idris stood in front of it, carefully scooping the water up in his hands—some spilling through his fingers—before he brought it to his lips. He drank as if each sip might be his last.

"You actually did it," Idris said. "I'm almost impressed. Of course, I'll have to throw you into a different memory now. One you'll never escape from."

"Do you remember what you told me back on the battlefield? That I wouldn't be able to beat you in a thousand lifetimes?" I wiped the blood onto my trousers and then showed him the number on the back of my hand. Nine-nine-nine-nine. This was the one death I couldn't waste, so I remembered all the ones that had led to this one. All that suffering had to amount to something. Else I was nothing more than a madman with a death wish. "Care to see if that's still the case after ten thousand?"

TWENTY THOUSAND
DEATHS

"You lied to me," I said, stepping closer to Idris. The door slammed behind me as it was closed by the wind. "The Third Wolven King's name isn't in your memories. And trust me—I looked."

"It isn't?" he asked, genuinely surprised. "Odd. I was almost certain it would be. What happened when you entered the oasis?"

"I arrived here."

"What? That's . . . how far did *they* go to hide what happened there that day?"

"They can do whatever they want." I stepped toward him. "Tell me his name."

"I don't know it. It should have been there. And if it's not . . . then their magic reaches far beyond anything you could ever fathom." He turned his head to the side and whispered, "If they can even influence people's memories . . . how can they ever be reached?"

"This is bullshit," I snapped, face hot. "If not here, then where could it be? Why is the third brother's name harder to find than all the others?"

Idris stared at me. "His husband erased his name from history as punishment."

"His husband?" I repeated. "The third Wolven King was married? To who?"

"Isn't it obvious? An endless abyss of loneliness isn't created without help and, judging from the memories of yours I've seen, his husband spent a millennium grieving. His love betrayed him, so he betrayed his love and rebuilt the foundation of this world out of spite." Idris snapped his fingers and Charles Domet materialized in front of me. The immortal man wore no smile, but then he never did. "Is it better to have loved and lost or never have loved at all? I'm sure Domet is very torn on this issue."

Rian's words about Domet rang in my ears: *"His parents are dead, he has no siblings, and I haven't seen him kiss someone, let alone sire a child. That shrine is everything to him."*

And then Domet's own followed quickly after:

"What are those for?" I had asked. *"Are they for a lady?"*

My question had been met with a chuckle. *"Not a lady, the lady."*

"Oh, no," I muttered, tilting my head upward. I suddenly felt very, very sick. "Patron Victoria was his sister, wasn't she? I burned down his sister's grave."

"Her full name was Lady Javi Victoria of Wolvenguard. And the last time anyone hurt her, Domet ruined the world in revenge. He didn't know which Wolven King killed her—still might not—because none of them took responsibility. So he treated them equally. Wiping out their names. Their legacies. Their empires. Took the throne they all craved so badly for himself. And then gave it away to a regular, ordinary man." He huffed. "Not even his husband—his one true love—was spared from his wrath. It's nothing short of divine intervention that you're still alive."

I was about to be sick. Of all the stupid things I had ever done . . .

what would Domet be planning for me in revenge? Now that I had severed all ties with him, I didn't even know if he was in Hollow. I had severely underestimated him.

"Since we've settled that . . ." Idris took another drink of water from the basin as the liquid slowly turned black, bubbly, and rancid. If he dipped his hands in it again, I half expected his skin to melt away. ". . . What's your plan, Michael?"

I steeled myself. I couldn't do anything about Domet until I got my body back. Until then, nothing else mattered. "Nothing in my life has been easy, but I won't fail here."

"Oh, you will. You've never stood a chance against me."

Idris kicked over the basin, letting the black contents spill all over the floor. It melted away and exposed a hazy vortex below, lined with teeth. The black liquid ate away at everything until there was a massive crater between us. Idris's features began to morph, elongating and twisting into something between a man and a dragon. A tail sprouted from his tailbone, along with two rainbow-colored membrane wings that shone in the light. His teeth were all jagged points, his dark skin was layered with greyish white scales, and his eyes were a brilliant red. Idris raised his hand as if summoning lightning and armor materialized over his body, shimmering in and out of existence with every heartbeat. He created a longsword from nothing, more akin to crystallized light than forged steel.

Idris pointed the blade at me. "You can't beat me, Michael."

"Can't I?" I gathered that warmth in my chest. "I learned a lot on that battlefield. Like what good and bad matchups for specializations are." I nullified the immediate area. "Two people fighting with nullify specializations is like stabbing yourself with a dull knife."

Idris's armor and weapons melted away.

"But here's the thing. We're in *my* mind. In here I'm king. You shouldn't have given me time to learn so much."

I clenched my fists and the walls around us fell like trees, thundering when they hit the ground. Four shadowy figures appeared, walking over the swirling vortex below as if it was solid ground. Each was one of the people I loved the most. Gwen was in the south, Serena was in the north, Naomi was in the east, and Trey was in the west. Each of them held chains that they threw at Idris, impaling him with the hooks at the end of each, and forcing him to the ground like a trapped animal. He fought. He tried to use his sword to slash through the chains that held him, but it passed through them like air.

I floated over the gap between us and landed in front of the wiggling dragon man.

"This shouldn't be possible!" He was thrashing. "I was in control!"

"You're right, it shouldn't. You had all the power, until you let me get wiser." The chains tightened around him, and he screamed in pain. "Us humans are nothing more than a collection of memories that form a personality, so of course understanding their defining moments makes someone easy to control. That's what happened to you in Rian's mind, wasn't it? Even a fool like me can put the pieces together, given enough time." More senseless thrashing. "I'm sorry it had to be like this. You shouldn't have tried to take over my mind."

"Do you even want to go back?" Idris asked through gritted teeth. "You haven't opened your *own* door yet. This might be your only chance—"

"I'm a broken man either way," I interrupted. "At least one path will let me be with my family."

Idris's dragon form faded away and only a mortal man remained. "Then do what you must. Purge my memories from your mind."

I plopped down cross-legged in front of him. "No, thanks."

"What?"

"I need you. I needed you when I ate your memories and that hasn't changed. Although it's a shame you don't know the third's name. I could have really used that."

"What else could you need me for?" he asked tentatively.

"Isn't it obvious? You're going to lead my body straight to a Wolven King without anyone knowing." I smiled at him. "And then, once Alphonse is in sight, I'm going to lock you in this room with the chains of delusions I'll never admit to and leave you here for all eternity." I paused. "Or until I need you again."

"And here I thought Rian was a monster." Idris shook his head. "How naïve of me."

"Naïveté can be fixed in time." I rose to my feet as I cracked my knuckles. "Now, where's Alphonse?"

INTERLUDE

THE WOLF'S CAPTIVE

Gwen had always believed that everyone wore a mask. Some, like Lyon, wore them with their families to hide that they opposed what they were supposed to be. Some, like Michael, wore theirs in front of the world, to seem something other than the fallible human they truly were. Gwen wore her mask every day. She never let it slip. It was her weapon, her armor, and her biggest regret. She had lied to everyone she had ever loved, to protect them from what she knew.

Her only moments of vulnerability were with her mother or brothers. She never took her mask off, but rather forgot she wore it in their presence. Those few moments of sanity made up for all the others. But as she stared at her brother's face with a different mind behind it, and they strolled through the Vargo streets toward the palace, she wondered if he was truly gone.

"The Abyss Walking point being near one of the lockless doors is an absolute riot," Rian said, hood up and hands in the pockets of a cloak he had traded for from an Ehamian sailor. "Is that always the case?"

Gwen nodded. "I believe so. There's one in the Church of the

Wanderer, and in Hollow Castle behind the painting of King Adrian the Liberator." Idris put his hand out and they paused to let a group of rowdy clan guards pass by. "But there are other connection points besides the doors. They just have to be set up ahead of time."

"So where are we headed?"

Gwen wondered how much to give away. Both Rian and Idris knew she was working for a Wolven King, but not which one. There was a massive difference between the first, second, and third for the beast immortals. Before she could decide, Idris said, "The Wolven Captive will direct us wherever her master tells her to. So, little bird, which are you working for?"

Since he asked directly, she replied, "The first."

Rian cursed and Idris chuckled. They had reached the palace gates. Rather than bother talking, lying, or scheming their way past the guards, Idris slammed their heads together. They hit the ground, too surprised to scream, and then the three of them continued unhindered.

"Why does the first want to talk to me?" Rian asked. "We've never seen eye to eye, but I thought he'd rather gargle lava and crunch on shards of glass than speak with me after I decimated his vanguard at Thousand Craters."

"He wants you to broker an alliance with someone named Scarlo, to fight the second. My employer plans an attack on them soon and seeks allies."

"And if I refuse?"

"He'll probably kill you," Gwen said tentatively. "He didn't say that directly, but his patience and tact have grown short recently. Anyone who's not useful is destroyed. If it's any comfort, your heart will survive in another. He wouldn't let it go to waste."

"I suppose that's better than having it be eaten by the Mercenary," Rian said with a sigh. "But if I'm doing this . . . I want something in exchange."

"I can't negotiate—"

"I want the Wyvern the Corrupt Prince captured and confined here to be set free."

Gwen ran her hands down her face as she let out a groan. "Seriously? The fucking Wyvern? Don't you have more important things to worry about?"

"The Wyverns hold a special place in my heart. I couldn't stop them from becoming endangered after Celona was shattered, so I want to help them whenever I can." Rian looked at Gwen with a soft smile. "Do this for me and I'll make sure Scarlo agrees to the alliance. He'll be the most difficult one to convince."

Gwen had no option but to accept Rian's conditions. She couldn't let her employer down, not given the price of failure. So she resigned herself to her fate—hoped she wouldn't run into the Corrupt Prince—and then said, "Do you know where it's being held?"

"Your brother said it was in the central gardens."

"That's this way." Idris turned to the left. "What? This palace hasn't changed much since I was last here. Sadly some things last longer than they ought to: repaired and updated but still only a shell of what they were."

The three of them meandered through the palace, cautiously keeping their distance from the servants and guards. But just like in Hollow, most assumed they were supposed to be here. It was the lie of conformity, which Gwen had taken advantage of multiple times. As had her brother. They were masters of taking advantage of an assumption.

The garden that held the Wyvern was beautiful, with willow trees paired with small green fruit trees. Rings of brightly colored flowers circled the steel cage the Toothless Wyvern was being kept in, hiding the chains that kept it in place. It was designed to look beautiful, as if that made up for being a prison.

Idris plucked one of the green fruits off the tree, snapped it in half, and began to devour the fleshy pink insides as Gwen and Rian went to the cage. The beast roared as loud as it could—barely enough to be considered a dying whimper—as they searched for a way to open it, but only found enough locks to make a thief despair.

"Destroy the locks," Rian ordered. He stuck his hand through the slits of the cage to comfort the whimpering beast within. "I'd do it myself if I could."

"Such a steep cost for a simple action," Gwen muttered. She reached into her mouth, pulled out a small black bead, and then put it into the main lock of the cage as if it were a key. The lock deteriorated into nothing within a few heartbeats. The Toothless Wyvern refused to leave the cage—despite it being open—until Rian lured it out with fruits. Idris did nothing to help, too busy gorging on the fruit himself.

"Calm, calm. We're not here to hurt you," Rian said softly, hands up as he tried to guide the Toothless Wyvern around the gardens. The beast lumbered around, taking a few steps, then hesitating and sniffing around. To Idris and Gwen, he added, "I think it's forgotten how to leap after being in a cage for so long. It should have bounded off the moment it was free."

"Captivity can be a comfort when you've been confined long enough," Gwen muttered.

"We'll have to take him with us."

"Seriously?" Gwen balked. "You want us to guide a blind Wyvern through the Vargo palace and then an Abyss point? Are you insane?"

"I'm a dragon, Gwendolyn," Rian snapped. "Do you think anyone in this palace could stop me?" He thumbed to Idris. "And with that monster by our side, we're unstoppable."

"Well, you're both about to be disappointed," Idris said, tossing a half-eaten fruit to the side. "We have company."

And it was the worst possible. Adreann and Emelia walked into the gardens side by side, arms interlocked like star-eyed lovers. Their easy smiles turned predatory when they caught sight of Gwen, Rian, and Michael—with Idris's mind—in front of them. Adreann pulled Emelia close, cackled, and then said, "My love . . . weren't you just saying how bored you were? I think we've found the perfect entertainment."

"I think so, my love."

"'My love'?" Gwen asked. "Can you two even feel something that strong?"

Their faces fell and they separated, dropping the charade. Adreann brushed dust and dirt off his shoulder where Emelia's head had been. But it was the former rebel emperor who spoke. "No quip, Michael? Has the return of your sister mellowed you so?"

Idris looked surprised, glancing back between Emelia and then Gwen. "Wolven captive, do I know these two?"

"Michael does."

"'Michael does'?" Adreann repeated with a tentative tone. "That implies he's not a Forgotten. So why doesn't he recognize us? Is it . . . *who* are you?"

"My name is Idris Ardel," he said. "Michael made a bad deal, and I've taken over this body. I have no desire to fight you two, but if I must . . . you will lose, and it will not be close. Think carefully about how you wish to proceed."

Adreann turned away from Idris to speak to Emelia. "You deal with him. If I hear Michael say something so arrogant again—even if it's not him—I won't be able to hold back."

Emelia rolled her eyes but stepped forward. "I may be harder to kill than you think."

"Immortal?"

A nod.

"True or beast?"

"True."

Idris whistled. "Good for you. But the unfortunate thing about true immortality is that since it takes *so* much to kill you"—he crept closer to her so he could see the cracks in her lips—"you have the pleasure of experiencing some of the creative things people have developed to contain immortals. Being trapped underwater constantly drowning is mundane, but it's a classic for a reason."

Emelia never backed down. Even apparent defeats had been strategic decisions. But cowardice was hard to misunderstand, and Emelia must have seen something that concerned her. She backed away from Idris, grabbed Adreann's arm, and pulled him away.

The giant of a man did not go quietly. "What are you doing? Royals do not flee, and we do not bow to Kingman. Especially not when they're trying to steal my property!"

"We can't win this fight. Maybe the Regal Mercenaries could, but *we* can't. Not without risking everything."

Adreann jammed his finger toward Gwen. "Don't make me do this. My honor and pride—"

Emelia grabbed the back of his head with both her hands and pulled him close to her. "*Our* pride. Do not forget we're in this together. Our marriage may be political, but our goals are not. Do you want revenge, or do you want the throne? Do you want progress, or do you want the status quo, forever? We cannot be great if we continue to be blinded by childish things."

"People don't speak to me like that," Adreann growled. "Not my father nor my sister nor my Kingman. What gives you the right?"

She raised her hand, showing the glass ring on her finger. "We're partners. Let's change the world together. We cannot die here. Do you understand?"

He put the back of his hand behind her head, gently playing with her locks of hair, holding her close. "I understand." Then he stared at Gwen and Idris. "We'll meet again, Kingman."

Then they flashed huge smiles and started to shout as loudly as they could, "Guards! Intruders! Help!"

Gwen was astonished as Emelia and Adreann—two of the strongest, boldest, and most arrogant people in Hollow—turned on their heels and sprinted out of the gardens. A stampede of soldiers shouting orders at one another ran toward them as Rian mounted the Toothless Wyvern as if it were a horse.

"I'll clear the way the best I can!" Rian said as the Wyvern began to creep toward the hallway. "Keep the soldiers off me!"

There was a group of six clan guards with hatchets and shields approaching. Idris stifled a yawn and then said, "Wolven Captive, can you open us a quicker path? Killing these soldiers would be pointless. Surely you don't value a few weeks of your life over their eternities?"

Those words coming out of Michael's mouth only made it worse. She had no choice but to reach into her mouth, pluck out a black ball as if it were an oyster's pearl, and then throw it toward a wall. Gwen hadn't had her powers for long, so her understanding of her limitations was minimal at best, but she did her best to guide the black ball in the right direction . . . only for it to consume everything within an arm's radius the moment it collided with something.

Now only two walls separated Gwen, Idris, Rian, and the Toothless Wyvern from the Abyss walking point.

"I'll distract the guards," Idris said, strolling toward the guards with his materialized sword across his shoulders. "What might Michael have said before a fight?"

Gwen wanted to rip his head off but swallowed her curses instead. "Something stupid."

"Delightful. Let me know if I live up to his standards." He lowered the sword, gripped it with both hands, and then smiled as the clear blade turned a royal purple. "Nullify this."

Idris made a sweeping horizontal strike, extending the blade dramatically and striking all the guards in one hit. They all collapsed into a single pile. The bottom half of their bodies were completely immobile, but their upper halves wriggled like worms.

"What did you do?" Gwen breathed, glancing back between the guards and Idris.

"Get the next wall."

Another ball out of her mouth and another wall disappeared in front of them. How much time was she sacrificing with every use of magic? She'd have to get her employer to tell her.

"My specialization is nullification—not magic nullification," Idris finally explained, seeing more soldiers run toward them. "If we focus, we can nullify just about anything. Contact, muscle groups, sight, hearing, smell—anything, really. But most people only use the magic variation. It's a shame, but knowledge of magic is power, and my allies and enemies alike would prefer most understand as little as possible."

"Contact?" Gwen asked as Rian led the Toothless Wyvern closer to their destination. "You can nullify contact? Does that mean you could theoretically catch magic?"

Idris nodded. "I'm surprised you made that connection."

"I didn't," she whispered. "My brother did it instinctively."

"Guts don't make you a great Fabricator."

"No, they don't." Another black ball from her throat and the last wall to the shrine was gone. The faceless statue, ever-burning cannister, and lockless door were in sight. "But it does make him frustrating for you immortals. He's figured out some of your secrets by accident."

Idris dispatched the next group of guards and entered the shrine, a scowl on his face. "Enough talk. Start the Abyss Walking."

Gwen took a coin from her pocket, flipped it into the air, and it vanished before it was halfway to the ground. In its place a tear opened in reality. It pulsated like a beating heart. Eham's black sand beaches were visible on the other side. No matter how many times she had traveled through these . . . they always made Gwen uncomfortable.

"Does your employer have enough weight on the other side to transfer my Wyvern as well?" Rian asked. He hopped off the Wyvern and placed his hand on its snout to stop it from lumbering forward. "Abyss Walking is more meticulous than other magic forms."

Meticulous was an understatement. Not only were the pathways restricted to certain places, but it had two costs, not the one of all the other forms of magic. The first was simple: an equivalent mass to the thing or person you wished to transport had to be sent through in the opposite direction. Her employer had called it the equivalent weight redistribution theory. The other rule was much harder to predict. One out of every thousand trips would fail—assuming the weight redistribution between points was correct—and whoever was being sent would be condemned to a certain death. She had been warned to never enter a tear if she saw a rocky landscape on the other side.

"My employer will be prepared," Gwen answered. "We're headed to Eham and then will voyage to the Reborn Titan. A mountain of sand will fill this poor shrine."

"Sand is the worst," Rian stated. "But I'll see you both on the other side. Is your employer going to kill me upon arrival?"

Gwen shrugged. "Your guess is as good as mine."

"Delightful." Rian sighed and then walked through the portal leading the Toothless Wyvern. Both flashed out of existence and neither appeared on the other side, but that wasn't abnormal. There was always a delay. But almost as if to confirm their arrival, black sand began to sift from the ceiling and into a pileup like an hourglass without edges.

"Your turn," Gwen said to Idris.

Idris tilted his head slightly, arms crossed at the tear. "And if I don't want to?"

Gwen silenced her immediate thoughts—all of which were various versions of "Fuck you, I'm not letting you walk away freely with my brother's body"—and went with a calmer response.

"Fuck you, I'm not letting you walk away with my brother's body," Gwen snapped. "You're coming with me whether you want to or not."

So *maybe* she hadn't gone with the calmer response after all. But it was right.

Idris flashed her a smile. "Fine, I'll come. Your employer will at least entertain me while I figure out what to do next."

"Just go through the—"

"Michael? Gwen?"

Shit.

Gwen whipped her head around and saw the three worst possible people standing in the doorway: Naomi, Chloe, and Serena. Naomi was the first to realize something was wrong, to Gwen's surprise. She would've guessed Serena. Normally she could read Michael's mannerisms like a book. But right now . . . she looked confused.

Naomi put a hand in front of Serena and then drew her sword. "That's not Michael. There's something wrong with him." Naomi kept her tone steady. "But that is Gwen. Which is a surprise, since she was kidnapped by a Wolven King. Gwen, what's going on?"

Serena interrupted. "What do you mean that's not Michael? He looks just like him!"

"Naomi's right." Chloe drew her spear, blocked Serena slightly, and then pointed it at Idris. "Something's wrong with him. Look at his eyes— they're not amber."

"Neither are Gwen's," Naomi added. "What is going on with that—" And then caught herself. "Talk! I don't know why your eyes are different, but I know that's really you, Gwen."

"Hello, Naomi," Gwen said. "You three should pretend you didn't see me." She thumbed at Idris. "I'll return him safely, and be rid of this abomination. Just give me time."

"I think we deserve an explanation," Chloe said.

"You do," Gwen admitted. "But I can't give you one."

"Enough." Serena pushed past Naomi and Chloe. Her demeanor was different. More aggressive and impatient. Had the crown changed her so much? Or did she truly need Michael to balance her out, just like she balanced Adreann? "You can have one day. If you don't bring him back by then, I will come and drag you both home. Whoever and wherever you are."

Gwen flinched. "Do you not know who I am, Serena?"

The infallible Queen hesitated, pursed her lips, and then said, "No. I'm a Forgotten. Michael is the only person I remember and even then, it was only his name."

"What . . ." Gwen trailed off. The specifics didn't matter. Not for her. Hollow and its politics and war had been beyond her scope since she began working full-time. If she wanted to help, she would have to restore her brother. "I'll bring him back to you. I promise."

Serena held up a single finger. "Then get to it."

Idris huffed and then walked through the tear. Gwen was close behind, wondering if she should say something more but not sure what. The pull on her skin and body felt more excruciating than normal before she rolled onto the scorching-hot black sand beach. Idris was sitting on the sand, relaxing with his eyes closed and hands behind his head. She pushed herself onto her feet with her forearms, seeing Rian was in the middle of a screaming match with her employer. The tear had snapped closed behind her.

"Where's my Wyvern?" Rian bellowed, on the verge of jabbing a finger against his chest. "He came with me through the tear. He should be with us!"

"He probably got lost," her employer said casually. "Abyss Walking isn't always as precise as we'd like. And if he's not here or back in Vargo— then he might as well be dead. He's gone somewhere none of us can reach."

"That's bullshit! Gwen swore that my Wyvern would be brought here in exchange for my cooperation. If that doesn't happen, I will take my talents elsewhere."

Gwen's employer ignored Rian, walking toward Idris. His shadow engulfed the relaxing man. "Idris? Is that you in there?"

"Yes," Idris answered. His eyes were still closed, and he waved the Wolven King away. "I had better be well compensated for taking out a major player. That boy will be lost within his own mind forever."

"My sincerest thanks." Gwen's employer extended a hand to pull Idris up. "You've done remarkably well, Idris. I'll send word to your other self. While it may be unorthodox to have two of you wandering around, I promise it will be—"

He never finished his sentence. Idris used the momentum from being pulled to his feet to ram his shoulder into the Wolven King. He was sent flailing to the ground and before he could recover—physically or magically—Idris planted his right foot on the man's chest.

"Alphonse," Idris said. He drew one of his flintlock pistols and pointed it at the king's head. "That's your name? You're the First Wolven King, and the asshole who kidnapped my sister. I've been waiting for an opportunity for us to talk. It's been . . . a long time for me. Imagine my surprise when Idris led me straight to you." Idris pressed down on the Wolven King's chest harder. "For someone so old, you're a little too trusting. But that's fine. I'll teach you how to mistrust everyone." He smiled like a maniac. "It's my specialty."

Rian, Gwen, and Alphonse were all visibly confused. Until Gwen noticed amber eyes had replaced the dragon's red. She put her hands over his mouth, gasped, and then looked at the sun to stop the tears from coming.

Michael was back, and he was face-to-face with a Wolven King.

THE KING'S FOOL

Imagine me—Michael Kingman, the king of the imbeciles and the bane of fools who thought they could do better than me—successfully planning to ambush one of the strongest beings in history. Improbable? Definitely. But so long as I won, the odds didn't matter.

Victory was a drug I rarely relished, but today I wanted the feeling to last. Gloating wasn't normally my thing, either, but I made an exception when I had my foot on the chest of a Wolven King, flintlock pistol aimed at his head, and the area around us nullified. If this was going to devolve into a fight, it would be with steel and flesh and nothing else.

"So, you shriveled-up dick, care to explain why you kidnapped my sister?" I asked. I took out another flintlock pistol and aimed it at Rian to make sure he didn't interfere. But the smoke dragon didn't so much as flinch. Even Gwen, who I had expected to show a little joy at my return, seemed frozen in place.

Maybe I looked awful, following my time in those endless death loops.

The hustle and bustle of Eham echoed behind me. Out of the corner of my eye I could see pirates and sailors unload the nearby ships, most of them flying the pirates' traditional solid red flag, except for about a dozen with the Machina Mercenary Company's logo. Why was a Mercenary company in Eham? Were they preparing for something? And if so, why didn't Orbis Company know about it? Usually the bigger companies sent word to one another to make sure no one intervened in their contracts. Especially if it was on this scale.

The Wolven King gripped my ankle. "I should have killed you on sight. How long have you been poised to take back your body?"

"Longer than you'd guess." I kept my body nullified, the warmth coming out of my body like waves crashing against a beach. It would no doubt cost me a lot of memories, but I would pay any price to get my sister back. "Well?"

"Do you really think I'll tell you anything while I lie on my back?"

"Do you really think I'll give up any advantage over you?" I mocked.

The Wolven King was silent.

"Gwen! Can you tell me what's going on?"

"I'm sorry, Michael." She looked away. "If I say the wrong thing, he'll kill Ma. I can't take the risk."

"Rian?"

"Not a chance," the smoke dragon stated. "I understand the difference in strength between you two, and I'd like to remain alive."

"You'll have to let me up, Michael," the Wolven King said. "We'll talk like gentle—"

I shot him in the head, white smoke wafting over my face. I waved it away as best I could and then looked down at the faceless man. There was a red hole between where his eyes should have been, but the wound quickly healed. I had suspected him to be a true immortal, now I knew for sure.

"Enough of this."

The Wolven King lifted me off him with a single hand before throwing me up in the air like a ball and then catching me deftly around the throat. My flintlock pistols hit the sand without a sound, and I struggled to lodge my fingers between his hand and my throat, desperately kicking to stay alive. So much for my having an advantage.

"Thankfully for you, your sister has linked your life to our contract, so I cannot kill you. Even if you deserve it." The Wolven King carried me around like a limp doll. "But if you ever try something as stupid as this again, I will do what I must. My pride is not something so easily broken or insulted without repercussions. Do you understand?"

I muttered nonsense at him.

"Do you understand?" he repeated, coming closer to me.

More nothings as I struggled to breathe.

"Do you understand, Michael Kingman? One more act of insolence and I will—"

I bit into his neck and then tore flesh, blood spraying everything around us. My body crashed against the black sand beach as the Wolven King instinctively tried to stanch the blood.

I wasn't proud of what I did next. But if eating a dragon's heart conveyed their powers, would the flesh of a Wolven King do something as well?

I swallowed his flesh and blood, nearly gagging on the stringy meat and warm bitter blood. The fact that Dark had done this so many times was terrifying. I'd rather return to the king's diet than eat another mouthful of human flesh, but the effects were immediate. Heat like a blazing fire rushed through my veins. Were my powers still connected to the warmth in my body? Or were these new powers—assuming I had gained some—triggered by something else?

"Delightful," the Wolven King said dryly. He took his hand away from his neck as the threads of skin connected and wove back together. "As much as I wish to applaud your tenacity . . . my magic is not fragmented, and you will not steal or inherit it so easily."

So the flash of heat through my body was bloodlust, not access to any new powers. Great. Now my body was playing tricks on me alongside my mind. But the Wolven King had let something valuable slip, suggesting that my magic and—potentially—all the magic I knew of were fragments of an interwoven system. And if that was the case, did that mean he held the abilities of all magic users? Fabricators, Weavers, Abyss Walkers, Spellborns, Insatiables, Alchemists, and whatever else was out there?

No wonder he was so confident. How could I overpower someone like that?

The Wolven King removed the bronze sash from his waist, let it flutter in the ocean breeze, and then morphed it into a long slender sword with a light-eating blade that consumed everything around it. The leopard pelt over his shoulders hardened into steel armor that left only a space above his heart unguarded. It was as if he was offering his opponents a target. "I may not be able to kill you, but shackles would look good around your neck and wrists. Maybe I'll send you to my brother's prison so you followers of the Lifeweaver can rot in silence together."

I raised my fists. "Come and try."

The Wolven King turned his free palm upward. A thin white light shot up into the air like a firework that left a trail but never exploded. I didn't have time to question what he had done before dozens of red-tailed pieces of Celona appeared in the sky. I wasn't a Hollow observer or expert sky watcher, but even I could guess that they were all headed toward us.

The first hit the water close by, spraying the four of us on the beach. The sound of hundreds of people screaming in the city nearby overwhelmed the sound of the crash. There was no warning for these attacks and even though the world had grown used to things falling out of the sky . . . we had all hoped for just a little advance notice.

"You are outmatched, Michael." Alphonse walked toward me. Each step was soft enough not to sink into the sand. "There are dragons and titans and behemoths and then there is me. I am not like the others. You cannot win this fight."

"The improbability of winning has never stopped me before."

I let the warmth cover my body, prepared to expel it or charge if needed. But as I watched the monster creep closer to me, I listened to my body. Had anything changed? I had learned that I was a nullify Fabricator on my own. What were the chances I could do something similar with another power? How did other magic users fight?

Two more pieces of Celona landed to our side, shaking the ground and blowing up sand. I nearly lost my footing but planted my feet again and kept my fists up. Fear was one of his many weapons and I would not let him see me as a coward.

The Wolven King lunged—almost floating over the ground—swiping at me with his blade. I ducked to dodge it and then drilled my elbow into his stomach. He didn't even feel it, striking my back with the hilt of his sword. It sent me to my knees, but I rolled out of the way before he could pierce my chest. He stabbed the sand and I jumped back to my feet, breathing raggedly, and kept my fists raised.

"Is that all you got?" I taunted.

"Goading your opponent isn't always the smartest plan," he said softly. "Some will succumb to rage, but others will strengthen their resolve." He slowly approached again. "I am of the second. My younger brother was a bigger bother than you could ever aspire to be."

"Oh, do you mean Zarack?"

The Wolven King sneered. "Two names? Wonderful. I'll have to find out how you learned them, and erase them. But no. Zarack is the middle child. You remind me of my youngest brother."

"Let me guess. Do we have the same defined chin and deep amber eyes?"

"No."

"Same name?" I smiled. "Bad luck if so. 'Michael' is such a mouthful to scream when they're being a little shit. Or so I've heard."

The Wolven King's knuckles were white around the hilt of his blade. "I take it back. You *can* get under my skin. But that's fine. Something else to work on in this immortal life I have been cursed with."

A vast piece of Celona crashed into the bay and threw up a giant wave. When it crashed onto the beach, it would swallow all of us whole. I only had a few minutes to win this fight. Less if I was unlucky.

"Michael!" Gwen screamed, finally interfering. "Get out of here before it's too late! Learn how to use Weaving! When Idris took control of your body, he laid the foundations of the skill. You should be able to use it as well! Your body remembers even when your mind doesn't. Think about what Trey can do! He's had Weaving—" Rian clamped a hand over her mouth, but Gwen elbowed him in the stomach and freed herself. "—training! He just never realized it! Meet us at the Reborn Titan when you have more knowledge of your powers! You can't win now!"

"I won't leave you!"

The Wolven King struck again, swiping and stabbing like a professional duelist. His first blow grazed my cheek. His second cut my side. Both wounds trickled blood, and I wouldn't be able to dodge forever. And with that wave coming . . .

"Go through the tear! Return to Vargo! Get Serena! Get Naomi! Get everyone you can!" Gwen screamed again. "We can't win this war alone. Please! We'll meet again one day!"

"Gwen, I—"

Two more strikes and two more wounds. One across my forehead and another across my forearm. The wave was curling upward, preparing to crash down on us.

"Go!" Rian tried to contain her, but Gwen wiggled out of his grasp. "You're the only Kingman left! Don't let them win!"

Her words struck a chord with me, and I looked at my sister. Her eyes were a deep brown. No longer amber. What the f—

The Wolven King cut my thought off, swiping vertically and nearly severing my hand. As I stepped backwards, the Wolven King clenched his fists and created another tear with cracked stone walls akin to a dungeon in the background. Gwen and Rian flew through it without warning, a chair and a few books flying out of it once they'd disappeared, and then it snapped shut. Alphonse stood, proud and unfazed, like a master dealing with a poor apprentice. He pointed his sword at me. "Let's finish this. Can you kill me and settle your sister's debt?"

Hate was a drug, pride was a disease, and victory had always been elusive to me. I was a master of nothing but failure, and I knew when to count my winnings and lay down my cards. Continuing this fight would only end in my death, so I dove for the tear in reality.

The Wolven King and I would finish our fight another day.

Water crashed down around me. I was sopping wet as I landed back in Vargo with a tumble and a thud, scraping myself on dull dry stone. Serena and Naomi were waiting for me, ready to bombard me with different questions. Chloe stared at my eyes. Was she making sure they were amber? What had I missed while I was in my own mind?

But, more importantly, what had just happened?

Why were Gwen's eyes brown?

THE DRAGONRIDER

Kyros Ryder had joined a cult. All things considered, it was a *nice* cult. One that was focused on reading, spreading knowledge, and discussing theology, but it was still a cult. At first, he thought they were just passionate readers who had a hard time separating fiction from reality. It was one thing to share and praise a story, but the moment Kai tried to critique one of his newfound group's favorite stories, he found himself in a series of long and rather boring meetings with a dozen people trying to explain *why* the story was brilliant and looking rather concerned that he didn't understand the masterful use of symbolism.

His new friends eventually settled on the excuse that hearing rather than reading the story might not properly capture the story's exquisiteness. Kai just thought the story was stupid. It was hard to suspend disbelief when a scholar who spent all day reading was somehow stronger than blacksmiths, soldiers, and hunters. And that a magic sword somehow gave him the strength of twenty men? Horseshit. The fact that the protagonist had the fairest maiden in all the land confess their undying love to them at the end only made it worse. Yet this writer was being praised as the reincarnation of Zafo Silvery—the greatest playwright Eham had ever bore witness to—and that only offended Kai more.

And that about summed up Kai's first week at the Institute of Amalgamation.

Joey had a better time. He ate well, had dozens of scholars jump at the opportunity to help him learn how to speak, and set fire to about twenty drapes in a common room when a burp brought up flames rather than air. He was still learning how to control his newfound fire dragon powers, but at least his farts were no longer flammable. Though Kai still made sure Joey didn't go near any of the rare books . . . especially after the book about the stupidly strong scholar had an unforeseen accident and only its ashes remained.

Kai was sweeping the ashes into a pile when one of his fellow initiates—Jaco, he guessed, by the smell of peppery perfume that arrived with him—stormed through the door as if trying to rival thunder. "Kyros! The council must see you at once."

Kai rubbed the crown of his nose. "Please tell me it's not about that story again."

Jaco was flustered, then said, "Sorry! I was shaking my head. I forget sometimes." He coughed. "It's about the letter you arrived with."

Kai had wondered when someone would finally get back to him about that. He had asked for information about it upon arriving at the Institute of Amalgamation, but rules and traditions and formal nonsense had taken precedence over scholarly inquiries. Knowledge seemed to be given freely only if it was for the benefit of the other parties. Knowledge about magic was even harder to get hold of. Hopefully this meeting would change things.

"Can you pass me my coat?" Kai asked as he reached for Joey to take his hand. His brother did so immediately, gently guiding him up off the floor. Joey was getting stronger and bigger every day. No longer was Joey the child he carried around or had to keep within reach out of fear of something happening. "Where do they want to see me?"

"In the heart of the library."

"Wonderful," Kai muttered. "Can you guide me there? The recent snowfall will have made the steps difficult to navigate on my own."

Jaco was more than happy to. He was a good man. To the point that Kai wondered if he might be *too* good. Not in a deceptive way. More akin to someone who might try to take advantage of him in the future, especially as he lacked family to fall back on. He was the third son of a twenty-strong family in Goldani and after the Fate Selection had deemed him "Barren" he had been given the option of either risking his life in a game of life and death to restore his luck or throwing himself into the gorge next to the capital and trying to find happiness in his next life. Only his foreign mother's compassion saved his life. And so a body in Jaco's clothes and wearing his signet ring *was* discovered at the bottom of the gorge, while the real one was exiled to the snowcapped Iliar mountain range.

Luckily, Jaco liked it here more than he ever had in Goldani. Something about the food had never sat well with him. Never mind the customs or obsession with luck and gambling. Honesty was one of his shining virtues, and maybe that was why Kai had been drawn to him. Hollow depended on manipulation and lies to keep its population docile, so finding someone who rejected all that was more refreshing than a cold swim on a hot day.

"Careful," Jaco said, suddenly grabbing Kai's arm. "I should have repaired that broken step, but it's difficult to chisel stone in the cold."

"It's fine. Don't scold yourself," Kai said. "The fact the masters leave us initiates to maintain the grounds while they spend their days inside next to fires is revolting. We all should share the work equally." He paused. "If anything, I should be thanking you for helping me with my chores. Why the masters assigned sweeping to the blind boy still baffles me."

Jaco chuckled. "It's nothing. I help you with the physical and you help me with the mental. Perfect trade."

"We're lucky we found each other."

The rest of their walk was in near silence, with only the odd grunt from Joey or Jaco near the more dangerous sections of their mountain home to break the eerie silence. Most of the time Kai liked the quiet compared to the endless noise of Hollow. Even in the gardens he often heard people hawking wares or speaking too loudly and bluntly. But Kai's love of tranquillity was constantly tested here. Every part of it seemed to be designed for an aesthetic purpose rather than one of substance. The five circular buildings with heated floors that made up the compound were connected by stone pathways that were constantly covered in snow or ice, even though the logical choice would have been to carve hallways to cover them. The only smart thing about this place was that their library descended into the mountain and would survive most disasters—magical or natural. And Kai suspected that was where the masters kept all their information about magical unification. If this plan didn't work, he would need to find the answers on his own.

It didn't work. His meeting with the masters immediately turned into an interrogation about what he knew, and none of them believed that his friend, a Kingman no less, had given him a letter from the Archmage— who turned out to be rather hated in the Institute of Amalgamation— containing secret information about the origins of magic. They threatened to expel him if he didn't back down. So Kai threatened to tell the local magistrate that the new recruits routinely committed light espionage for whichever country they came from. The standoff was resolved only by one of the kindlier masters Kai considered too good to waste his days among the cult.

Either way, Kai would not be expelled so long as he kept the Institute of Amalgamation's secrets.

It was a bittersweet victory.

And as Kai found himself playing with Joey and honing his new abilities—Joey had been able to transform into a dragon once or twice, but never for long—something *wrong* happened in his room. Nearby books and the only chair that didn't wobble were sucked through a hissing whirlpool in the air and two people tumbled through, skidding to a stop at the edge of Kai's bed.

"Hello?" he asked carefully.

The whirlpool snapped shut with a hiss. One of them held the other's mouth closed as they struggled to free themselves.

"Sorry for the intrusion. My partner here had too much to drink." The man had a slight accent. His voice was familiar. Heavy like a dragon's growl, every syllable distinct and clear. "We stumbled into the wrong room. We'll be leaving—"

"Wrong place, wrong time. I understand completely." Kai clenched his fists, anger welling in his chest. "I don't know why you're here and I don't really care, truth be told." Kai pulled his brother toward him and then put his hand over his eyes, instructing him to keep them closed until Kai said, "But unluckily for you, I never forget a voice."

"I—"

"Goodbye, Rian."

"Wait, don't—"

Sound forced Rian to his knees, the incessant buzzing driving the dragon to claw at the skin around his ears to ease the pain. Kai advanced toward him, continuing to shoot sound at him, but careful not to hit the other. There were no guns or swords or axes in the Institute of Amalgamation, so Kai would have to end his life another way. He settled on a dull letter opener that he had been meaning to ask Jaco to sharpen, but something about how the blade sounded as it slid through Rian's ear and pierced his brain made Kai glad he had chosen to wait.

Kai spat on his corpse and then said, "Rest in peace, best friend. I'll always remember your courage."

"Kai, that was brutal! Didn't know you had that in you." It was Gwen Kingman's voice. She sat upright, muttering curses to herself. "Murder aside—where am I?"

"The Institute of Amalgamation." Kai pulled the knife from Rian's ear and wiped it off on the man's robes.

She groaned as she came to her feet. "Too far to travel by conventional means. But I have to do *something*. I can't let my employer win so easily." She hesitated. "And we'll have to do something about Rian's body. Can't leave his heart lying around."

"I have no idea what's going on. Care to explain?"

"Oh, sorry. Yes, absolutely . . ." She trailed off. There was something heavy, small, and metallic in her hands. "Kai, would you be able to leave here for a bit? Do you have a friend that might be able to cover for you? Michael is going to need our aid and I've just thought up the perfect way to help."

There was a belief in the older days of Hollow. That if a Kingman ever came to you, it was a prelude to your doom. A guarantee that your life would be cut short if you followed them. But Kai was a loyal friend. He was only ever going to answer such a request one way.

"How can I help?"

PART 3:

BARGAINING

27 DAYS UNTIL THE FINAL DEATH OF MICHAEL KINGMAN

"Death has seen me, and I them. They were my first friend,
my first mortal enemy. We have brushed up against each other many
times, but when we finally meet I will beg for more time, though know
I was given more than enough to learn how to live."

—Deliana Dawnstar, the greatest single-feathered
Raven in Hollow history

41

THE STENCH OF DEATH

Serena insisted that she tend to my wounds while Chloe explained to the clan guards that I wasn't the one who had attacked them and Naomi gathered Orbis Company. It was a sweet thing to do and reminded me of our connection before she became a Forgotten. Or it would have, if someone had taught her to disinfect or stitch wounds without the bedside manner of a serial killer.

"Stop wiggling!" she shouted, gripping a handful of the hair on the back of my head to steady me. Her other hand held a soaked cloth of alcohol. "You're being a child. This would be over already if you just stayed still."

That was easy for her to say. People often agreed that the cure was better than the disease, but this might be one of the situations where the reverse was true. She gripped my hair harder and then patted my forehead with the soaked cloth like a toddler with a toy hammer.

"Stop! Stop! Stop!" I pleaded. "That's enough! I'll be fine, I promise."

Serena scowled at me but put the cloth down. Only to pick up a clean strip of cloth and wrap it around my forehead. Like the other bandages she had applied, it was too tight and would have cut off my circulation if I hadn't sneakily rewrapped them when she got distracted looking for a wet cloth. My only reprieve was that nothing needed stitches. I could only imagine how painful that would have been.

"There," she said, smiling. "All done. That wasn't so bad, was it?"

I managed to give my thanks clearly and appreciated the warm smile she gave me in return. "You didn't have to do this. Queens don't normally tend to their Kingman."

"I know," she said, tidying everything away. "But I wanted to. Is this another one of those things that could be seen as weakness?"

"Anything that reveals emotion is seen as weakness when you wear the crown."

"Why?" Serena asked. "Why does a ruler have to be cold and calculating rather than loving and compassionate? If I were a commoner, I'd hope to have a queen who cared for those around her, not one who shoved her problems off to others."

"Me too, but . . . that's not how it works."

"If you agree, why are you trying to make me do the opposite?" Serena countered.

"I'm just trying to protect you," I muttered.

"From?"

Everything.

But I didn't tell her that. Thankfully for me, Naomi returned with the rest of Orbis Company at that moment. Dark was the first through the door, shoving Naomi out of the way once he saw me. His eyes were burning red, and both of his fists were clenched.

"I heard I missed a few things," I said as Dark walked in. "What—"

Dark punched me in the jaw, sending me tumbling over myself. Alexis grabbed his arm, holding him back as Serena stood, screaming obscenities. I couldn't make out the words. It felt like water was lodged in my ears and everything was murky and dull.

Titus hauled me to my feet as Serena and Dark screamed at each other. He slapped my ears and they popped—sending a streak of pain up my neck—but my hearing returned instantly.

"—imagine being so embarrassed about losing a fight that you take a swing at someone who had nothing to do with it!" Serena had one hand on her hip and a finger in Dark's face. "Have you always been this immature?"

"Fuck me sideways," Naomi muttered from the entrance to the room. "Has anyone ever talked to Dark like that?"

Cassia interrupted before Dark could shout back. "You both did what you thought was necessary. Enough! Is that clear?"

"But am I not your employer?" Serena said, arms crossed. "You do what I say. Not the reverse. And there will be repercussions."

"No," Dark stated. "I'm not some Raven you can discipline. I'm a Mercenary, beyond your reach. If you think differently, take it up with someone who cares. Do you understand your position now, you silly Forgotten?"

"What happened to client is king?" I interrupted, pressing forward.

Dark put his face in mine and bared his teeth. "Careful, Michael."

I didn't back down. "Or what? Going to hit me again? Your threats don't scare me anymore." I leaned closer to whisper into his ear. "Swallow your pride. It's not time for us to write the ending to this tragedy quite yet. Unless, of course, you want to start the final fight earlier than foretold."

Dark picked me up by the collar, and I laughed and laughed. I had already seen the worst this world had to offer, I had died thousands of times in my mind. This was nothing. I told him as much.

Dark didn't like that—he *really* didn't like that—and threw me to the ground. But rather than lash out in anger, he sniffed loudly. "Why do you suddenly reek of death?"

I met his gaze, slowly rising. "Do you really think there's only one way to become a monster? You advance by devouring others. I advance by failing until my weaknesses become strengths. And after what I've been through recently, death doesn't scare me anymore. So why would you?"

Dark didn't cower, but he did turn to Serena, bowing deeply. "My apologies, Queen of Hollow. I lashed out in anger after being bested in combat by the man who took control of Michael's mind for a period of time. I hope you can forgive my transgression. And if not"—he lifted his head slightly—"I will step away from my protection duties."

Serena looked to me for advice, so I shook my head slightly. I didn't trust Dark, but when he was tasked with protecting Serena, at least I knew he was on our side. Without that . . . well, I could see him taking a rival contract and kidnapping her out of spite. With every heart Dark ate, he became more inhumane and uncaring. Would he turn on Orbis Company, if they tried to control him?

"You may remain my bodyguard," Serena said, voice wavering. "Your strength is unmatched, and my anger is not that severe."

"Thank you, Your Majesty." He stood straight again. "I will not let my anger cloud my judgment again."

Doubtful, but Dark apologizing was such a rare sight—genuine or not—that I didn't want to ruin the moment by saying something stupid. Go, me. Maturing and all that shit.

"Now," Dark began, hands carefully folded behind his back. "We need to hear what happened to Michael." He glared at me. "And don't skip a single detail."

As if. I recounted the tale as quickly as I could, and no one stopped me to pry even into clear omissions. Like what I was looking for in Rian's memories or why I had consumed Idris's memories. All that they cared about was that a Wolven King had my sister and Rian, and Machina Company were preparing for something big. It made Cassia take a few of the gems on her fingers to ease her anxiety.

"I'll let headquarters know Machina Company has been seen in Eham," Cassia said. "I'll reach out to the leader of Machina Company— Gregor Two Horns—as well but I wouldn't expect a response. If they've gone this far without warning other Mercenary Companies, it's because they don't want to."

"Would Regal Company know and be willing to share the information?" Titus asked.

Alexis made a clicking noise with her tongue. "I'm not sure we should ask for anything from Regal Company right now."

"Why?"

Alexis didn't answer, so Dark turned to her, shadows moving around him. "Alexis, what happened?"

"Jay Prince is dead," I said, sparing her.

A chorus of disbelief echoed around me. Only Alexis and Cassia were silent. But Dark laughed. Loud, boisterous, and deeply insubordinate. "Michael," he said. "That's not possible. Regal Company protects him, and my father also has a personal investment in him. There's no way he could die without Vargo being razed to the ground the moment Regal Company found—"

"Angelo killed him to prevent a war starting between Regal Company and the First Wolven King."

"The same Wolven King that currently has a fleet of Machina Company Mercenaries with it in Eham?" Cassia asked.

I nodded. "I thought it was impossible myself. That Angelo would kill someone who called him son. But I think he was trying to avoid a war between Mercenary companies. Whatever he's planning . . . it couldn't have possibly accounted for that."

"Wait," Serena said suddenly. "If my fiancé is dead, does that mean I'm free? Can I walk away from the throne? Please tell me—"

"Jay Prince isn't dead," Dark insisted. "I refuse to believe it. For all we know, Michael's trying to manipulate us. I want proof."

"Proof? Dark, are you insane?" I asked. "We'll become suspects the moment we even insinuate that Jay Prince is dead! We can't do anything suspicious until they announce it, and even then we have to be careful."

"Get me proof and we'll talk. Until then . . . let's all get some rest." He took an audible breath. "We could all use a break."

Orbis Company left after that. Whether it was smart to seek proof Jay Prince was truly dead—he was—or smarter to make plans and an escape plan for Serena if Regal Company sought retaliation, we had a plan. Chloe returned as they were leaving and had Naomi catch her up on what had happened. Her scorn for the situation was clearer than paint on a blank canvas.

Serena made me guard her room, pressing the issue because she trusted me. Chloe disagreed, choosing to guard the exterior door herself but letting Naomi, me, and Serena stay inside together to ease the Queen's fears. It was a compassionate choice that allowed me to sleep and be near Serena after such a long day.

For some reason I thought of my brother, Kayleigh, and their child as I rested my head against the pillow on the floor near Serena's lavish bed, exhausted. My body was stiff and sore, but my mind was active, and I dreamed of Ryder Keep.

Kayleigh was asleep, lying in an ornate yellow-and-black feather bed with a carved dragon headboard. It looked nothing like the ones I had seen—more cute and feathery than lean and bitey—but not everyone had the unfortunate pleasure of learning that firsthand. Lyon was next to her in a rocking chair holding his newly born son. The baby looked like a blob with a sketched-on face and was still utterly perfect. He had wispy blond hair and bright blue eyes, having clearly escaped the Kingman family's legacy. I couldn't be happier for him, smiling ear to ear as tears streamed down my face.

My brother, all nerves and half-formed smiles, gently rocked his son. "I'm so scared to be your father," he said softly. "I grew up without mine, so I don't know how it's done. All I have is hope that I'll do a good enough job."

The baby was perfectly still, eyes closed. "I hope you stay healthy. I hope you don't experience loss too young. I hope you have all your toes." He chuckled, and then grew more serious. "You definitely have all your toes. I already checked." He resumed rocking. "I hope you love me even when you're mad at me. I hope you find your place in the world without too much difficulty . . . And I hope you forgive me for my past."

The baby gurgled and Lyon went on. "You don't have the Kingman eyes. And I doubt you'll ever feel indebted to the Kingman family. I never wanted all that pressure, and yet . . . I made that choice for you, because I was scared to be a part of it myself. Will you forgive me? Will my family? Only time will tell."

"You did what you had to, Lyon," I said. "And I love you. You're my brother, always."

Lyon looked up as if he could hear me, smiled, and then returned to caring for his child.

The dream turned darker as I fell into a deep slumber, and broke only when I was awoken in the morning by Naomi. She asked why I had been crying in my sleep. But as I felt my face, the remnants of tears like painted-on war markings, I couldn't remember who I had been dreaming about, or why I doubted I would dream of them again.

CAESURA

I had a headache, and no plan for the day. Naomi had suggested going to see what the barren tide had exposed on the beaches, and I had agreed. It was something to do while I tried to figure out our next move. Symon had invited himself along, even though he thought the whole trip was a waste of time, complained about how badly his wheels moved through the sand, and constantly critiqued the smell of the sea, noting how he missed Hollow's smell. Which was stupid, because it always smelt like fish guts and bad perfume. Who missed that?

"I hate few things more than these tiny grains of pain that get stuck in my boots like a porcupine's quills," Symon moaned as I pushed his chair down the sand line. Naomi was trailing slightly behind us, stopping to admire every brightly colored shell she could find. So far, her collection consisted of an opal-colored spiral and a muddy-red scallop. "Can you imagine how wonderful a beach would be if it was smoother and less drippy?"

"Drippy?" I questioned. "What about this place is drippy?"

"Look at your feet!" Symon said. "Look at how they sink into the sand. How is that not drippy? Your feet should be firmly planted on the ground at all times."

"What about when you jump?"

"What about me makes you think I jumped a lot before my injury?"

"Noted." I stopped pushing him, turned him so he faced the sea, and took a seat next to him on the sand. I stared at all the holes on the beach, wondering where they went and if they were anything more than homes for fish and other aquatic things when they were full of seawater. "Do you think there are any hidden treasures in those crevices?"

"Doubtful," Symon said. "They're probably just small sinkholes. You'd likely get crushed by water if you tried to enter them."

"Ah, that's unfortunate. Who knows when I could have used a secret way into Vargo."

"There are no secret ways into Vargo," Symon said. "It's actually one of the big advantages of this city, despite the constant worry about moonfall creating tsunamis. The only way into the city by sea is through the iron gate, which is controlled from within by the Vargo clan." Symon pointed to the ring of land that surrounded Vargo's bay and the iron door that connected the two pieces. "You have to ask permission to enter, and that can take weeks."

"I'm aware," I said as I let a handful of sand slip through my fingers. "Alexis and Cassia were stuck at Maiden's Rest for a week, returning from a job by sea."

Symon hesitated. "When you initially told me you captured Rian, I thought you were lying. But I went along with the lie because it was interesting." He chuckled awkwardly. "I don't know what's more surprising—that you told the truth, or that none of us believed you when you finally did."

"I only lie when it's necessary."

"I know," he said softly. He closed his eyes and let the morning light warm him. "I need to ask you an uncomfortable question, Michael."

"I was thinking about it," I answered, already knowing the question.

"Giving you a dragon's heart would heal your body, but . . . would you really want to become a dragon?"

"I don't think *want* has anything to do with it. It's just me trying to make up for my insecurities," Symon explained. "Envy is hard to control when everything is going well, but after my injury—despite surviving it—I . . . I don't know. Part of me just wants my old life back. Eating a dragon's heart might be the only way."

"But it won't be the same. You'll be an immortal."

"I know," he said. "There's always a cost. But that cost doesn't scare me. Research, books, and stories were all I had for as long as I can remember. When my family failed me, fictional characters comforted me. Helped me momentarily escape my harsh reality. And even if I live forever . . . I can always find something to do with an immortal life. Someone has to be around to chronicle it all, don't they?" He pushed his hair back with his fingers. "I always wanted to tell the greatest story ever told. Maybe this is my way to do it. And maybe I can do it without losing myself to my pride. I seem to have a better perspective these days."

"Really?" I countered. "Because last I checked, you were still an asshole."

"And you're still a whiny man-child with delusions of grandeur."

We both smiled.

"If the time comes and you have a dragon's heart in your hands and I'm nearby . . . consider it. That's all I'm asking."

I didn't want to give him hope, so I said nothing. Living forever was a cost he could easily comprehend, but if Symon ate a dragon's heart, he would become a target to Dark. Like Joey. Could I really wish that on one of my friends? Maybe if I could stop Dark, I'd think differently, but right now . . . I didn't know what to do. So many decisions and so little time.

"Have you two picked a season for your wedding yet?" Naomi called out as she approached, a few more shells in her hand. "Because I can give you some more time alone if you want."

"That depends," I said, regaining some of my composure. "Have you told Chloe you're in love with her yet?"

Symon snorted next to me. "Oh, Naomi, that's adorable! Do you two braid each other's hair and clean each other's weapons? Or has it not progressed to that stage yet?"

Her face dropped, eyes narrowed, and she pushed her tongue against the inside of her cheek to hide a smile. "I hate you both. Next time I'm letting both of you die."

Symon was taken aback. "I'm sorry. Did you catch me when I fell out of Kingman Keep? Because my broken spine would say otherwise."

"Well, I'm definitely not going to now!" She chucked some broken shells at us and we dodged them as best we could, laughing as we did, and enjoying a momentary respite. When Naomi decided we had suffered enough, she plopped down next to me, kicked off her boots, and wiggled her toes in the sand.

"Why does this feel like the turning point in a symphony?" she asked softly, staring out into the sea.

"Because it is," Symon said without elaboration.

I pulled my knees up to my chest. "I've decided I'm taking Serena to the titan. With or without Dark or Orbis Company's help. Waiting around for Regal Company to announce Jay's death, or wasting time trying to prove it, will only delay the inevitable." They let me continue without interruption. "Maybe the fruit there restores her memories. Maybe it doesn't. Maybe I get another shot at saving Gwen and taking down the Wolven King. Maybe I die trying. Maybe I find the third brother's name in the process. Maybe I don't. But waiting here gains us nothing." I exhaled. "None of you can talk me out of it."

"You'll need a ship," Symon said. "Have you got one?"

"Not really. I was thinking of stealing—"

"Chloe can get you one," Naomi interrupted. "Probably on the condition she goes with you as well. Small sacrifice to make."

"I'll talk to her about that, then," I answered. "At least if I act, Serena and Gwen will have a chance."

"This will be different, Michael," Symon pushed. "If you go rogue, you'll make an enemy of the world. Regal, Orbis, and Machina Company will be after you. No place on this planet will provide you safe harbor. You'll be a fugitive who kidnapped a queen for as long as you live. And you won't live long."

"I'll do whatever I have to to save Serena and Gwen." I got up and brushed off the sand. "I'm already the Dragonslayer and King Killer, why not be a worldbreaker too?"

"So dramatic," Naomi huffed with her hand in front of her mouth.

"Always." I glanced at them and then the iron gate. "I'm going to go find Serena and Chloe. Talk to them about it." I hesitated, glancing at Naomi. "Ready to die at sea with me?"

Naomi glared at me, trying her best—and failing—to hide her smile. "What if I don't want to? What if I want to have a normal life instead of this suicidal fever dream?"

"So you're going to let your two best friends leave you behind?"

She groaned. "I can't believe the only two people I actually like are determined to be martyrs. Do I have some sort of weird—"

"I'm sitting right here," Symon interrupted. "I can't walk, but I'm not deaf."

"Fuck off, Symon! Fine. I like you, too. And Trey and Serena and Gwen and all you assholes." To me, she added, "And I guess I like flirting with death, too."

I didn't deserve to have Naomi at my side—I told her as much—and she jabbed me in the side. "Damn right you don't."

"As much as I would like to join you to the titan and back . . . I think I'll have to remain in Vargo," Symon said. "I'd only be a burden at sea." He shuddered. "The thought of falling off the ship and drowning fills me with a cold dread."

"I'm sorry, Symon."

"Apologizing doesn't suit you, Michael. Remain the arrogant child with delusions of grandeur I expect you to be or else I'll grow bored." He straightened up as best he could. "When you return, you'll give me your story. Is that understood?"

"Perfectly," I said.

"Good." Symon hadn't turned to face us yet. "You two should get going. Meet with Chloe and Serena and plan your next move." He paused. "I think I'm going to remain here for a bit longer. Please send someone to get me whenever you can."

Staying longer with him would only do more harm than good. I couldn't make him feel better. So, I turned away with Naomi and we trudged up the beach back to Vargo's palace.

"He was crying," Naomi said when we were well out of earshot, climbing a narrow set of stairs. "Should we try to find a solution that would let him come?"

I shook my head. "Our sympathy would just make him feel worse."

"Are you sure about that?"

I wasn't.

We returned to the palace and went straight to Serena's chambers, where she and Chloe were arguing. As usual. The subject of their dissent was the only thing that ever changed. This time it seemed to be about Gwen.

"If Michael's sister is in danger, why are we just waiting here? We should go and get her!" Serena said as she paced in front of her bed. Chloe was sitting at the table nearby. Both had their backs to the door and didn't hear us enter—too engrossed in the argument. I softly closed it behind us and then locked it, not wanting their words to be overheard.

"It's not that simple, Serena," Chloe said through gritted teeth. "Gwen's situation is complicated, and we can't afford to just rush in like fools. Let Michael handle it. You have a country to govern."

"Crown this. Crown that," the woman I was bound to mocked. "Am I just a personification of a crown, never to do what I want?"

"The crown takes precedent. You are a queen." Chloe rose to her feet. "You have a duty to the people. Start taking that seriously."

"Forget the peo—" and then she caught herself, seeing me and Naomi standing in the doorway. "Michael. Naomi. I didn't hear you two enter."

"Sorry for intruding," I said with a slight bow. Naomi tried to calm

Chloe but was batted away with a carelessness only the truly seething with rage could manage. "I've come to pick up last night's conversation."

Serena took a seat. "That's what Chloe and I were discussing. She disagrees, but I would like to offer you a solution to all our problems. I will travel with you to the Reborn Titan and help you save your sister—thus allowing Orbis Company to continue protecting me as well—on the condition that once you have whatever you need from my memories, you let me walk away."

I struggled to form words. Luckily, Naomi gave me a chance to recover. "Abdicating isn't that simple."

"Isn't it? I've been reading up on Hollow's history and politics," she began. "Royals abdicate all the time. Why not let my brother have the throne? He clearly wants it."

I was still tongue-tied. Every part of me wanted Serena to abdicate, but . . .

Like a piece of Celona falling from the sky, my ass was saved by an unforeseen event.

The door swung open, and Jay Prince stepped in with Liam and Ciara Noble behind him. Naomi swore while Chloe's and Serena's mouths dropped open like seagulls' beaks. And I nearly shat myself at the sight of a man I had seen suffocate in front of me. After I shot him.

Jay was less put together than he had been previously: his short black hair beginning to curl, hiding his abnormally large ears. The bone tattoo that covered his face was as striking as ever. Dark black lines bringing out all the angles and curves, almost as if it had recently been touched up or re-tattooed. But his presence should have been impossible. He had died. I had checked his pulse. Jay Prince had been murdered by Angelo. What was going on?

"Michael," Jay Prince said as he put his hand on my shoulder. "I had a feeling you'd be in here. It's been a while, hasn't it?"

"Understatement of the century," I muttered, staring at him. Was this a body double? A trick? How was he standing in front of me right now? "Why are you here?"

"To see my beloved," he said softly. He gave my shoulder a squeeze and then advanced toward Serena. Liam and Ciara kept Naomi and me within arm's reach. Jay bowed deeply in front of Serena, kissed her hand, and then said, "Forgive me for taking so long to visit, my love. Duty has consumed my every waking moment. Are you well? Have you recovered from your bullet wound?"

"Mostly," Serena answered. "Some soreness and dizziness when I rise too quickly."

"Better than dead," Jay said icily. "I feel I must make up for my absence. I've let the romance die. I'm still working on balancing duty and pleasure. Will you accompany me on a date through Vargo?"

Serena didn't glance at any of us. She was the eager girl who had wandered down to the docks alone, overruling whatever crumbs of the dutiful queen Chloe had tried to implant in her mind. "What would we do?"

Jay smiled wide enough to show his bright pink gums. "Something that makes us feel *alive*."

39

THE MIGHT OF THE
MERCENARIES

Their date was calm, cordial—romantic, even. Serena and Jay spent
the morning enjoying a picnic at the beach, nibbling on Vargo delicacies sweeter than fried dough or multi-fruit jam before walking along the
waterline, laughing and chatting. They attended a show that replicated
the Queen's meteoric rise from unknown in her father's shadow to the
triumphant charge she led through the streets of Hollow after defeating
the Heartbreaker Serial Killer. I remembered events differently—a little
more blood and fewer poetic musings—but the troupe must've forgotten
to get my version of the events. And while they dined and wowed the
crowds, Ciara and Chloe stayed by their sides like dutiful guards.

Papa Noble and I watched from afar. Always out of sight, but close
enough to jump in if trouble arose. For Papa Noble to be on guard duty
himself was a divine rarity. But at least we could talk without arousing
suspicion. We were at a table outside a tavern, enjoying small cups of

scaro with the midsummer sun beating down on us, the only slight relief coming when the breeze came in from the bay.

"They look good together," Papa Noble said, admiring from a distance. He gently twisted the glass, letting the liquid spiral around its small confinement. "A noble queen and a man who has crawled up from the bottom. I wonder what ballads will be created for them. Heroic? Passionate? Tragic? This is the part I love the most . . . the tentativeness before the tale is written. There is so much beauty in uncertainty."

I glanced at them. The way he shone next to her. How Vargo's citizens treated him as if he was already theirs. Selfish in making sure his brilliance and charm were unhindered and amplified Serena's own. The light to my darkness. The acceptance to my disdain. We were total opposites. "Jealousy" wasn't a strong enough word to describe how I felt about him. Maybe that was why I had lashed out, shot him in cold blood and pretended it was strategy. And why I had been so angry when he had returned. Alive. Unbothered. His light was one that hid darkness in its very core, while I was a void that devoured everything around me.

"There's beauty in everything," I said after a long pause.

"Only if you avoid the thorns." He took a sip from his glass. "But that's not your path. You're covered in them. Pricking anyone brave enough to venture close."

"I hate these types of conversations. Full of pause and double meaning. It's why I loathe poets. They lie and claim it's artistic. At least mine are practical." I looked at the leader of Noble Company. "Can we begin the real conversation now? Or must we wait for them to share a kiss?"

"It is better to wait for the opposing party to be at their most vulnerable to press."

"If you think a kiss will break my will, you vastly underestimate me."

"We're here precisely because I *don't* think so little of you." Papa Noble adjusted in his seat, crossed one leg over the other, and then interlaced his fingers. "Do you have the information I asked for?"

"Yes, though not from the source you imagined." Serena and Jay were dancing now while street musicians played. "Angelo doesn't care what the Wolven Kings are doing, so long as they don't get in his way."

"Not too surprising. So what do they want?"

"To rule the world, destroy each other, and reclaim whatever they lost." I huffed. "Kind of boring, no? Old men always want their lost power."

"The difference is that they are worldbreakers. Walking calamities that make you and me look like ants," Papa said in a rare moment of introspection. I'd thought he would have denied any such thing to the heavens until his last breath. "If they truly are going to war with each other, my company will need to prepare—"

"Don't bother," I interrupted. "I'll deal with them myself."

"What childish arrogance to think . . ." Papa's eyes met mine. "You truly are an oddity, Michael Kingman. You're not lying. Every part of you thinks you can do it. What delusions do you cling to?"

"Beautiful ones," I said. "Are we done here? Since you won't answer my questions, this conversation is pointless."

Papa smiled like a devious fox. "Are you sure you don't want to try asking me something? A curious boy like you must have *something* nagging at the back of your mind. Maybe concerning life and death?"

"I'm good," I stated. "Death is death."

"We all meet the unwavering hunter eventually," Papa drawled, obviously disappointed. "For a Kingman . . . I'm surprised you haven't wondered where Liam is."

"Am I supposed to keep track of your children for you?"

"No. But all the greatest strategists should recognize a distraction. Alas, you do not." My eyes went wide. I glanced back toward Serena and no longer had sight of her. Jay, Ciara, and Chloe were gone as well. Papa laid down a few claxo on the table for our drinks. "We decided . . . that examples must be set. For you. For Vargo. For any that might ever oppose us. You will no longer be allowed to see the Queen. You are too dangerous to be in her presence any longer."

"What have you done?" I growled.

Papa rose. "To the Queen? Nothing. She will remain in the palace until her wedding to Jay Prince and be pampered beyond belief. To those who have made my life more difficult? I conquered them."

I couldn't stammer out a response, my mind trying to figure what he had done and who he had hurt. Where was Chloe? Naomi? Symon?

"You'll find my message in the bay," he said, thumbing behind him. "Oh, and Michael. Don't do anything rash. You'll see the Queen again in twenty-seven days, at her wedding."

I ran toward the docks, half tripping over my own feet as I pushed through crowds still in shock. The bay was filled with floating bodies. All the rebels in the Vargo prison had been massacred. Most still in the clothes they had worn that night. There were over a hundred. Maybe *hundreds*. There was so much blood in the water that it had formed a thin coating over the surface. And just so there was no mistaking who had done it . . . Liam stood on a wooden barge waving the Regal Company banner back and forth. Their sigil fluttered proudly in the breeze as bodies washed up onshore, carried in by the waves with every gentle ebb and flow.

This was not a declaration of war. But a reminder. That Mercenaries were above common feuds and petty squabbles. They could do whatever they wanted without fear of reprisal. They were the new nightmares in a world that was killing off every myth our ancestors had feared. But, for all their bluster and pride . . . did they forget I was a Mercenary as well? Did Regal Company think I would do nothing, and they could keep me away from Serena? They wanted to rule? To shout that they were untouchable?

Fine. Let them try to conquer me.

TICK TOCK

Everyone aside from Titus, who was preparing tea in the galley, gathered in Cassia's quarters on the *Freedioso*. It was the only place we couldn't be watched by Regal Company. It was cramped, and I was sitting on the floor, while everyone else perched on a chair or the bed with Cassia. My eyes kept falling on the crystal goblets filled with amber liquid near her desk, but I knew it was only a temporary fix, not a long-term solution.

I didn't want to end up like Domet.

"Regal Company has custody of the Queen. Delightful." Dark rubbed his brow. "Is there any way to get to her without starting an open conflict with Regal Company?"

"Doubtful," Chloe said. "Jay wasn't trying to be subtle. She's his way to unparalleled power . . . We suspected he had dubious intentions, but I didn't expect them to come out so quickly. Or for him to be so direct." She closed her eyes. "Before Serena became a Forgotten, she was confident she would be able to control him. She knew something about him that he would rather submit to her than let get out . . . Does anyone know what it could be?"

"Any chance it's how that asshole came back to life?" I questioned. "Because I saw him die. He was choked to death by Angelo Shade."

"It's not," Dark said. "New Dracon City calls Jay Prince the Merchant of Death because of his rumored inability to die. Proving that he actually can't die would only increase his legend."

"Is he an immortal?" Chloe asked.

Dark shook his head. "No, he's something else. His body changes slightly each time he theoretically dies. I was never able to figure out what was going on."

"Have you killed him before?" I asked.

"Yes," Dark admitted. "About half a dozen times. Hence wanting proof of his death."

Naomi scratched at the back of her hand. "So the only person who can stop Jay—a potential immortal—from taking over Hollow and stopping Angelo Shade is currently a Forgotten. Could she have left a note behind or got a tattoo to secure the information?"

"Someone would have seen a fresh tattoo when they were taking the bullet out of her," Dark said. "And judging by Chloe's face . . . I have a feeling the princess wasn't the note-leaving type, was she?"

"No," Chloe confirmed. "She wouldn't have taken any chances with the information."

"All Fabricators have a way to preserve their most important memories," Cassia said as she swirled the crystal glass in her hand. Some of the amber liquid sloshed over the edges. "What was hers?"

"It's complicated." Dark and Cassia motioned for Chloe to continue. "Serena only had two tattoos. One she stupidly got as a child, and another on her ankle in memory of Davey. She used to keep diaries, but Prince Adreann snuck into her room to read them, so she stopped. Instead . . . her idea was to hide her memories in plain sight." Chloe cursed and put her hands behind her head. "You all have to understand—Serena didn't see or do things normally. She was the head of the country. She thought in terms of decades and generations and—"

"Get to the point, Raven," Cassia snapped.

"Music," Chloe spat out. "Serena hid her memories in her songs. The lyrics, the tunes, and even the titles were all meant to correlate with something for her. But I don't know the cypher."

"Does anyone?" Alexis asked softly.

Chloe pointed at me. "Serena told me—long before Michael entered the Endless Waltz—that if something happened to her, he would be able to figure it out."

As always, all the eyes in the room were on me.

Stuttering, I said, "I mean, it should be easy, right? All I would have to do is look at her most recent musical notes and . . . how many pages of notes are there, Chloe?"

"The month we were on the road she filled seven journals front to back."

Dammit, Serena. Why did she have to be so prolific?

"Do we have a backup plan for when Michael inevitably fucks it up?" Cassia asked.

"Our other option is the fruit growing on the titan," Dark said. "But that plan is a little more complicated with her under Regal Company's control . . . We'd be kidnapping her. And they would respond the same way we would: by trying to kill every last person in this room."

"Imani would never approve us doing something so drastic," Cassia stated. "It's a shame, but our contract might be—"

"What if they didn't know Orbis Company was responsible?" I asked.

Everyone looked at me.

I got to my feet. "Right now, we have two options: finding the leverage she has on Jay by deciphering her songs, or going to the titan and trying to restore her memories. Both take time we don't have. Since Orbis Company can't be connected to kidnapping Serena . . . it seems our best option is to stall Jay while we get the fruit and bring it back. But what if I proposed something else?"

Alexis nudged Dark. "Does he really think he doesn't have a flair for the dramatic?"

I ignored her. "I'll go rogue and kidnap her. We'll steal a boat and leave Vargo. Then both Orbis and Regal Company will hunt me down. It can be framed that I'm in love with her and couldn't let her go through with marrying Jay. If I get caught, well . . ." I smiled at Dark. "Kill me creatively, alright?"

"It's official. He's insane," Alexis said.

"He's always been insane," Naomi added. "This is just plain stupid."

Cassia was doubled over with laughter. "Merciless sea, I say we do this. Just so I can watch Michael drown trying to leave through the gate."

"Then teach me how to pilot a boat so I can survive," I pleaded. "If anyone else has ideas that don't involve giving up or throwing Serena's life away, I'd love to hear them."

"Michael," Dark said, voice level. "Do you know what would happen if you went rogue? If we were forced to hunt you down?"

I did, but I shook my head to make myself seem ignorant.

"We would be forced to strike your name from our company's registry. You would no longer be a member of Orbis Company but a Mercenary without a company. The Worldeaters would put a bounty on your head to set an example. And if they did that, you would have no allies on this continent or the next. You would be at war with the world."

"And?"

"Assuming you don't die just trying to leave Vargo, your only chance would be for Regal Company to forgive you. Which they would only do if Jay forced them to. And that requires Serena's information. And getting that will require an obscene amount of luck on its own." Dark laughed, and it caused everyone except me to recoil. "You've pulled off miracles before—I'll give you credit when it's due—but you never went up against Mercenaries. We stand side by side with God."

"The Kingman family holds God to account. If I'm not scared of them, why should I be of you?"

"Why are you doing this, Michael? She doesn't remember you. And even if she does recover what was lost . . . she'll still end up with Jay. This path leads to either heartbreak or death. Is she worth it?"

"I wasn't there for her once when she needed me. This time I will be. I'm her Kingman." I put my hand over my heart. "Till death do us part."

"And I thought the Ravens were ridiculous," Alexis muttered.

"I'll ask one last time." Dark rose to look me in the eyes. "Are you sure? If you do this, we will be your enemies. And to protect the company . . . we will kill you."

There was no fear left in me. I would make sure Serena could choose her own way in life, just as I had. Because if I couldn't do this, who was I but an impostor? Some things had to be done. No matter the risk.

"Just tell me what I need to do to get to the titan."

"So be it." He took a map off a nearby table and handed it to me. "This charts the most direct route. If you can . . . I'd follow it closely. And remember we'll be right behind you. And we won't hold back."

I took a deep breath and looked around the room. Dark, the Black Death, wielder of multiple Fabricator, Weaver, and Spellborn specializations, would be coming after me. Along with Cassia, captain of the *Freedioso* and renowned navigator. Alexis, the best shot this side of the Iliar Mountains. Titus, whose cooking gave soldiers a second burst of life no matter the conditions around them. And Chloe. She would never—

"I'll be going with you, Michael," Chloe said abruptly. "I won't abandon Serena either."

"Chloe, you don't have—"

Naomi groaned dramatically with her hands behind her head. "Try not to get either of us killed, will you?"

"But—"

"You won't get past the gate without me," Chloe said. "Unlike you, I have navigational training. And with Naomi we'll be able to control the wind. Out there, it'll be an unparalleled advantage."

Cassia downed the rest of her drink. "She's not wrong. At sea, the current and winds are the only gods sailors pray to."

"Maybe you'll actually stand a chance," Dark said as he went to open the door. He nudged us out of the room. "Best you three leave. The less we know about your plan, the better. Michael, remember our agreement." His eyes were redder than wine. Redder than blood. Red like a forewarning of calamity. "If you can, bring me what I need, and I'll make all your problems disappear."

Chloe and Naomi glanced at each other, visibly confused. I lingered in the room, staring at Dark, wondering if I could defeat him if we finally came to blows. Then I joined Chloe and Naomi out on the deck, still wondering, and the door slammed behind me, and I felt free.

"So which boat are we stealing? Or should we try to stow away somewhere and grab a boat once we're free of Vargo?" Naomi asked, sitting on the railing. "I'd like anything where I don't have to share a room with Michael. He snores."

"Every boat and cart will be inspected once they discover Serena is missing. We'll have to steal one. Opening the gate will be the bigger issue." Chloe pointed toward a building on the cliff face, barely visible. "It's controlled by the guardhouse. And I don't know how we'll get someone up there and back without missing our chance to escape. Or leaving them behind."

"The landing might be rough," Naomi muttered. "But assuming the wind isn't too strong, I can probably jump to the boat. How many guards are usually stationed there?"

Chloe bit her lower lip. "Half a dozen. Maybe more. Hard to know until you get there." She paused. "Will you need help?"

Naomi shook her head. "Doubtful. I just have to get past them and push a button, right? I can do that." She stretched her arms back until something cracked. "I haven't flown in a while. I wonder if I'll touch the clouds."

"So that's the gate. What about the boat?"

"I have an idea where I can find one," Chloe said. "But I doubt we'll have all the proper necessities for sea travel ready in time. It'll be hard to find a black boat cat, but if I'm captain . . . I can't have a ginger or tabby. They clash with my stars, and with that kind of bad luck, we'll likely sink before we reach Maiden's Rest."

We stared at her, speechless, but Chloe kept going.

"Make sure both of you step on the boat for the first time with your dominant side. It's very important." She raised a finger. "And never snap your fingers or say 'I'll see you when I get back' to anyone before we depart. More bad luck." She looked us up and down. "Good thing neither of you are natural blondes or we'd have to bathe you in whale's blood before departure." She chuckled. "It *really* smells. And because it's almost high tide, there would probably be a shortage with all the ships going out."

I turned to Naomi as Chloe kept muttering, blissfully ignorant we were even there. "Did you know?"

She shook her head. "How was I supposed to? Who thinks someone is that *superstitious*? I guess everyone has a character flaw. But why couldn't it be biting her toenails or something?"

I shrugged and then interrupted. "Then there's Serena." Chloe snapped back to reality as I looked toward the palace. "Is she still being kept in her room?"

"They've moved her to the inner sanctum. One of the noble siblings is guarding her. We'll have to take them out to get to her."

"I'll handle that," I said. "It's about time I showed Jay and Angelo that they've been underestimating me anyway."

Both of my lovely companions tilted their heads at me, as if mentally deciding who was going to pinch me and wake me from my delusional dream. It was Naomi. "Michael. It's one of the noble siblings. You'll need Chloe's help or—"

"We're about to be chased across the sea by two Mercenary Companies. If I can't take out a single Mercenary by myself, then none of this has any chance of succeeding. Believe it or not, I have to do this."

"Do you have a plan?" Chloe asked. "Because your ability to nullify magic is useful, but it's not guaranteed that they'll have chosen the Fabricator. Especially if they foresee you coming for her. Besides guns, are you good with any other weapon?"

"Just my fists," I admitted. "But I've always been a brawler and a fool who could take a beating. I'll bring her back. I promise."

37

ETERNALLY YOURS

Naomi prepared to open the gates and Chloe found a boat while I prepared to storm the Vargo palace. I had no idea where she'd get one but knew by the time I had Serena, she'd have something waiting in the harbor in spot thirteen. It was close to dusk by the time I was ready. While it would be more dangerous to head out to sea at night, it might slow Regal and Orbis Companies down. So many variables . . . and so many ways I could end up in that grand cathedral where I had seen Dawn off. Would someone be there for me, too?

The guards at the palace gates were gone, as were most of the bustling servants that made this place resemble a beehive rather than a cemetery. Only a warning had been left behind in bright red paint: *The Kingman will be killed on sight.* So much for subtlety.

I walked through the palace with my revolver in hand, checking every turn cautiously before exposing myself. I expected to see visions of my ancestors more than any real person. It seemed impossible they had cleared everyone out, but they had. Even Vargo was no match for Regal

Company. And I was about to make an enemy of not just them but Orbis Company, too.

There was no time for hesitation, so I continued down the path I had chosen. Getting to the inner sanctum meant passing through a large indoor garden that was a series of stairways and plateaus. Whichever noble sibling was here would be waiting for me there. Sure enough, Liam Noble was. They had left the Wood Weaver to stop me. I would have to show them what a mistake that was.

"You actually came," Liam said, from the final step on the only stairs that led to the main area. Serena would likely be in there. "We took bets on it. Jay won."

I said nothing, keeping my distance. I didn't know whether it was better to engage him in close combat or try a shot. Either way, I spread the warmth over my body, everything nullified.

"I need to know . . . are you here as a Mercenary of Orbis Company or as a rogue apprentice?"

"Rogue," I declared. "I'd burn the world down to give Serena her chance at freedom. Dark will come for me . . . but I'll deal with him. I know his weakness."

"We expected that." Liam gestured toward the scythe across his lap. "Jay asked me if I wanted more backup as they prepared for our return to New Dracon City . . . but I can handle you. You are a fly who needs swatting."

I imitated a mouth with my hands. He didn't like that, sneering at me. "You all are returning to New Dracon City? I thought the royal wedding was supposed to be held in Vargo."

"Originally," he said, still baring his teeth. "But after you failed to protect her, we decided to take matters into our own hands. New Dracon City will be safer. And it's gorgeous in autumn. The fallen leaves coat the city in a ruby blanket so bright and wondrous, it cannot be imitated in art."

"Shame she won't see it."

"If you say so." Liam rose to his feet, scythe in hand. "As you have declared yourself rogue, I have no obligation to keep you alive. You will die here, Michael. Unless you leave." He cracked his neck. "Jay wanted me to offer you mercy. He doesn't want Serena upset."

I holstered the revolver.

"There's my answer. But why would you put your one advantage over me away? You don't really think you can beat me in a fair fight, do you?"

"You'd think by now people would stop underestimating me." I raised my fists and took a defensive stance. "But don't worry, you'll learn like all the rest. I know that style you're using. One Strike, right?"

Liam took up a stance with his scythe.

"I'd be curious to hear who trained you," I said, pacing. "I doubt it was Master Veeto. Maybe their apprentice Joji? They were pretty proficient—extremely paranoid, but proficient. My father told me how they trained weaknesses into their disciples. Just in case they ever got too cocky and tried to take out their master." I flashed him a canine smile. Let him believe that I was mad rather than calculated. "I wonder if you have those weaknesses, too."

"I was warned you'd try to get into my head," Liam said. "You'll have to do better."

"Better." I repeated the word a few times. "People have been telling me that for *years*. Since my father was executed for a crime he didn't commit. He was set up by Angelo Shade."

"Are we going to fight or are you going to keep yapping?"

"To be fair, I enjoy talking more than fighting." I yawned and made Liam scowl again. "Usually fights end up with me bloodied or damaged or—"

Liam rushed me, closing the distance between us in a flash, drawing his scythe back. I ducked right before he took my head off, air rushing across my neck as he cut the space above me in half. As he attempted to recover, I punched him in the stomach—hoping he'd wheeze and drop the scythe. Instead he grunted and then brought up the back end of the scythe, hitting me in the jaw and knocking me onto my ass. Liam was relentless, going for the kill, but I rolled out of the way and the blade struck the ground rather than my chest.

He got it out as I returned to my feet. But that was when the tree branches began to move toward me, slithering through the air. I broke any that I was able to as I kept one eye on Liam, watching from a distance, a large bleeding cut down his forearm. The pain that powered his Weaver magic. That was the issue I hadn't figured out how to solve yet. How to beat someone who got stronger whenever I hit them?

The tree branches stopped closing in on me and I resisted the urge to double over to catch my breath. Instead, I stood tall, a smile on my face. "Is that it? I didn't even nullify the area."

"Most pain is finite," Liam declared. "But more is always around the corner."

"I guess the real question is how much pain to inflict on yourself without becoming too weak or vulnerable in the fight." I adjusted my footing. "Oh, is that what you Weavers have to balance? Rather than worrying about the long-term effect, it's all short-term for you."

"You're learning," he said.

Which meant me nullifying the area was worse for me than it was for him. Liam would progressively injure himself during a fight to use his magic, so by taking that away, I was at a disadvantage, facing a healthier foe. But so long as I could hold off his magic and his scythe, he would weaken gradually. Then I could end it with a single attack.

This time I rushed him, sliding across the grass and then kicking at his chest. It connected, though he tried to block at the last second, and I tore his jacket open, sending buttons flying. The butt of his scythe found my throat and knocked the wind out of me. I was scrambling on the ground, alternating between heaving and trying to catch my breath again. His scythe got my upper thigh as I recovered, and I hobbled away before anything worse could happen.

The tree branches swayed as I dove into the widest area of open grass I could find. If he was going to use his Wood Weaving . . . I would at least see it coming. Liam followed me, stopping near two trees as the dusk light faded and darkness overtook the sky. Only the moonlight from Celona and Tenere illuminated our stage, no other trace of flame around.

"You've done better than I thought," Liam said, trailing his scythe across the ground. "Any last words?"

"As if my story will end he—"

The ground beneath me exploded. Roots from the nearby trees surrounded me like spears coming up from the earth. They entangled me, tying up my limbs, as clods of dirt fell around me, obscuring my view. I shouldn't have been so cocky. Not until I had completely secured victory. I had to return to the state of mind of the conqueror who charged across a battlefield to protect those he loved, dying ten thousand times with a smile on his face. Kill the arrogance in my heart, so the logic could manifest.

Liam whistled as he strolled over to me, swinging his scythe like a toy. "What were you saying?"

There was a tree root around my mouth like a gag. I chewed at it, swallowing splinters of wood as if they were water, ignoring the tingling sensation in my throat. For him to do something this impressive meant he had hurt himself badly. But he wasn't walking with a limp, his already hurt fingers were still in splints, his hands looked normal, and he wasn't bleeding. Where and what was the injury?

"You're resilient. I'll give you that." The Mercenary stopped in front of me, pushing my chin up with the flat edge of his scythe. "With a little more training you could have been a great Mercenary. Maybe you could have even started your own company." He clicked his tongue. "I would have liked to see that."

I tried to spit insults at him, but it only came out as muffled screams.

"May you meet the Wanderer in death, Kingman."

Liam raised his scythe and brought it down on me in one fluid motion. But before it connected with my neck, I bit through the tree root and leaned forward. Instead, the scythe severed the roots that held my wrists and feet in one clean strike. Wood flew, but I continued forward and drove my fist into his crotch. Whatever his injury was, this one was going to hurt just as much.

He doubled over, still holding his scythe, and I did what I was best at:

brawling. I'd been a street rat for ten years and knew how to take hits as well as give them. I delivered a right hook to Liam's jaw, planted my foot, twisted, and then used my momentum to follow up with an elbow to the same spot. Then, before he fell, I ducked and jumped forward, making sure my uppercut connected with the bottom of his chin.

The Mercenary hit the ground with a thud, the grass muffling his fall. His scythe tumbled out of his hands, his tongue stuck out of his mouth, and his eyes were rolled back into his head. The fight was over. And I had won.

I stepped over Liam and walked toward the inner sanctum before pushing open the door. There was no movement inside except for curtains blowing from the wind. A lump of blankets was in the middle of the extravagant bed, which had so many pillows on it that there was only enough room for one person to lie on it comfortably.

"Serena," I said, limping into the room. "I'm sorry I'm late. You in there?"

No response.

"It's Michael." I sat down on the edge of the bed, wondering how to bandage my cut leg. "I've come to get you out of here."

Only the wind answered me, so I fell onto my back, relaxing in the momentary comfort the bed would provide. If Serena followed me out to sea, this might be the last one I'd see for a long time. Or maybe ever. Who knew if I could ever return to the continent?

"You don't have to come with me if you don't want to," I said. "I can't promise that it'll be safe or nicer than marrying Jay Prince . . . but your life will be your own. And there's a . . . ah, damn, why does that cut hurt so much? Sorry. Where was I? There's a chance we could restore your memories. To be honest, I don't know if it'll work. But I'm willing to find out if you are."

Serena appeared over me. She ripped off her sleeve, tore it into long strips of cloth, and then wrapped it around the cut on my leg.

I sat up. It didn't hurt like last time. "Who taught you how to do that?"

"Chloe," she said as she finished tying it. "If you were me . . . what would you do?"

"I can't answer that for you. If I did, you'd just be following my desires. And that's not the"—I gulped, swallowing the word "relationship"—"*friendship* I want with you. If we're doing this, it's as equals."

She took a seat on the bed next to me. "What're the odds I get my memories back?"

"Low," I said. "Dark is more confident in it than me . . . but I've tried to cure a Forgotten before and failed. I know how hard it is. It'll take a miracle."

And I doubted God would be merciful to me or those I loved. After my family had been at war with them for a millennium.

Serena twirled her hair around a finger. It was a new strange habit she had picked up since becoming a Forgotten. The days of rubbing her left wrist were long gone. "So, I can either be safe and confined or free and looking over my shoulder for the rest of my life." She exhaled loudly. "Delightful choices."

"If you come with me, you'll see my life is one delightful choice after the other."

"If I come with you, will I find out why I fell in love with you?"

"No, you'll experience it."

"What an ego," she said accusingly. But the smile that followed was soft. A push that gave her room to pull back. "As if I could ever fall for a man like you."

"You say that as if it hasn't already happened." I shrugged. "Once, twice, thrice—no matter how many times it takes . . . you will always fall in love with me, Serena. It is a truth so poignant, God themselves balks at it." I held up my wrist. "We are bound by fate and we chose each other anyway."

"As if." Serena reached under her bed, grabbed an already full bag, and slung it over her shoulder. "Let's get on with it, shall we?"

"Just like that?"

"Just like that," she repeated. "The way I see it, if I stay here, I'll spend the rest of my life imprisoned in rooms like this with people who only see me as the Queen of Hollow. If I go with you, I see the world and can be anyone I want to be. A queen or a sailor . . . a lover or a loner. The possibilities are endless." She held out a hand to help me up. "And maybe I really will fall in love with you again. If you're lucky."

As I took her hand . . . I saw the woman I had fallen in love with for the first time since she had become a Forgotten. We were going to do this together. As we always should have.

Let the consequences come at us as they wanted.

SEABOUND

On our way out of the palace, we made sure to tie Liam Noble to the nearest tree. It wouldn't stall him for too long, but any slight delay might be the difference between having an army on our back or half a dozen ships. By the time we made it to the harbor, there was a commotion coming from the palace, but Chloe had a boat and was preparing to leave as we boarded.

It was bigger than I'd expected. The copper-bottomed ship had a single mast, a black cat figurehead, and no cannons. But it did have a lot of harpoons on board. If we got into a fight, we might have to board our enemies rather than try to take them out from the ship . . . I suddenly had doubts we'd make it out of the bay—much less to the titan. Was this little ship really going to take us all the way there?

Chloe was waiting for us on the deck. The four of us—once Naomi joined—would be the only crew this ship would have.

"How can we help?" Serena asked as she dropped her bag onto the deck.

Chloe pointed to the ropes holding our boat to the dock. "Free those and then raise the anchor. Michael, help me with the mast." She pulled at a rope that made the sails unfurl. "This is going to be rough with only three of us."

"How'd you get this boat?" I asked as I did as she told.

"It's my inheritance. I just claimed it."

"Inheritance?" I questioned, following Chloe up to the wheel. "This is Efyra's?"

"No."

"Then whose is it?" I pressed. "Is it your father's?"

"Something like that." Chloe took the wheel. "Now is not the time, Michael."

"I just want to know whether we'll have some angry owners after us, along with two Mercenary Companies. It's nice to know who might try to kill us once we're—"

"It's Erica's ship," Chloe snapped. Serena shouted that we were free and hopped onto the deck. "She gave it to me because I asked for it. I've never asked for something from *her* in my life and she owed me."

"Why does Erica owe you?"

Chloe slammed her hands against the wheel. "Because I became a Raven! Because I have gone to extreme lengths to protect her daughter, and because unlike my mother, I have remained silent for years. We really don't have time to get into this now. I have to signal Naomi."

"I get that. Tell me what I need to do and I'll do it," I said. And then, because I'm a moonstruck fool, added, "I just don't understand why you're being so weird about—"

Chloe grabbed me by the collar and snarled, "Because I'm King Isaac's bastard daughter. He had an affair with my mother, and Erica has hated me ever since I was born, even though I've never done anything to disturb her precious family. If you say another word about this, I'll cut out your tongue. Understand?"

I nodded wordlessly. Holy shit, Gwen had been right. Efyra and Isaac had an affair, and Chloe was the result. How had they kept it hidden?

Her existence made succession so much more complicated. There was no law in Hollow that said bastard children gave up their family rights. And there had even been instances of bastards inheriting over legitimate children. If she had been born before Serena, she was the rightful Queen of Hollow, and if she was younger, she was Serena's successor rather than Adreann.

Lightning started to crackle over Chloe's body, jumping between her fingers and arms to her chest and face. She illuminated everything around her as Serena ran to my side, oblivious to what I had just learned.

"What's the signal?" I asked, voice cracking like a boy's.

"This."

Chloe slammed her fist against an open palm and lightning rained down from above. Bolts hit five nearby ships, and they burst into flames. The smoke and force of the explosions around us caught our sails, propelling us out of the dock at a high speed toward the gates. Chloe took the wheel as chaos spread. I was amazed by her strength. If we had been back in the church now, I doubted I would have emerged victorious.

As Chloe manned the wheel and the sail caught the wind, we braced ourselves on the railing of the boat. We were cutting through the bay at a high speed, toward a metal gate that hadn't even begun to open. And having seen how long it took, if Naomi didn't press that button soon . . . I'd drown, and the others would be enjoying a long stay in a secluded room. For someone who was still learning how to swim, I must've been delusional to declare war against two Mercenary Companies and then set out to sea.

"That gate has to open!" Serena shouted amidst the fluttering of sails and the shouting coming from Vargo. "Is someone opening it?"

"Naomi's got it!" Chloe kept us hurtling toward the gate. "She won't fail."

The gate didn't so much as open an inch.

"C'mon, Naomi," Chloe muttered. And then louder, as she hit the wheel, she said, "C'mon, Naomi! C'mon!"

Serena grabbed my hand and held it tightly, and I clung to her.

"C'mon!"

The piercing sound of the gate opening made me flinch as the other two cheered for Naomi. It was a good thing she wasn't around to hear. It would have made her already sizable ego bigger.

"Can we make it through?" Serena asked, seeing how narrow the gap was, still holding my hand.

"It'll be close, but I think we'll—"

We hit a wave right before we made it to the gate. It launched us upward, and suddenly we weren't on the water anymore, but in flight. We sailed through the gate and I saw the greater unclaimed world for the second time in my life. After spending years imagining it, the water still blew away my expectations. It was crystal clear with a slight blue hue. I could see the schools of monotone fish and the monstrous finned creatures with jagged teeth swimming far below us among brightly colored coral that would make most painters jealous. I saw sunken ships down there. Some were split in two as clean as any knife strike, while others were fragmented and had been overtaken by the coral decades ago.

It was all so wondrous. And if wasn't for the fact that we had yet to hit the water again—and the boat might shatter on impact—I would have been in awe rather than screaming like child as I clutched Serena. She couldn't stop laughing as the wind blew her hair back. Chloe was trying—and failing—to steer us midair.

"Where's Naomi?" Chloe shouted. "We need a gust of wind to blow us forward or we're going to—"

I caught a flash of something, let go of Serena, and ran past Chloe toward the edge of the ship. I kept one hand on the railing as I threw the rest of my body over, extending my arm out. Naomi fell past me like a piece of Celona and caught my hand at the last second, our fingertips grazing each other's, the force of catching her nearly breaking the railing. I threw her up and over, then followed suit.

Even I could be brave when I needed to.

"Naomi, we need—"

"On it!" she interrupted, hands on her knees. She pushed her hand through the air and a powerful gust of wind accompanied it. The sails gained new life, becoming fat and full, and we lifted over the coral and ship bits that were sticking out of the water and onto safer sections of the sea. We still landed hard, water sloshing onto the ship, but we had, for the moment, survived the Madness Reef.

Naomi collapsed on the deck, breathing heavily. She shooed Serena and me away when we tried to check her for injuries, so Serena followed her example and sat down to tie her hair back into a ponytail. I went to Chloe's side, my eyes on Vargo as hers were on the horizon.

"Are we being followed?" Chloe asked quietly.

"Not yet," I said. "But the moment Orbis Company has to . . . they'll come after us."

"Half a day to a day at most, then." Chloe spat to the side. "Our best bet is to bypass Maiden's Rest. They'll expect us to stop there to resupply, but if we don't . . . we might be able to make it to the Palmer Archipelago safely."

"Do we have enough supplies to make it there?" Serena asked.

"No," she said frankly. "We'll need to fish for food. And hope for a heavy rain."

"Brilliant," Naomi said. "From one fire to another." She sat up. "Is it even safe to stop at the Palmer Archipelago? Aren't they called the tyrants of the sea? I can't imagine they'll like a bunch of pirates stopping to restock."

"We're not pirates!" I said.

"Yes we are," Chloe declared. "Regal Company will have bounties on us before the week is up. So, for all practical purposes, until we make it to the titan and see if we can restore Serena's memories—we're outlaws. Assume every ship we see is an enemy and will sink us on sight. Every legitimate port will deny us entry, and the ones that don't will charge a fortune to keep our identities a secret."

"What are we going to do if we can't stop for supplies?" Serena asked. "The titan is too far away for us to reach without them."

"We, reluctantly, will have to follow Dark's map," Chloe said through gritted teeth. "Though it doesn't account for going through the archipel-ago either. For some reason. Even though it would be faster." She took a deep breath. "Instead, his map leads us to the abyss."

"I thought we couldn't pass through the abyss."

"We can't," Chloe confirmed. "But we can skirt by it without getting caught in the sinkhole. If we can find a port near it, then we can pass our-selves off as inexperienced sailors and dock there. All the islands this side of the Sleeping Cities are run by the Palmers, but I doubt they'll have ships that far north unless it's for tax purposes. So, we restock, slip past the tyrants, and onward we go."

Naomi was up and beginning to light some of the lanterns that ran along the railings as the moons reached their apex in the sky. "What're the odds things go that smoothly?"

"From what I've seen . . . zero," said Serena.

We settled in for a long journey, quiet and each alone with our thoughts. Until a man came up from the lower decks, dazed and con-fused, a cute black cat perched on his shoulder. It was Sebastian Mar-gaux, attempted Queen Killer. I glanced around in shock and saw we were all stunned to see him, none except Chloe able to move. She quickly subdued him, pinning him with his arm behind his back. The injured man didn't even try to fight her off.

"Absolute shit luck I have," Sebastian muttered as he realized whose ship he had hidden on. "Anyone want to tell me where we're headed?"

TASTE OF THE SEA

Being out at sea was strangely comforting. Within a day we had settled into an easy routine. The only major debates were what to do with Sebastian and where everyone would be sleeping. Chloe had wanted Serena to sleep in the captain's quarters alone. Serena had wanted to sleep with me and Naomi in the crew quarters. Chloe shot that idea down. In the end, and after a lot of bickering about proper etiquette, they decided that Chloe would take the captain's quarters, while Serena would stay in the connected chart room. Naomi and I were relegated to the hammocks below deck. But after sharing a bed in Kingman Keep, neither of us was worried about it.

My compassion for Dawn's brother found its limits with the five of us confined to a small wooden area. So I advocated for the logical thing: locking Sebastian in the brig, throwing the key over the side of the ship, and waiting for madness to consume him.

Only Naomi—who relished in making me uncomfortable—said that was inhumane and monstrous. Sadly, Chloe and I agreed with her after our initial shouting match had ended with Serena forcing us to our knees with her Fabrications. We settled for putting him in a separate room, someone keeping watch over him as the others slept, and having Chloe get as much information out of him as possible during the day.

With those two minor arguments settled, we split most of the duties as evenly as possible. Chloe spent most of her time at the helm of the ship, and—after teaching Naomi—the two of them split their time between steering, navigating, sleeping, and eating. When I wasn't cooking what limited supplies we had, or fishing, I tried to meditate and further explore my memories, hoping to unearth something new in Idris's memories. In three days I didn't gain so much as an inkling. Another problem that I didn't have enough time to solve.

Serena spent her days reading and trying to reclaim as much of her previous knowledge as possible. While she picked most things up quickly, it still came as a surprise to all of us when she would ask the names and functions of common items. Such as a hammock, or a bowl, or even a bucket and sponge. She didn't much like the purpose of the last items, lamenting that the sea would do the cleaning for us. Chloe disagreed.

She also, much to my displeasure and Naomi's snickering, wanted to know more about the Kingman family. So I told her stories. Most about my ancestors and what they had done to deserve to remain at the side of the Hollow family for a millennium. To my surprise, she didn't still love her childhood favorites. Instead of idolizing the Mother Kingman or the Noble Kingman, she was drawn to the Unneeded and the Kingman Who Walked Away.

No matter how much I tried to hope differently, I knew she was different . . . no longer the person she had been. Even when we had been at war, she had carried Lucky with her. But now that knife was lost somewhere back in her room in Vargo, along with her memories. It hurt my heart in ways I couldn't comprehend on my own . . . so, most nights, Naomi helped me talk through my feelings, coming to terms with what we were and what I had to be. And even knowing what I had to do didn't make it any easier.

As we sailed on the fifth day, I longed for a chance to get away from the ship, if only to clear my mind for a few hours. Being this close to someone I loved, who didn't remember me, was infuriating. Especially since she followed me around like a lost kitten whenever she wasn't reading or learning things from Naomi or Chloe. That morning wasn't any different.

"So," Serena began as she lay on her back, book held over her face to block out the sun. "No one knows how Fabricating works? Just that you have a specialization, you can create whatever your specialization is, and it costs you memories? Because that's stupid. It's like walking around with a gun to your head and hoping it doesn't go off."

I held my tongue and moved the fishing lines a little, hoping to get something to bite. Naomi was listening from the helm, laughing at Chloe's failing attempts to talk to our prisoner. "Knowledge is power. The less we have of it, the better it is for those who have been influencing the world from behind the curtains. We just have to be careful about it."

"No one's tried to figure it all out?" Serena put her book down. "No one in Hollow was even a little bit curious about how Fabricating works? Like how someone's specialization is even determined?"

"We know that part," I said. "Kind of. It's through our bloodlines. If you combine certain specializations, you can create others. Apparently, some High Noble houses seek out good pairs to get the children with the specific specialization they want."

"Such as?"

I rattled off the combinations the Archmage had told me about back in Hollow. It didn't stop Serena from questioning everything. "But that doesn't make sense! How did my family end up with three different specializations if it's all based on our mother's and father's blood?"

I paused. "I . . . I don't know."

It didn't make sense when I considered my own family. I was a nullification Fabricator and Gwen was a non-Fabricator. If it was solely based on our parents' blood . . . how did we get the specializations we had? Was there more than luck involved? Did our grandparents' blood affect it as well? Where was the missing piece?

"How Fabricating works is one of the big mysteries of this world," Naomi said from the helm. "The High Nobles always liked to think they knew how it worked, but all the arranged marriages to get children with specific specializations were crapshoots half the time. It was the unsung secret of Hollow that you just did whatever the Fabrication masters said even if it didn't make sense." She smiled at me. "If anyone tells you they know how Fabrications work . . . they're a liar."

Serena fell onto her back with a loud huff and then held her hand out as if trying to pluck the sun from the sky. "I don't get it. None of it makes sense." She sat up abruptly. "And why did Hollow have such a twisted obsession with blood? Blood oaths sound disgusting. Am I going to have to do that?"

"No," I said quickly. "They're an old, outdated ideal at this point meant to show your ally or potential ally that you mean them no harm. Besides, the king or queen never does them. Their partner does. And I think your mother, Erica, did . . . two, maybe, in her time as Queen of Hollow? Once with the most senior of the Merchant Princes in New Dracon City and once with a frustrated High Noble to settle a land dispute a little bit after your birth, when civil war was a possibility. And that was rare. Normally a Kingman would take the oath rather than their Royals."

"Delightful," Serena said with disdain. "More rules to memorize and follow." She closed her eyes and let the sun warm her body. "I have another question. What is going on with the stowaway below deck? Why are you all so bent on keeping him away from me?"

"He tried to murder you!" I said. "Or he worked with the people who tried to. He may be the current leader of whatever remnants of the Hollow rebellion there are."

"So?" she countered. "Does he still want to murder me?"

"Chloe will find out," Naomi called down. "She's excellent at getting information out of people when they don't want to talk. Without hurting them, no less! It's magical to watch, not so much to experience."

I stared at my friend and then mouthed the words "Did you confess yet?" at her. She answered with a sharp turn of the ship that nearly sent me over the railing and into the water below. Ha. I'd get her to confess to Chloe sooner or later. She couldn't hide her feelings for the one-eyed Raven forever.

Serena didn't miss a beat. "If he doesn't want to murder me, will we let him go?"

"It'll be up to Chloe," I said. "She's the most senior Raven here, and your protector."

"Well, I hope he is," Serena stated. "I'd like to talk to someone from Hollow who's a little less biased than all of you."

"Everyone is biased," I said, uncomfortable. "But we'll see what happens. Honestly, I can't imagine Chloe will let him go without a good reason. The risk is too great."

"That's stupid." She lay down again. "Holding someone's worst day against them is childish. It's not as if we've not tried to kill each other before."

Naomi snorted loudly and I nearly choked. There wasn't a single person on this ship who *hadn't* tried to kill me before. And yet I was in love with one of them, another had become my closest friend, and the third was a valuable ally. Maybe I had been too harsh on Sebastian because of what he had done. What was a little attempted murder between friends?

"I'll talk to Chloe about it," I said, headed below deck. Naomi and Serena quickly changed the topic to one I was glad to avoid: how people became Mercenaries. The ship's interiors were a little cramped, but as I neared the room we were keeping Sebastian in, I could hear Chloe and him in mid-conversation.

"—all I need you to do is swear fealty to Queen Serena and we'll let you go. So long as you wear this bracelet." She pulled out a stone link with glints of the green crystal embedded into it. So Alexis and I weren't the only ones who had explored the discoveries made during the Heartbreaker's attack on Hollow. Had Hollow weaponized the crystal in other ways, too? "Let it go, Sebastian. Serena wasn't responsible for Dawn's death."

"I don't care if she was or wasn't anymore. Dawn is dead and nothing will change that," the High Noble said, chained to the hull behind him. "But I have no desire to kneel to a queen who has enabled monsters like the Corrupt Prince to gather power. And now that she's a Forgotten, she should step aside. Let another lead Hollow into the future."

"Who would you suggest? Because last I saw, there was only one noble that could."

Sebastian moved his tongue from cheek to cheek in his mouth. "Maybe we should change the system. Get rid of the monarchy. It's worked for Goldano and New Dracon City."

"Maybe we should," I said, creeping up behind them. "But if we could find someone else to take the throne that wasn't Adreann or Serena, wouldn't that be better?"

"Who else has a claim?" Sebastian snapped.

Chloe jumped to her feet, shoving me into another room. When the door closed, I expected to have her slam me against the hull—all threats and violence—but all she did was stand opposite me, her hands trembling as she said, "Michael. Whatever you're trying to insinuate—don't."

"We have to talk about it at some point."

"No we don't. For my sake as well as Serena's. You know me well enough to know I don't want the throne. But will she think the same? I'm a stranger to her. I want her to trust me. Not consider me another threat."

"I get that, but the throne could be your birthright. Why run away from it?"

"You'll never understand," she said quietly. "I always knew you never would. Maybe that's why I always kept you at a distance, but if you're my friend—"

"Yes?"

"—then you'll let this be. Please. I've never wanted anything from my father. I didn't even know who he was until I was sixteen. I don't want his throne. I just want to serve."

"Then serve the people other than Serena. Let us walk away from this."

"You're being selfish," she snapped.

"And you aren't?" I countered. "We're all selfish. But sometimes we can't afford to be." I exhaled. "And maybe this is your sacrifice."

"You think I haven't made sacrifices?" Chloe said. "You think I wanted to be a Raven? To never find love or marry? Nothing about my life is in my control except for this. And that's where I'll make my stand. Whether you like it or not."

The intelligent part of me told me to stop pushing—to let her have this secret in peace—and I did . . . kind of. Some lines were meant to be crossed, and, sadly, this might have to be one of them. If only to help someone I cared for deeply. "Ravens can't marry. But would you take the throne for a chance at love?"

Chloe's hesitation, hand on the doorframe, gave away her answer, if only to us other lovelorn fools. But rather than admit a painful truth, she said, "Negotiate with Sebastian. Convince him to agree to our terms. I'm tired of spending all day talking to him. I've almost forgotten how the sun feels on my skin."

She trudged back up to the deck. I wasn't sure whether to feel happy she trusted me to talk to Sebastian or annoyance because she hadn't answered my question. If she was in love with Naomi, this whole thing could be over by sunset. There were times to keep secrets for friends and times when two people in love needed to admit it to each other. But on the flip side . . . if she was in love with another . . . then it could be one of the toughest conversations of my life.

I'd get the answer out of her eventually. I focused on Sebastian for the time being. There was no point in feigning a position of power, not after he had made statues beat me up near the docks, so I took a different approach—fake friendliness.

"It's hot out there," I said as I strolled back in. Barrels of rum were suspended from the roof by taut rope. Of all the stores we needed for the voyage, it was probably the least useful. But sailors always made sure their drink was well stocked on a ship. "So, why didn't you leave when you had the chance? Why stow away on a random ship?"

"Why do anything?" he countered. One-Eye, the black-coat cat Chloe had acquired for our voyage, had taken a liking to Sebastian, curling up on his lap throughout his imprisonment. "It seemed the right decision at the time. I didn't want to give in and do what you told me to, so I chose another option."

"But why?" I asked again. "It was a stupid decision."

"Are you sure *you* want to lecture me about bad choices?"

"Absolutely. I'm a hypocrite for a reason." I smirked, and he didn't like that. I dropped my charade, twisting my father's ring. Somehow talking to Sebastian was like talking to my younger self. "What do you want to do? Kill me? Kill Serena? Find Rian and kill him to avenge Dawn? What's your move here?"

Sebastian hesitated and then asked, "Rian? Is that who killed my sister?"

"Yes," I admitted. "And I last saw him in Eham."

"Is that where you're all headed?"

"We might pass it on the way."

Sebastian extended his hand for the bracelet as best he could against the chain restraining him. "Give me the bracelet. I'll wear it. But Rian is mine when we run into him again. Is that understood?"

"Perfectly." I unchained Sebastian, clamped the magic nullification bracelet on his wrist, and then helped him up. He shook slightly but remained upright as One-Eye rubbed against his right leg. Sebastian was as prideful as I had been. "Revenge is a powerful drug, isn't it?"

"Stronger than you could ever imagine until it starts running through your veins."

"Try not to let it consume you," I muttered, knowing he wasn't listening to me. He was probably thinking up ways to kill Rian. Just as I had with King Isaac and Angelo. "Retaining your humanity is more important than revenge. Killing the object of your hatred only continues the cycle of hate. Only once you break it can you truly grow."

Sebastian didn't hear me, nor did I repeat myself, and we each continued thinking we were doing what was right, even if we both were in the wrong. None of the women were talking to one another when we saw the sun again and the tension in the air felt heavy and sticky, like one wrong word would cause the entire ship to explode.

"Sebastian's with us now," I said to Chloe as he leaned against the railing of the ship. "He wants revenge against Rian."

"And when he gets it?" she asked.

I shrugged and looked toward the sky. "Guess we'll find out."

She put her forehead to the railing. "It never gets easier."

"No, it never does."

And since we rarely got the chance to relax and catch our thoughts, Naomi spotted something on the horizon that demanded our immediate attention. "We're near the abyss!" she shouted.

"Prepare to drop anchor!" Chloe ordered. She patted me on the back and looked toward our destination. "Time to see if you can pull off the impossible once again, Michael."

CROSS-EYED

The abyss was the first thing I'd heard about when I arrived in Vargo. It was like a lingering secret that everyone was too scared to talk about sober, but while drunk . . . it was all they could theorize about. I mean, how could they not? There was an impossible sinkhole in the sea that water drained into and had no end. Was it the result of a piece of Celona hitting the ocean? A home for some mythical behemoth? Or something even more sinister? I had no doubt it was connected to the Wolven Kings somehow. It was too perfect a scar not to be one of their many wounds on this world.

Approaching the abyss was a feat in and of itself. Approach too quickly and a ship would be caught in the currents and dragged in, taking the crew with it. Going too slowly was even more dangerous. The abyss was surrounded by stone walls, almost like half-open gates, and as many ships smashed against the barrier as were destroyed in the abyss. Both were guaranteed death. No one had ever managed to cross it.

Luckily for us, Chloe was a skilled helmsman and Naomi was able to control our direction and speed better than most, thanks to her wind Fabrications. We were all tentative as we approached the small still-water bay where we could drop an anchor in without risking our ship floating away. But once the ship was safe, the hard part began: finding a way to cross the abyss. Apparently this was up to me.

No pressure.

I kicked off my boots, yanked my shirt over my head, and then walked the plank. My toes clung to the edge of the wood as my sight was focused on a single sliver of land surrounded by mist that extended over the abyss. Of all the places I had been to, this felt the most bizarre and magical. How had this formed? And how had it remained like this? Shouldn't the seawater have eventually filled it up?

"I'll come with you," Serena said, beginning to undress. Chloe quickly intervened, pulling her shirt back down before it made it past her forehead. "Oh, come on. We shouldn't send him in there alone! And me going makes sense! You and Naomi need to be here in case something happens with the boat."

"We don't know what's in there," Chloe said. "Michael will handle it. He's faced worse before and come out on top."

"I'm like a suicidal cockroach," I admitted. "Despite my best attempts, the world hasn't come up with a way to get rid of me yet." When her expression didn't turn from a stern grimace, I added, "Seriously. I'll be fine. I'll just scout out the area and be back. Promise."

She was like a small child, pouting as she crossed her arms and looked away from me. "Fine. But be back before I realize you're gone."

"As you command, Your Majesty." I bowed deeply. "Sebastian, any desire to join me?"

He waved me off. "Not unless Rian is in there."

"Doubtful." I turned toward the abyss. "Here goes nothing."

I held my nose before I jumped off the plank, the springy wood bouncing up and down as I left it behind me. The water rushed past me as I sunk into the bay, the shock of the crisp coldness reaching my skin only after I had stopped moving and began to swim upward. I broke the surface, savoring that first breath, and then kicked a few times before I could stand and walk the rest of the way to shore. There was no sand here, only sharp rocks all the way.

I waved back to the ship to tell them I was well, and then made my way toward the abyss itself. Black howling wind met my advance the moment my toes touched the sliver of land that extended over it. I nullified my body immediately, my arms over my face as I tried to push forward, but it whipped me backwards and sent me tumbling back to the water like a ball.

Sitting in the shallow water like a fish flopping on land was embarrassing, but it didn't compare to how overwhelmed I had just been, trying to cross. I had felt the black wind before, in Dark's memories. But why was it here in reality? Was there some connection to this place and the world I experienced when I was in someone's memories?

I didn't have answers. But I did have a stupid amount of persistence and an uncanny ability to charge headfirst into things without thinking. So that's exactly what I did. I charged the black wind over and over and over again—got blown back multiple times—before eventually recognizing it wasn't working. Nullifying the area didn't work. Nor did trying to punch or crawl through the black wind. And eventually the black wind grew tired of my nonsense and began to intensify, swirling over the entrance to the abyss until it resembled a black door.

Naomi landed next to me with a soft plop thanks to her Fabrications. She hauled me to my feet and out of the shallow water. "Nothing working, eh?"

"Absolutely nothing." I scratched my head, still staring at the black wind. "It doesn't make sense. Is the magic operating on its own without someone controlling it? And if so, how?"

Naomi shrugged and then charged the black wind herself. She was slammed back as well but was able to flip herself in midair and land more gracefully than me. "Shith," she cursed. "Bith my tongue. I donth thinth we're crothing here. Noth unleth we're misthing something obviouth."

We searched the area and found nothing but water, small sharp rocks, and the black wind that prevented us from advancing. Naomi was preparing to return to the ship, when I tried one last desperate move: I shouted into the abyss.

"Hello!" I screamed into the endless darkness. The roar from all the waterfalls nearly drowned me out. "I want to cross. Can you open the path for me?"

Nothing.

"We won't bother you!" I added. "We just need to get to the Reborn Titan."

Nothing again.

"Please! I have nothing to offer you in exchange, but wouldn't you like that warm fuzzy feeling you get after doing something nice? It'll be wonderful!"

"C'mon, Mikel," she said around her bitten tongue. "Leth head back."

I grudgingly accepted nothing I could say would get a response—assuming something or someone was even listening—so I returned to the ship with Naomi. We climbed up and hauled ourselves over the side. Neither Chloe nor Serena looked happy, but Sebastian was cackling away. Even One-Eye looked smugger than normal.

At least someone was enjoying themselves.

"This was a waste of time," Chloe muttered, already preparing for our departure.

"It was worth a try," Serena said softly. "It would have cut days off our voyage if it had worked. I guess we can't solve every mystery out there."

"Guess not," I said, staring at the abyss one last time.

We left without fanfare. The abyss was impassable for a reason. But by the time the sun had set, and the abyss was far away, a piece of Celona flashed blue across the sky before turning sharply and falling into the sea just beyond the horizon.

The voice that resided in the pieces of Celona fell from above like melting snowflakes, barely reaching our ears before disappearing. "You should not have tried that. I will mourn your deaths as if you were my own children. Goodbye, Naomi Dexter. Goodbye, Chloe Mason. Goodbye,

Serena Hollow. Goodbye, Sebastian Margaux. Goodbye, Michael King-man. I will remember you all."

The wave from the fallen piece of Celona came on quickly, blocking out the moons and sending us into perpetual gloom. It was so high it scraped the clouds, dragging the wispy remnants down as it slowly turned inward toward us. A ship killer was coming for us and we only had minutes to decide either to outrun it, get over it, or prepare for our ship to be destroyed and face whatever came next.

DISASTER

Disaster, as it were, was an eight-letter word. And each letter perfectly described how we were all feeling as we watched the ship-killer wave come to sink us.

D was for disbelief.

"What the fuck!" Naomi screamed at the top of her lungs, eyes fixed on the approaching wave. "What is going on? You all heard that? What's happening?"

I was for ineptitude. Mainly mine, as I was unable to do anything but stand slack-jawed.

Thankfully for us, Chloe must've mentally been prepared for something like this and was already in action, shouting orders in a tone that left no room for negotiations or questions.

"Naomi—cut down as much sail as you can! Serena—grab that length of rope and tie it around your waist with the 'sailor's pride' knot I showed you. Then do the same to me! Sebastian and Michael—prepare the heart of the ship! Now! We'll barely be able to outrun this!"

S was for sarcasm. Which was surprisingly absent.

A was for action. Which we all sprung into at Chloe's commands. Naomi launched herself into the air with a dagger in one hand, slicing away as big a piece of cloth as she could. Serena had already tied the nearby length of rope around her waist—double- and triple-checking the knot—before doing the same to Chloe, who was at the helm, trying to keep us on the straight and narrow. It didn't take a prodigy to understand that if it hit us from the side we were done for. At least head-on we had a chance.

Meanwhile, Sebastian and I prepared the heart of the ship, readying it for use and checking it for cracks and holes. It was standard equipment for all ships on the Gold Coast: a square of pumice designed to be sealed so tight to the ship that it could keep water out for ten minutes. After that, it opened like a book and could be used as a floatation device. It could comfortably fit four grown men. Uncomfortably, it could fit seven.

Sailors told stories of crews who had sabotaged the heart of the ship at the last second, jamming the locks and hinges when their captains refused to save as many as possible. Something about the thought of their superiors slowly drowning in a stone box after selfishly abandoning the crew was too appealing for many crews to ignore, which explained why the survival rate of ships facing ship-killing waves was almost zero.

But we were allies and there was enough room for all of us. Maybe we could survive this. If we got lucky and no one developed a sudden sickness of the mind when the wave hit our ship and we all locked ourselves in a tight stone cube that did little to guarantee our lives. At most, it would delay our deaths.

S was for silence, in which we all did our duties as the wave grew closer and closer. It wasn't long before drops of seawater started to spray me. Our time was running out.

"Naomi!" Chloe shouted. "Right before the wave hits, launch yourself into the air as high as you can! Use the sails to delay your descent."

"I can take someone with me," Naomi said as she hit the deck with an armful of cloth. "There's no need for you all to squeeze into that box. There'll be more air if—"

"Naomi," Chloe said softly, yet with the strength of a scream. "You need to live so all of us can. If that box doesn't open again on its own, you'll need to bust us out. Is that clear?"

She nodded, likely hundreds or thousands of things she wanted to say in her mind. Would this situation force her to admit her feelings to Chloe? Sadly, not. She turned away, tied the cloth around her waist, and then took fistfuls of it in her hands.

T is for timing. Something we all lacked when we desperately wanted it.

In the face of all the chaos and in the shadow of the wave that was about to crash down on us, Naomi leapt into the sky—a sharp whistle marking her path upward—and disappeared completely. Chloe and Serena jumped over the railings in tandem and shoved Sebastian, One-Eye, and me into the box. We closed the metal door, pulled a chain, and then fell into the water just as the wave crashed down on us, throwing us around like a feather in the wind. Our screams were lost in the madness.

E is for emptiness. Emptiness of the mind. Emptiness of the heart. Emptiness of the body as we were tumbled about. I held Serena, pressing her head against my chest to shield it from banging against the sides . . . and then water began to seep in through the cracks instead. Sebastian was screaming at Chloe to yank off his bracelet as she tried to plug the holes, and I concentrated on the girl in my arms.

R is for regret. Regret at words unspoken. Regret at actions untaken. And regret at the better decisions we had not made.

My warmth covered both of us and I closed my eyes and hoped we might live. And then the back of my head slammed against the pumice behind me, and the darkness welcomed me into its arms.

INTERLUDE

BIG BROTHER

Trey burned the Hanging Gardens to the ground with enough grain alcohol to overrun the gutters of the east side. His oppressors arrived too late with their firefighting Fabricators to stop the blaze. Instead, they watched from the neighboring districts and did their best to prevent the fire from spreading. They succeeded—but the whole city saw his declaration of war against the nobility. The fire burned for a day and night and by the next morning the sun shone hazily through black smoke thicker than anything during the destruction of the Militia Quarter.

Wanted posters for Big Brother appeared quickly. A question mark on it rather than a crude drawing of his face. His bounty was higher than the Black Death's. Higher than the Emperor's. Higher than Michael Kingman's. And Trey didn't even kill a king.

Trey knew that would have bothered Michael.

Michael's mother found him in his supposedly secret hideout before the ashes were cold, arriving like a nightmare to ruin his daydream of overthrowing tyrants. Trey was only relieved that Michael wasn't there too. For whatever reason, he was the one person he could never quite cut off. Though he would have to, if his war was ever to be fully complete.

"Treyvon Wiccard," she howled from the doorway. One of Trey's men stopped her from entering, but they both knew she could plow through him if she wanted to. Her meek days ended long ago. "We need to talk."

Trey waved her in as he continued eating fried dough that squished rather than snapped when he bit into it. Juliet towered over his table, and his stomach churned. Her presence reminded him of his late mother. Yet their anger was not the same. Hers was righteous while his mother's had been chaotic.

"Read this." Trey handed her a neatly folded letter.

"Why?" she asked, and read it faster than he ever could.

"Michael sent it before he went out to sea. Haven't heard from him in a bit, though."

Juliet rubbed her brow and muttered something under her breath. "Unbelievable. How is it that Michael has a natural instinct for rebellions, of all things?"

"Kind of funny, isn't it?"

"'Funny' isn't the word I'd choose." She joined him at the table. "But I came here to talk to you. How far are you going to go?"

"No more kings. No more queens. No more nobility." He looked into her eyes. "No more Kingman."

"Do you know what system you'll leave behind if you destroy this one?"

"I don't care," he admitted. "Ruling isn't for me. I only seek to end injustice. Others will do what I cannot."

"So an exchange of tyrants, then?"

Her words sent a prickle up Trey's spine. "No."

"Oh, I'm sorry," she mocked. "That's what I thought it was. Good men always want to enact change, and usually discover ruling is harder than destroying. If you're serious about leaving Hollow better than you found it—then find the backbone to rule or the wisdom to create an institution that may succeed when others have failed."

"I don't want to rule," he muttered. "I won't become what I hate."

"Therein lies the conundrum. How do you remain the same man without compromising your beliefs?"

Trey hesitated. "Why are you lecturing me about this?"

"Because I believe in you."

Those words were a curse, when Trey couldn't forget his own mother's whispers in his ear: That he was worthless. That he killed both her and Jamal. That he was unworthy of love or praise. That he was broken beyond redemption.

Juliet continued, "My eldest son has chosen love over duty. My middle child has found his own way and my youngest is missing. So I've decided to bet on someone else—you." She leaned forward. "Hollow always needs a Kingman."

"I am not a Kingman. I'm a nobody."

She tsked at him. "The Kingman family is ending. Lyon's child has been born a Ryder. Michael and his descendants will carry the name but not the position. And I'm not certain Gwen even wants children. So, I think it's important to find an alternative."

"I don't understand."

"You don't want to rule because you're worried you'll become something you hate?"

Trey nodded.

"What if you had someone at your side who would promise to make sure you never compromised?"

"You mean you want me to keep the Kingman family in place?"

"No. I want you to take the idea of the Kingman family and make it better."

"Do you . . . do you want me to make it an organization? A calling rather than a duty?"

"Now you get it." Her smile grew broader. "Come, Trey. I've something to show you."

Trey and Juliet returned to Kingman Keep. The days of being a cobweb keep had long since passed and now the entire area shone. Its restoration had been a labor of love, the great hall was alit with dozens of candles, and the table in the middle had been set for a dozen. Other, smaller tables were nearby. This place could easily fit and feed a few hundred if they sat shoulder to shoulder. The hearth was burning brightly, a pile of wood that would last all winter next to it, ready to be burned at a moment's notice.

Trey ran his fingers over the polished grain of the chair that sat at the head of the table, remembering what it had been like to eat with his family and wondering if he'd ever have the chance to do so again.

Juliet's sudden descent down a nearby staircase brought him out of his reverie. She had a small bag slung over her left shoulder, was dressed for travel, and had a dagger strapped to her shoulder and a sword on a belt around her waist.

"I'm leaving. Going to continue the good fight in the Warring States, I think," she said. "Being in this city has been a painful reminder of what my life was . . ." Her eyes lingered on the painting of the Kingman family that hung above the hearth. It was battered and flaking, and David Kingman's face had been torn out of it . . . but it was the only semi-complete painting of the Kingman family that remained. ". . . and I can't live with that regret anymore. I need to do something. Be something other than a Kingman."

"W-What?" Trey stammered. "What about your children—"

She didn't shout or cut him off, just smiled sadly. "None of them are coming back here. They've all chosen or been forced into other paths. If they need or want me, they'll find me again. I've sent them all letters. But if you want this place for an orphanage, an institution that'll carry on the Kingman name, or another symbol to destroy—well, do with it what you will." She tossed him a key ring with dozens of brass, gold, and copper keys on it. "It's yours, Trey."

"This is too much," he said frantically. "I don't want this. I operate out of the shadows. I'm nobody. I'm not—"

Juliet hugged him and Trey stiffened as if it would break him in half, but very slowly softened in her arms until he returned her hug. It felt nice.

"You're a good man, Trey. You got dealt a shitty hand in life, but I believe in you. And I'll be there for you if you need me." They separated. "Be good, alright?"

"Thank you," he said.

Juliet ruffled his hair before she left and then disappeared into the city of Hollow, alone and nameless. Her part in the Kingman legacy was over and now it rested on Trey's shoulders. Would he destroy it? Reinvent it? Or let it wither away and die?

There was no time to come up with an answer. A tear in reality appeared in front of him with a snowy landscape on the other side of it before Gwendolyn Kingman and Kyros Ryder heaved the body of the smoke dragon through it. Joey Ryder followed them with his eyes closed, licking a sugar-coated icicle. A nearby table flew back through the tear as if exchanging one thing for another.

They stopped dead in front of Trey, silent.

"Who killed him?" Trey asked when no one spoke.

Kyros raised his hand proudly. "I avenged my best friend."

"Good for you." A pause. "Gwen, you just missed your mother." He thumbed in the direction she had just left in. "She's leaving Hollow. Do you want me to get her?"

Gwen shook her head, kicking Rian's body under a nearby table. The heart had yet to be extracted. "I can't interact with her, or my employer will punish me. This is already a big enough act of rebellion. He'd kill me if he found out I was gathering one of his enemy's allies."

Trey tossed the key ring onto the nearby table. "Why are you three here? Something happen?"

"Michael is going to need our help soon," Kyros said. "And we're going to give him the support he needs."

"I'm busy." Trey scratched the back of his head. "People are depending on me here. I can't just leave them without warning."

"That's fine," Gwen said. "Do what you need to. I have to dispose of Rian's body, make another stop for an ally, and then figure out what we're going to do with his heart."

"This feels like bullying."

"Does it?" Gwen countered sweetly. "Then good. Because it is."

"Always knew you were scarier than Michael." He sighed dramatically. "Doesn't matter, really. It'll give me time to delay making a decision." Trey glanced back down at the key ring. "Destroy, change, or wither away. Which one will it be?" And then to the others, he said, "Alright. Who we beating up this time?"

32

A NEW DANCE

Her lips felt hot pressed against mine as a steady pounding on my chest lifted whatever water had been in there out of me. My eyes felt too heavy to open, my arms too flimsy to move, and my heart barely a fleeting whisper.

"Live," she begged. She pressed her lips against mine again and exhaled deeply. "Live. Please. Live."

I wanted to tell her I was too tired. That she expected too much of me. But whenever I tried to speak, nothing came out but mouthfuls of regurgitated salty water. She pried open my eyelids and forced me to look at her. The moon behind her haloed Serena's head and her warm smile gave me the strength to push myself up.

We were floating on a sheet of pumice that had been twisted into a makeshift ship. The sails Naomi had flown upward with had been repurposed to power it. The Ravens were lying on their backs, still struggling to catch their breath, while Sebastian was curled up with his knees to his

THE VOYAGE OF THE FORGOTTEN   315

chest. His face was covered in claw marks, bloody gashes left by One Eye. We were all soaking wet.

Serena hugged me tightly. Then she broke the hug, holding me at arm's length as water dripped on me from her wet hair. Had she always been this beautiful? Or had the seawater made me mad?

"You almost died."

"'Almost' is the key word there," Naomi muttered. "I've seen him drowned, stabbed, sliced, and hung, and the cockroach always gets up again. He's luckier than anyone I've ever met."

"Sorry," I said, ignoring Naomi. I was trying to hide my blush as Sebastian looked on and the others began to recover. "It wasn't as if I was trying to."

"I don't care. You're not allowed to leave my side again, understand?"

My heartbeat was in my throat. "Some things are beyond my control. I don't know—"

"Do I look as if I care about the logistics?" Serena rolled away from me, one knee up against her chest as one of her hands covered her face, a faint frown seen through her fingers. "You should be a stranger to me, but I know how I felt when you were holding me. So, from here on out . . . you will stay with me. Do I make myself clear?"

"Serena," I whispered.

"Must I command you?" She got to her feet and looked onto the horizon. The last remnants of our ship were vanishing beneath the waves. "It's one of the few benefits of being a Forgotten. I do what I want. Regardless of the consequences. Just this once . . . maybe you should follow my example."

I wanted to. We could run away. We could be free, escape Hollow politics, and the curse that had plagued us for all these years.

"Fine." I extended my hand for her to help me up. "I promise to be at your side until my last breath."

Serena yanked me off the ground with a smile. "See? Was that so hard?"

If only she knew. "I suppose not."

"Are you two finished?" Sebastian asked, wincing whenever he twitched unexpectedly. "Because we're still stuck in the middle of the sea with no food or water or anything except this stupid pumice boat."

"There's an island about a day's float away," Chloe said. She pulled out Dark's waterlogged map and held it up to the stars to navigate our path. "It's not marked with a name like the other Sleeping Cities, so I'm not sure we'll be able to find a ship there, but we don't have any other option. The next-closest island is a few days away at best."

"What a gift from the Wanderer," Sebastian muttered, still nursing his injuries. I would have to ask, if the opportunity presented itself, if he had Woven this ship. It seemed like the only possible explanation.

I had always been so scared of magic. Too nervous to willingly experiment with my abilities, but sometimes . . . when I wasn't overwhelmed by it all . . . the thought of learning more about magic seemed fun. Even if the costs were high. Who hasn't wanted to learn magic?

"Are we going to talk about what happened?" Naomi asked. "We heard a voice after the piece of Celona passed over us. What was that?"

"A Wolven King," I said. Everyone's eyes were focused on me. "When I fought Gwen's employer, he was able to direct pieces of Celona at me. I think one of them aimed moon-fall at us when we tried to cross the abyss. But it wasn't the first king. I would recognize his voice."

"So it was the second or the third," Chloe determined. "But why attack us? It sounded as if they were trying to—"

"Punish us," Sebastian said. "As if we were violating holy ground."

"One of them must be imprisoned there," I said. "It would explain why another king would try to stop someone from entering it."

"That's a big leap in logic without much proof, Michael," Serena said tentatively. "Did we see anything that might back that statement up? What did the First Wolven King say when you ran into him? Did he give any indication of his plans?"

I shook my head. "Only that they were headed to the titan."

Sebastian rolled over and made it clear he was done with the conversation. The black cat joined him, lying on his neck.

"What should we do in the meantime?" Serena asked as Naomi blew a small gust of wind into the sails, and we sped off to the east, navigating by the same red star sailors used.

"This," Chloe said, curling up next to Naomi for warmth. "Enjoy the night sky while it lasts. It may be cold, but we're together, and in the morning the sun will burn us alive. Oh, and no one stick their fingers in the water. There's enough of Sebastian's blood around us to attract sharks, and the last thing we want is missing extremities."

Sebastian coughed.

"*More* missing extremities," she clarified.

Everyone was too tired to argue. Chloe and Naomi curled up together, both snoring lightly. Serena was next, falling asleep with her head on my shoulder. I tried to join them in a world where pain and discomfort didn't exist . . . but sleep never found me. As if reality wanted me to experience every moment of this pain. So I was forced to focus on other things. Like continuing to improve myself and my magical abilities.

"Sebastian," I whispered. "Are you awake?"

"No," he shot back.

"Teach me what you know about Weaving."

The High Noble rolled over with his eyes wide-open. "Oh, how the waltz has changed. I won't be as easy a teacher as your others were. You'll need to know how we noble rejects fought for our survival." He grinned. "I'm going to make you beg for mercy."

NEW MAGIC,
NEW MICHAEL

The girls were exhausted, so when Sebastian and I began Weaving training, neither of them heard me scream, or felt the boat rock when he stabbed me in the side with a piece of pumice. It was only a flesh wound and would heal in a few days at most. But when he pushed me into the water, I began to wonder if this was just an elaborate ploy to feed me to the sharks.

"This seems unnecessary," I said, treading water. "Didn't Chloe say blood in the water would attract sharks?"

"That's the point," Sebastian stated. "Your mind has to fear death while your body fights for survival. With Fabrications, you're searching for abnormalities in your body. With Weaving, we're trying to force your body to bend the world around it to its will. That means sink-or-swim situations."

My body was painfully numb and I shivered if I stopped moving for even a moment. Streaks of dark water dripped from me with every stroke I took to keep my head above the water.

"Begin the Fabrication process," Sebastian ordered. "Normally we wouldn't have to do this, but your specialization is rare, and I doubt you'll find anything you can manipulate in nature."

I muttered a string of curses as I gathered the warmth in my chest, and lost it almost immediately as something brushed against my calf and made me lunge for the boat. I shouted as Sebastian kicked at my fingers and pushed me back into the water.

"Don't be such a coward!" he hissed. "It was probably just an eel. If it were a shark, you'd be underwater and full of holes by now."

Sebastian was brave for a man not in the water. Especially since I could *feel* something moving around me. Something big. Something patient. A true predator. And as someone who had only just recently grown confident enough to swim in the water . . . I was certain this wasn't a slimy eel or a common red fish waiting for an opportunity to strike. Hopefully, the seabed wasn't too far down, since I had a sinking feeling I might be seeing it soon.

Once I had reclaimed the warmth in my chest, I said, "I got it back. What now?"

"First, focus on the pain. Know it from the inside out. Every nick and cut and how your body responds to it."

I focused on the cut in my side. It was a horizontal slash that went across my side just under my chest. It was jagged and twisty and shallow. My head was pounding, the skin under my nails felt raw and sore, and the spaces between my toes were sweaty and blistering.

"Got it? Good. Now twist that pain into something tangible in your head like armor or a sword," Sebastian began. "Imagine it covering your body or being held in your hand. Then *will* it into existence using that pain. Make it real. Think of it like the fire that shapes metal."

It couldn't be that easy . . . could it? I sent the warmth to my hands until it felt hot enough to boil the water around me, and then let that warmth extend from my palm, slowly shifting into a wide flat disc like a porcelain plate. Oddly enough, the wrinkles in my fingers disappeared as if I wasn't in the water and nothing felt . . . wet anymore. Just tepid. I tried to move the warmth down to the soles of my feet and make the circular plates under them . . . and I rose up until I was standing on two invisible platforms on top of the water. Blood and water dripped down to the sea below as the cold wind blew against my goose-bumped skin.

"What's going on?" I muttered, moving my feet slightly. The plates were attached to my feet and followed me wherever I went. "How can I be doing this? This is Weaving?"

Sebastian nodded. "Weaving allows you to manipulate your specialization. With enough practice, and enough pain, you can create and control anything."

"Is there a ratio of pain to ability?"

"Nothing beyond a lot of pain equals a lot of power. A jammed finger lets me move a stone statue for a bit, but a broken finger lets me control one for a whole day. Oh, and if you fall asleep, all your Weaving abilities will cancel out."

"Delightful," I muttered. I held out my empty palm, focusing on the pain and imagining a dagger in it. "C'mon, dagger. Show up and—"

Two tentacles grabbed my ankles, yanked me down and onto my face, and then dragged me under. The shock expelled all my breath in a torrent of bubbles. I couldn't make out whatever was dragging me down except for a blur of grey and purple in the sides of my vision. But it didn't matter what it was, so long as I got away from it. Everything was cold and splintery, but I focused on the warmth in my chest, moving it back to my hand. I focused on holding a curved dagger until I felt something hard in my hand, and slashed at the tentacles, hoping it would be enough to cut off the whatever-this-fucking-thing-was's connection with my ankles.

To my surprise—and horror—the dagger went through the tentacles without severing them. But the bluish-purple tentacles grew grey and lifeless as if all the blood had stopped flowing through them. Its hold on me grew limp and I shot upward as it continued to go deeper and deeper into the ocean without noticing I was free.

I frog-kicked back up to safety, throat burning with pain. The breath when I broke the surface didn't feel as good as it had in the past. Maybe I was getting too used to drowning for my body to feel relief at not any-more. Symon was leaning over the edge of the makeshift boat with an eyebrow arched.

"Kind of thought you wouldn't come back up," he said softly. "You're really hard to kill, aren't you?"

I pulled myself up and into the boat. None of the others had woken up and were still snoring peacefully. If they could sleep through this, I doubted anything short of a natural disaster would wake them. "What would you have told them?"

Sebastian shrugged. "No idea."

I drew my knees to my chest and hugged myself tightly to ease some of the chill. "Do you really hate me so much that you would laugh at my death? I know I wasn't the best friend for Dawn for a long time but . . . she forgave me, so why can't you? Or do you hate me because of my rela-tion to Serena?"

Sebastian laughed in response. "Hate you? I couldn't care less about you or your Queen, Michael. You've been a means to an end for me ever since I got this." He tapped Regal Company's brand on his neck. "I want my freedom, for the world to know my name, and never to bow to an-other man. Nothing less will make me happy."

"Freedom calls to us like a primal urge we can't suppress," I mused. "It's not wrong to crave it when we don't have it, but . . . freedom is noth-ing if you're alone. You can be a monster if you want to be one, Sebastian. But it won't make the quiet moments any less painful . . . nor will it calm the doubting voices in your head. Freedom won't bring you peace just as power won't bring you love."

"Whatever." Sebastian turned away from me. "Good night, Michael. May we see morning together."

His childishness reminded me of myself months ago. All he had was a goal with no direction and a hatred he hadn't let go of yet. If he didn't move on, it would consume him. But rather than sleep like the rest of my companions, I closed my eyes and tried to reach the never-ending halls in my mind to just get a little more time. To think and consider my next move. To come up with a way to defy fate. But dawn came sooner than later, and seagulls broke my focus and brought me one step closer to the day of destiny where I could be forced to die, kill, or watch Tenere shatter above.

When it happened . . . would I choose to embrace the apocalyptic love Angelo and Dark had? And would the world break because of me?

FRACTURED TRUTHS

As we got closer to the island, its weird features slowly came into view. The sand on the beach was black and every trace of habitation was overgrown with weeds, flowers, and tropical plants. A once-elaborate dock had rotted away, leaving only a few planks of wood to show it had ever been there, and the beach was covered in broken wood, rusted cannonballs, and knickknacks that had no doubt once held sentimental value before being claimed by the sea. When the waves started to pick up, Serena held my hand as we rode them in to the shore.

Naomi, Sebastian—who held the cat—and Chloe had swum to the beach and were trying to dry off as best they could without stripping down. They had streaks of sand on the napes of their neck, down their arms, and covering their feet. It clung to them like wet paper, and as we made our way to their side, I was already growing annoyed by the very idea of spending anything more than a fleeting moment on a beach. All this damn sand was finding its way into crevices of my body that hadn't seen the sun in a decade.

"Anyone have any idea where we've washed up?" Serena asked. She had done the smart thing and taken off her shoes. "Besides being somewhere in the Sleeping Cities."

Chloe flicked specks of sand off her eye patch before putting it back on. "It's some no-name village. Best bet is to head inland. If we're going to find anyone . . . it'll be there."

"Why is this place called the Sleeping Cities anyway?" I asked. "I think I slept through most of my Ehamian history lessons."

"You wouldn't have learned about it as a kid," Chloe said, leading the way up the beach. "It was only named the Sleeping Cities . . . a little over twenty years ago? Most of the initial information was speculative and proven wrong in the decade that followed. And no self-respecting Archivist teaches rumors."

I chuckled, wondering if Symon would agree. "What was it known as before?"

"Torda, the City of Orphans."

My heart skipped a beat, and Sebastian and Naomi nearly fell back in surprise. But it was Sebastian who spoke first. "Torda? This was known as Torda? Are you positive?"

Chloe nodded slowly. "Positive."

I put my hands behind my head, digging my nails into my scalp. "I . . . I . . . What happened here? I need to know."

"Why?" Naomi asked. "What's so special about this place?"

"I think my friend Omari was born here. His last name is Torda. He once told me that he had his own legacy to live up to, but . . . but I never asked what it was. I should have helped him." I wanted to scream so much, it made my throat ache. "Please. Tell me what happened."

"It'll be better if you see for yourself," Chloe said.

We made our way further into the island and away from the monstrosity of a beach, the others drying out as we walked. The paths that had once led inland were overgrown with long, floppy green plants and bamboo. Towering trees shaded us and Chloe hacked through whatever flora blocked our path with a handcrafted machete Sebastian had created from one of the ship's sharper edges. The air was wet, we heard strange bird sounds, and we were all sweating so much, it was as if we were still in the water.

After Chloe cut through a particularly obnoxious plant, we saw Torda proper. Or what remained of it. Every building was covered in a strange orange moss, a muddy river ran through the middle of it, and fireflies flew lazily. There were skeletal remains everywhere, some more decayed and broken-down than others. The stench of dead bodies had long since faded away, replaced by a sweetness from rotten tropical fruits. It was a long-forgotten graveyard.

"How does something like this happen?" I muttered, staring at a discarded toy. It was a doll, its hair intricately braided . . . obviously once cared for, but its face had been burned beyond recognition. I saw small bones nearby and the implication made my stomach churn.

"The Hollow government was told that the gas from a nearby volcano eruption poisoned the entire island," Chloe said as she, Naomi, and Sebastian carefully moved bones out of the main pathway and into neat piles. Serena stuck to my side like a wet cat seeking warmth. "No one believed it, but the Gunpowder War had just ended and the King and Queen didn't have the energy or the ability to look into it further."

"I thought the point of rulers was to protect people," Serena said through gritted teeth. "How could they let this happen? How could they let this go unanswered?"

"Because Torda's allegiances were weird. They were an independent colony, like most of the islands in Eham, but had always been closer to the Gold Coast than others. If Hollow had tried to intervene, both Eham and the Palmers would have responded. And Hollow didn't have the resources to do anything but lick its wounds after the Gunpowder War." A hesitation. "We were lucky to survive."

"This is bullshit!" Serena screamed. "Everyone let this destruction go unpunished because they liked the status quo? That's corruption at its finest." No one responded, so she continued, "Is the real reason known? Or are the secrets lost to everyone but its destroyers?"

"If there's any trace of it . . . it's here."

Serena clenched her fists and stormed into a building with a rusted sign that read: *A sanctuary for all people.* I debated following but remained with Naomi and Chloe. Both had taken seats on a fallen tree trunk that had crushed a house in two. Sebastian poked at the various limp flora with a stick and paid none of us attention.

"She'll calm down," Naomi said, seeing my and Chloe's faces. "She's going through a lot. Before this, she had a lifetime to figure out what kind of queen she wanted to be. Right now, she's had . . . what? A week? Two? Every injustice she sees seems like the end of the world."

"But shouldn't it?" I asked. "We've all seen terrible things happen in Hollow. We saw questionable rebels hanged by a tyrannical private military force daily. We saw rebels cut down civilians in the street to sow chaos. We've seen people have their hearts torn out. And yet we continue as if it's normal. Maybe Hollow needs a queen that hasn't been jaded."

"A jaded heart will keep her alive. Taking everything so personally will only cause her pain. We need a queen who is compassionate yet practical."

"I don't know." I kicked a branch into the jungle. "We may not be able to solve every problem, but maybe we can solve this one. Besides, *I* need to find answers. Omari doesn't deserve to bear this weight alone."

Chloe and Naomi started collecting bones, arranging them off to the side with reverence. I went into a random building, expecting nothing, but hoping for a clue as to what had happened. I searched through the destruction without finding anything helpful. The official story was easy to disprove. There was too much needless violence and destruction for this to have been gas. The old clothes thrown across floors were threadbare and moldy, kitchen utensils were rusted or falling apart or covered in dried blood, and family paintings were torn in half. Whatever had happened here was personal.

When I couldn't search any longer, I made my way through the abandoned town toward the largest building still standing. If growing up in Hollow had taught me anything, it was that the biggest building usually held the most important people or things. Humanity had never learned to be subtle. And I doubted Torda had been different before it became the Sleeping City.

It was clear upon entering that this building had once been the central hub of the city. There were rooms filled with dozens of beds, a kitchen that could rival Hollow Castle's, and a dining hall bigger than any single room I had ever been in before. The hallways had once been lined with pictures, but only the frames remained. There were hundreds of small bones, so many that I had to stop looking at the floor whenever I heard something snap beneath my feet.

I was still exploring when Serena found me, carrying a heavy leather-bound book. "Michael, I think I found something."

She put the book down on one of the tables that were still usable, and I flipped it open to a random page. Every page that wasn't torn out had the same sentence scrawled over everything else in jagged, bold lettering obscuring everything below it: *I'll erase you. I'll erase you. I'll erase you.*

"Well," I said, rubbing my brow. "This confirms this wasn't an accident."

"But gives us absolutely no specifics." Serena slammed a fist against the table. "How can an entire city be erased like this?"

"They must've been persistent." An unsettling thought flashed through my head, and I dismissed it. Angelo was from the Gold Coast, but what reason would he have to destroy Torda? His hatred was aimed at the High Nobles. "I don't think there's anything here that can help us figure out what happened. Everything was too thoroughly destroyed." I closed the book. "My friend Omari probably has the answers we want. But he's in Hollow."

"How'd he end up in Hollow? Did he ever tell you?"

"Not really," I muttered. "I never asked him . . . and at the time I thought that was for the best. Everyone who got close to me . . . they left. So, I kept him at arm's length while I called him family." I couldn't help but laugh. "I'm kind of pathetic, aren't—"

Serena hugged me, until my body relaxed in her arms. "If you knew him well enough to call him family, then you did know something about him. You're not the kind of person to use that word lightly. So, think. Is there something you're forgetting?"

My mind was blank, preoccupied with her fingers gently twirling my hair, so all my words came out unfiltered. "He was a former Skeleton. He bought his freedom and came to Hollow with his adoptive brother."

"How old is he?"

"Maybe a year or two older than us."

"So, he was old enough to have been in the womb when Torda was destroyed?"

"Yes," I said without hesitation. "Which means his mother survived whatever happened here. And I don't see how people who could do *this* would willingly leave a loose end."

"Even the greatest strategist can make a mistake . . . and they must have if Omari lived." She stopped running her fingers through my hair and rubbed my back instead. "Let's think about it from a different angle. Everything you've said about Hollow makes me think that even ten years ago, people could see how far it had fallen. If Omari was from here and bought his freedom, why would he go there?"

"I . . . I don't know. Why would he go to Hollow?"

"Maybe it was to—"

"Michael! Serena! Get out here!"

We ran out as fast as we could and saw Chloe, Sebastian, and Naomi staring through the canopy of treetops at the sky. All were awestruck, and Chloe silently pointed upward. There was a solar eclipse happening, an orange ring and flare around a perfect black dot in a sea of dark blue.

"We knew it was coming," I said. "So it started early. The watchers must've got the date wrong . . ."

The solar eclipse and the dark sky around it were in a small fracture, like a spidery crack that had spread and widened after someone tried to open it. Beyond the boundary, the sky was the same as it always was in the daytime. Bright blue, thick long clouds lazily traveling across it, and light from the sun illuminating everything. But whenever something got close to the fracture in the sky—bird, cloud, even light—it was sucked in, erased from existence in half a blink.

"There's a crack in the sky," Serena muttered. "Why is the sky broken?"

"Our world seems so desperate to crack and crumble, so eager to get rid of us for the damage we've done to it," Naomi whispered. "This must be a wound from one of the Wolven King's battles," she added, uncertain but desperate for any reason that might make sense. "What else could have caused this?"

"One man could've," I answered. "Angelo Shade."

"But what is this?" Chloe asked. "Another shattering like Celona?"

"It's a memory," I said, head pounding and words flowing out of my mouth without thought. As if they were another's. "Of what the sky looked like when this scar was created." I felt a splintery pain, filling my ears and throat like my stomach was about to toss up whatever was inside it. Something was *wrong* with me. More so than normal. "It's a reminder that we are mortal. Nothing more than temporary visitors to a world that will outlive us."

Someone gripped my shoulder. "My love, are you well?"

I turned to face Serena. To tell her that I was fine. That the pain was only temporary. But it was not her freckled face and auburn hair and green eyes that greeted me, but a woman with black hair and brown eyes. Katherine Naverre, Angelo's deceased wife. As young as she had been when I saw her in Dark's childhood memories. Chloe and Naomi were gone as well, replaced by a younger version of Papa Noble.

"Michael, Michael, Michael," someone said. Tidy, clean, and always presentable in his Scales uniform . . . Angelo Shade smiled ear to ear. "So you finally triggered that memory I gave you back in Hollow. I'm *so* proud of you."

"Can you be any more condescending?" I sneered.

"Of course, but let's make this quick. Your mind is not a hospitable place." Angelo grew serious and then pointed toward the crack in the sky. "I did this. This was an early attempt at opening one of the lockless doors." He chuckled. "Which I assume you know about by now or else you are *much* farther behind than you should be."

"Why are you telling me this?"

"Because," my former foster father said, "the traps have to be set or you'll never ensnare yourself." He stuck his hands in his jacket pockets. "The lockless doors can only be opened during a solar eclipse."

I hesitated. "And if you can't open it . . . you'll just shatter Tenere and open it that way?"

Angelo nodded. "You see? Your death is inevitable. A leaf changing colors on the branch, waiting to fall and be crushed."

"I can run," I stated. "If you can't find me—"

"I only have to find Serena," Angelo interrupted. "Because you're a fool for love. A martyr. You'll die to save her life. Just as I would for Katherine and Dark would for Zahra." He smiled softly at me. Too tenderly for me to look at it directly. "It's over, Michael. The ending has already been written. Has been since you fell for a young girl with auburn hair. If only you hadn't, maybe this story would be different." Angelo and the others began to fade away. "Goodbye, Michael. When we meet again . . . I can't wait to see which of us will be the hero, the villain, and the fool left out in the cold."

I closed my eyes, tilted my head upward, and counted my breaths. Every exhale was a statement that I was here. That I had lived. That I deserved to be remembered. But Angelo was right. Unless something miraculous happened . . . love would be the death of me.

29

PRIDEFUL

The sun was setting, filling the jungle with an orange light, as Chloe and Naomi were coaxing a small fire into a raging inferno. We had all taken off our boots and set them by the fire to dry. Fish impaled on sticks were roasting on the open fire. I sat down next to Naomi. That conversation with Angelo had left me exhausted . . . and the interrogation from everyone about it had left me bruised and broken. How could I tell them my death was guaranteed? How could I tell the woman I loved that she would kill me? How could I do anything but hide the truth? Only the information about the solar eclipse saved me, and even that felt bought and paid for in blood.

"Do you think we'll ever know what truly happened here?" Naomi asked, staring at the fire. Serena and Chloe were having a strained, back-of-the-neck-rubbing conversation next to us. "How so many died? And for what?"

I took a split fish and held it over the fire, turning it slowly. The fire was so hot that the fish quickly browned and flaked. "Could've been Skeleton Coast slavers."

"You think they would come this far?"

"Omari was a former Skeleton." I checked my fish and decided it needed a little longer to cook. "If he was born here, he had to get there somehow."

Naomi began to peel her steaming fish apart with her fingers. "Some days I feel bad for our parents." She paused to blow on the meat. "Can you imagine trying to protect a child in this fucked-up world? I can barely keep myself sober most days."

"I don't know," I said. "You seemed to get clean from Blackberries easily enough."

"Only because they're rarer than heroes in Hollow nowadays." She popped some meat into her mouth and said as she chewed, "Thankfully for me . . . I like drinking more and I was barely a dimmer when I stopped taking Blackberries. I can only imagine what the East Side is like with all those dragon blood–consuming lunatics around."

I took my nearly blackened red fish off the fire, thinking of Trey. He had been able to bring some normality to the Rainbow District by controlling the tweeker population. But without Blackberries to sedate them . . . the East Side was likely chaos. But I had faith in him. If anyone could do the impossible, and bring real change to the city, it was him.

"Maybe my mother will give me an update in her next letter. I am curious what's going on in Hollow without us."

"No doubt my ex is terrorizing everyone with Serena out of the city."

"Can you really call him your ex? That seems too polite for someone who shot you in the stomach."

"What else am I supposed to call him? That's what he was, and I did my part." She lowered the fish, suddenly looking disgusted. "All for a crown I don't even want anymore."

"We were all young and stupid once. At least you learned from your mistakes."

Naomi glared at me and I stuffed my face with the fish, periodically spitting out bones. "Since when have you grown past that stage? You may not be a total prick anymore, but I'd hesitate to call you wise just yet."

I smiled and nudged her playfully with my shoulder. She bumped me in return and nearly knocked me off the stump I was sitting on. We finished our fish in silence, wondering if things would've been different if I had grown up somewhere else. Or whether I'd be a different shade of fucked-up.

No matter where I went, it was always the same story of children acting like adults. At most they had a few years to laugh and live without worry, but then the world would force them to grow up or die. When all this was over—Angelo dead, Serena safe, Hollow at peace—I hoped children could be children again. It was a simple thing, but I'd had my childhood stolen from me, and I wanted to spare others the same thing. Hopefully, my children . . . no, I wouldn't sire any children. Not with the unwavering hunter coming for me. I quietly wiped away tears at the thought.

"Queen this, Queen that! How about you treat me like a human being rather than an instrument to wear the crown you care about so much?" Serena screamed at Chloe, silencing all the conversation around us. She was on her feet, hands clenched tightly and veins bulging in her forehead, while Chloe sat on a fallen log, staring straight ahead.

"You have a duty to the citizens of Hollow," Chloe said, emotionless. "I am sorry you were dealt a terrible hand, but there's no excuse for throwing a tantrum when I am trying to catch you up on important things."

"Every conversation with you is a lesson. We never discuss the scenery or feelings or music . . . just responsibilities, power structures, and which dead assholes I need to be thankful came before me! I am a person! Not a crown!"

Chloe rose to look her in the eyes. "You are Queen Serena Hollow, and whether you like it or not . . . you *are* the crown. Every action you take is a statement on the world stage. Every person you slight risks starting a war. The sooner you accept this life, the sooner you can come to terms with what it will be like if your memories do not return."

"You told me I would have a choice if my memories don't return," Serena said through gritted teeth. "If I wanted to walk away from the throne . . . would you let me?"

"No," Chloe said without hesitation. "Without you, Hollow will fall, and I cannot let that happen . . . or every sacrifice that has been made for our country in a millennium will be in vain. One spoiled selfish woman will not—"

Serena slapped her across the cheek. Chloe looked dumbstruck as she gently touched the reddening mark.

"Fuck your country," Serena said slowly, clearly. "In all your hurry and worry to make me a good queen . . . when did you give me a reason to call Hollow home? Why would I sacrifice my life for a place I've never seen or been to?"

"You grew up in Hollow," Chloe whispered. "I . . . I . . . I just—"

"I may have grown up in Hollow, but I was reborn on the sea." Serena gestured to everything around us. "But I do have to thank you for one thing . . . I'd rather die here than ever set foot in Hollow again."

"Serena," I said, "maybe—"

She swatted me away, her glare without compassion or sympathy, burning with rage. "Don't touch me."

"I . . . I'm sorry."

"I'm going for a walk. None of you follow me." She took a deep breath and turned away. "I need to think."

"It could be dangerous out there," I said as she walked away.

Leaves fluttered down and fruit smashed into the ground around us, an invisible force pressing everything down. Serena was using her Force Fabrications on us. It wasn't enough to force us to our knees, only be aware of its imposing presence.

"I can take care of myself."

The Forgotten Queen of Hollow wandered into the darkness, disappearing as the fire that had been built so high and fierce slowly lost some of its strength. The four of us were left staring at the darkness, wondering if she would return. "Well, you two really fucked that one up, eh?" Naomi said.

Chloe and I were fuming separately—me kicking at nothing while lightning began to spark off her body. I was the one who broke the si-

THE VOYAGE OF THE FORGOTTEN 335

lence, angry, and said the last thing I should have. "Maybe she doesn't have to be queen."

"Michael," Chloe growled. "Don't finish that thought."

"Why not?" I turned to her. "Serena suffered enough *before* she became a Forgotten. Maybe this is our chance to let her be at peace. To finally find her own path."

"And let Adreann take the throne?" Naomi asked. "Are you insane?"

I glared at Chloe. "No, someone else could be queen."

"What are you—"

"Naomi. Sebastian," Chloe interrupted. "Leave us." And when Naomi didn't, she added, "Please."

Naomi did so hesitantly, sulking away. Sebastian put his arm around her shoulder and left with a laugh and whisper about nobodies sticking together. When they were out of earshot, Chloe said, "Do you really want to go down this path again?"

"Yes. Why can't you take the throne? You're dutiful and wise and— most importantly—not a Forgotten. Take it. We'll all support you."

Chloe picked up a stray twig from the floor and then snapped it in half. "Thanks for making it sound *so* easy. Do you even understand what you're asking of me? I'm a worthless bastard who only ever said 'Sorry' and 'Excuse me' and 'Thank you' to their father. I'm not fit to be queen."

"Do you think any of us are fit to be anything other than fuckups?" I asked. "Look at me. Look at Naomi. Look at Serena before she became a Forgotten. Nothing ever came easy to us, but we've done our best because that's all any of us can do."

"You're asking me to be the Queen of Hollow," Chloe said. "The 'best someone can do' led my father to put a gun under his chin and pull the trigger rather than live another day with the guilt and stress of ruling a country." Another twig, another snap. "Are you so desperate to save Serena that you'd sacrifice me to do it?"

"I would burn the world down to protect Serena," I admitted. "But I'm not trying to sacrifice you to the stone throne. I'm asking you to consider it because our country is broken and . . ." I kicked at the ground and cursed. ". . . and I don't think the Kingman and Hollow families are ever going to make things better."

Chloe stared at me. "What did you say?"

"I think it's time the Kingman and Hollow families stepped away from the world stage. For the greater good. Maybe we were needed in the past, but not anymore. It's time for others to step up. It can't just be us trying to do good anymore."

"Wanderer have mercy," Chloe muttered. She rubbed the fragment of the stick in her hand as if she were trying to start a fire with it. "Do you realize what you just said?"

"I'm well aware."

"What changed? I never thought you, of all people, would utter those words."

I told her the quick version of what I had learned in Idris's memories. She listened raptly and by the end only had one question: "So if you're willing to walk away from your legacy, why force one on me that I've never wanted?"

And just like that . . . our conversation was over. I had no justification, and it was selfish of me to keep trying. She could choose her own path. Whatever that was.

We waited at the bonfire all night for Serena to return. Sebastian went to sleep first, not wanting to appear a hypocrite in caring about someone he had tried to kill weeks ago. Naomi sat with me for a bit, until she went to comfort Chloe, who spoke to me only once—asking whether I had seen Serena—and then lay down. We all heard her sob herself to sleep.

I debated going out to search for Serena, when a branch snapped and I jumped to my feet. "Serena?"

No response. Just faint snoring and the tossing and turning of the others fighting heroic battles in their sleep.

"Serena," I said calmly. "Do you want to talk?"

Only it wasn't Serena, it was Sirash. The skin on his face was discolored from the burns he had suffered from the Hollow Educator, his green eyes flaked with gold were prominent, and he held a metal lantern in his hands. But as he stepped into a pocket of moonlight, I saw that the Skeleton tattoos on his hand were gone—replaced by a bony hand instead. All the flesh had melted away. He was a hybrid between a Skeleton and a human. Was it just his hand? Or had more of his body turned to bone?

"Sirash? What are you . . ." I stared at the metal-frame lantern and then the silver necklace around his neck. Memories of Mocking Bird returned to me. "You're not—"

"I am," Sirash interrupted. "Wrath, to be specific. The castle educator was the previous Waylayer to hold that title." He brushed his hands over his side as if reaching for a pistol. "You know how it is—you keep what you conquer."

"How did you get here?"

He shrugged. "Doesn't matter. Only that I am."

"Are you here for me?"

Sirash nodded. "It's time we settled some old arguments. Come with me."

"And if I don't?"

Snakes seemed to slither toward me, but as I rubbed my eyes and blinked rapidly to make sure I was seeing things right . . . I realized they were the roots of trees. Liam, one of the four noble siblings of Regal Company and a Wood Weaver, emerged from the darkness to stand in the moonlight next to Sirash, a dagger pressed against his side. The trees moved around him.

"If you move a muscle or attempt to fight back, I will stab myself with this dagger and then use my Weaving to bring down all the nearby trees before you can nullify me," Liam said in a monotone. "If you want your friends to live, you will come with us."

"What's to stop me from beating your ass once we're a safe distance from them?" I asked, hands still at my sides. My thumb was brushing against the holster of my revolver. I only had one bullet. I should have used it on him when I had the chance.

Liam knocked his free hand against his crotch with a metal clonk. "I came prepared."

"Really?"

"Really," he said. "I won't underestimate you again. My father made sure of that."

I hesitated, glancing toward Naomi, Sebastian, and Chloe. Dawn was hours away, it could be a while before anyone looked for me. If I went with him, I might be on my own. But if I was going to die in twenty days anyway . . . why not take a risk or two while I still drew breath?

"Let's talk."

ON TRAMPLED PATHS

Once we were out of the clearing, the darkness overwhelmed us. I struggled to walk in a straight line without tripping over my feet, made worse
as so much littered the ground. Liam kept a hand tight around my shoulder as he guided me forward, digging his uncut nails into my flesh. I
would never be able to find my way back. Wherever we were going . . . I
would have to hope the others found our trail in the morning.

"So, what's the plan here?" I said as I ducked under a low-hanging
branch. "I know I'm probably Regal and Orbis Company's biggest walking curse right now, but I doubt you'll kill me until Serena is recovered."

"You're correct in that assumption."

"Are you going to torture me?" I asked. "Because the Ravens were
pretty good at it, and I didn't break then. You'd have to do a lot worse
than threaten my toenails, my teeth, or my tongue to get anything out of
me about Serena."

"We're aware," Sirash said. "That's why I'm here. To break you."

I wrenched free of Liam's grip to face Sirash. "Why are you doing this, Sirash? I can understand you taking a shot or stab at me, but not hurting those I love. Focus your revenge on me. No one else."

"You have no right to make demands." Sirash unsheathed a slender knife and used it to raise my chin so the tip was parallel with the soft part of my throat. "You made me this monster. I could've walked away from all this hate if you hadn't forced me to go to the castle with you that night. I wouldn't have killed Wrath and inherited his position. So shut up and take the consequences."

"I may be an asshole, but at least I admit it. Grow up, Sirash. Stop blaming others for your problems. No one forced you to drive a knife into the castle educator's throat."

Sirash slammed me against a nearby tree. I didn't even bother fighting back, staring into his eyes instead. "Shut up."

"Why?" I asked, holding his gaze. "Scared that I'm right?"

"I'll—"

Liam separated us, forced us to the ground, and then clamped his hands over our mouths. We both struggled to free ourselves, but he nudged his head toward something, and we stared as deformed creatures crept toward us. They weren't Mercenaries, and just the sight of them made me want to scream to warn my friends.

Their clothes were minimal, loose, and threadbare, exposing all the rough, oozing stitches around their major ligaments. Their birdlike noses were covered in warts, their hair was thinning and patchy, and none of their skin was a single shade. Some had the arms of a man who had spent a lifetime on the Gold Coast or in Eham combined with the fair coloring of a winter man from the Warring States. It was as if they were an amalgamation of body parts scavenged over a lifetime, and they stalked through the jungle like creatures who had mastered hunting in the night. They snuck past us as we held our breath, and only when they were completely out of sight and earshot did Liam yank us up.

"Those were Skeleton Coast slavers," Sirash whispered unprompted. "I wouldn't mistake them for anything."

"We have to warn my friends," I said. "They were headed right for them."

"We're not babysitters," Liam countered. "If you want to be a hero, you should have thought of that before you decided to come with us."

"I won't walk away from them!" I turned to Sirash. "Can you just walk away? Do you really want to let others suffer for what you did, when we could save their lives?"

Sirash was silent, twisting his bony hand to admire all the angles. "You know nothing about what it was like to be a Skeleton."

"You're right, I don't." I got to my feet. "I don't know why your hand is made of bones instead of flesh, nor do I know what being a Skeleton entails beyond identifying as former slaves and your bone tattoos. But the details are unimportant . . . I won't let others enter a life of pain if I could've stopped it."

Branches twisted toward my neck as if preparing to hang me. "Good thing what you want doesn't matter," Liam said, though Sirash wouldn't meet my eyes anymore. "You made a deal, Michael. You can fear the monster men all you want, but if you try to run . . . I'll destroy everything on this island."

I took a deep breath, played with my father's ring, and said, "Then let's make a new deal."

"A new deal?"

"I have something you want. Help me save my friends and whatever it is—it's yours."

Liam chuckled. "You're a terrible negotiator, Michael. Usually someone defines the terms before making an offer. What if I want your life? Would you give me—"

"If you want it"—I stepped toward him—"come and get it. I'm right here. I already beat you once, are you that desperate for a rematch?"

Liam didn't back down. Not that I expected the Mercenary to. We were all prideful and stubborn people. But rather than let this devolve into a fight, he smiled widely. "Fine, Michael. Let's go protect your friends. And in return, you'll come with us willingly and help me . . . acquire something nearby."

"'Acquire something'?"

"Yes. You'll see. I don't want to ruin the surprise. Now let's go play hero."

We chased after the slavers. It was hard to traverse the jungle in the dark, but we caught up to the monster men as quickly as we could, catching them lingering just outside the light of the dying campfire. They were pointing toward the treetops, whispering to one another in a language I was unfamiliar with. I assumed it was Skelial.

"How should we handle this?" I asked. "Is there magic on the Skeleton Coast? Could they be magic users?"

Neither Sirash nor Liam answered my question. My continued ignorance of the greater world seemed to be one thing all my enemies liked about me.

Instead, Sirash said, "Go in quick and brutally. Don't assume they're dead unless their necks are broken, hearts are torn out, and heads are mush. I've seen them break a neck before and then continue as if nothing happened."

"Are they as pain resilient as tweekers?"

Liam shook his head. "We're almost positive they feel pain but don't care about it. Tweekers don't feel it. Two completely different things."

"Understood. So, who wants to—"

Sirash did. My former friend scampered up a tree, disappeared in the leafy madness, and then appeared above the Skeleton Coast slavers. He dropped on them, impaling one of them in the head with his dagger as he landed, donkey-kicking another, and then jamming his bone hand into the face of the third. Liam cursed, vaulted over a broken tree, and joined the fray. He scratched at the back of his hand hard enough to draw blood. The pain let him manipulate a nearby tree root to grow massively, tripping and entangling the monster men as they tried to recover from Sirash's surprise attack.

The one with the dagger through his head yanked it out nonchalantly and then began to wave it at Sirash, who ducked and weaved around his attacker's blows, then eventually twisted his arm behind his back to reclaim his dagger and stab the monster man repeatedly until he could be mistaken for a well-used archery target. His target slumped to the ground, mumbling nonsense as blood filled his mouth.

I leapt to tackle the monster man who was quickest to get up. We wrestled, both taking turns with our backs to the ground as Liam impaled the third monster man with a thousand branches. It died in midair, as punched with holes as its companion. The remaining one realized it was outnumbered, punching me in the face with a fist that felt more metal than flesh, and tried to run away but tripped over the roots before it could get anywhere. Sirash flung himself onto it, choking it to death with his hands. And then, when it stopped moving, he drove his dagger into its head, heart, eyes, and groin to make sure it stayed down.

I was panting as Liam helped me to my feet. Sirash was on his feet soon after me, breathing shallowly as well but keeping his eyes focused on the body at his feet.

"Well," Liam said as he wiped his bloody hands onto his pants, "that was easier than I thought it would be."

"We got lucky," Sirash said. "These were all raw recruits. We wouldn't have been able to beat those of higher ranks."

"Skeleton Coast slavers have ranks?" I asked.

Sirash glared at me. "Yes. Not that you would care. You never once bothered to ask me anything about myself."

"I apologized for being an asshole back in Hollow." I rubbed the back of my neck. "How long am I going to be critiqued for things I regret? What can I do but apologize and move forward? Will I always be a selfish prick in your mind?"

"Like—"

"Hey," Liam interrupted. There were torches flickering in the darkness. "People are coming to investigate. We should go. Unless Michael wants to make a scene."

I put my hands up. "I'm coming willingly. I've done everything I could here."

We marched through the jungle with an increased pace, Liam either trusting me not to run or not having the time to care. The sun was beginning to emerge from its slumber, and it was clear Liam wanted to be gone before it was risen.

I stumbled through a prickly bush and onto still-warm sand, slipping and landing face-first on it. I spat sand out and looked up. We were on a beach, a ship anchored just offshore in front of me. It wasn't Regal Company's massive behemoth that I had seen in the harbor of Vargo but a small two-masted frigate.

"Did Daddy not trust you with the big toys after letting me escape?" Liam hauled me to my feet and yanked my head back from the roots of my hair as his sister, Ciara, slithered over to us, trailing a net behind her. Guess he had to make a show of force in front of her. Wouldn't want his pride to be wounded further. "I guess he made you bring your sister too. Does he not trust you on your own anymore?"

"No," Ciara said. "He doesn't. But thankfully for him you're a nuisance, not a world-breaking threat."

"Yet."

"Ever," Liam said as he kicked me over. The sand against my face was worse than the pain from his hit, and he held my hands behind my back to keep me still. "Ciara, how do you want to do this?"

"Like this." She yanked the net forward so it was right in front of my face. I was immediately overwhelmed with the pungent and distinct smell of sulfur. Then, as I tried to squirm away from Liam, I saw what their surprise was.

Bombs. They had brought bombs. And judging by their smiles, I was about to become the world's most dangerous piece of bait. There was nothing I could do as they stuck the bombs to my skin with a sticky clear liquid. When they ran out of bare skin, they tied more around my biceps, ankles, neck, and chest. By the time they were done, I was lying perfectly still on the sand, too scared of setting them off to move.

Ciara helped me to my feet, and, for once, I accepted her aid without fighting.

"If you think I'm walking into the jungle with these strapped to my chest, then you have another—"

"That's not the plan," she interrupted, taking my revolver from me. "We're going to do something much more . . . direct."

Ciara turned to the jungle and shouted, "Serena! We have Michael here. He's our hostage, with enough gunpowder strapped to him that he'll leave no trace if we set it off. You have until dawn to surrender to us or the sunrise won't be the brightest thing you see this morning!"

This was a joke, right? How was she supposed to hear that? She could be anywhere on the island. I said as much, but Ciara haphazardly pointed the gun in my direction and said, "She heard us. I guarantee it."

The moons were falling in the sky, getting closer to the horizon with every passing heartbeat. Soon the sky would begin to brighten and my life would end. Liam and Ciara didn't bluff—Dark had taught me that much about Mercenaries—but when they struck, I would retaliate. At the very least . . . maybe I could take them out with me. Assuming, of course, they didn't have some sort of backup plan to make sure I took a solo journey to parts unknown. Maybe that was why Sirash had been brought in. I could take them out, but could I kill Sirash as well?

No, I couldn't. And there was no point in trying to convince myself otherwise.

While we waited for Serena, Liam paced back and forth, creating a deep line in the sand. He bit his nails with an increased ferocity every time he gazed into the jungle. He looked like a man about to snap, but I didn't know why. I had to find out.

"Getting nervous, Liam?" I asked, debating whether I was brave enough to wipe sweat off my forehead. "Are you worried about me? I didn't know I meant so much to you."

"Shut up," he snapped. "It's not you. It's this place."

"You've been to Torda before?"

Saying the name caught him off guard. He bit off too much of his nail, taking some skin with it and causing it to bleed. He waved the hand away and let a few droplets crash into the sand. Ciara was talking to Sirash and would have stopped the conversation if she had heard us. I would have if the positions were reversed.

"Were you here when it was ransacked?" I asked. "Do you know what happened here?"

"I wasn't," he said quickly. "But my father was. Before we were Regal Company. Back when—" He stopped, catching himself from saying anything else.

"Back when what, Liam?" I pressed. "Back when you were known as something else? Back when you were working with someone else?" Despite my predicament, my confidence spiked. "Who destroyed Torda?"

Liam sucked on his teeth. "The Reaper."

I had heard that name before. It was the title for the leader of the Waylayers. "Do you know who the Reaper is? And if Regal Company didn't destroy this place, how do you know they did?"

"No one knows who the Reaper is. Not even Papa. And he saw the daemon in person," Liam lamented. "Papa and his crew were hired to catch anyone who got away during the massacre, but . . . no one did except—" He cut himself off again, eyes suddenly lingering on Sirash. "It doesn't matter. I've said too much."

"Why hide the truth from a dying man?"

Ciara approached me from behind and said, "Because you're annoyingly persistent. And if you manage to escape, we don't want Papa even angrier with us." She stood next to her brother. "Liam, I hope you didn't give too many family secrets away."

"I didn't. I'm not stupid. Just a little unsettled in this place. As you are aware."

"As I am aware," she stated. "Not much time left, Michael. Maybe we underestimated how much the Queen cares for . . ." The rustling of leaves caught her attention. "Or maybe not."

Chloe emerged from the bushes with finger streaks of mud across her cheeks. She was weaponless and barefoot but calmer than she had any right to be. As she trudged through the sand toward us, I was struck by the memory of the woman I had first met at the Shrine of Patron Victoria before the Endless Waltz. She had seemed meek then. No longer. She stood like a conquering hero in front of these Mercenaries.

"Release him," she ordered, stopping out of reach.

"We will, the moment Serena is on that boat," Ciara replied. "We have orders to bring her back to Vargo. It can be a kidnapping or voluntary. That's up to you."

"If we refuse to give her up to you?"

Ciara aimed my revolver at me. "He dies."

"You think Serena will come with you if you kill him?" Chloe crossed her arms, leaning more on her left leg. "Because that's delusional."

"We're aware it won't be willingly," Ciara said with a sigh. "But we can contain you on this island until we can capture Serena. And, honestly, the odds are higher that you'll end up a Forgotten fighting us than successfully drive us off. We're Mercenaries. We know how to wage war."

Chloe dug her toes into the sand and cracked her knuckles. "Well . . . when you put it like that . . . I suppose our options *are* limited." She stared at the Mercenaries. "But we're not naïve. Serena won't give herself up unless you guarantee that Michael will be released unharmed."

"The longer you stall, the lower his odds—"

"Serena will give herself up at the Reborn Titan. If we can guarantee neither of you will murder Michael once you have her."

Liam and Ciara glanced at each other, visibly amused and annoyed but wearing smiles nonetheless. "That is . . ." Ciara hesitated. ". . . that is more reasonable than we expected. You realize that if you don't show up, we'll murder him?"

"We're aware."

"Then so be it," Ciara said, holstering the revolver. "Two days from now we'll meet at the Reborn Titan."

Chloe nodded. "We'll count Michael's toes and fingers when we see him again."

"Wouldn't dream of hurting him." Liam grabbed me by the back of my neck and steered me away from Chloe toward a small boat. As I was dragged away, I hoped Chloe would give me some sign that she had found Serena and I wasn't about to die, but I was met with a blank stare. I had to hope Serena was well.

Once Ciara and Sirash had joined us, we pushed off the beach toward the boat waiting for us offshore. Being an extremely curious person with the self-preservation instinct of a suicidal ant, I couldn't help but ask, "Why did you agree to meet them again at the Reborn Titan? Why delay the exchange?"

Ciara began to take off some of the bombs she had stuck to my body using a brownish liquid that burned my skin and smelt worse than rotten fish. But it was Liam who replied, "Don't you remember, Michael? You owe me a favor and we plan on capitalizing on it."

"What do you need me to do?"

Ciara yanked a bomb off me, tearing skin and hair from my legs. She paused, holding it just below my face. "You're going to kill someone for us."

27

LIE TO ME

They put me below deck in a cramped room with water dripping from the ceiling. Rather than confine me with chains or rope or whatever, they did the civilized thing and left a bomb attached to the doorframe. It would undoubtedly go off at too rough of a wave crashing against the side of the ship, let alone me tampering with it. The only people who could get in and out of the room without risking my life were Liam, Ciara, and Sirash—something they made painfully clear to the crew when we boarded. Because even if they were all members of Regal Company . . . every Mercenary had a price. All I had to do was find it and my escape would be guaranteed.

Which meant Liam, Ciara, and Sirash were responsible for taking care of me. And to my surprise, they did. Liam brought me water and stale bread shortly after throwing me in there and then Ciara brought dried fish and apple slices for lunch. Sirash just opened the door every so often, sneered at me, and then left. By the time darkness fell, the musty boards of my room started creaking, and my stomach was grumbling, I expected Liam or Ciara to visit again. I was hoping for Liam. Ciara was too calculating and cold to give up any information, but Liam—even after I had proven he shouldn't underestimate me—still had a loose tongue. And since I had lost my chance to learn what had happened on Torda, I needed to get it out of him or Sirash.

But not even in my wildest dreams had I expected Sirash to stagger in drunk. He had a half-drunk bottle of rum in one hand, a knife between his perfectly straight teeth, and a rhythm he maintained by snapping his free hand and tapping his feet. Guess no one told him snapping his fingers was bad luck while on a ship. He collapsed against the door once it was defused and chugged the rum as if it were a miracle cure-all and he was a plague victim.

"No food?" I asked from the other side of the tiny room.

"Nah, I got something here for you," he said as he rummaged through his pockets. He tossed me a long flat piece of bread that seemed harder than a brick. But as I nibbled on the edge, I found it tasted like olives and salt rather than sawdust. "Pretty good, right?"

"Better than most of what we ate back in Hollow," I agreed. "Even before I was a Mercenary, I was always amazed at the food they all ate. It was different than commoner or noble food. More flavorful, more accessible, more—"

"Real," Sirash interrupted. "It's always been more real. Some say it's because they travel the world and take the best techniques and recipes from other cultures and infuse it with their own . . . but I always thought it was because of who they were. Mercenaries aren't scared of anything— well, the good ones aren't, at least—so they're honest to a fault. It shows in everything they do. Even their cooking." He snickered and then added, "Back on the Skeleton Coast the older men used to joke that a Mercenary would be the best lay of your life. I think they were just intimidated and wanted that power for themselves."

"Did you ever want to be a Mercenary?" I asked as I chewed.

"I did before I found Arjay and came to Hollow. Even applied at one point." He took a swig. "It was a small company called Dahei's Rejects.

They turned me down for, like, twelve different reasons. I applied to two of the bigger ones, hoping their requirements were lower. They rejected me, too. Realized then how hard it is to become one. Guess it has to be, when they have immunity from every government on the continent."

I didn't know how to ask this, so I went aggressive and bold and hoped it would work. Sirash and I had been straightforward with each other in the past. "Why are you here, Sirash? Why did you become a Waylayer? Why did you leave Jean and Arjay in Hollow? What is going on with you?"

"Do you love her?" Sirash countered. "The Hollow Queen?"

Lying wouldn't help me here, so I told the truth. "We've been bound together since we were children," I began. "We were raised to support and cover each other's flaws no matter what happened. Be it noble politics, magical serial killers, pirate adventures, plague, or war. It's hard to explain how I feel, but . . . I'm connected to her. As if we're fated to be together. It was never meant to turn into love, but, to be frank, I'm a moonstruck fool . . ." I took a breath. "I fell for the one person I shouldn't have."

Sirash held the rim of his bottle against his chapped lower lip. "That kind of love is dangerous. How far would you go?"

I hesitated but then said, "I don't know. But I suppose we'll find out together, eh?"

"I suppose." He took a swig from his bottle. "Which question do you want me to answer? That's how you do it, right? Question for a question."

One chance, then. Better make it count. "What happened to your hand?"

Sirash let out a small chuckle. "Heh. Jumping right in. How much do you know about Skeletons, Michael?"

"Not much," I admitted. "You all have those bone tattoos, and you are all former slaves or indentured servants or whatever noblesque bullshit they call it to justify owning others."

"That's what most people know." Sirash cradled his bottle. "But it's more complicated than that. Us Skeletons come from all over the world. It just depends on how unlucky you were on any given day to be caught by the slavers. But once you're shipped down south you begin your thirteen years as a slave. The first thing they do is ask you to choose a body part for the tattoo."

Sirash rotated his hand completely, showing off all the yellowish bone. "They advise the children to pick something less painful, but some of the stupid ones try to be brave and go for the face or ribs or head. Some even die in the chair, though it's rare. Our inksmiths are too masterful to let it happen often. They actually hold a higher position than the slavers do. For a long time, I had assumed it was because the craft was hard to master or understand, and I was right—to a degree—but it's because every tattoo is identical to the thousands that came before it. No variation. That kind of skill is uncanny, don't you think?"

"Why must they all be the same?"

"Because they bind us to the coast forever." Sirash drained his bottle and then wiped his glistening lips. "They tell us we will serve for thirteen years from our arrival and marking. Not a day more. After that, they let us go. They call it borrowing time, but it's all lies."

"I don't understand."

"How could you? It's not *your* problem, is it? Just mine." He gritted his teeth. "I served my thirteen years and left. I was one of the lucky ones who was there from birth. The slavers claimed me as their own. The man who collected me said the last thing my mother saw before she died from blood loss was me screaming and being carried away." He exhaled. "I killed him the day after I was freed. Shot a bolt through his back while he was on top of a woman. To this day I still feel bad for her. She didn't deserve to have his deadweight collapse on her."

"Sirash . . . I—"

He held a finger to his lips. "Not yet, Michael. I'm almost done." He let the drops fall to his tongue. "The lie is that it's only thirteen years. It's true they let us go after that but . . . that's just the beginning. When the voices in your head begin and your true employer starts talking to you. It's faint at first, but it gets louder and louder and louder."

"True employer?"

Sirash stared into my eyes, twisting his head like a snake preparing to strike. "The voices tell me you know his name, so I won't break my oaths by saying it out loud." He pulled back slightly, inhaled, and then said, "Zarack, the Second Wolven King. The one trapped in the abyss. We're his Skeleton army, bound to serve him for all eternity. Not even death can set us free, for when we die, we cross the abyss and take a seat at his side. Waiting for the day he'll set the world on fire."

I gulped audibly. "You're lying."

"No. I'm not."

My head was spinning. If Sirash was telling the truth, then things were much worse than I had imagined. Alphonse and Gwen were preparing a grand army to destroy Zarack, while Zarack had been amassing hundreds of thousands of Skeletons in his own army for a millennium. Their battle could destroy everything, or at the very least scar the world once again. Two of my loved ones were indentured to serve two different Wolven Kings and . . . there was no clear path to save either.

"Our tattoos turning to bone shows us that he's getting ready for something," Sirash explained. "All of us who can are expected to return to him as soon as we can. So here I am . . . ready to serve my master."

"Can't you fight it? Why are you listening to someone you've never seen? You're stronger than that!"

"No," Sirash said softly. "I'm not. He'd drive me mad if I tried to fight his commands. Or worse . . . take over my mind and kill Jean or Arjay as a reminder never to disobey him. I couldn't take that risk."

I blinked back tears that were beginning to form. "Maybe I can nullify the magic in your mind. You don't have to do—"

Sirash's voice changed. A deeper and more primal one came out of it. And his eyes turned colors, from a green flaked with gold to pure bright gold. Just like Domet's. "Yes, he does, young Kingman. You cannot save him. Not unless you help me destroy my brother Alphonse. And then I'll set him free. I'll set *all* of them free."

Shivers ran up my spine, but for some reason . . . it wasn't fear. It was *excitement*. The more these immortal kings revealed themselves to me . . . the more I knew I was doing something right.

"Zarack," I said, smiling. "Pleasure to meet you. I'm sure you've heard of me. I just slapped your brother silly and I'll be the one to punch you in the face when we meet. Did you keep me from crossing the abyss, or was that another brother?"

"My youngest brother tried to kill you for trespassing," Zarack admitted. "But I was the one who stopped you from meeting us face-to-face. It's too soon for that, young Kingman."

"Why? Scared of me?"

The Wolven King snarled. "No. When we meet, you will be in desperate need of something from me. But fear not, young Kingman . . . it may be sooner than you think."

I lunged toward him. "You better hope it's not. Because I'm coming for you and your brothers. Do you hear me? Your time in this world is up."

But Zarack was gone. Sirash returned, slumped against the wall as if he had fallen asleep. His eyes fluttered open, some painful twinge through his body forcing him to grab his head. I wanted to learn more, but the door opened and in strolled Liam Noble.

"I told you to slow down. That stuff is strong." Liam kicked at Sirash, who groaned in response. "Whatever. You're coming with me, Michael. It's time to fulfill your promise."

Liam dragged me out of the room. Silently, and ignoring my protests, he hauled me through the ship and threw me into a much larger room. I skipped across the floor before slamming into a desk. Ciara was seated at it and looked over as Liam closed the door behind us, bolting it to make sure we would be undisturbed.

"We're almost to our destination," Liam said . . . tentatively. The blustering man was almost a shadow of himself.

"Are you sure you want to do this, Liam?" Ciara asked as she leaned back in her seat, tipping two legs off the ground. "Papa won't be happy."

"Papa doesn't need to know. Besides, if he dealt with it himself, I

wouldn't be forced to find someone who can read the King Script and
have them do it for me."

Ciara ran her fingers through her hair, silent.

"Is someone going to tell me what's going on?" I asked from the floor.

The two noble siblings glanced at me and then said in unison, "I suppose we'll have to."

Liam stood over me, hands in his pockets. He looked on the verge of
tears. "You're going to kill my mother for me. She's in the cage my father
left her in."

DOPPELGANGER

It was midnight when we reached our destination. The moons illuminated our journey and hung high in the air like lanterns. The water looked like the dredges of paint-water in a cup from the deck of the ship, and if it weren't for Liam pointing it out, I might have missed our destination. There were ruins hidden in the water and pure white coral that surrounded the stone like a cage of bones or a tangle of vines . . . and among the coral were the Moon's Tears flowers that gave off a steady white glow.

Up until this moment, I had thought they grew only in Hollow. To find them here made my mind reel with possibilities. Were the flowers more important than I realized? Where else did they grow? And what did it mean? As always, I would have to seek the answers later. Right now, it was about surviving what came next.

Liam tied a rope around my waist as Ciara ordered her crew to drop anchor and I walked the length of the plank. It would be an easy swim— or so they said—to the ruins. Hopefully they were right.

"Once I'm in there, what am I looking for?" I asked.

"My mother will be in the deepest part of the ruins," Liam said. "Behind a door that will only open if you know the King Script. That's why I needed you. You'll likely run into traps, but nothing too dangerous."

"Are you sure you want me to do this? What if your mother can be saved?"

Liam shook his head. "She can't be. Papa sealed her in there because she was infected with . . . I don't know. Something that made *him* afraid of her. He told me she was no longer his wife and that I should consider her dead. That she'd kill me if I ever gave her the chance." He paused. "This happened right after Torda was destroyed. I was five and it was the hardest lesson I ever had to learn."

"Liam . . . I . . . ," I said, trailing off. What could I say? Changing topics was the only move to make. "What is this place? If it holds King Script, that means it's related to the Wolven Kings. Is it another hidden tomb?"

"No. We suspect it's something else."

"That's very descriptive." I walked to the end of the plank, my toes clutching the edge. The breeze blew against my bare chest and I hoped the water wouldn't be too cold. "If I'm doing this, I deserve to know whatever you do."

"We think it's an armory," he said as he tossed me a sheathed dagger. "But, honestly, you'll know more than we do the moment you start exploring. You can open doors we can't."

"What's stopping me from lying to you about what I find down there?" I asked.

"Because you want to know the answers as much as we do," Liam snapped. "You could lie to us, but then you'll be left with information you don't fully understand. You and Dark are at war with Angelo . . . and based on recent events, you may be at war with Dark as well. Any misstep is their victory. So, lie if you want. But is it really worth sacrificing the war to win the battle?"

"Fair." I shook out my legs. "Do you want me to bring something back as proof she's dead?"

Liam nodded. "She wore a silver necklace with my name on it. Bring that back . . . and I'll tell you whatever you want to know about Angelo as thanks."

Ciara nearly fell over. "Liam, you can't! Papa would—"

"Papa isn't here," Liam said. "And if he wanted me to be loyal forever, he wouldn't have forced a young boy to forget about his mother. I've waited a lifetime to find out what happened to her and now I will."

"Does that mean you're coming with me?" I asked.

"No," Liam said softly. "I don't want to remember her as something other than my loving mother. Whatever is down there isn't her . . . but at least this way she can rest."

"What about you, Ciara? Fancy a swim?"

The other noble sibling sneered at me.

"What a shame. It would have been lovely to bond some more."

"Go, Michael," Liam whispered. "Don't make this harder than it needs to be."

"What's your mother's name?" I asked.

"Laymi."

I put the dagger between my teeth and dove into the water feetfirst.

Bubbles popped and rushed to the surface at my side. The rope pulled me up, but I wanted to think that my frog kick helped me get there faster. My face felt cold as I broke the water and my hair clung to my forehead as if stuck with honey. I swam toward the radiant white coral structure nearby. If it weren't for the Moon's Tears guiding me, I wouldn't have been able to spot it from the water. When I reached something solid, I climbed up it and untied the rope around my waist before throwing it over a once-proud pillar of stone.

Most of this place was held together with prayers and old stone that was too stubborn to give up after a millennium of water erosion. The stone was as smooth as silk, while the white coral felt like rose thorns when I ran my fingers over them. In the center of the floor was a metal trapdoor, and I yanked it up with great difficulty, straining my muscles to get it open enough to tie the rope around the handle and make sure I wasn't imprisoned down there. Once it was secure, I took a breath and jumped down into the darkness.

I landed with a plop, water splashing around my ankles. The walls were made of the same weird glowing green crystals that lined the hidden chambers of the Royal Crypt in Hollow. I carefully trudged down the corridors, searching for any strange strings of letters, but came up with nothing except slime that had found a home in the cracks. My path grew tighter and tighter the farther I went in until I could barely walk without my shoulders scraping against the walls, forcing me to crawl on my hands and knees until I entered a wider area.

Much like the wall in the secret corridor in the Royal Tomb, another wall covered with symbols stood in my way. Rather than waste my time pushing them as I had last time, I put my hand against the wall and spread my nullification over it. When it didn't crumble, I cursed and crossed my arms. The same trick wouldn't work twice. So, I began to examine it. It was almost a perfect replica of the previous one, with the same images and pattern, except for one very noticeable difference. The letters *HWLJQXEW* were written around it in a repeating pattern. It was easy to guess that whatever it said was the key to unlocking a path forward.

I knew only one word—"Alphonse"—which translated into *GVHRQXJE* and would have to decipher as much as I could with it. Using my knife, I scratched out what I knew, and the phrase repeated all over the wall. Code breaking wasn't something I had any familiarity with—my style of thieving had always been more hit-and-run—but if Angelo could do it, so could I. I would not be outsmarted by the same man twice.

I had most of the letters, so I was able to translate *HWLJQXEW* into *P**SONE**. And with the second and last letter being the same . . . the word jumped out at me. Only because I knew it all too well—*PRISONER*. If I was right, this place wasn't an armory, it was a jail. And since this was a world where dragons and titans existed, who knew what I might let out if I opened the wall. Could I come across a behemoth next?

But whatever lay beyond wouldn't get past me. It was just another myth to fall at my feet.

I found the closest image to a prisoner in the bottom left corner—a birdcage—and pressed against it. The wall buckled almost instantaneously and rumbled out of the way.

Every new place I came across made me feel more ignorant of how magical the greater world was . . . more than I could have ever imagined. So, to stand in a mirrored room beneath the sea that looked nicer than many buildings constructed in the last decade left me speechless. It was pristine, without dirt or dust or rust tainting any of the mirrored surfaces. Liam's mother was nowhere to be seen, and only my unblinking reflection greeted me. It made me wary to take a step, as if they were going to leap out and grab me.

And then my reflection did step out of the glass and join me in the room. It was in many ways a perfect replica of myself—messy brown hair, Kingman amber eyes, strong jaw, tall but not towering, and muscle that had been forged surviving on the streets of Hollow. The only difference was it lacked the crown brand . . . that and it seemed a lot happier than I was.

"Hello, Michael," it said in a deep voice. "It's wonderful to finally meet you."

I pinched myself, and when it remained, I groaned loudly. Nightmares never went away easily. And this one wouldn't be any different. "Are you Laymi?"

"Laymi?" my reflection repeated. "I have some of her memories, but no. I am not her." It reached into the mirror and pulled out a small box of knickknacks. It slid it to me with the heel of its boot. "The remains of the people who have died in here are in that box. Take what you want. I'm not greedy."

I rummaged through the box and found a tarnished silver necklace hidden among the tangles of threadbare clothes. It all smelt like bone dust and iron. But at least I had what I had come here looking for. I pocketed the locket. "What are you, then?"

"Does it matter?" my reflection said.

I shrugged. "I guess not. Are we going to have to do some back-and-forth nonsense or can we get straight to the point of whatever this is? Are you trapped down here or something?"

"To a degree," it said. "I'm not really here. Just a fragment." It gave me a canine smile, a darkness surrounding it—me—like a halo. "Consider me a memory of what once was."

"And what were you?"

"It's hard to say for certain. I am old. Very old. Or the part of me that is real is old. What I am is . . . complicated." The monster turned its back to me, grazing fingers along the smooth glass. Spiderweb-like fractures crackled out wherever its fingers passed. "This whole thing was a countermeasure. But since it's no longer needed, and the seal has been undone . . . this masquerade is coming to an end. As is my existence, I suppose. A shame."

"You're going to have to be clearer if you want me to help you, or else I'll just leave. I've seen enough to report back to those who sent me here."

"Have you?" it taunted. The monster changed before me. Its amber eyes turned pale green, its hair grew longer and redder, and its features more feminine. Serena. The one person I couldn't walk away from. Identical to her, but for the missing tattoo on its left wrist. "Are you sure you don't want to stick around?"

It already knew the answer. "What do you want?"

"Influence."

"Influence," I repeated, teetering on my heels. "Interesting desire. Tells me nothing, though. But I can infer some things on my own: you couldn't have predicted my coming here, so you're taking advantage of the situation. But . . . but you know enough about me to know about her . . . or at the very least guess. So, how do you do that?"

"It's a gift," it said. "I am what you might call a . . . memory connoisseur. I can see what others cannot. And I use that power to bring about change to the world. I am like the weather. Blameless but unpredictable. I did not break this world. That honor goes to another. I am a mere collector."

I hesitated, remembering Nonna and what I had seen about Dark. "Can you show me memories of events that have already happened?"

Its canine smile didn't look too foreign on Serena's face. "Absolutely. But be warned, only the first taste is free, and my expertise does not come cheap. What do you want to see?"

There were plenty of options, but only one that nagged at my mind like a burrowing parasite. "Show me the night before Prince Davey Hollow died. I was with him, and I need to know what happened."

The mirrors shattered outward, bits of glass hovering all around us as if we were walking through a sea of stars as the walls disintegrated into pools of blinding light. The monster in front of me changed form once again. Into the last person I expected to see—Angelo Shade. Had he been there that night?

Before I could ask any questions, the ground beneath me collapsed and into Angelo's memories I went.

25

BEHIND THEIR EYES

Despite knowing it wasn't *him*, having a smiling Angelo stand in front of me made my blood boil. Yet, this wasn't the man I was used to. He was younger, his hair was darker, and he was flashier—with more jewelry than I had ever seen on him before. This was him before he lost Katherine, or maybe before he found her. The brash young man, not the careful mastermind he would one day become. But why was this version here, if the one I was used to was smarter in every way?

"Do you like my choice of form?" it asked.

"Was he there that night?" I asked cautiously.

"Obviously. And I don't appreciate you ignoring my question." The monster snapped its fingers, and the scene began to change around us. "Don't do that again."

My city appeared around me. The castle sprouted up from the ground like flowers after a long winter. It was a morphing tower of stone and metal, a room clarifying around us until it was clear we were in the Star Chamber . . . where my father took the blame for a murder

Angelo committed. But why were we here the night before that assassination?

As the painted walls came into focus, we stood by the door as Angelo and Vance Shade stepped out of the metaphorical mist. They were standing near the hidden entrance to the Royal suite, examining the out-of-place eighth piece of Celona. Angelo looked the same as the day I met him eleven years ago. As did Vance when I had last seen him . . . one of the perks of being immortal. Age was just a number.

They were in mid-conversation.

"Not a bad kill zone," Vance declared. "Best option will be for me to wait on the ceiling in a partial dragon form and use my Fabrications to hide. I'll shoot the boy with your revolver and drop it into the hand of the first person who walks in."

Angelo was at the head of the table, tracing the wood grain with his fingers. "That will work." He paused. "I'll figure out how to frame whoever it is. It shouldn't be hard. This king is a weak man and will succumb to grief once his son is dead. His Kingman will be a pain, but he'll be too preoccupied keeping the country stable to see my plan coming."

"You underestimate that family, Angelo," Vance warned. "If it were that simple to destroy them, someone would have. Most attempts to corrupt their ideology have been in vain."

"Yes, well, that was before," he said nonchalantly. "They've never faced someone like me. Or have you forgotten what you created, dear sweet Father? I am a monster fit to kill God."

Vance seemed amused, running his tongue over his massive canine teeth. "I haven't. Although I don't understand why, after all the help I've given you, you still refuse to join me in fighting the immortals and focus on killing insects instead."

"You'll have my son soon enough," Angelo stated, drawing his coat tight around him. "Make him your Godbutcher, while I will finish what these High Nobles started. It works out for you, doesn't it? This chaos will only draw more of them out."

"That's the hope, at least," Vance said. "Still. Such a shame. All your potential wasted."

Angelo opened the door to the rest of the castle, passing through me and the monster like we were made of mist. "Yes, yes. Spare me. Finish this one last request, then go and claim Davis and hopefully I will never have to see you again."

"Our deal will be enforced. But I'm surprised you were so willing to make it," Vance mocked. "You'll give Katherine's son to the monster you ran from most of your life. What would she think of that?"

Angelo shrugged. "I never wanted children. His purpose was to be with his mother if I could not, so she wouldn't be lonely. With her gone . . . he's disposable."

Angelo closed the door behind him, leaving the darkness dragon in the Star Chamber to await his target's arrival. We followed Angelo as he walked the hallways almost aimlessly. He muttered things to himself, but no matter how close I got, I couldn't make out the words. None of the castle guards paid him any attention, the Scales emblem on his shoulder enough to deter them from asking questions. If even one of them had, they might have saved the prince, my father, and the Hollow and Kingman families.

"As informative as this is, I already knew most of it," I said. "Is there a particular reason you're showing me this?"

The monster shrugged. "I'm not omniscient. I can only show you what I have. This is the only memory I have of that night. He wanted information from me and was willing to give this up to get it."

I stopped walking. "What did he want from you?"

It kept following Angelo and forced me to do the same or risk losing sight of them both. "Information about forgotten things," it said once I had caught back up. "The Wolven Kings. Their names, their fates, and so forth."

"You know the names of the Wolven Kings?" I clarified.

It nodded. "I would be a terrible collector if I did not. Do you crave them, too?"

I had to swallow my yes, focusing on the man I hated the most instead. If only because I remembered what this monster had said before we began—only the first taste was free. And clearly any price would be paid in memories.

"Did he learn them this night?" I asked.

The monster shook its head. "No. But he did discover something just as good."

My heart sunk as two boys came bounding around a corner and slammed into Angelo Shade. The three of them were knocked to the ground, and as the amber-eyed boy told the adult to watch where he was going . . . I saw Angelo's dull grey eyes fall on him and his scorn quickly turn to fascination.

Angelo discovered me, the night before Davey died. The son of the Kingman he would have signed a death warrant for, the Kingman he would try to use against Hollow and its citizens. And, like everything else that night, I couldn't remember what had transpired. How much pain could have been prevented if I could have remembered?

"My apologies, sir," Davey said as my younger self helped him to his feet. "We were not paying attention to our surroundings."

Angelo didn't kneel to anyone, so he stayed on his ass and hid his insolence behind shock. "The fault is all mine, Your Majesty. Please accept my sincerest condolences. I mean no disrespect, but . . . what are you two doing up so late? It is past midnight."

My younger self went pale and tongue-tied. Back then I saw honesty as the only answer, having been raised on stories about my noble and heroic ancestors. The younger me would have been ashamed to see what I had become. A villain masquerading as a hero, using family and love to justify what he did.

Davey saved me from whatever poor excuse I was about to spit out. "We are participating in a training exercise set up by the Captain of the Ravens. My father wants me to be prepared at all times, so we were woken in the middle of the night and given a mission."

Angelo didn't believe it, but didn't call us out on it either. "Then can I be of some assistance? It is the least I can do, and I cannot imagine there are any rules against it, since good Kings and Kingman *always* know when to ask for help."

Davey hesitated, mouth slightly agape. "That is very kind of you, but we are looking for something very peculiar hidden in the castle, and I doubt—"

"Why not ask me? Unless it's a secret?"

My younger self interrupted. "We're looking for a key."

Davey whacked me upside the head and quietly—or as quiet as kids can be—told me to shut up. It was very unbecoming in a boy who would become king. Especially in the presence of a monster like Angelo Shade.

"A key?" he asked. "What kind of key are you looking for?"

"It's a key for a door without a lock."

I wanted to strangle my younger self. So stupidly trusting, and to Angelo of all people? Had I always been his perfect little pawn? Was this meeting why he adopted me and my siblings? I had learned so much about him, but not his plan for me. Had Dark been telling the truth about his endgame? Is that why he kept me alive for so long, but was prepared to let me die on the executioner's block?

"Every door that needs a key has a lock. Is it a riddle?"

"We think so," Davey lied quickly. Even years later I knew his tell . . . scratching the back of his neck. "But, sir, I think we should solve this riddle by ourselves. There's no shame in asking for help, but I imagine an adult will easily solve a riddle meant for us."

Angelo smiled sweetly. "How mature of you. It can be tempting to take the easy way out. I wish you two the best of luck."

Davey grabbed my younger self and hauled him away from Angelo, disappearing down the dimly lit corridors. The smile on his face slowly faded into a neutral glare. Angelo stuck his hands in his pockets, took a deep breath, and then walked on. Me and the monster followed in silence. But just because I was out of his sights didn't mean his night was over.

Angelo made his way to the main foyer of the castle, stopping in front of a once-exquisite painting of King Adrian the Liberator. Most of the details around his face were lost to time and some notoriously bad restorers who had modeled him after King Montagne's likeness rather than the historical texts. Yet, the background was still masterful. The colors were bright, the lines distinct and bold, and the fact it had survived so long was one of the many reasons it had been given a place of honor on the main staircase.

No one was around—not a rat scurrying beneath the steps, or a dead fly in the corner—so maybe that was why Angelo spoke to Adrian.

"You were so smart, Adrian." Angelo paced back and forth in front of the painting. "You were a brilliant tactician. You hid every trace of the Wolven Kings from the world for over a millennium. And obviously some secrets slipped out . . . it was a millennium, after all . . . but the big one, the one you did your best to hide, was discovered by your own grandchild. Sort of ironic, isn't it? Undone by blood."

Angelo ran his hand through his hair, ruining his pristine tidiness. He moved the painting to the side, exposing a jagged tunnel into the wall behind it. It was the path to my childhood fort, my escape route whenever I couldn't deal with being a Kingman. My heart sank as Angelo crawled down the tunnel. The monster and I followed, walking through the walls.

I had found it by accident one day when I was exploring the castle, hoping to unearth some secret my ancestors had left behind. All good things were hidden in plain sight, and yet I was still surprised when I looked behind this painting and it wasn't a bare wall. Only the Kingman and Hollow children knew of this place—we had all sworn to keep the secret, and somehow I knew Adreann and Serena always had. Childhood promises were sacred things.

So how Angelo found it I will never know.

The tunnel opened out into a darkened room holding a lockless door. It was surrounded by Moon's Tears, their thick branches bearing star-shaped fruit. Few, if any, of those fruits had ever fallen to the ground without intervention by human hands, and none rotted no matter how long they were on the floor. I had checked back on one fallen fruit for over six months.

Angelo left the tunnel with a grunt, pushing himself up with his fore-arms. He brushed off his clothes and then approached the door as if it were going to open and swallow him whole if he didn't treat it with respect. He stepped out and plucked a Moon's Tear off the vine, then rubbed the petals between his fingers.

"Katherine," he whispered. "I'll see you soon. Because if a boy can find this place and almost solve its mysteries, so can I. Adrian can't hide the key from me forever."

And then it all disappeared around us, filtering away like smoke blown by the wind until only darkness remained. The monster stepped into my view, rubbing its hands together like a street merchant trying to entice me into buying their goods. "Fascinating, wasn't it? Can I tempt you with something else?"

I said nothing, unable to trust myself to say no. This . . . thing could answer all my questions at the cost of a few of my memories. But . . . I put my hand over my heart and felt Dawn and Jamal hovering around me, reminding me where I had come from and what I still had to do.

"Are you sure?" it persisted. "There are so many things I think you'll want to see. Like the First Kingman."

I backstepped in shock. "What? You know who the First Kingman was?"

"Absolutely," it sang. "After all, I was the one who stole them away from the world."

"What do you—"

The monster snapped its fingers and a misty apparition appeared be-fore me.

It was shorter than me, if only slightly, but it stood tall and proud and made me think of my father. Every aspect of its features was hid-den except for the amber eyes that pierced me to the heart. Just a few heartbeats with them and I could learn so much. I could finally get the validation I had spent my life craving. They had set the standard we all followed . . . If they were proud of me, then nothing else mattered.

The monster circled me. "I'll give you all the First Kingman's mem-ories I have. Limitless knowledge. In exchange for a paltry memory.

Something you wouldn't even notice. I like collecting beautiful things, and this memory would be so—"

"Not interested," I breathed out like I was gasping for air. "I don't know what you want from me, but I don't want you to have it."

It moved its jaw as if it were unhinged. "Are you sure? Think, Michael. This is an opportunity you can't refuse without some thought."

"I think it is," I said, gaining confidence. "Everything I've seen suggests that you can only take the form of people in memories you've stolen. So you know who I am . . . and maybe even what I've done. I doubt your price will be paltry." I exhaled. "This is a trap, isn't it? There's something you want from me."

"Clever," it said.

"Whose memories do you have that you can take my and Serena's forms?"

"Do you really want to know?" it asked. "It won't be who you expect."

"It never is."

The monster rubbed the back of its neck, its features slowly distorting again. Its hair grew longer and brighter, going from pitch-black to rosy auburn, and I swore. Serena appeared before me again, the monstrous smile spread across her face.

"Serena? But she knows about the tattoo on her . . ." I hit my thigh with the bottom of my fist. "She keeps it concealed most of the time. Just because she knew it was there doesn't mean it would show up in your copy. And the bran—" Another hit to my thigh. "She always saw the best in me. The brand made me a traitor and she never saw me as one. Even when she thought I had killed her father."

"Do you want to know what memory she wanted? Or the one I took from her?"

I answered with my question. "How and where did she find you? How many other places like this are out there in the world?"

A shrug. "Does it really matter?" When it saw my eyes narrow, it added, "Let's just say there are many secrets in the Hollow castle that still haven't been discovered. And now, because of her, there is one less."

Serena wasn't stupid. If she'd met this thing, then it had shown her something for free and then tempted her with something of practical value to force her to give a memory up. But what . . . ? There was still one mystery.

"You gave her information about the Wolven Kings."

The monster jumped up and down, clapping erratically. "So clever!"

"Which means if I ask you to show me the same scene, I can learn what she did. And then we don't have to go to the titan and get the fruit." I paused. "We can defy destiny and then choose our own path."

It bared its teeth at me—shiny and white. "Do you want to see what I showed her? It'll cost only a single memory. I'll even tell you what I want in exchange. Just like I told Serena."

"What did it cost her?" I asked.

A small red ball formed over the monster's fingers. He spun it around, passing it from finger to finger. "The memory of the moment that she realized she wanted to be with you rather than fulfill her duty as Queen. She was cocky. She thought that single memory couldn't do too much damage. That she would still love you when it was gone . . . and she did. But she no longer had the guts to act on it. Duty prevailed."

If I spoke, I didn't hear what I said. All I could hear was my heartbeat reverberating in my ears. If she still had that memory when I'd confessed my love on the balcony, would she have run away with me? Would we be free now and together somewhere our last names didn't dictate our futures?

"Funny, isn't it?" It spun the red ball of light a little faster. "Life is a collection of inconsequential choices. But take the right one out and a person can change into something they wouldn't recognize. So, Michael, would you like to gamble that if I take a single memory from you, you'll be the same person afterward?"

I didn't respond. I could barely keep my thoughts straight.

"Or perhaps you don't care about the memory she saw," the monster taunted. "Maybe you care about the memory she gave up. Would you like to see the moment she decided love was more important than duty?"

I shook my head. That memory had to remain a mystery, if only to prevent me from going down the same path.

"What a shame. So: the memory she traded her own for?"

"What would you take from me for it?"

"I want the moment you fell in love with Serena Hollow," it said, accenting each syllable.

I was unable to process its request. "That's a little hard to do, since I don't know when—"

The monster snapped its fingers and the darkness transformed around us. We were in the King's Garden now, in the middle of summer, the sun high in the sky as cicadas chirped to each other despite two children's laughter overwhelming everything around them. Me and Serena's younger selves sprinted through a field of wildflowers, petals blowing up into the air. We pushed and chased each other playfully. It was all so innocent. An easy smile formed on my face as I remembered the happy moments of my childhood.

Serena won our play fight, tackling me to the ground with her arms wrapped around my waist. I landed with a laugh as Serena pressed my chest down with her hands. "I win!"

"Never," my younger self protested, struggling to get free. "You cheated."

"Being superior in every way isn't cheating. It's hard work."

"Oh, really?" My younger self jabbed her in the side. She yelped and lost her balance as I pounced and pinned her down. Serena's face was redder than the petals around us. "What was that about being superior?"

"Let me go," she demanded, suddenly growing serious.

"Not until you admit I won."

Serena repeatedly jabbed me in the side to less-than-stellar results. I kept her firmly in place. "Admit it, Serena. Nothing you can do is going to make me—"

She stole a kiss and cut my gloating off. I froze, no part of me understanding what she had done, what it meant, or even why I liked it so much. As a child, I had seen my parents kiss. I had never seen the appeal until this moment. And I wanted to do it again. With Serena.

Right up until she pushed me off her while I was floundering. I lay on my back, awestruck, as she stood over me smiling. "What was that about nothing you can do?"

My younger self sat up. "That was definitely cheating!"

"All's fair in love, Michael." And she sped off, blushing and smiling so widely. At the time I'd thought it was the summer heat that made her flush, and now . . .

The scene stopped and the monster stood in between our younger selves as they were suspended in mid-stride. "How adorable."

"How do you know this was the moment?" I asked defiantly. "What makes you the expert about how I feel?"

"Because this is what I do, Michael Kingman. For over a millennium, ever since the Wolven Kings were overthrown, I have watched and waited and learned from all those who have entered one of my prisons. I watch the lives of all those I have collected over and over and over again, finding their moments of weakness . . . of bravery . . . and love. I am an observer. The *perfect* observer. This is the only reason I'm alive."

"You're immortal," I declared, unsurprised.

The monster shrugged. "That should be obvious."

"So you know Domet?"

"Domet?"

"The Lifeweaver."

"You've met the Lifeweaver?" The monster snarled at me, using Serena's face. It was a mistake, and brought my beating heartbeat back to a steady rhythm rather than the ruckus mess it had been. The peaceful scene around us slowly distorted, flames overtaking everything. "Tell me everything."

I hesitated. "You can't see him in my memories on your own? Isn't that how you found this scene?"

"The Lifeweaver is exempt from the usual rules," it hissed. Serena's tongue became longer, more snakelike. "Has been ever since he damned humanity with his pettiness and anger and created all of this." The flames around us grew higher, brighter. "And what an ugly name to use. Domet. Yet, it's quite befitting of that monster."

And just like that, I had an advantage.

"Then maybe we could agree to a better trade of information."

"Never," it growled. "If you know who the Lifeweaver is, then he has his claws in you. You are more dangerous than you could possibly imagine. He creates living weapons. The only thing worse would be to inherit one of the wills of the Wolven Kings." It stopped, suddenly very human-like in its hesitation. "I have to stop whatever he has planned for you."

And just like that, my advantage was gone. Dammit, Domet. Who was this man, truly?

I nullified my body, worrying that the flames might suddenly become real. "Who are you to him?"

"Don't you get it?" it said with a flourish. "*I* am the Lifeweaver. He fragmented his mind and locked most of it away in these prisons in a misguided attempt to come to terms with what he did in the Wolven King War." It snarled. "Drink, as he discovered, was not effective enough to bring peace to a broken man."

"I don't believe you," I said in confusion. "That doesn't make sense. How is that even possible. It's just—"

"If you still want information, the price has changed," it said. "I want your name."

"My name?"

"Yes. Your Kingman name. It's the only thing that might stop whatever the Lifeweaver has planned for you. Because if he's active again . . . the world will shatter around us."

"That's it?" I asked. "I haven't gone by 'Michael Kingman' for a while now. It would be a nuisance, but I—"

"No. I will take the world's memory of you. Once the deal is complete, you'll have one day to say your goodbyes, and then Michael Kingman will be erased from history. Your family won't remember you. Your friends won't remember meeting you. Even your dear sweet Serena will forget the object of her devotion."

I tilted my head. "How do you have the power to do that?"

"I am more than just a seventh of the world. All that you need to know is that I am serious. I have done it before, and I will do it again." It gritted its teeth. "You are dangerous, and I will not let the world be manipulated by the Lifeweaver again."

"I don't believe you," I said. "There's no way you can— Wait, the First Kingman. Everything about them has been erased from history. We don't know their gender, their name, how they died, or where they came from. The only reason we know anything about them is what they're credited to have done with King Adrian the Liberator. Was that Domet? Did Domet erase the First Kingman from the world?"

The monster stared me down. "The First Kingman understood the deal they made."

"Liar."

Another snap of its fingers and the flames around us turned to smoke. As it wafted away, another scene appeared around us. We were in a dark room with only a single candle on a table. King Adrian, long before he wore a crown, sat at one end of the table, across from a person made up entirely of moving darkness—just like the man Dark had manipulated his own memories to protect. King Adrian wore dirty clothes that were riddled with holes, had his greasy auburn hair slicked back, and had a large burn mark on his right cheek. It was bad enough that I knew it would never heal completely. Though none of his royal portraits showed the injury.

"If we do this," King Adrian began quietly, "we'll be starting a rebellion. We'll be declaring war against King—" My ears popped, and I missed the name. "I know this is important, but what if there was another way? We'll be risking everything."

The body of darkness said nothing, but Adrian nodded along regardless.

"I know. I know. But can we really be that selfless? I'm a follower of the goddess, not a hero."

The darkness reached out and took Adrian's hands in their own.

"Me take over? I'm not fit to be in charge. I didn't have enough confidence to correct my masters. What makes you think I can rule a country? I'm not a leader, I'm just some poor pathetic loser who couldn't . . ." Adrian choked on his words and rubbed his eyes. "I can't do it. No matter what you think."

The darkness said something that made Adrian recoil and then look down, blushing deeply.

"Maybe I can do it . . . No, maybe *we* can do it." Adrian extended his hand. "Promise me. If we do this, we're in it together. From now until the end of time. King and King's man."

The darkness shook Adrian's hand and the man who would be king smiled widely.

"What?" he said with a laugh. "You don't like how it sounds? Fine. Together forever. A King and his Kingman." He paused and took a deep breath. "The world must change, and we are the poor fools who have been forced to do it. I hope our descendants will be proud of us."

The monster in Serena's body sat on the table, legs dangling over it. "There's the promise that destroyed a nation. If these two knew what would happen . . . I wonder if they would have gone through with it. Dreams are nice to talk about, but they do tend to turn bloody. Tens of thousands died"—the monster hovered its hand over Adrian—"to make this man king."

"Why was the First Kingman erased from history?"

"As if I'll tell the Lifeweaver's weapon anything. You know my price."

My voice didn't waver. "As if I'll give up my life to you for so little."

"Then we have nothing left to talk about." The monster hopped off the table. "At some point you will seek me out again. You will need me and my knowledge. And no matter your question, my price will not waver."

I was so close to saving Serena—to earning her freedom—and now it was impossible without the fruit at the titan reborn. If it even worked. I wished there was another option, but I wasn't giving up what this monster wanted. I was Michael Kingman, and even if I was a Mercenary of Orbis Company for the rest of my life, my family would always be more important.

"Don't hold your breath."

The monster huffed and we returned to the room full of mirrors. It was so bright in comparison to where we had been, I was blinded. The monster paced in front of the mirror it had emerged from. "Don't think that you can send in an ally to learn what you need. I will not trade what Serena saw to anyone who has ever met you."

"A little dramatic, no?"

"No," it said. "Necessary." And the monster vanished back through the mirror.

When it was clear it was gone, I smashed my elbow into the glass. It shattered into a thousand pieces along with every other mirror in there, pouring down on me like a torrential rainfall. It had made its position very clear, and the last thing I wanted to do was let the Mercenaries waiting outside ask it questions in turn. It had done enough damage to me and my family by taking Serena's memories and trading information with Angelo. Something like that would happen again if I left this place intact.

It couldn't actually have been a fragment of Domet's mind, could it?

No, it must've been lying. But if it wasn't . . .

. . . no matter that it was, I had work to do. Like telling the Mercenaries outside that there was nothing here but broken mirrors. I gathered up some broken glass, chipped off a piece of one of the mirrors with the King's speech engraved on it, and made my way back to the surface. By the time I emerged into the real world, the sky was beginning to lighten, turning the world a bluish grey. Regal Company's ship was still anchored nearby, and the life rope was still tied to the trapdoor. I undid it and pulled my way back to the ship.

Liam and Ciara were waiting for me. Ciara took the knife from me instantly, as if daring me to fight them. Liam simply stood there cross-armed with an eyebrow raised, waiting for me to tell them what I had found. Sirash was nearby, chugging water as if his life depended on it. And after all that rum—maybe it did.

"I don't know what you two were hoping for, but I didn't find much," I began, pulling out the broken pieces of glass and the piece of the mirror's frame from my pockets. "The only thing down there was a room full of broken mirrors with the King Script all over the frames. It looked like it had already been pillaged, but I brought back whatever I could."

I returned Liam's mother's necklace to him. He took it gently, licked his thumb, and then tried to rub some of the tarnish off it. I gave the piece of the mirror to Ciara. Her lips made a thin line as she walked over to the edge of the ship and tossed it in. "Nothing but junk. I hope that necklace was worth it, Liam."

"It was," he cooed. He stuffed it into his pocket and then said, "The wall with all the markings on it was open already?"

I nodded. "It looked like one of the sigils was the key, but I'm not sure—"

"It's obvious he's lying," Ciara interjected.

"I'm aware." Liam looked up at me. "Michael, let me be honest for a moment. Whatever you saw or did down there isn't *that* important to me. But I'm going to ask you some questions and expect truthful answers, as per our deal. Am I clear?"

"Perfectly," I mumbled.

"Does Angelo know all the names of the Wolven Kings?"

"No, I believe he's still missing the third."

"Did he get the first two names, thanks to whatever it is down there?"

"He got something, but I don't think it was a name."

"Did it come at a price?"

"Yes."

"And do you know the names now?"

I shook my head. "The price was too steep for me."

"Was the price one of your memories?"

"Yes."

Liam ruffled his hair and then soured his face. "Whatever this world is trying to hide, they're doing a great job so far. Luckily for us, we know where another one of these armories is." He exhaled. "Last question: Which sigil opened the wall?"

I told him, and he nodded. "Wonderful. Your turn: What do you want to know about Angelo Shade?"

THREE DEATHS

Liam and I were in a war of attrition, handing each other cups filled to the brim with scaro as we drank from our own chipped ceramic cups. Ciara had thought Liam's agreement to give me information about Angelo absolutely insane and refused to participate . . . but had made sure Sirash was in the corner of the room, taking notes. We invited him to join us but apparently his stomach couldn't handle the smell, let alone the taste. The swaying boat didn't help his situation either. But, on the bright side, we were anchored in an inlet with a volcano at the center of the island where broken statues washed up onto the rocky beaches. It was a common place for fishermen, pirates, and merchants to rest before crossing near Eham. And, frankly, any island without a settlement had some kind of volcano. Not all of them dormant.

Knowing my luck, this one would be active.

I was on my third cup before Liam said anything. "Alright," he began, wiping his mouth. "Where should we begin?"

"Torda," I growled. "What happened to Torda?"

Sirash recoiled violently.

"One of the lockless doors is in Torda, hidden amongst the vines and moss," Liam said. "Angelo wanted it, back when he was a nobody with his eyes on the stars. Before his ship was renamed the *Lady Katherine* . . ." Liam drank again. ". . . he hired Regal Company to wipe out everyone on the island. Only two people escaped. A pregnant woman and a young boy."

"My mother," Sirash whispered.

Liam nodded. "And Jay Prince. Angelo let him name himself . . . he was only a kid. He thought a prince was a higher rank than a king."

"Why were they allowed to live?"

"Who knows." Liam leaned back in his seat. "Angelo raised Jay as his own son. 'Ward' might be a better term, since I don't know if Angelo ever saw Jay as something more than another pawn for him to direct. Because even a man like Angelo understood he couldn't do everything alone." A pause. "But eventually he met Katherine, married her, and had a son of his own. Do you need the specifics of that, or will the quick version suffice?"

After the third cup, scaro tasted less like tingly wine and more like well-used back-alley bathwater. But if I remembered correctly, it turned into something *beautiful* after seven. If I could make it that far with my sanity and stomach intact.

"I think I remember how it goes," I said, knocking back what remained in my cup. "Boy met girl, boy fell in love with girl, boy married girl. They had a child, she died, and he became a maniac obsessed with bringing her back. That sound about right?"

Liam made a clucking noise with his tongue. "More or less."

"So what happened with Jay Prince, then? How is he alive?"

Liam stopped suddenly. "Oh, so it was *you* who killed him. Delightful." He filled his cup until it was overflowing. "We agreed to talk about Angelo. Not Jay."

"What if I guess what happened?"

"Be my guest," Liam said as he sipped more scaro.

"His body died but his memories didn't. The Jay Prince I met is gone, but his mind was somehow transferred into another body."

"Bold claim. But do you really think something like that could be done without people knowing about it? It's almost like another way to become immortal."

"If there's anything I've learned, it's that what I consider possible is only a fraction of what can be done in this world." I poured more into his cup. "So am I right?"

"Yes," Liam said. "This is the seventh Jay Prince that I've met. Dark has killed him four times, he was poisoned by a Merchant Prince, and another demise was from an infection. Yours was the seventh. An honor."

Back in Vargo, Dark had claimed to have killed Jay half a dozen times rather than four. So, who was lying? And was it maliciously or ignorantly? Who did I trust more: the drunk man in front of me or my Mercenary mentor who held more secrets than I did? The answer was obvious.

"How is it done?" I asked.

"Patchworkers have the ability to take out people's memories. Angelo likely found a body that looked like Jay's, extracted his foster son's memories, and then put them in the lifeless husk. It was probably fairly difficult without quick access to the body vault he has in New Dracon City." Liam smiled at Sirash. "But shouldn't you be talking about this, assassin? After all, you're the Patchworker who did it."

My tongue felt heavy in my mouth, but Sirash spoke before I could even stammer out nonsense. "All Skeletons are Patchworkers," he began. "Thanks to our tattoos. But none of us understand how it works until *he* starts talking to us. That was the first time I ever did it. Angelo hired me as a Waylayer and . . . it is what it is."

I gritted my teeth. "He's a Waylayer, too, isn't he?"

Liam and Sirash nodded together. "Was that just an educated guess?" Liam was impressed. "Maybe you know more than I suspected. How wonderful." There was a knock at the door and he stood. "This might be the end of our conversation, Michael. Your friends have finally caught up."

Which friends?

I had barely made it to my feet when Orbis Company strolled through the door. Alexis was first, with a shrug, followed by a chuckling Cassia. Titus gave me an apologetic look, and finally Dark strolled through with his hands in his pockets and darkness weaving around him. His shadow elongated and took hold of mine, and although it didn't do anything, it felt as if my feet were nailed to the floor. My Mercenary mentor stared into my eyes.

"With me, Michael. No one else follow," he ordered.

Like a return to my state in Hollow, Dark and I left the boat together, jumping over the wooden railings and into one of the ankle-deep pools of water that had become a graveyard for washed-up half-broken statues. We climbed up to the highest point silently, slipping and sinking until we reached the top. Lava was quietly bubbling in a hole below us, and the hazy outline of the monstrous humanoid titan towered in the distance. Even so far away, it nearly blocked out the moons and all the stars in the sky.

"You made it farther than I thought you would. My bet was we'd catch you in the Palmer Archipelago. Imagine my surprise that you went to the City of Orphans. Did you discover any hidden secrets there?"

"Not really. How'd your dragon hunt go?"

"I killed two more. They attacked me and Orbis Company on our way here," Dark explained. Lightning jumped up and down his arms. "Didn't stand a chance. Not as I am now."

"Which ones?"

"Water and Nullify."

My breath caught. That was a lie. A stupid, pointless, overconfident lie. And now I knew the truth. All of it—finally. "What are we doing here, Dark?"

"Waiting for the end. It's coming." He exhaled and it was all white whispers. Not from the cold around us, but from his ability to create ice. "When we reach the titan, we'll be fighting the remaining dragons, a Wolven King, and who knows what else. The odds are against us."

"And yet we continue on."

"And yet we continue on," he echoed. "Do you have the name yet?"

I shook my head.

"Shame," he said flippantly. "I'll do my best to kill all the dragons while you get the third name from Skelly. Committing genocide might not be the nicest way to achieve our goals, but at least it won't end in your or Serena's death—"

"I want to thank you, Dark," I interrupted. "You're not the man I want to be. You kill, you maim, you devour those around you . . . but you're the realist who raised me in opposition to the idealist I idolized. In some ways you're the big brother I always needed. I wouldn't have been able to accomplish half of what I've done without you."

"Sentimentality doesn't suit you."

"Better not to leave words unspoken." I gulped. "Dark . . . after everything we've been through, did you really think I wouldn't notice that you lied to me back in Vargo in that chapel?"

Waves crashed against the rocks below in a steady rhythm.

"Omit. Ignore. Manipulate," I continued. "You lie like I do. It's about the words unspoken, not false words said. When you changed tactics— twisting truths and making narratives that are easier to swallow—I caught on immediately. All I lacked was the proof to call you out on it." The brand on my neck was throbbing. "We both know the dragon method you described couldn't happen in time."

Dark clicked his tongue and it echoed away from us like a dying man's dream.

"I learned about the solar eclipse in the City of Orphans. It's another element needed to open the lockless doors. That's why you were so confident I was going to die at Serena's wedding. And here I thought it was because I'd do something stupid to stop it," I explained. "Combined with the fact that you couldn't possibly have killed Nullify because no one knows where he is . . . you aren't going to risk losing a chance to revive Zahra. The next solar eclipse isn't for a few more years. You saved my life in that church to control me. Just as Angelo did after the Kingman riots. But you didn't want me to become anything more than an apprentice Mercenary: you couldn't risk me getting away."

"What makes you think I don't know where Null is?"

"What other information could you have been looking for when you sought permission to enter the King's archives? Mercenaries have access to more information than any King. Unless it's about a missing Evoker. One no one has been able to find since my father's execution."

He huffed. "Good memory."

"I was taught by the best." I stared him down. "It's time to be honest with each other."

Dark pulled out pastel-colored square candies wrapped in a faded pink cloth from one of his pockets. He handed one to me and I bit into it without hesitation. Dark wasn't the kind of person to use poison, so I relished the squishy tart flavor as if it might be my last. And, frankly, it might be. Now that I knew the truth, why would Dark ever let me run wild?

"If Skelly doesn't have the name, then you'll continue this dream a bit longer," Dark said. "But if he does . . . you'll have to decide which of you will die to open the door for us."

"Us?" I chuckled. "So you're working with Angelo. Or at least helping him until the door is open. After that, will you only be able to bring either Zahra or Katherine back?"

Dark was silent, chewing his candy. The sea breeze blew against our skin, cooling the sun's heat.

"There's no other way, is there? Either Serena or I will have to die?"

"Either one of you, or Tenere will shatter," he muttered. "This isn't a story where happy endings are plentiful. Someone has to die for Zahra or Katherine to return." He turned to me. "And we both know who that will be, don't we?"

"The hero, the villain, and the fool left out in the cold. How wonderful to know which role is mine." I rummaged through my mind for anything that might change our fate and asked the only question left. "What if I refuse? What if I fight until the end?"

"Even worms struggle when they're on the hook." Dark gestured around us and let the eerie silence and slow, steady sound of waves breaking against the beach command the conversation. "You're alone. There's nothing—"

A dozen lightning bolts struck Regal Company's ship out of nowhere, thunder booming just slightly behind it. Fires sprang up across the deck as Mercenaries struggled in vain to douse them while statues in the bay started to twitch, move, and then climb up onto the ship and attack. Turns out, I wasn't alone after all. My friends had finally caught up to me.

"What the—"

I rammed into Dark, yanked the revolver out of his holster, and then aimed it at him.

Dark tilted his head slightly to the side, cursing as he saw the spilt candies as he got to his feet. "You know there's a ship full of Mercenaries behind us, right? You really want to do this?"

"I think I do."

"Better men than you have tried and failed," Dark said flatly. "Give me the gun and I'll forget this happened. I'll make your death easy. Don't forget who the real enemy here is, Michael. I didn't kill your father and destroy your family's legacy. Do you really want him to win?"

My body was already nullified. "This isn't about winning. It's proving a point. If I keep following you . . . you'll destroy the man I want to be. This isn't personal . . . it's about being able to look at myself in the mirror."

"You're already looking in the mirror." Dark extended his open hand at me, urging me to reconsider. "Don't make this harder. The more you struggle, the more Serena will suffer."

I hesitated and then turned the gun around and offered it to Dark butt-first.

"You're doing the right thing," he said with a smile as he reached for it. "I'll protect Serena. She doesn't have to die alongside you. Sacrifice—"

I grabbed Dark's wrist with my spare hand as he went for the gun, pulled him close, and then headbutted him with my nullified body. Blood spurted from his nose as I spun around him and then kicked him in the ass and into the volcano. A blast of black smoke shot up almost instantly and a deep congested growl echoed around me as if I were in a monster's stomach. Death wouldn't claim him that easily, but it was still a lingering hope. The lava might slow him down. I ran down the mountain as fast as I could, kicking up rocks behind me. I wasn't stupid enough to think I could beat him alone, but I had to take a stand. I wouldn't be the perfect little sacrifice he wanted me to be. I'd fight until the bitter end.

"Michael," the monstrous figure that shot out of the volcano rumbled. There was a terrifying calmness in his voice. A surgeon's stillness combined with a natural disaster's carelessness. Two pairs of varicolored membranous wings were sprouting out of his back. "Remember that you are mortal. Remember that you will die. Remember your death. Struggle all you want. We will be reunited in due time."

Maybe. But until there was no hope, neither Dark nor his father would claim me. I would defy both, a fool for love until the very end.

23

LAST MAN STANDING

Tendrils lunged at me from the ground, but I batted them away with nullified hands, splatting the darkness to the ground like spilt ink. I made it to the pools at the bottom of the hill as a thick black mist poured out of the volcano, destroying any flora it came in contact with. I splashed through the water, following the trail of lightning toward Cassia's ship. Whatever Chloe was doing—as lightning rained down around me—it was the only safe place to be. Dark's screams became echoes as I climbed up the ship's side, feet getting tangled in the knotty ropes. If this volcano was going to explode, it wouldn't be too much longer before it did.

A horde of blue-sash sailors were waiting for me when I made it over the side. They formed a half circle around me, armed with spiked poles and firebombs made from strips of cloth and bottles of alcohol. I hit the deck with a sharp inhale of breath, putting my hands on my knees to collect myself.

"Michael." I jumped to my feet as Alexis made her way over to me, one gun drawn and aimed at me. Cassia and Titus were next to her. My friends were nowhere to be seen, but the attack on Regal Company continued without pause. "It's over. Give up and you won't be harmed."

"You made your choice, Alexis?" I asked. "Are you sure this is what you want to do?"

She said nothing, but Titus put a hand on her shoulder and said, "Where's the Queen, Michael? Tell us where she is and you won't be harmed. You made it further than we expected, but your adventure is over. We have a job to do."

"I know," I said dryly. "Client is king, right?"

"If you come with us quietly, we'll ask Regal Company to spare your life," Cassia said. "There's no point in you dying for the Queen. You are a Mercenary, and you are valuable to us." She snickered. "Or so I've been told."

I chuckled, thinking about what I had just done to Dark. "No, I don't think I am anymore. Not to Dark, anyway. I've made my choice, and I'm happy with it, but it definitely forfeited my place in Orbis Company."

Alexis's jaw tightened. "What did you do, Michael?"

"I defied Dark." They remained composed. "And kicked him into the volcano."

All three of them went bug-eyed. Even if they didn't know the specifics of what Dark was, or what his goals were . . . they were all smart enough to fear him and understand what I had just done wouldn't be solved with an apology and a hug. I had declared war against one of the most terrifying people in our world.

"Dark is a monster," I said. "And I refuse to let him continue unopposed."

"Are you joining his father?" Alexis asked, emotionless.

I shook my head. "No, I'm choosing the third option. I'm going to stop both Dark and Angelo from achieving their desires. Both will bring ruin to this world, and I refuse to settle for the lesser of two evils."

"And how do you expect to do that?" Cassia mocked. "No other company will take you in. You have no army. You have no land. You're a Kingman in name only. And your strongest ally—the Queen of Hollow—can't remember who you are, nor the bond you used to share. What are you but a rogue apprentice Mercenary?"

"I'm just a persistent imbecile, not some great hero," I said, pride swelling in my chest. "But in Hollow they call me the King Killer and the Dragonslayer. I ended the Hollow rebellion and stopped the Heartbreaker Serial Killer. I have dined with immortals, outsmarted calamities, and defied fate. People have underestimated me ever since my father died. So, listen carefully when I say I will become a Mercenary King. It's not a wish, it's a statement."

"Do you even understand what a Mercenary King is?" Cassia said quietly. "It's not something you become so easily. For starters, you need to form your own Company and . . . and it doesn't matter! You're nothing more than an apprentice!"

"Give me your vote and I won't be one any longer," I declared.

The blood drained from Cassia's face. "What are you . . . How do you know that?"

I tapped my temple. "I've gained some knowledge since we last met. Want to ask me those questions from the exam again?"

"Anyone can find the answers to questions already asked."

"Then ask me new ones, or give me another test to prove my worth," I dared. "Or are you scared I might succeed and be an apprentice no more?"

Cassia bit her thumbnail with a sickening crunch. Embers and ash were beginning to fall from the volcano at an increased pace. It wouldn't be much longer before the bang. The shadows were getting more active, too. As if excited for someone's arrival.

"Can you really stop him?" Alexis shouted. "Can you stop whatever Dark's doing in my sister's name?"

"Yes, I can. I promise."

Alexis hesitated for a moment and then turned and raised her guns at Titus and Cassia. Both swore at her but put their hands in the air. Cassia ordered her crew to stand down as well. She was too good with guns to miss at that distance—and too quick for them to take the gun from her without someone getting shot.

"Alexis! What are you doing? Are you insane? He's a nobody!"

"He's the only hope I have left," Alexis said as she backed away from them. "Michael, with me. You've got a plan?"

I jogged past Titus and Cassia to her side. "Absolutely."

"All of you, tie each other up and get below," Alexis said, hands steady. "Don't make me shoot anyone, Cassia."

Cassia scowled, but Titus looked like a proud if frustrated father. Neither answered Alexis but slowly ordered everyone to do as she said. Only Cassia's quartermaster remained on deck, instructing Cassia to tie her hands to the mast, which the Mercenary did. The quartermaster wasn't leaving the ship in our hands. Not even if it meant remaining out in the open as a prisoner. And because I wasn't a fool, I double-checked the knots myself. They were tight enough.

"What now?" Alexis asked quietly. Regal Company was still dealing with the lightning and stone statues. "Where are your friends?"

Serena popped up over the side as if in answer, a smile on her face, and extended her hand to demand my help. I helped her over. Then Naomi and Chloe, who immediately began running around, tying knots and unfurling sails, while Sebastian went toward the ship's wheel with his eyes closed. One-Eye was hunched on his shoulder like a judgmental furry parrot. Naomi sprang upward into the sails and ropes. Before I could ask any questions, Serena embraced me tightly enough to crack my back.

"I was worried about you," she said softly.

"I was worried about you, too," I said, breaking the hug. "But we really need to be going. Dark's coming after me."

Naomi landed next to me, spools of rope in her hands. Her hair was hidden by a bandanna and she was dressed for sailing. "What did you do? And why is Alexis our ally now?"

Alexis collapsed against the side of the ship, the ramifications of her actions finally catching up with her. She was chuckling to herself like a madwoman.

"We defied Dark," I stated. "I couldn't keep helping him. So I made it clear where I stood."

Naomi blinked a few times. "Are you mad? Why would you do that? Dark is . . . Dark. I'd rather chop my fingers off than argue with him. He's fucking *insane*."

"Understatement of the year," Alexis mumbled.

"What she said!" Naomi said. "Why did you suddenly grow a conscience now?"

"I don't know," I said, shaking my head. Serena put a hand on my shoulder to comfort me, but all it did was make me regret what I'd done. I put us all in danger—massive, world-ending danger—because I couldn't pretend to be his dog anymore. Maybe it was foolish to continue struggling when my death was all but guaranteed . . . but wasn't it better to die on my feet than on my knees?

"Excuse me, Your Highness!" Sebastian called down from the upper deck. "But we really need to get going!" He pointed at the fires slowly going out on Regal Company's ship. "Raise the anchor!"

Naomi dropped everything and skidded toward the metal chain that disappeared into the murky water below us. She began to heave it out of the water pull by pull, and despite being strong enough to do it on her own, Serena and I joined her to make it go quicker.

We had it halfway up before Sebastian screamed again. "Chloe! Are we all tied down?"

"Yes!"

"Naomi! Hit us with a gust! We have to get out of—"

The volcano erupted. Smoke, lava, and rocks burst out of the opening and into the air. The sky was obscured by thick black smoke and the area around us darkened as if the sun would never rise again. My ears were ringing and I lurched forward, staggering, as we fought to pull the anchor up. The moment we had it locked in place, I tried to scream and tell the others, but I couldn't even hear myself over the roar of the volcano and the sound of rocks hitting the water around us.

Naomi's blast hit the sails and I flew back and nailed my back on the bowsprit. Serena and Alexis had been lucky enough to avoid going anywhere, both holding firmly to the railing as the ship was propelled forward at a nauseating force. Naomi had tethered herself to the mainmast so she could create wind for the sails, moving her hands back and forth as if pushing some invisible force. It was as if we were in the center of a hurricane, and for just a moment I was grateful I couldn't hear anything.

And then my ears popped, and I heard the screams around me, my own included. Well, at least that explained why my throat felt raw. As we sped away from the island, I turned around to give it one last look. Lava was already covering most of it, burning and encasing anything it touched. From this side it was impossible to see if Regal Company's ship had escaped before the volcano erupted. If anyone had at all.

Once we were far enough away that ash no longer fell from the sky, Naomi stopped and collapsed to her knees, sweat drenching her. Chloe was at her side, forcing her to drink water and running through the basic questions as she did, making sure Naomi was still Naomi.

"What's your name?" Chloe asked.

"Naomi Dexter."

"Who are your parents?"

"Bryan Dexter and Evie Browne. Both dead."

"Do you know who *they* are?" Chloe asked, pointing toward the three of us as we made our way over to them.

Naomi groaned dramatically. "Queen Serena the Forgotten, Mercenary Alexis the Trueshot, and do I really have to name that dumbass?"

We all chuckled. Naomi seemed fine. Or, at the very least, not a Forgotten. After what had happened to Serena, we were all on edge. Chloe asked one more question. "Who am I?"

"The most important person in my life," Naomi said, grabbing the back of Chloe's head and pulling it down to kiss her. Despite Chloe's initial shock, she returned the kiss tenfold. I smiled broadly, happy that my friends had finally found each other.

They separated, lingering so close to each other that they shared the same breath.

"I didn't *know*. I thought . . . *I thought* . . . ," Chloe breathed. "How long?"

"A long time," Naomi said before kissing her again. "Sorry it took me so long to act on it. I got lost on the way. Thought a crown was more important than you."

"It's fine, I'm—"

"Sorry to interrupt the lovefest down there, but we have a problem!" Sebastian screamed as he began to turn the wheel sharply to the right. "We've got a follower!"

All four of us went to the side of the ship and looked back. Sebastian was right. We were being pursued by Regal Company's ship. Its dragon-head figurehead was covered in ash and soot but prominent as always. Regal Company was coming for Serena, and Dark was coming for me.

So much for a clean getaway.

PART 4:

DEPRESSION

"I fear the hunter who has stalked me since birth.
I see them in the wrinkles on my parents' faces, in the bones
my friends break, and in the eyes of my lover as she ages.
I have tried to run from them, but they remind me of my fate
no matter where I go. After a lifetime of hiding,
I have decided to meet them on my own terms."

—Mercenary Bottles of Machina Company, age 23,
five days before he committed suicide

ONCE MORE
WITH FEELING

Death, it seemed, was inevitable as we watched Regal Company's ship trail us at a steady distance. It was comforting in a way. We had lived these past few weeks constantly looking over our shoulders and never sleeping deeply. Now we could face the end together without saying a word, knowing this was it. We wouldn't get out of this unscathed.

Naomi was the first to move. "If I increase the wind, we might be able to—"

"No." Chloe took her hand. "You might become a Forgotten. You've lost enough memories getting us this far. We'll come up with another plan."

"Like what?" Naomi snapped. "We can't fight back."

"Are you sure?" Alexis said with her arms crossed. And then to the quartermaster, she asked, "What are the weapon capabilities of this ship?"

The quartermaster rattled off the number of cannons, harpoons, and gunpowder barrels, and even boasted that she had a dozen statues below deck. But there weren't any others in the water nearby, and, judging by Alexis's face, it wouldn't be enough to stop Regal Company, let alone Dark. We were outnumbered ten to one. And that was the wrong side to be on against Mercenaries. One of them equaled ten others at least.

"Then what can we do?" Naomi asked. "I won't die without a fight."

"What if I try to sink the ship with my magic?" Serena suggested. "If I use enough, it might—"

"That's not happening," I declared with a finality in my voice I didn't know I had. Serena opened her mouth but swallowed her words instead when she saw my eyes. Using Fabrications strong enough to sink a ship would steal a lot of memories from her, and to be frank . . . I didn't know what would happen. Would she become a fresh Forgotten and lose the memories she had gained recently? It wasn't acceptable to me. We'd find another solution.

"Regal Company won't stop until they catch us," Alexis mumbled. "Failing to would insult their Company, and the noble siblings would sooner fall on their swords than let that happen. Papa Noble doesn't like failure or compassion. Only victory."

"And all Dark cares about is Zahra." I put my hands behind my head. "No one on that ship is stopping for any reason."

"Would Dark stop if their mission was complete?" Serena asked quietly.

Alexis shrugged. "It's hard to tell. Ciara or Liam might force Dark to stop, but it's complicated. Dark has an . . . influence over others." She scratched at her wrist. "We're Mercenaries. We respect the strong. Dark's obsession is infectious, and his strength is unparalleled. It's hard to say what Dark can and can't do."

Chloe asked the question I didn't want to, maybe out of mercy. Or pity. "Would Regal Company stop if they had Michael?"

"Without a doubt." Alexis couldn't look me in the eyes. "They'd resume eventually. But Michael could delay them for a long time. Hours . . . days . . . weeks . . . ?"

I took a deep, deep breath. "I guess that gives us an option, then."

"Not happening," Serena said frantically. "You're not giving yourself up."

"Dark will stop once he gets me, and you all can continue to the Reborn Titan. If I can delay them long enough, then you can get the fruit and restore your memories. Or you could get the Third Wolven King's name and we could barter for our freedom." I looked at her and smiled faintly. "Your continuing without me is the only thing that makes sense."

"No, no, no!" she repeated like a toddler throwing a tantrum. "There has to be another way. Right, everyone?" She looked around and no one would meet her eyes. "You won't let him do that . . . right?"

The blood drained from her face when no one spoke up or acted differently. Giving myself up was the only thing that made sense, and we all knew it.

"You swore you wouldn't leave me again," she hissed, her eyes welling up. "You *swore*."

"Serena, I'm sorry. I didn't . . ." I closed my eyes and tried to steady myself. "Mercenaries are ruthless. They will never stop. This is the only thing . . ." I trailed off, remembering that Mercenaries didn't stop once something was in their sights.

"Alexis . . . release Titus, Cassia, and the rest of the crew. Tell Titus I want to eat something." I nodded absently. "We should all eat before this happens."

"Are you giving up?" she asked.

"No. But families eat together, and that's what we should do before we get there."

The others were all confused by my resignation that we might not be able to outrun fate, Regal Company, or Dark. But they accepted what I wanted to do. Cassia, Titus, the quartermaster, and the crew were released from their bonds, and while Titus whipped up a proper meal for us all . . . Cassia and I struck an agreement. We would use her ship in the upcoming battle, but none of her crew would fight. When I asked what would happen if Regal Company bombarded us, all she did was shrug and say she doubted Dark would resort to such brutish methods. Which likely meant our odds were truly nonexistent.

We ate soon after. Titus prepared a feast of fish and greeneries: seaweed-seasoned oysters, fatty bluefin with brined olives, seared flatbread, grilled peppers stuffed with pink and yellow tropical fruit, lemon-soaked snails, dark liquor, white wine, and a fish so thoroughly drenched in orange juice it felt more like a drink than something chewable. We drank and laughed, telling stories long past dusk and into the twinkling starlight. Doom had a wonderful way of lightening the mood. We had no need to fear the day of our death: it had come. But we could embrace the final moments.

Everyone slept while they could, watching as the titan in the distance slowly and surely blocked out more of the sky until it was all we could see. The titan was humanoid in nature, but akin to a personification of a mountain in the middle of the sea. It had plateaus and even trees growing on it, with jagged bones jutting out of various parts like splinters. It was covered in moss and had coral reefs growing on parts of its knees after spending hundreds of years underwater. There were faint traces of rusted pauldrons and gauntlets interwoven into the titan's stone flesh as other discarded bits of its armor floated in the water nearby like metal rafts. There was a massive scythe in its hand. A tool to slaughter. A tool to sweep across the battlefields and wipe out hordes of enemies with ease. It was as frightening as it was beautiful.

As morning approached, only Serena and I were on the deck. We had talked through the night.

"What's it like to be a Forgotten?" I asked, elbows on the railing, staring off into the distance. Everything felt at ease around us. A pleasant breeze. A full stomach. Friends who had followed me until the end. It was more than I deserved. "Is it . . . weird?"

"It's hard for me to express how difficult it is. I remember *nothing* about my previous life. Except your name and how it felt to be in your presence. My heart danced at the sight of you. My nose recognized your scent—a city after a storm. The bards tell us true love is eternal, that it can never be lost, but . . ." She twirled her hair between her fingers, and my heart ached not to see her rub her left wrist instead. "I don't know if I'll ever understand what we were. Or remember the private moments we shared. But you are the only person I want."

"Serena . . . I —"

"So if I am to be Queen . . . I need my Kingman. But I don't care about crowns or legacies. I just want to be happy." Then she added, "You make me happy. So while I may not be the exact girl you loved . . . will you fall in love with me again?"

"I've always been yours."

"Good." She blushed. "Then let's make some new memories, shall we?"

We kissed. Softly, like sailors testing the waters to determine the temperature. And when we separated, she whispered, "Another."

The next was more passionate. More familiar. Roughness interspersed with care. "Another," she demanded.

Each new kiss brought more fervor. After each, she demanded more. Like a spoiled child who could never have enough. A hunger that could never be sated in a single life. We savored every memory before they had a chance to fade away. I was a willing companion, kissing her every time she said, "Another."

We were greedy. Careless. But for a moment, in the stillness before dawn where the light had yet to illuminate the sky, we were all that mattered. Our fears were eased as we held each other, no longer wondering about what would happen when we reached the titan. Because, maybe, just this once, a Kingman and Hollow could have a happy ending.

THE MERCENARY
AND THE TITAN

Our ship crashed into the Reborn Titan's left foot. Cassia and her crew stayed on the ship while the rest of us misfits leapt off. Regal Company, Dark, and Sirash's ship barreled into the same foot. Shards of rocks rained down on us as we struggled to remain upright while the ground beneath us shook. Sebastian bent his pinky back well past the point of breaking, screaming in pain as the nearby stone statues rumbled to life and formed a wall between us and the incoming wave of Mercenaries. The forces of nature clashed in a crescendo of stone and steel.

The noble siblings bounded over the statues, weapons shining in the early light before they were stopped by Chloe's bolts of lightning and Naomi's blasts of heavy wind. Naomi and Chloe urged us to continue upward to the titan's forehead as they held back anyone who crossed Sebastian's line. The battle itself was only a momentary distraction. Winning wasn't our objective. Surviving was. We could likely stop Dark and Regal

Company from destroying us . . . if Serena remembered the leverage she'd had before becoming a Forgotten, and if not . . . well, happy endings were overrated, right?

We said nothing as we circled around the titan's foot, looking for any path upward that didn't require free-climbing up the smooth, slick surface. There was a small opening in the titan's sole that we crawled through. The inside of the titan's leg was hollow, with splinters of bone crisscrossing all the way up like a spider's web. Everything around us smelt like ground-up corn, and around the edges were steps that circled all the way up. We took them at full speed, not looking back to see if we were pursued. The clank of our footsteps echoed all around us.

We emerged somewhere near its lower back where a bone had curved out and back like a crescent moon. The entire area was covered in a field of Moon's Tears that shone brightly even with the sun so high in the sky. I didn't recognize any of the other flora in the area. It was a strange mix of brightly colored and odd-shaped fruit, spiky cacti, sun-dried fish bones, and thick vines that covered the tree like armor. Almost as if a once-tropical island had dried up.

Serena looked around. "How do we continue?"

There was no obvious path to take. No ladder or rope. "I think we need to get back into the titan. If we can reach the spine, we could follow that all the way up."

Serena nodded, and we began to search for another entry to the titan. All the moss made it hard to see any opening or cracks into it, forcing Serena to scrape away whatever she could with her forearms and hands. It wasn't long before the moss had tinted her skin red and green. I did the same, albeit slower, trying to figure out where the original path had been. We weren't conquerors, braving the unknown. Rather we were followers treading hidden paths. And no path was ever completely hidden.

I stopped and looked around again. There was a path to the forehead, I just had to—

And there it was.

It looked so innocent: a tree had slumped against the titan's back and grown toward the sun. But no moss covered it, and the vines fell in front of it like a bead curtain, gently swaying in the wind. I tapped Serena on the shoulder, pointed, and we made our way toward it. We pushed the vines aside and crawled through the hollow trunk and into the titan once again. Sunlight filtered in through pinprick holes all over its torso and back.

The towering spine greeted us when we emerged into the open interior. I couldn't see the top of it, a hazy darkness waiting for us above and below. A spiral staircase wrapped around it just like the legs. But this one was less secure, planks of wood instead of the solid stone below. Bone spikes jutted out of the spine randomly. They wouldn't be the best handholds, but it was better than nothing. And it was much better than free climbing.

I went first, one hand on the spine, while I took each step slowly and carefully. The planks trembled under my weight as the ropes that held them to the spine went taut. Serena followed, one hand on my shoulder and the other on the spine. And so we continued . . . too stupid or too proud to consider any other option.

"Do you think we'd die if we fell from up here?" Serena asked.

No part of me wanted to look down and see for myself, but I said, "Almost definitely."

Serena muttered a few curses under her breath. "I'm starting to think I may have a fear of heights."

"Terrible time to figure that out."

"Right?" She laughed awkwardly. "Was the old me scared of heights?"

"No," I said. "The old you wasn't scared of anything."

"I don't believe that. Everyone fears something."

"Not you," I asserted.

"Just because you didn't know it doesn't mean there wasn't something."

"We'll have to agree to disagree."

"I suppose so." She hesitated, squeezing my shoulder tighter. "Do you think this me will still be here if I eat the fruit and all my memories are restored?"

"Why wouldn't it?" I paused, one of the planks buckling under my weight more than the others. When it held, I continued. "It's not as if you're dying."

"I mean I sort of am," she said. "Everything I've heard about the old me is so different. She was a queen, prim and proper and noble, and I'm just some wannabe wanderer with her head stuck in the sand. If she returns, I'll disappear . . . And that seems a lot like death."

"If that were the case, then becoming Forgotten would also be death."

"Isn't it?" she countered. "The death of a personality seems like a death to me. Just because someone's heart remains beating doesn't mean they're alive."

I didn't respond. If Serena ate the fruit and it restored her memories, would it kill this version of the woman I had fallen in love with?

"Do you miss her?" Serena asked quietly. "The old me?"

"It's complicated."

"It's fine if you do. You knew her so long. I—"

"I love every version of you. The quick-tempered free spirit who always speaks her mind and the contemplative, quiet, and slightly manipulative Queen I grew up with. They're both you. You will always be Serena, the love of my life."

I left it unsaid that I hoped she felt the same. We were broken people. Ones who wore whatever masks they needed to survive any given day. Some days we manipulated and lied. Others, we re-created childhood fantasies about saving the day and slaying dragons. It was all real. It was all necessary. No part of us would have made it this far if the others didn't exist. We were exactly who we needed to be. Not for the world to find comfort in us, but for each other.

She glanced away, a blush creeping up her cheeks. "So dramatic."

"Concerning you?" I smiled. "Always."

We walked out of the spine and into daylight. The wind howled around me like a lingering nightmare. Serena was right behind me, clutching at the back of my shirt like a lost child. There was a rocky path from the neck to the top.

"Almost there."

"Almost—"

Branches shot out of the ground as Liam Noble landed in front of us. He was covered in self-inflicted wounds, the dagger dripping in his hand and onto the grass below. His breath was short, and he held a hand over his ribs. Maybe one of the stone statues had got a good hit in. "It's time for a rematch, Michael."

I put my hand in front of Serena, urging her to continue to the tree while I dealt with Liam. But she stayed, unwilling to leave me alone. "You already lost to me once. Really think you stand a chance now?"

"Who knows," Liam admitted. "But that's why I brought reinforcements."

Rocks descended from the top of the titan, rumbling down the trail in a pitter-patter as Sirash appeared, twin daggers in his hands. He pointed the tip of one at me. "Here we are, Michael . . . two thieves trying to steal more time . . . reunited again under the stars."

"Is that the guy that kidnapped you?" Serena asked, nudging her head toward Sirash.

I nodded and then to Sirash said, "You sure we have to do this?"

"We'd only re-tread the same old paths if we talked again." There was something in the back of his throat. Words he wanted to speak. He was doing everything to contain them. "I'm here to complete a job. There's a bounty on your head and I'm here to claim it. At least it'll be a friend taking you out. Doesn't that make it better?"

"Not really."

"As if either of you are getting close to him," Serena growled. Everything around us began to shake—the titan included. Yet, as I nullified myself to make sure I could remain upright . . . Sirash and Liam never faltered. The knees of neither buckled under the pressure. "Michael, please tell me you're nullifying the area."

"Someone must've nullified their bodies before they came up here."

Serena cursed, releasing the pressure around us as Liam pressed the dagger to his throat, slicing a thin red line from his jaw to his collarbone. Roots began to bulge up from the trail, bursting out of the ground like popping veins. They shot toward us, binding us like ropes before I expelled the warmth out of my chest—nullifying the area—to set us free. The roots withered away, wilting like cut flowers in a vase as Sirash jumped toward us, daggers aimed at our eyes. I shoved Serena down and took the brunt of his attack myself, my back sliced from dimple to spine. The shallowness of the cut was my only saving grace, because my sweat-stained shirt did little to protect me.

Serena, never one to act like a damsel, grabbed Sirash's arms before smashing him to the ground. His daggers fell out of his hands as he groaned, then slid across the grass. She tried to pin him, but a lifetime of thieving and running made him too slippery to hold for long, and he was easily able to roll away and to safety.

"C'mon, Sirash," I muttered as Serena helped me back up. "Let's talk."

"No talking," he spat. "I'm never talking to you again. All you do is lie and manipulate and trick and make me—" Sirash sucked in a breath, hands moving to his throat as if he was choking. His irises turned golden. And then his hands moved away from his throat and jammed into the ground like stakes. When he pulled them out, the hand of bone had streaks of silver running through it. "Michael Kingman. For some reason, this tool cannot or will not do as he should. So I'll do it myself."

Sirash's entire demeanor was different. Still instead of jumpy. Proud instead of tentative. Every move was purposeful. Important. Zarack, the Second Wolven King, had taken over Sirash's body. A parasite that assumed control of its host.

"Assassin!" Liam shouted. "Stop all this grandstanding and stop Mich—"

"Did I speak to you?" Zarack asked flatly. Liam froze. Mercenaries weren't used to being talked down to. Especially not one with such a high position in an infamous company. "What right do you have to order me to do anything?"

Liam stood straighter. "I am Liam Noble, one of the four commanders of Regal Mercenary Company and—"

"I loathe Mercenaries. Never trusted them before the war and especially not during. They promise you the world and only deliver a city. Void Company was such a disappointment." Zarack ripped out one of Sirash's molars, and then flicked it at Liam like a coin. It hit the Mercenary in the shoulder, sticking to his clothes like a barnacle to a ship. "Your services are no longer required. I'll deal with the Kingman and Hollow myself."

The tooth exploded into shards of bone and smoke, and blew Liam away and off the titan before he had a chance to say anything. My ears ringing, I never heard a splash or a scream. Just an absence that couldn't be filled with hope or despair at another life being lost.

"Now . . ." Zarack adjusted Sirash's jacket. "Where were we? Ah, yes, you two are going to reverse my brother's plans and justify your lives. You're going to kill a Wolven King today."

THE ASSASSIN
AND THE TITAN

Back when we were young and stupid—well, *stupider*—Sirash and I used to count the stars after the bells stopped ringing in Hollow and the moonfall either passed over us or hit something. It was the only time the city was calm. The hustle and bustle paused as everyone said their prayers, composed themselves, and did whatever they needed to stave off another brush with death. We used to pretend that every star was a coin, one we could take for ourselves if we could just climb high enough.

That all changed after we worked with Dark. After Sirash had been taken prisoner by Scales. After I had lied to him about what happened to his brother. After I had let one of my only friends down. My mistakes started his downward trend. The path that led him to becoming a personification of wrath. A being who barely lived for himself. I had always regretted how I took advantage of him . . . so when Zarack took over his body, redemption was my only goal.

Sirash was going to get his body back. No matter the cost to my own. But this wasn't a battle I could win with my strength. I was going to show why I talked while Sirash shot.

"I know my brother has your sister captive," Zarack said, pacing in front of the trail. If we tried to rush him, we'd be caught easily. "So here I am, offering you revenge. I'll tell you what he most regrets—what tethers him to life—and then you'll be able to—"

"Sirash!" I interrupted. "You in there?"

Zarack's face fell. "*I* am addressing you. Offering you a chance to—"

"Shut up," I snapped. "I'm not talking to you. Sirash! I know you're in there. You're really going to let someone take over your body? You're stronger than that. Force that asshole out of your mind! You're in control. Not him!"

Zarack was snarling at me. All primal, no regal. "How. Dare. You. Ignore. Me."

"How dare I?" I feigned surprise. "How dare *you*? You interrupted our conversation. Don't you know how impolite that is?" I looked down on him. "How vulgar. What kind of king doesn't have basic common courtesy?"

Zarack was breathing shallowly, fists clenched tight. With every inhale, the wind howled around us, and with every exhale, thunder boomed and lightning struck the water below. A true natural walking calamity who could reverse the rules of nature to his will.

"You're too much like him," Zarack growled. "The deal is off."

"It was never on, since I never even listened to your terms."

"I'm going to kill you."

"Get the fuck in line." I thumbed all around me. "You're maybe tenth or so if you're lucky. You immortals always like to act tough, but none of you can handle me. You have strength and I have my poisonous tongue. Adept at pissing off anyone and everything."

Zarack didn't respond. More lightning struck around us, inching closer to where Serena and I were standing.

"I once made a priest with a ten-year vow-of-silence record break their oath to scream at me. I made a chivalrous knight kick a puppy just to get out of protecting me. I'm *really* good at making people emotional. And the angrier they are, the sloppier they get. And do you know why that's such a useful skill to have?"

Zarack flinched and grabbed his left arm, which was now shaking violently.

"Hard to focus around me, right? Yeah. All Sirash ever needs is an opening. It's all he ever needed. Every con, every steal, every pickpocket. He always knew how to take advantage when I made an opening. It's why we were such a good pair." I spat at the Wolven King. "Sirash, do you hear me? It's time to share our winnings!"

Zarack fell to his knees and screamed. The clouds above us split and cracked as if someone had broken them with a hammer. And as the echo of Zarack's wails died out, he stared upward, breathing heavily. His eyes were green flaked with gold again. Sirash was back.

"Despite how many times I've experienced it," Sirash breathed, "it never ceases to amaze me. You make everyone angry so easily." He chuckled. "You're one-of-a-kind, Michael."

I ran to my friend's side, helping him stand. He wobbled and then leaned on me slightly. "Good to see I can still impress you after all these years."

"We'll have to reschedule our fight," he muttered. "Don't really want to collect your bounty anymore." He nudged his head toward the tree. "But you've still something to do, right?"

I nodded.

Sirash plopped back down. "Then go do it."

"You'll be fine?"

"Always am." Sirash sucked his teeth. "Zarack's still in there. Screaming at me. I can tune him out a little right now. Not sure how long I'll be in control, but I'll do my best."

"That's all I can ask for."

"Suppose so." Sirash waved me off. "Hurry."

I clasped him on the shoulder, then went to Serena, grabbing her hand and beginning up the path to the top of the titan.

Thieves have this superstition about looking back. That if you spend your life thinking of what's past, you'll never have the confidence to forge a path forward. Sirash had always been good at following that rule. I had always been bad at it. He used to make fun of me for it all the time.

So, when I looked back to make sure Sirash was fine, I didn't see him. Didn't hear him move. There was no trace of him. Except for a piece of the titan that was crumbling at the edge, as if something had recently fallen from it.

THE KING AND THE TITAN

We reached the apex of the titan, hand in hand. There was nothing up here but rocks and grass and the tree in the middle of the titan's forehead. The roots were thick and sprawling and the pitch-black leaves let no sunlight through. Four heart-shaped fruits hung from the branches, dangling like cocoons. Alphonse, the Wolven King, lay against the trunk of the tree, gently batting a ball of ever-changing light between his hands. Skelly's heartless body was at his feet, shattered into thousands of jagged remnants of bone.

"I always hated my brother's titans." He got to his feet like an old man, with a groan. "They have no honor or sense of duty, like the dragons, or a strong malleable urge for freedom like the behemoths." He sighed dramatically. "They just want to be the strongest, the proudest, the whatever-est. Luckily for my brother, wars forge paths to new pinnacles, and so the titans followed him, always eager for more."

"Couldn't tame Skelly?"

"Couldn't. Wouldn't. Shouldn't," Alphonse droned. "Does it really matter which?"

I shook out my arms. One more fight. One more step in forging our own path forward. "Suppose not."

"Seriously?" he asked, amused. "I didn't think you'd want to duel again." He whipped his sash into the air like a ribbon and it solidified into a longsword that sucked light into it. His leopard pelt hardened. "My youngest brother's name is no longer here. I've destroyed every trace of it. Are you sure you want to fight a pointless battle? You have no chance of winning."

"Losing is good for my ego. Makes sure I never become complacent." I raised my fists. "Maybe it's because I fear one of my friends plunged to his death, but I'm not really in the mood to back down right now. And I doubt you're going to just let us take the fruit anyway."

"You are correct." Alphonse stabbed his sword into the tree, slowly corrupting the roots and life from the inside out. It turned ashy and flaky, a slight breeze more than enough to make it all wither away. The infection was slow and methodical, but we didn't have much time before it destroyed the fruit on the branches. "My youngest brother's name cannot get out there."

"Then I guess that's all there is."

Alphonse nodded. "You will be conquered here."

I smirked. "As if. I've still got fourteen days until I die."

"What are you—"

I rushed the Wolven King, pinning the immortal against the trunk of the tree, leveling blows to his midsection. Alphonse responded with a blow to my knee that caused such a loud *crack* in the air, I felt as if the sky itself had shattered. My breath left my body, squeezing my lungs till they hurt. Another kick to my face and I collapsed like a sack of wheat. And then I got back to my feet, wiped the blood from my mouth, and smiled from ear to ear.

"Is that all you've got?" I goaded.

"Shut up." Alphonse punched me again. And again. And again. His rage consumed him. Overwhelmed his senses. Narrowed his vision. With one hand around my neck to hold me still, he continued his onslaught. So even an immortal like him could be so mundane. "You are an ant beneath my feet."

I couldn't stop smiling as he hit me. "Dumbass."

He paused. "What?"

"Dumbass," I repeated. "Don't you understand how a con works? Never take your eyes off the queen."

Alphonse whipped his head around.

Serena was in front of the tree with one of the heart-shaped fruits in her hands. She winked at the king and then took a big bite. The juice that trickled out of the sides of her mouth was as black as the leaves. Her eyes went wide and her body went limp, and I was past the king so fast I caught her before she fell and gently lowered her to the ground. Her body shook uncontrollably.

"Serena! Talk to me!" She stared at me with vacant eyes, trembling violently. It took all my strength to stop her from slamming her head against the ground. "C'mon, wake up."

Serena stopped convulsing and her eyes closed. I put my ear to her mouth and felt her breath against my skin. Her heartbeat was steady, too. Whatever that fruit had done to her body or mind, she had recovered. When she woke up, I would learn which Serena would return to me.

Alphonse stood over us, fists clenched and faceless head scrunched together like one big wrinkle. "You remind me of my youngest brother. It made me careless."

"Not a lot of brotherly love there, then," I said between painful breaths. The pleasure of outsmarting an immortal was starting to wane, pain resonating through my body. "Ready to go another round?"

"Yes." He yanked the sword out of the tree. "But this one will be much—" Alphonse paused, staring at my shadow as it elongated to an unnatural degree.

Everything blackened around us as I held Serena in my arms. A bolt of darkness leapt out of my shadow and then re-formed into something unmistakably human and familiar: Dark. He didn't show any signs of having fallen into a volcano. He was exactly the same as before except his clothes were singed, his body was covered in blood splatter, a pair of black wings were sprouting out of his back, and he had burning red eyes. Eyes that infected the skin around his face with pulsating red veins like the corruption had back in Hollow. Any trace of grey had been washed away. And so the monster finally became fully formed.

Dark held his revolver parallel with the king's head. "If it makes you feel better, Michael is a wonderful distraction."

And Dark emptied the entire cylinder into the king. Two above and four below the neck. The king was speechless as he hobbled backwards, and with one stride forward, Dark kicked the Wolven King off the titan. The immortal fell wordlessly below and, as with Liam and Sirash, I never heard a splash.

Dark blew smoke away from the tip of his revolver, knocked the cylinder out, and began to reload it. "So you actually made it here."

"I did. How long have you been in my shadow?"

"Since we parted, before the volcano erupted," Dark stated. "Can't say I was very fond of having to live in your shadow for so long . . . but at least it gave me a shot at killing a Wolven King."

I looked him up and down. "Nice wings. I thought you didn't like turning parts of your body into those of a dragon."

"We're at the end," he snarled. "Didn't think there was a point in holding back anymore."

"I'm glad," I said, drawing my revolver. "I must scare you if you're meeting me with everything you are."

"Oh, this isn't everything." He clicked the cylinder back into place. "Best to have some secrets, right?"

I nullified my body, a comforting warmth easing my aching muscles. This might be the last time I ever felt it, so I enjoyed the heat and memory of the days before I realized what kind of Fabricator I was. To be so young and naïve . . . Had I finally grown into a man I could be proud of? Maybe, in the end, that was all that mattered.

"Are you ready, Michael?"

"As I'll ever be." I exhaled and smiled widely. "Come on, Dark! Show me the Black Death!"

"Good." His hands rose up slowly as if conducting an orchestra. The shadows cast by the black-leafed tree elongated toward me. "I wouldn't want you to ask for forgiveness now. You were never more than my plaything."

Darkness.

It was all-encompassing. All-consuming. It was everywhere and my senses were gone like a fleeting thought. I lost sight of Serena. Forgoing common sense—that Dark was still in front of me, armed with a gun and hatchet—I reached back for her, just to know she was still well. I stumbled and landed on my belly, clawing at the grass. There was a boot on my stomach in moments, pressing me down, and then a gun barrel against my shoulder.

Dark's voice pierced the darkness. "You never stood a chance."

There was a bang, a wave of heat through my body, and then immense pain. But without my sight, I didn't know what had happened. Only that everything seemed heightened and the pulse in my neck felt like someone pounding drums. What had he done to me?

"Enough!"

The darkness fizzled out around us as Dark's body slammed against the ground, an invisible force pressing down on us. I was holding my shoulder, and I could stand, but even I noticed how the titan rumbled around us. Pieces of it fell off and into the ocean below.

Serena was on her knees, one hand clutching her side as the other was pressed against her cheek. Her snarl sent shivers down my spine, and as she stood, I knew in my heart this was Queen Serena. She walked cautiously over to me, smiled, and then ran her hand over my prickly hair.

"You got a little tan," she said softly. "It looks nice." And then, wide-eyed, she saw the blood running red through my fingers. "Dark *shot* you. Michael, are you okay?"

I hugged her tightly with the arm that didn't feel about to fall off, holding back tears. "Are you really back?"

She hesitated and then returned my hug. "I am."

"Do you remember why we're here?"

Serena pulled away. "I do. We came to the Reborn Titan to restore my memories. You brought me, because you wanted me to have a choice in what my life became, and I am so grateful, Michael."

Her tone was odd, less happiness and more remorse. "Serena, what aren't you telling me? Did I do something wrong?"

"No, of course not. I did, Michael. I lied to you."

"I . . . I . . . I don't . . . What did you lie about?"

"I never had any leverage over Jay Prince. It was a trick . . . one you and he both fell for." She brushed a few strands of hair behind my ear. "I'm sorry, Michael. You did all this for me, but I can't stop the inevitable. I must be the Queen of Hollow."

"No," I whispered. "There must be something else we can—"

Serena kissed me and silenced my protests. It tasted bitter and felt clumsy—like a hummingbird pecking at a tree. Only once she pulled away did I realize she was crying. "This is the way it has to be, Michael. You said it yourself—we're Kingman and Hollow. We can't be together. And we were fools to ever think differently."

"There has to be something we can do. We can run away. Go somewhere where Hollow and Kingman don't mean anything. We can . . ." My words faded away as she shook her head, and I knew this wasn't the happily ever after we had fought for. This was the tragedy we had hoped to avoid.

"I love you so much, Michael," she whispered as she held my head against her chest. "But this is how our story ends. With us doing what we must to save those we love."

"I'm sorry," I said between sobs. "I couldn't protect you."

"It's fine," she said. "Because *I* can still protect *you*." Serena turned her head toward Dark. The invisible weight on my shoulders disappeared. "Mercenary, let's make a deal."

"Talk quickly," he growled.

"I'll go with you if you spare Michael's life, and that of everyone on the *Freedioso*. Regal Company will spare them, too."

"You know I can't agree to that," Dark explained. "Michael needs to die for—"

"I'll die in his place."

"Serena, don't—"

She used her Fabrications to force me to my knees, and as hard as I struggled to nullify my body, nothing happened. Dark must've shot me with a green-crystal–laced bullet. I was useless with it in my body. I dug through my open wound with my fingers, prying apart muscle in search of the bullet lodged in my shoulder. The pain was mind-numbing, but I pushed through it in desperation.

"I'd like to propose a new deal. I'll give you the third name as well. I've always known it. I just never realized it until now."

Dark blinked at her as he ran his tongue over his teeth. The shadows around him hummed like a horde of insects. "We still need a Kingman to open the door. The third name without him won't do—"

"I only have to die by Kingman hand, right?" Serena motioned toward me. "And—tell me if I'm wrong—but aren't all Skeletons Patchworkers? And can't Patchworkers reattach body parts and extract memories?" She smiled painfully. "Take his arm and attach it to another to fulfill the requirements. Just let Michael live. I'll abdicate the throne. Whatever it takes."

"Maybe I misunderstood who the true fool in your relationship was," Dark muttered. "But if you're willing to die in his place . . . I'll agree to your terms."

"Swear on Zahra's memory you'll stay true to the deal."

Dark bared his teeth at her but said, "I swear."

"Then so be it." And to me: "Don't cry, Michael. I can't give you much, but I can give you this freedom. Don't take it for granted."

"Please don't do this," I begged. "We can find another way."

"No, we can't. But the memories I have of you will be enough to last a lifetime. Just this once, fate wins." She kissed me on the cheek. "We were outplayed. We've had everything we needed from the beginning. We just didn't understand it. I'm sorry, Michael."

Serena walked back toward the black-leafed tree as I searched for the bullet in my shoulder, fighting the overflowing guilt in my chest from letting her down.

Dark approached me with a sickening expression on his face, hatchet twirling in his right hand. "Left or right, left or right. Which one should I leave him, Serena?"

"Leave him the left," she answered quietly. "That's his dominant hand."

"Fine by me."

Butchers are efficient. So it only took two hard clean strikes from Dark's hatchet and a twist to sever the tendon, muscle, and bone from the rest of my body. I tried to use the pain to dig deeper for the bullet, but I could barely stay conscious.

Dark hung my severed arm above me like a gutted rabbit and let me watch as blood dripped down it and onto the grass below. He tossed it to Serena—who caught it awkwardly—and Dark cleaned off his hatchet on his pants, squatting next to me. He froze the exposed bit of flesh where my arm had once been with his Fabrications and likely saved my life. I would have bled out in minutes if it had been allowed to flow freely.

But he wasn't done. Dark turned his right hand into a dragon's hand and then delicately lifted my chin with one of its talons, until we looked each other in the eyes. "Kingman have amber eyes. So, just in case the arm isn't enough"—he smiled broadly—"I'll be taking one of these as well."

The last thing I saw with my left eye was Dark's talons above and below it. Then there was a pinch, pain, blood, haze, and darkness.

RESTING PLACES

When I opened my eyes—or, well, eye now—and saw the glittering white cathedral around me, I wondered why I was here. Was I being sent off to whatever came after life? I had been beaten physically, broken mentally, and lost a lot of blood. Maybe I had escaped my fated death by leaving early.

But as I walked down the central row between the wooden pews, I found Rian sitting at the front, arms extended over the backboard. He wasn't in his black flame-trimmed robes, but rather a simple pair of trousers and an ornate maroon shirt with a floral pattern. Smoke wafted off his body like a dying candle. His eyes were hard as he stared at the iron metal door in front of us like a painter admiring his greatest creation. There was an empty plate next to him. He must've eaten while he waited for me.

"I've been waiting *forever* for you, Michael," Rian stated coldly. "This place is a nightmare. What took you so long?"

"You're dead?" I asked, suppressing a laugh. "Who did it?"

"High Noble Kyros. Alphonse accidentally sent us to him, in the Institute of Amalgamation. I never stood a chance with that bullet in my shoulder."

I smiled as I put my hands in my pockets. "You're not going to make me fake sympathies, are you?"

"No. I'm just here to talk." A pause. "I remember the first time I was told about this place, and I thought it was a good idea." He leaned his head back and exhaled loudly. "We're such stupid children. This place shouldn't exist."

I stood in the aisle. "Isn't this place in my mind? Why are you acting like it's real?"

"Because it *is* real. This is the crossroads between life and death, where it's sometimes possible to wait for someone you have a connection with before passing." He looked at me like I was an imbecile. "Did you not know that? So ignorant."

"You sound pretty chipper for a man who has to see *me* before heading to death." I returned his look. "How sad. An immortal lifetime and I'm all you've got?"

"Don't think so highly of yourself," Rian countered. "It's not as if everyone can send people off. Only those with a connection with death."

A connection with death? What did that mean?

"Your childhood trauma will reveal itself soon," Rian said, getting to his feet. The iron door began to creep open, just wide enough for someone to slip through. "I could tell you more about everything—the Wolven Kings, this place, the immortal war—but I don't think I will."

"Feeling a little bitter Kai killed you?"

He flipped me off. "If I can ask anything, please don't let Dark eat my heart—assuming he hasn't already. I don't want him to have access to my memories."

"Your memories?"

Rian nodded. "Our hearts contain traces of our personality as well as our abilities. Not enough to alter the new host's mind or anything but . . . enough that it hurts me to think Dark would have information that I hid from everyone, myself included." He rubbed his eyes. "Damn those kings. It's all misinformation with them. I wonder if I would have joined them, knowing how it would all end."

"Do you regret it?" I asked. "Does it make all the good moments less sweet?"

"No, my life was worth every quiet moment and every painful breath," he answered quietly. "Time is fleeting. And I could never accomplish everything I wanted to. But even though it's ended so . . . sadly . . . I'm happy about the moments I was here. Every shout at the sky, every step in the sinking sand, and every smile that no one else understood. Just because I didn't get to see the fruits of my labor doesn't mean I regret it. My legacy will ripple throughout the world. Even if it's just my heart transferring powers to another."

"How noble of you," I muttered.

He yawned and then strolled toward the door, wagging a finger at me. "That's what you never understood, Michael. Your life is yours to squander or embrace, but your legacy belongs to the world. So don't worry about such silly things. Enjoy your life while it lasts."

"What if I have to decide between my legacy, life, or love?" I shouted right before he crossed the threshold. "Which is more important?"

Rian stopped but didn't look back. "Isn't it obvious? Love is the only thing that can conquer death. And sometimes . . . if you're lucky . . . love can become a legacy."

The smoke dragon stepped through the door and disappeared into the light. He didn't look at peace, as Dawn had been, but . . . he seemed content. A blinding light spread out from the door and overtook everything around me and—I hoped—would send me back to life.

I had no idea what would be waiting for me, but hopefully it might include Serena. Maybe I could still save her. Maybe we could still be happy. Maybe love could save me from the legacy I had always been enslaved to.

A GIFT GIVEN FREELY

Reality slapped me in the face with a breath of hot air and a crack of pain down my forehead. My vision came back slowly in my right eye, and I awoke on a feather bed in the middle of a sunlit room. A balcony door had been left open, letting the breeze flutter the thin curtains lazily. Everything was clean and warm, the wooden frame and floor polished to an enviable degree. My heart was beating rapidly as I held my left hand over it, hoping to calm it down. I was alone and unrestrained, so it was hard to tell if I had been saved or imprisoned.

I tried to swing my feet over the bed, but pain rippled through my body the moment I did, and it took everything I had not to fall out of bed. All I could do was grit my teeth and slam my closed fist against the headboard. Once I could breathe again, I lifted the blanket to observe my injuries. Deep-purple-and-blue bruises covered my chest. I looked as though I had run through a dye party without a shirt on. Everything below my right elbow was gone, but the nub had been patched up better than Dark's makeshift ice treatment, with stitches and stained gauze.

There was also an eye patch over my left eye's socket, and I could feel the throbbing pain of its vacancy.

But no matter how much pain I was in . . . I was alive. I could still save Serena. I could still stop this from happening. Well, assuming I could walk again at some point soon. There was a ruckus outside of my room, so, moving gingerly, I looked around for anything I could use to support myself and found a hand-carved cane leaning against the bed. I propped myself up with it and hobbled toward the door, used all my strength to push it open, tumbled forward, and caught myself on the railing before I went over it.

All the noise in the bar below stopped as all eyes fell on me. Titus, Cassia, and Alexis mingled with cheerful patrons who looked like stereotypical pirates—flashy jewelry, colorful bandannas, loose sweat-stained clothes, and wooden appendages. They spoke in hushed tones as they sipped from dirty glasses.

Titus raised his overflowing glass toward me. "The dumbass lives!"

They cheered loudly enough to shake the place. Even Cassia looked up from the book she was reading with a slight smile on her face. Alexis was behind the bar, filling glasses until they were overflowing. Two very, very beautiful women and a man built like a boulder ran up the stairs and carried me down them despite my protests. They sat me down at a table in the middle of the room and it wasn't very long before Alexis and Titus joined me. Both put small vials of a goldish liquid in front of me and wouldn't let me say anything until I'd downed them. It was scaro and made my throat burn with the fire of a thousand suns as it slithered down my throat.

"What's going on?" I said as I pounded my chest. "How am I still alive? If my injuries didn't kill me, all of you should have."

"You're a Mercenary, did you really think we'd abandon you?" Alexis asked.

They wouldn't want me to answer that honestly. "How long have I been out?"

"Nearly a week," Titus said. "Honestly, we all thought you were dead.

Had to feed you my miracle broth like a newborn babe. You must be—"

My stomach growled loud enough for both to hear. "Can I get a platter and a pitcher of water over here?" he called. "The dumbass is starving!"

Nothing seemed important after a barmaid put down a plate of barbecued meat, baked beans, and thick slices of a pinkish fruit that tasted sweeter than peaches. I didn't have the willpower to say anything until half of it was gone, shoveling it into my mouth with a spoon. "Why haven't you killed me?"

"Did you forget we gave you permission to go on this suicide quest?" Titus joked. "You did what you had to. None of us hold it against you."

"Except Dark."

"Except Dark," Alexis muttered. "Dark is a different story. But if he's not willing to kill me for betraying him, the others won't let him kill you."

"Very comforting." I gnawed on one of the fruit slices, regretting eating so quickly. "So where is Angst and Gloomy, anyway?"

"With Serena. We're still tasked with her protection, ya know? They're probably close to Vargo by now." Titus leaned back in his rickety seat. "The rest of us stayed here. With you."

"As jailors or friends?"

"Both."

I took a big gulp of lukewarm water. "What happens next?"

"Dark will likely bring you up on insubordination charges once we're reunited with the rest of Orbis Company," Titus said. "If he had convinced Alexis or me to flip, you'd be in chains, but he couldn't, so here you are. Free for now."

"Will he get the votes?"

"Doubtful. We've all been there. Everyone has a story and, in the end—no matter the outcome—we've all come back to Orbis Company." He smiled at me. "At least you did it for love. Most of us were more selfish than that."

I drummed my fingers on the table. "Where are Naomi and Chloe and the stone fool?"

"Chloe is with Serena. Decided it was best to leave you in our care and protect her until the end. Naomi is here, but she's running an errand. She'll be back tomorrow." Alexis rubbed her brow. "Sebastian is convening with the pirate council, trying to gain position in their ranks. Say what you will about him, but after we got him to the titan and allowed him to claim a statue army . . . he's become powerful and respected."

"You should ask the other question you want to."

"Then just tell me the answer."

Titus lifted three fingers and we waited for three more shots to be delivered. I reached for it with my stump, paused, and then took it with my good hand. We clinked glasses and drank together. It burned just as much as the first two.

"Serena will be wed to Jay within the week," Alexis said. "He'll be King of Hollow. And now that Dark has all three names . . . he'll open one of the doors when he gets the chance. Likely at their wedding."

"I failed," I breathed as if it were my last.

"You did," Titus agreed. "But the odds were stacked against you."

"Is that supposed to comfort me? I'm supposed to be the guy who defies fate."

Titus belly-laughed, and Alexis put her hand over her mouth to stifle her own.

"We're Mercenaries," Titus said. "We all defy fate and do the impossible daily. If you didn't, you wouldn't have been chosen to join us. But we all fail sometimes. And that, too, is no different for you." He hesitated. "This one will just hurt more than others."

"I can still save her," I declared. "Maybe I can get there in time and—"

"Enough, Michael." Titus covered my trembling hand with his own. "It's more than a week's journey to Vargo, and by the time you get there she'll already be dead. I'm sorry . . . but it's over. You have to let her go."

"What if I can't?" I asked meekly.

"That's the thing . . . you don't really have an option."

I didn't protest or rebel or throw a tantrum. Where was I going to go with a bum leg, one and a half arms, one eye, and my body covered in bruises? I was a fool, but one who understood my options were limited. And right now this was a complete and utter loss. Even if my life had been saved, nothing felt right about this. So I sat back in my chair and watched the world move around me. Titus and Alexis stayed with me for a time, trying to tell me stories that would put a smile on my face. As amusing as hearing about Titus's legendary quests for rare ingredients was . . . it all felt so hollow.

Pirates came up to me every now and then, wanting to hear how I'd lived after getting butchered like an animal by Dark. Most of them weren't too thrilled with the abbreviated version and were even less impressed when I tried, and usually failed, to give the longer explanation. In the end, when someone asked, I muttered that it was because of a woman, took a drink, and stared into the distance. They all nodded in understanding and returned to whatever they had been doing. Being dramatic had its advantages every now and then.

When it was dark and most of the bar had retired for the night, Cassia finally made her way over to me. Miraculously, she didn't have a book or old map in hand. "I would have brought you a drink, but I have a feeling you may black out if you drink so much after your recovery."

"Who's to say I haven't already had enough to black out?" I asked as I swirled the cloudy liquid I had been sipping for a while.

She smiled at me gently and it felt like a viper waiting in the grass before it struck.

"Are you here to taunt me?"

"No," she said. "I'm here to offer my sympathies."

"I didn't know the great Cassia ever felt sympathetic."

She shrugged and drank. "Miracles happen every now and then. And since you'll be around for the foreseeable future, it seems pointless not to be there when you're feeling down."

"What makes you think I'll be around for much longer? I heard Dark is going to bring me up on charges of insubordination."

"That motion will fail. Do you enjoy talking nonsense, or are you really that insecure?"

I pushed my tongue against my cheek. "I just wanted to hear you say it."

"Prick." And then she added, "Maybe you did learn something from Dark after all."

"I hope not. He's a monster."

"Understatement of the century. He likes to claim it was only one, but I've seen him sink multiple Palmer battleships on his own." She paused. "Back when he was at his weakest."

"Have you ever thought about stopping him?" I asked. "If we all know he's a monster, why let him carry on? We could end him!"

"Dark is my family. All we have is Orbis Company and the fellow low-lifes we've attracted." Cassia put her wine bottle down on the table. "And family is hard to hold to the same standards as we do others. Becoming a Mercenary was the smartest thing Dark ever did. Else I imagine he would have been hunted down by other companies by now."

"Mercenaries won't take contracts on other Mercenaries?"

Cassia shook her head. "Each company is responsible for taking care of its own and holding them to whatever standard they deem appropriate."

"So it's up to us to stop him when the time comes."

"*If* the time comes," she corrected. "And no, don't suggest hiring a Waylayer or something else stupid."

"Why not? They hunted us down in Hollow just fine."

"The rumor mill tells me you two are on a special list."

"A special . . . Wait, did you say the two of us? Me and Dark?"

"Obviously," she said. "Was there someone else responsible for killing Mocking Bird?"

I murmured nonsense and then asked, "What is this special list?"

"It's better you don't know."

I gestured to everything around us and then to the bruises all over my body. "Have I missed the part where I don't deserve to know things when they involve me?"

"You're on the Reaper's list," Cassia said with a roll of her eyes.

"I've heard of them," I said. "The head of the Waylayers?"

Cassia nodded. "It means they are the only ones that can take a contract on you. On one hand, it means you only have to worry about one Waylayer. On the other hand, it means that if a Waylayer is coming after you . . . it's the Reaper. The worst of the worst."

"Wonderful." I wanted to pull my hair out. "Is there a way to get off the list? Or perhaps to be put on a 'don't try to murder me anymore' list?"

"Sadly, the only way to become exempt is to become a Waylayer. You have met their biggest requirement. You could try to join them if you want. There's no rule you can't be a Mercenary and a Waylayer."

"I've met their requirement?"

"You have. You killed a Waylayer. And usually they fill the void in their ranks with the person strong enough to kill one of their own. It's something we agree on—you keep what you conquer."

"I . . . I didn't kill a Waylayer, though. Dark did."

"You helped. Besides, they won't extend another invitation to Dark." My expression must've been enough to reveal my next question, so Cassia continued, "His grandfather was War. And I'm assuming you already know how that ended."

"If they accredit me with Mocking Bird's kill, where's my invitation?"

"They must've given it to the wrong messenger."

"A shame." I reached for the wine bottle and Cassia snatched it away from me. "Really?"

"Really," she said, and then downed what remained. "Michael, are you going to do something stupid in retaliation?"

"Against Dark or Jay Prince or Angelo?"

She hesitated and then said, "Any of them."

I leaned back in my seat. "I can't do anything to Dark and we both know it. If I did, it would jeopardize my position in Orbis Company. And the moment I do that, I'm a dead man walking. So until I get aid or permission, I'm biding my time."

"That's very mature of you. And Jay?"

"What can I do?" I asked. "I'm too far away to stop Angelo's plan from succeeding. What can I do but begrudgingly appreciate the time I've been given?"

"If you want to talk, let me know. You're family, and we look after our own."

"You've been tasked with supervising me while Dark is with Serena, haven't you?"

She smiled as she rose from the table. "Guilty as charged."

"Cassia, one last question. If I wanted to do something, is there anything I could do?"

"Convince Orbis Company to declare war on Dark, Angelo, and Jay." Cassia patted me on the shoulder as she left. "Good night, Michael. Try to get some sleep."

The party I had interrupted earlier was slowly winding down, and since I had slept in so late, I wasn't very tired. I decided to go to the beach outside the bar. The sand was as dark as a starless night and felt just as cold between my toes as the place in my dream had. Mist settled over the water and, for once, I couldn't see what swam beneath the crystal-clear water. For so many years I had dreamed of sitting on the beaches of Eham, finally free from my obligations as a Kingman . . . And now that I had my freedom, all I wanted to do was go home.

I scooped up a handful of sand and then let it fall through my fingers. "As if I'd give up so easily. No more hiding. Let's finally find out who the real monster is, Dark." I pushed my thumb down on a deep-purple bruise and let the pain give me focus. "How do I devour him?"

A WAGER OF KINGS

Sebastian woke me up first thing in the morning by leaping onto me and shouting, "The dumbass lives!"

His elbows dug into my side, his knees into my chest, and the pain of his landing on me nearly made me puke. It took everything I had to shove him off me before I emptied yesterday's mistakes all over the floor. Sebastian didn't care as I wheezed for air and water, cackling like a schoolchild as he sat the wrong way on a nearby chair. All his fingers were wrapped in makeshift splints and he had a hook prosthetic to replace his lost hand. But, weirder than anything else, he had created or found a leather carrier for One-Eye. The black cat meowed at me, his head poking over Sebastian's shoulder.

"When we finally got to the top of the titan and saw you lying there . . . we thought you were dead. There was so much blood. Nothing Naomi could do woke you. She slapped you and cursed so many times— I learned a lot of new phrases—that I thought the suicidal cockroach finally ate a bullet. But it gave me the push I needed to confront the pirate council about my application into their ranks. Didn't want to die with my dreams unfulfilled."

I didn't bother sitting up, keeping my head on the fluffy pillow. "And?"

"And turns out being able to summon a stone army in a place called the Sea of Statues makes you quite formidable. I'm one of the top thirty now," he said with a toothy grin. "Twenty-seven, to be exact. And that's without a crew, ship, or any kind of loot! Imagine how far I'll rise in time."

"Congratulations, Sebastian. I'm happy for you. No longer after revenge?"

"Revenge would have been sweet, but it wouldn't have brought her back. It gave me the energy I needed to move forward while I was grieving." His tone grew serious. "You shouldn't have saved me after what I did to Serena, but I'm glad you did. This life feels more like my own than the one in Hollow ever did." He stuck his hand out for me to shake it. "The way I see it, we're allies for life."

I finally sat up and shook his hand. "Allies for life."

"You don't seem very happy to have gained one of the most notorious pirates in the world as your ally."

I wanted to pull my knees to my chest or bury my face into a pillow and scream. But instead of showing weakness, I said, "I lost. How can I be happy about anything right now?"

"From what I heard, she did it for you. Her actions show a love most people never know."

"I was the one who was supposed to sacrifice myself for her. Not the other way around."

"Ah, so you're selfish. Making the sacrifice for the one you love is easy, but being on the receiving end of one is much harder. You have to live a life that justifies what she did, and that's a lot of pressure to have on your shoulders."

I put my legs over the edge of the bed and began to massage the muscles there. "I've lived with a weight on my shoulders for as long as I can remember. This is nothing new."

"It is when it's from the one you love."

I didn't respond.

"The way I see it," Sebastian said, "you have two options. The first is to live a life without regrets, becoming the man she thinks you are rather than the man you are."

"And the other option?"

"You reshape the world so the two of you are together regardless of the consequences."

I stopped massaging my legs. "If I make any move after she and Jay are married, I'd be declaring war on Hollow and likely Regal Company. I doubt even Orbis Company would stand by me." I exhaled. "Every friend I have ever made would be an enemy."

Sebastian leaned over the chair and ruffled my hair. "I told you. Allies for life. Your war is my war and mine is yours. So even if you're alone, you'll have me."

"Very reassuring," I said flippantly, suppressing a smile. Sebastian was insane, but he was honest, and that was hard to come by. "That doesn't help with the whole declaring-war-on-my-city thing, though."

"Would you do whatever it took to save her if we could get to Vargo before they were married?"

"Obviously," I said without hesitation. "But we can't. We're over a week away and their wedding will be within the week."

"We'd get there in time if we cut through the abyss."

Silence. I raised my head to see the huge smile on his face. "Are you insane? Last time we tried that, a rogue wave nearly killed us. And that's without the Wolven King at the bottom of it that's likely to tear out my eye if they get the chance."

"Impossible odds, yes, but I'm willing to bet you can find a way to pass."

"Or die trying."

"Or die trying," he repeated. "Is it worth it, for Serena?"

"I'd reshape the world to be with her," I replied, and every part of me meant it.

"So, are you willing to take the chance to save her?"

Sebastian already knew the answer, but so there was no uncertainty, I said, "Yes."

"Then let's get to work!" Sebastian went to his feet. "I'll find a ship—might steal, might buy, doesn't matter, really—for the voyage. It'll only take a day to reach the abyss and five days to reach Vargo once we pass through it. That gives us a few days to prepare, and time for you to get permission or whatever it is you need from Orbis Company to do this."

"Right," I muttered. The timeline would be tight, unless rather than crossing it, we . . . I was getting ahead of myself. First things first. "I'm still an apprentice Mercenary. They won't let me go anywhere unsupervised. And I doubt they'll let me declare war on Regal Company to save Serena."

"Then you know where you need to begin."

"Sebastian," I said as he put his hand on the doorknob. "What do you gain by helping me?"

"Fair question," he said. "You'd think I'd be satisfied to be a pirate but . . . I'm not. To reach the top, I need to do a few more miraculous things, and crossing the abyss just seems like the next thing to do. I'm simpleminded like that."

"At least you're honest."

"Cheers to that," he said with a chuckle before bounding down the bar's steps like a drunken madman.

I sat on the edge of my bed for a bit, wondering if I was doing the right thing by turning my back on the life I had been given. Just trying to cross the abyss was dangerous enough. Even more so when I was confident a Wolven King would be waiting for me. If I succeeded, I was still going to have to invade Vargo, interrupt a wedding, and then get Serena out of there while a company of Mercenaries tried to stop me. It was a suicide mission . . . and yet I felt more alive with that flicker of hope burning in my chest than I had all yesterday at the thought of a long life. Was I a fool? Obviously. But I was a fool in love, and I wouldn't give up so easily.

The first step was to become a full-fledged Mercenary, and only Cassia could help me with that.

None of my Mercenary friends were in the bar downstairs—which probably explained how Sebastian had got to me—but the bartender was helpful enough to tell me where they had gone. There was some sort of meeting today and it was all hands on deck except for their apprentice—or maybe "wounded bird" was more appropriate. All I had to do was not get lost among the crowds of pirates and assortment of interesting games they seemed to be playing.

I would have knocked before entering but decided that they wouldn't let me in if I did, so I barged in with a smile as I said, "Whoa. Whoa. Whoa. How come no one invited—"

Alphonse the Wolven King was at one end of the table. Tai, the leader of Orbis Company, and Imani, his second-in-command, were at the other side. Every single member of Orbis Company was in the room, maintaining a defensive distance between their leader and the Wolven King.

I lunged at Alphonse like a rabid animal, but Naomi caught me mid-flight and then slammed me against the wall, holding me up against it by my collar. Imani, Titus, and Alexis helped pin me against the wall as I struggled to free myself. "Alphonse! I swore if I ever saw you again, I'd devour your fucking heart!"

The Wolven King rose to his feet slowly. "Mercenary Tai, I thought you said this child wouldn't throw a tantrum in my presence."

"He wasn't supposed to know where we were." Tai rubbed his brow. "Cassia, you told me he was barely able to walk."

"He was. Yesterday. Barely made it out of his room," Cassia said. For the first time in her life she hadn't been reading during a meeting. "This kid is the biggest pain in my ass."

"My apologies," I growled. I nearly got my bicep off the wall, but Imani slammed it back down. Having four people restrain me was very annoying. "I'm fairly hard to kill. Ready for round three, Alphonse?"

Alphonse shook his faceless head at me and returned to his seat. "Should we continue negotiations, or do you need to deal with the Kingman first?"

"Imani," Tai called out. "Is he moving if we continue talking?"

"Not a chance," she answered, pressing down on me harder. "Kingman is secure."

"Like fuck I am." I thrashed out but they held me even more firmly. "I'm going to devour your heart, Alphonse. And then I'm going to—"

Naomi clamped her hand over my mouth and then whispered into my ear, "Shut up, Michael. This might be the only chance you get to hear this. Trust me, alright? I'm with you."

I exhaled heavily into Naomi's hand but relaxed slightly. Naomi was my friend. I trusted her. Besides, it wasn't as if I could go anywhere. I was too heavily constrained to do anything but watch and listen.

"Where were we?" Tai asked.

"Events at the Reborn Titan—Regal Company being delayed by an army of statues—leave me reevaluating my younger brother's defenses at the abyss. I need more allies to be sure that obliterating him will be successful. Which leads me to reluctantly seek the Black Death's assistance."

"What? Why?" Alexis whispered, horrified.

"What my subordinate said," Tai clarified.

"The Black Death's reputation precedes him, and he's growing stronger every day. I think he could be the turning point that helps me stop my brothers."

"If you want him so badly, hire him. He isn't cheap but—"

The Wolven King folded his hands neatly in front of him and silenced the leader of Orbis Company. The pressure in the room seemed to grow heavier, as if every movement was constrained by thick mist. "Do I look like the sort of man who hires others? I don't need things with thoughts or dreams of their own. I need perfect soldiers who never disobey my commands."

"Then I'd advise finding another," Cassia interrupted. "Dark doesn't listen to anyone."

"He wants Dark bound to him. Just like the younger Kingman is," Tai stated.

The room fell silent.

"Dark is family," Imani said quietly. "Even if he makes us mad at times."

"Then I suppose that issue is settled, isn't it?" Tai rose to his feet. "I'm sorry we couldn't come to terms, but Orbis Company is family, and we will not—"

Alphonse turned to me, interrupting Tai, and said, "Michael, do they know that Dark and Angelo may shatter Tenere in a few days?"

The sudden silence was deafening.

I spoke, but I was muffled by Naomi's hand over my mouth. Surprisingly, Tai indicated Naomi should let me speak. Better make this count.

"He's telling the truth. Dark is going to help Angelo Shade shatter Tenere unless Serena and I kill each other. Right now they're trying a loophole using my eye and hand to fake a Kingman, but if it goes to shit, they're going to shatter Tenere instead." I took a breath as they let me go. "Dark and Angelo are trying to open the lockless door to bring back their beloveds. If we don't do something soon, we might be dealing with another Celona." My eyes fell on the Wolven King and a smile crept to the edges of my mouth. "Which I doubt you want. That's why you're trying to get Orbis Company to bind Dark to you." I turned toward Orbis Company. "If you want my opinion, rather than give in to the whims of the immortals, send me to Vargo to kill Angelo, stop Dark, and let's be big damn heroes who save the world without anyone dictating our destiny."

"Alexis," Tai said slowly, "can you back Michael up?"

The Azilian Mercenary nodded.

"Release the imbecile," Tai ordered. The others let me fall to the ground. "Michael, be honest with me, since I've clearly underestimated Dark. Can he be beaten?"

"Yes. Though I'm the only one who can do it."

"The arrogance of this boy," Alphonse drawled. "I just told you *I* wanted him as one of my soldiers and you think you can stop him?"

I stood straight. "You've all treated Dark as if he were some monster who cannot be defied, and I'll admit there were times when I was terrified of him. But I've fought him. Even when I was powerless and magicless. If anyone stands a chance against him, it's me."

"Children always sound so confident, but they crumble under pres-

THE VOYAGE OF THE FORGOTTEN 439

sure," Alphonse countered. "I doubt this imbecile can do anything. He's just going to take the Hollow Queen and run away. He isn't worthy of anything! He cannot—"

"Then I'll prove my strength." I gestured to what lay beyond these walls. "Machina Company is on Eham, right? Put me to a test. Me against a hundred of them. If I win, Orbis Company helps me raid Vargo, save Serena, capture Dark, and kill Angelo." My eyes fell on the Wolven King. "And you can go back to whatever prison you escaped from in shame."

"You won't succeed."

I squatted so our eyes were equal. "Watch me."

"If by divine intervention you do succeed, you won't stop them without my help. Vargo is too far away and—"

"I'm going to cross the abyss," I said. "That should give me a fighting chance at making it there on time, won't it?"

"It's impossible," Alphonse shouted, slamming his hands on the table. "You cannot—"

"I can do anything! So sit back and watch the show." I looked at Tai. "Do we have a deal?"

"Absolutely," he said. "You defeat Machina Company and cross the abyss, and we'll help you storm Vargo." He cracked his knuckles. "Usually I try to avoid fights with Regal Company, but I need a good old-fashioned scrap every now and then. Otherwise my instincts will wane." He turned to Imani. "Prepare the feast for our apprentice, will you? Dawn tomorrow sounds like the perfect time for it, and I'm sure Gregor will find some of his members up for the challenge of stopping our apprentice. Prepare yourself, Michael. You'll need to."

Most of Orbis Company left with chuckles and disbelief until only Naomi, Alexis, and Alphonse were left.

The Wolven King adjusted the pelt over his shoulder lazily. "Your commander made a mistake. How shameful to put so much trust in a child. You won't beat a single Mercenary of Machina Company—never mind a hundred."

I shrugged. "I don't know. I tore through the battlefield of the thousand craters easily enough. That oasis you and your brothers were at was beautiful."

The Wolven King stopped suddenly. "What did you say?"

"What?" I chuckled. "Trouble hearing, Alphonse?"

"I'm going to command Machina Company to destroy every trace of you so there's nothing but memories left."

I bowed dramatically. "And what a wonderful legacy that will be."

The Wolven King left without another word, probably to save himself the embarrassment of letting me get the upper hand. Even if there was a decent chance it would end with me sprawled out on the ground somewhere with a few bullets lodged in my chest. But what was death to me at this point but an inevitable outcome?

"Dramatic as always, Michael," Naomi said with a smile. "So, how are you going to survive this?"

"I can't. Not without help anyway," I muttered. "I'm going to win by goading the third brother into attacking me with moon-fall during the test. Something made him attack us when we tried to cross the abyss before, so I bet I can get him to do it again."

Naomi smacked me upside the head. "What if it wipes out the island? What if you *can't* get him to attack you and you have to fight a hundred Mercenaries on your own? Do you ever think before you speak? How do you expect to pull this off?"

"First, I need to get the third brother's name. It wasn't in Idris's mind nor was it at the Reborn Titan, so there's only one place left to try." I tapped the side of my head. "The night before Davey died, I think we figured it out. I think we found his name, learned who shattered Celona and whatever else they've been trying to hide from us for a millennium."

"But you chained Idris up in the depths of your mind and the meditation isn't working. How do you expect to find him again? Last time you'd nearly lost your mind after King Isaac died." Her face grew grim. "Are you going to try and go insane or something?"

I shook my head. "I need a Patchworker." I explained what I had learned from Sirash and Regal Company—that they could manipulate body parts along with memories. Naomi asked the obvious question:

"Where do we find one?"

"The Wolven King has the abilities to do what we need, but . . ." I rubbed my brow. "I doubt he'll help us. The only other one I know is Sirash."

"He's working with Regal Company. There's no way he—"

"He's in Eham," I said. "And he'll come for me. I know he will."

"How can you be so certain?"

I stared out the window at the pale blue sky. "Because he's my friend."

15

A LIFE IN MOMENTS

My Skeleton friend found us while we were eating fish-head stew and watching pirates play games of chance with extremely squishy vegetables. They could have been rotten for all we knew, since the salty taste and sour smell from the stew overpowered everything else. Sirash approached us loudly, his clothes still dripping wet streaks of sand across his bare skin and strands of algae wrapped around him. It looked as if he had walked across the bottom of the sea to get here. He plopped onto the ground next to me and I handed him the rest of my soup, which he ate silently. Naomi poured the rest of hers into Sirash's bowl as well.

Sirash didn't speak until there was nothing left. "Tastes like shit." He put the empty bowl down with his bony hand. "But it's better than most of what we ate in Hollow. Have you two noticed there's not many redfish around here?"

"I think redfish only live in rivers." Naomi leaned back to enjoy the sunshine. "My da could make the crispiest redfish you'd ever see. Add a little salt and lemon and . . ." She kissed her fingers. "Divine."

"I liked it smoked," Sirash countered. "Hung up all day long wrapped in seaweed and it flakes apart so easily." He stared at the pirates. Their game of chance had turned more violent, with sudden sleeve pulls and many threats of cutting off fingers. "I wonder if I'll ever get another chance to have it."

I didn't give him any reassurance, because I didn't want to lie. To give him false hope. But . . . had that life ever been that good? Stealing from tourists? Struggling to make payments on the asylum? Shouldn't our golden days have been better? I had clung to those memories, and yet . . . I don't know if I'd ever want to return to them. When would my best days start? When I was dead and gone?

"Do you think we're adults now?" I asked. "Or are we just kids pretending to be?"

Naomi shrugged, but Sirash spoke slowly and carefully. "You know what the worst thing about growing up is?"

"No, what?"

"Realizing nothing will protect you from the future. That the skills you may have spent years perfecting are useless and friends you've stayed up all night talking to may be gone from your life in the blink of an eye. Life isn't a story. There's no foreshadowing from the beginning of your life to the middle . . . just the end."

"I guess a ruinous fate is all we have left to look forward to."

"At least we saw a part of the world together. That was nice." He breathed in through his nose. "How did you figure out I was still around?"

"Everything between us in public will be backwards," I said, repeating the old words he had told me in Hollow. "You knew back then what was going on with the Waylayers and the Wolven King, didn't you? That's why you distanced yourself from me. It was out of mercy, not hate. Did you think you'd be ordered to kill me?"

"Doesn't matter now, does it? At least that part of it is over."

"No, it's not. I need a favor, Sirash."

Sirash groaned. "We tried to kill each other last we met . . . and you're already asking for a favor? Is our friendship nothing but an opportunity for you to get things out of me?"

"You're laying the guilt on pretty thick for a man who tried to kill me. The way I see it, we're even. We've done terrible things to each other as well as kind ones. This is our fresh start." I tried to scratch the back of my head with my missing arm. "Don't get me wrong. Probably not the smartest thing to instantly ask for a favor. But . . . you know how I am."

"I do," he said softly. "I definitely do." He rolled over onto his side. "What do you need, Michael? Connections with the Waylayers? Information from them? What could you—"

"I need you to manipulate my memories with your Patchwork abilities."

Hesitation. "What do you want me to do?"

"I need to be knocked out long enough to search through my memories. And I also . . ." I twisted my father's ring with my thumb. ". . . and I also need you to remove some of my memories. Can you put them in vials for others to witness?"

Naomi jolted up. "What? Why?"

I thought about how to phrase the next sentence so it didn't seem like I was giving up or planning too far ahead. But . . . I guess a fool like me had always been obsessed with my legacy. I just wanted to leave something behind for them all when . . . when I was forced to succumb to a fate I could never outsmart.

"It's a contingency plan," I said.

"I can do that. It'll take time, but while I'm working on that, you'll have time with your memories. Be quick, though. You won't get a warning when I'll remove you." Sirash rolled over onto his back and then exhaled. "Do you know which memories you want removed?"

Seventeen memories for ten people. A parting gift for those I held close.

My mother would get the first conversation we had after she saved my life in the church. When we had spoken about duty, fate, and love. It was a quiet moment. Too tender to be anything truly noteworthy, but special to me all the same.

Gwen would get the memory of us reading together in the Archmage room, basking in the silence and comfort of each other's company.

Trey would get the memory of when me, him, and Jamal all ate red-fish together on the banks of the Hollow River on a hot summer day.

Naomi would get the memory of the day we had spent singing badly and laughing loudly in a cart on our way to Vargo. She punched me in the side when I told Sirash but didn't keep arguing that I was doing the wrong thing. Or giving her the wrong memory.

Sirash would get the memory of how I felt when I had discovered he had gone missing. It wouldn't make him forgive me, but I wanted him to know the truth. He didn't act as if he cared but didn't look me in the eyes for a bit afterward either. There was a conflict in his heart, and I didn't blame him for it. Our relationship was complicated.

Kai would get the memory of how grateful I had been after he had saved me in the Kingman Keep riots. Even though the price had been great . . . I thanked him for his decision every day.

Chloe would get my memory of learning what the Kingman legacy entailed. What it meant to stay by my Royal's side for all eternity, sworn to defend the throne. Since she was without a Kingman herself . . . I hoped she'd appreciate knowing what it was like to have one.

Symon would get the memory of me lying to him when I recounted my story and exchanged truths with him. Every lie. He'd be furious that I had conned him, and my only regret was that I wouldn't be able to see his reaction when he learned the truth.

Dark would get more than one. A collection of seven of my great-est moments. Things that truly defined who I was and how I had been. Idris had been able to infect Rian's mind, so who said I couldn't infect Dark's? To ensure he would never escape me. To never let him forget me. I couldn't kill him, but I could make him regret ever crossing me and my family.

And Serena, well . . . there are some memories that are meant to be relived over and over again with friends until those tales are written into the heart of the world. And then there are some memories that are too sweet and too delicate to be shared with anyone but the ones involved. Telling Sirash and Naomi had been hard enough. But that memory . . . that comfort . . . those gentle touches and soft whispers in the night where we were the only two people in the world who mattered . . . I have no desire to share it with anyone else besides her.

Leave me this.

"And then I need one more favor," I said, once Naomi had finished writing down all the memories I wanted extracted. "I need you to give me your Skeleton hand so I can cross the abyss. The Wolven King won't let me in without it."

Naomi's jaw hung open and Sirash's face wasn't much different. "Are . . . are you insane, Michael? If I give you my hand, you'll have his voice in your head. You'll be a marked Skeleton. You'll—"

"Is there any other way to cross the abyss?" I interrupted. "I need your hand. Besides, that'll free you from your fate, won't it? Let me take on your curse. Let me do some good while I still can."

Sirash gritted his teeth. "I didn't ask you to do this. It's not your burden."

I shrugged. "No, it's not. But why don't you let me carry it for a bit?"

"I . . . uh . . . thank you, Michael. Maybe I judged you too quickly."

"You didn't," I admitted. "I'm an asshole. But heroes have to learn how to be heroes at some point, don't they?"

"I suppose so." He coughed. "Shall we do it here?" Sirash began to cloak his hands in wispy, swirling darkness. The sight of it made my heart rapidly convulse. Whether out of fear or anticipation, I didn't know. "We can go somewhere else if you want."

"Better here than in a dark alley somewhere." I leaned backwards. "Ready?"

Sirash plunged his dark hand into my chest as if squeezing my heart to control the rhythm as his other pressed against my forehead. The world melted away—Naomi promising that she'd look after me while I was asleep—and for the last time I went in search of the truth.

14

BEAUTIFUL LIES

Some days I wanted to punch my mind in the throat because it made no sense. Or maybe it was Sirash's influence that made it so weird. Not that there were ever proper instructions for how magic worked. Even the Archmage's information had been vague and directly in opposition to what Domet had taught me during the Endless Waltz. Nature or nurture? Which was responsible for people getting their specializations?

There was no plane of light, sea of darkness, or perfect cathedral waiting for me this time. Instead, it was a labyrinth filled with staircases and doors leading in all directions and orientations. Some were upside down, some were at an angle, and some were an optical illusion and got smaller and smaller the closer I got to them. Everything seemed to be made of smooth river stone.

I cupped my hand around my mouth and then said, "Echo!"

"Echo!" my own voice repeated as it got further and further away until it was nothing.

That would never not get fun. But it was time to get serious. I had to figure out how to reach my door of desire. Behind it, I would learn what had happened the night before Davey died and what the third's name was. Without it, I was just a pawn in Angelo and Dark's war.

So, where to begin? With the closest door, of course.

It opened into darkness. As did the next. As did the one I had to climb up a wall to get to. As did the upside-down one without a door handle. After I opened about a dozen doors, I realized I was being distracted by an elaborate illusion meant to keep me preoccupied. I was rather insulted there weren't at least a few traps. So the question became: How did I escape and how did I find whatever it was hiding?

"You're forgetting about me and the forest," an upside-down boy said from above. He was sitting on the edge of a staircase, legs swinging freely. There was a birthmark on his temple, and he had messy auburn hair and height he hadn't grown into. He was dressed in the regalia only the royal family wore for their Kingman binding ceremony: perfectly white trousers, ornate golden gloves with the fingertips cut off, a blue-and-gold military-style jacket with gemstone buttons, and a black lace veil over his face. "Can you say my name this time? Or am I just the hallucination boy again?"

"Davey," I muttered. "Why are you here? Are you in my mind?"

"Obviously." Davey hopped down, twisting in midair, before landing gently. "It's all wonky, because someone's messing around with it. Normally it would be cleaner."

"Delightful. Maybe I can—" My eyes widened. "Wait. You're acting like Idris was in Rian's memories. You're too smart. Too insightful. Did Davey leave his memories in my mind?"

"No. I belong behind your door. I'm a part of your core desires," Davey explained. He snapped his fingers and one door off in the corner of the labyrinth lit up in bright red. "That door leads to it. Along with the other memories you've been hiding from yourself. Are you ready, Michael? Will you finally seek the truth of your own life?"

I glanced around at all the sets of stairs and doors. "Why does my mind look different? Where's the plane of white? And why are you my guide instead of Dawn?"

"Your mind was broken back then," Davey said. "Well, *more* broken. Dawn was the hammer that left a crack that we could use to unearth everything else. But her part in this story is over. You need to solve the final mystery now—what we learned the night before I died."

"How? My memories aren't corrupted anymore, so I must've forgotten them. Those memories can't be recovered."

"What makes you think Fabrication use is responsible for your memory loss? Trauma is just as effective."

I opened my mouth, hesitated, and then said, "So whatever happened that night, my mind wants me to forget about it. Does that mean if I go through that door . . . I'll have to face my past traumas? Is it going to be that night?"

"It's the Kingman Keep riots."

Fuck.

"Fuck," I said out loud.

"You know I can hear your thoughts, right?" Davey mocked.

"Shut up." I waved him off and then stared at the door to my memories. "I relive that day in my nightmares. Why would doing it this way give me a different result?"

"Do you know what trauma is, Michael?" When I didn't answer, Davey continued, "They're lingering memories of past mistakes. Diseases without cures. Your dreams force you to relive these moments until you shatter or develop new personality traits to cope with what happened. You need to conquer your past to move forward."

"And if I don't?"

"Then you will be broken forever. You didn't forget Serena. Since you know your memories aren't corrupted anymore, either you magically forgot the night we went in search of a door no mortal can open *or* your mind hid those memories to spare you unbearable pain." Davey gestured to the door. "Only one way to find out which one."

"A door no mortal can open," I muttered. "We went looking for one of those doors Dark told me about. Did we open it? If we did, then that means we had the Wolven Kings' names. But there isn't a crack in the sky above Hollow like there was in Torda . . ." I stopped, mind racing too quickly. "A path through my trauma. How delightful."

"It won't be easy, facing the worst days of your life over and over and over again . . ." The child prince trailed off. "I won't judge you if you can't do it. But this is your only chance."

The door to my own memories seemed bigger than all the others. It was all I could focus on in this strange, mesmerizing place. As if, now that I'd seen it, it was calling to me like an alluring lullaby.

It was the correct path to take. Even if it was the last place I wanted to go. I cursed, steeled my resolve, and then screamed as loud as I could.

"To your traumas it is," Davey said with a smile.

"Let's go and see what makes me my own worst enemy."

We entered together and let the blinding light beyond it devour us. When the haze settled, we were in Kingman Keep right before its fated downfall. Its splendor was astonishing, dormant memories freezing me in place as I stared up at it in awe. Kingman Keep was once a lighthouse in the perpetual gloom that lingered over Hollow. Well-maintained Moon's Tears covered half the keep, rather than the overwhelming vegetation of it now. The observatory at the top of the keep was pristine and operational, whereas the three towers that clung to the main section were like sprouting fungus. All the houses in the area were immaculate, lit from within by warm fires and light laughter. And yet, as we walked toward the servants' entrance, I saw the crowds of angry rioters waiting outside the main door with makeshift weapons: old swords, worn hatchets, pitchforks, and torches that made their smiles look darker and deeper than usual. Every person in the crowd would soon try to kill me and my sibling.

Davey was silent as we entered the great hall. There were only four people in there: me, Gwen, a kid a few years older than me, and Lothar Bryson, Emelia's father, who would abandon us and break his oath to our father. He looked as he always did: light blond hair, pale skin, and a body that had been forged by war and pain. Gwen was a miniature version of the adult she would one day grow to be. I had no idea who the kid dressed like a hero with leather armor, chain mail, a metal helmet, a shield on his back, and a short sword on his hip was. Besides Lothar, he was the only one who was armed.

My younger self was comforting Gwen as she cried into our mother's red scarf.

"What should we do? They won't actually attack us . . . will they?" the pretend hero asked Lothar as both stared at the main entrance. We could hear the crowds shouting and pounding from inside. The boy was doing his best not to waver in the face of overwhelming odds. But all I saw was a scared kid playing pretend.

Lothar ignored the boy, too focused on shouting for his daughter.

"Lothar! Please! Tell me what to do!"

The pale blond man stopped as if frozen by a Fabricator. He craned his neck around so he could look down at the boy and something changed in his demeanor. Disgust? Annoyance? It was hard to tell, but, knowing what he was about to say, we should have realized that he was a liar.

Lothar kneeled in front of the boy, put his hands on his shoulders, and said, "Stay here. I'll reinforce all the other doors so no one can get in. You'll be safe in the meantime."

"Are you sure?" the armed boy asked tentatively, looking at the main door. "We could go somewhere else and wait for—"

"No," Lothar interrupted. "This is your home. Let no one force you out. You're Kingman, not cowards."

Those words felt like a blow to my very being, and it nearly sent me to my knees. Those words that I paraded around like a sacred oath . . . a calling . . . the poisoned ideology that had given meaning to my life and being and had nearly corrupted me . . . were said by a man who wanted us dead to save his own daughter. I had been so desperate for guidance . . . Would I ever grow into a man I could be proud of?

The boy bought into the words as well, nodding as Lothar ran off. We didn't see him again that night. And the next time I did, the Corrupt Prince slashed his throat in the Royal Gardens.

"Where did Lothar go?" my younger self asked. "Is he getting help?"

The boy nodded. "He's reinforcing the doors to make sure no one else can get in. He told us to stay here and wait. We're Kingman, not cowards! And we will not abandon our home."

The gears were moving in my younger self's mind and I wanted to hug him. To tell him he didn't have to live up to our ancestors. We could be something else. Something we were proud of. Rather than trying to fake it. But the damage was already done. The bell had been rung. And so this night would be the first of many that created Michael the King Killer. The boy who couldn't cry out of fear of failure. He'd find his family again one day, but not for a long, painful time.

My thoughts were interrupted by the rioters. The main gate opened by an unknown force—Lothar, I now knew, trying to save his daughter—and the rioters swarmed into the keep with vengeance on their minds. They didn't even try to hide it, two men swiping at the boy with their swords before he could say anything except:

"Run!"

The horde overwhelmed the boy, piling on top of him. My younger self hauled Gwen to her feet, and they sprinted away to safety. Blood ran freely where the boy was as spears of blood punctured all those around the boy like a blooming flower showing off its core. Screams echoed throughout the keep as I slammed the kitchen door behind me and Gwen, lowering the wooden lock as I did.

Gwen was in tears, screaming for the boy.

"He'll be fine," my younger self said, ushering Gwen away from the door and toward the servants' entrance, hearing frantic footsteps approaching. He hesitated, then pushed Gwen into the pantry instead. "Stay here. Hide behind the wine barrels. I'll distract them and come back for you."

Gwen tried to stammer out, "No," and "Don't go," but it all came out as gibberish through her heavy sobbing before the approaching rioters forced her to hide. My younger self locked the door behind her, searched the nearby cabinets for any sort of weapon—settling on a ladle—before brandishing it at the four rioters as if it were the finest sword in all Hollow.

"Hey!" my younger self shouted. "Get out of here!"

Normally pride would prevent adults from backing down to children, but all they saw was an opportunity and approached my younger self like addicts searching for a high. I wouldn't have been surprised if, in that moment, they thought gold ran through my veins, not blood.

They attacked together and I really stood no chance. The first attack cut me across the chest. The second stabbed at an angle, through my neck and into my chest. And the third—

—pain splintered through my head, forcing me to my knees.

"Don't look away, Michael!" Davey screamed at my side. "You have to see it!"

I tried to pry open my eyes as the rest of the rioters stabbed my younger self. But . . . but it didn't make sense. My memory must've been wrong. My wounds in the Kingman Keep riots had been severe . . . but these were beyond anything any mortal could survive . . .

More pain blotted the scene out.

"Face the truth, Michael! Think about it! How did you survive the Kingman Keep riots?"

"I don't know," I muttered, on the verge of passing out. "This memory can't be right."

"Fine!" Davey said angrily. "Maybe you will admit it in another memory."

Kingman Keep melted away around me as the tunnels beneath the colosseum sprouted up instead. The blackened and burnt bodies from the rebel attack on the Militia Quarter surrounded me in the musty, damp corridors. But one body stood out among the dozens of others. One with a black and steel ring on its middle finger. The body was indistinguishable otherwise—all its features burned away—and—

—I was screaming with pain.

"Another? Because I have plenty!"

Another memory began. We were underwater in the Hollow River as a body floated weightlessly downstream. It was still for too long for anything to be salvageable. Too waterlogged for too long to be saved. And yet, as a woman dove for the body, there was no doubt in my mind that they would live. But how could that be possible? How could someone drown and still live? Unless they were—

—more pain, and I curled up in a ball, pleading for it to stop.

"Dozens of times, Michael," Davey said, pacing in front of me. "You're a liar, but do you know your greatest lie? Because I do."

Moments flashed around us. A cold body in a pool of blood being discovered by children. A body falling from the rooftop of the Church of the Wanderer, burned black one moment but healed before it hit the ground.

"Stop," I begged. "Please."

"You can't keep looking away. Face the truth. Admit what you are!"

"I can't. Something is wrong with my mind. This isn't how any of it happened."

Everything disappeared around me as I struggled to my feet, head pounding, fighting to recall what had just happened. An endless stretch of white, and a green-and-white–striped house, lay in front of me. It was flat and boarded up, a place that was never seen yet passed by daily. A house from my childhood that I had tried hard to forget. It had witnessed one of my greatest shames, one that Symon had found out about, forcing me to confront this place once again. It was empty inside, except for a lone red-and-grey door covered in chains. The door to my desires. Three sets of chains crossed over it, in three Xs.

"But it is! And do you know why things happened this way, Michael? Why you lived when others wouldn't? It all comes back to *that* night." The red door to my desires began to shake as if something was trying to get out. "That night you can't remember. The night before I died. The night you became an—"

"Fine!" I screamed, warmth flooding out of my body without restraint or control. But rather than embrace it, I smothered it, clawing at my skin and leaving long red streaks across it. "You're right. It does all come back to that night. That night I can't remember. That night before you died. *The night I became an immortal.*"

The chains to the door melted away and then swung open. It sucked me inside, and I tumbled through like a ball bouncing down steps to show me where my tragic story truly began: the night of my first death. But first . . . first I had to admit what happened on my second death. And, in some ways, that was more important than the first.

ME AND YOU

Hey.

It's me, Michael Kingman. The narrator of this tragic tale.

It's nice to be able to talk to you directly. And I know I just broke the pacing of this story, but . . . I think it's better we see this next scene together like this. Just imagine me sitting across from you in a big cushy black chair. Can you see my dirty face? Can you see my amber eye and the vacant socket where Dark stole the other eye from me? Can you hear my rough voice? Can you see the one-armed fool I've become? Can you finally see the real me? I hope so. Because I see you. I always have. After all, all of this has been for you.

There's been a wall between us until now and I'm sorry about that. I never meant to keep you at a distance, but . . . when you hate yourself the way I do . . . you develop methods to cope. You learn to project yourself in certain ways to make everyone hate you. As if that would justify how I felt about myself. I'm sorry to be the bearer of bad news—if you've ever thought about doing the same—but . . . it doesn't work. When you hate yourself, there's nothing you can do to ease that pain but learn to love yourself instead. I never learned how to and maybe that's why everything will end this way.

No doubt you've been waiting for this moment.

Where you finally learn *everything* about me.

I'm sorry it's happening like this. I didn't mean to lie to you, but I did. And to be fair, I lied to myself a lot, too. Some things weren't worth remembering. And I thought my many deaths might be something we could skip over. Something we might ignore. That, for some reason, I was unable to die when others would a thousand times. I wouldn't be surprised if you already suspected before this moment. You didn't really think I could survive an explosion, drowning, or multiple stabbings thanks to my magic, right?

I'm stalling. I know I am. But . . . damn . . . can you just close the book here? Let me be the villain you hate or the hero you don't understand . . . anything other than the lonely boy you're about to see. I guess if you're still here you're going to see this story through until the end. I mean, I've already done everything in my power to make sure you didn't get this far. That you'd never see the *real* me, however much I want the world to remember my name. But your persistence paid off. Congratulations. I guess we have that in common.

This isn't about the night before Davey died. This is about the green-and-white–striped house. The night before Davey died is the crux of my story—the shining emblem that'll explain everything—but at the same time . . . it won't explain why I'm writing this. What happened to me in that house will explain it all. I never thought I'd be an observer to it until I began to write these words, to slide into Symon's account, but . . . but it is what it is.

I guess there's no point in delaying it now, is there? Let me tell you when I discovered I was immortal. I was thirteen when I planned to kill myself in the green-and-white–striped house.

I hated myself because the city hated me, and what my father did. I thought my life wasn't worth living. That I would never amount to anything. That if I were to die . . . I might as well do it on my own terms. I just wanted to end the pain. I wanted to be at peace. It took me weeks to pick out a nice secluded spot. Somewhere I knew I would never be found. Especially not by my brother or sister or Angelo. I spent another two weeks practicing my knots and then another figuring out what stool I would need to make sure the fall would break my neck.

After months of prep, I decided to do it on a random sunny day when the breeze was pleasant. There was a festival going on, but for the life of me, I couldn't tell you which one. I said my farewells to my family as usual and went to do what was necessary. Only I never made it there. I got sidetracked in the Great Stone Square watching an argument between a young boy from the East Side and a Low Noble. The noble exemplified everything I hated about them—proud, unapologetic, and quick to anger—while the boy was meek, calm, and just wanted to leave without causing an incident. He even offered to repay the noble whatever the cost was as compensation for scuffing his shoes. But the noble wanted more.

So he called the nearby Advocators to help him get what he wanted. He wanted proper compensation. He demanded blood . . . for a pair of scuffed shoes. I don't consider myself a hero—just a fool who was already planning on dying that day—but I intervened in the only way I knew how. Dramatic asshole that I was, I punched the noble in the jaw and sent him sprawling to the ground as all the Advocators looked on, absolutely shocked.

Then I ran away. And the noble followed, screaming for my head. The Advocators followed as best they could, but I lost them by the time the Low Noble and I crossed the bridge to the East Side. I wasn't thinking clearly, so my body raced toward the house I had planned to visit that day. And the noble followed. When we made it there . . . the noble pulled a gun on me and aimed down the sights, screaming that I had better plead for forgiveness if I wanted to live. That I was nobody and no one would mourn my death.

And considering how much I wanted to die that day . . . I didn't argue with him. I smiled and told him not to miss. And he didn't. The bullet hit me in the chest and the last thing I remembered was him walking toward me with a smoking gun as I tried to stanch my wound, wondering why death hurt so much.

Then I took a breath and opened my eyes to find the Low Noble checking my pockets. My wound was no longer bleeding profusely. The noble—caught off guard by my sudden return to health—scrambled backwards, stumbled over the stool I had laid out so carefully, and then cracked his skull on the messy floor. He was dead before I'd got to my feet. And there I was, a kid who had failed to die, with the body of a Low Noble in front of me. A death sentence not only for me but for my family as well.

I'm not proud of what I did next . . . but the noose was already set up, and what choice did I have? I emptied the noble's pockets, took his gun, and then hung the noble in the spot where I had planned to die.

You must understand that justice is blind in Hollow. That perception is everything. If the scene is painted correctly . . . any lie can become reality. And so I set the stage as best I could and left the note meant for my family for his and made myself scarce.

Two weeks later I learned his identity. His parents said he had always been troubled and that they wished he hadn't committed suicide but that he would be remembered for all eternity. I forgot his name a week later. As did most of the city. No trace of his identity survived.

Some lies are sweet but turn bitter. And some are always bitter but masquerade as honesty. This moment in time was neither. This was just pain. And so I forgot it. Sent it to the back of my mind like an unwanted guest. As I did with every other moment that resulted in my death, twisting the truth into something I could believe.

How many times did I suffer injuries and then conveniently forget to mention them again? How many deep breaths did I take to return to life since this all began?

I hope you've been counting.

And now that you know the truth. Hopefully . . . once all this is over . . . you will forgive me for my lies. I never meant to twist the truth like this, but some things are inevitable. Some things are dictated by fate and can be broken only with a miracle. And, sadly for me, God chose not to intervene on my behalf.

Now let's see the start of this twisted, bloodstained story together.

UGLY TRUTHS

My memories took shape like flowers sprouting toward the sun as I composed myself for whatever was about to happen. The buildings were uniform, pristine, and ornate. I instantly knew I was in the Upper Quarter of Hollow. Especially when Domet's odd redbrick house with its broken clocktower materialized. Conqueror's Fountain was the last thing to pop out of the ground, shooting water wildly in all directions and shrouding the immediate area in a faint mist.

The eight-year-old version of myself was last to appear. Carried by the younger counterparts of Serena and Davey Hollow. He was bleeding profusely from his head—*our* head—and his eyes were glazed over. Death was coming for him, fast, and not even the best surgeon would guarantee that he'd live. So maybe that was why they were bringing me to Domet, the Lifeweaver. I had never seen his powers firsthand—except in Idris's memories—but the little I knew suggested he could manipulate one's life span to a certain degree. But how did Serena and Davey know that? And why was I so wounded?

Serena used her free arm to pound on Domet's door. "High Noble Domet! High Noble Domet! I know you're in there! It's Princess Serena Hollow! I need your help!"

Silence.

Davey joined in with knocking of his own. "Please, High Noble Domet! We know what you can do! We need you to save a Michael Kingman's life! You're his only hope!"

Morning birds were beginning to sing the dawn chorus as my own life was headed toward an eternal slumber.

"Lifeweaver!" Serena shouted. "We *know* your name. Get out here!"

The door swung open and slammed against the nearby wall like a gunshot going off. Domet was standing there, disheveled in a robe that barely made it past his mid-thighs. He had a bottle of wine in his right hand and a trail of empty bottles littered the path from the entrance to his foyer. The immortal man's eyes were sunken and distant and yet at the sight of the three of us . . . his eyes turned flinty and fearful.

"What did you do?" he growled. "A Kingman flirts with death and two Hollows know a name their ancestors would have killed to keep hidden? Why are you here? What happened?"

"Does it matter?" Serena countered. "Save his life! We know you can."

"Who told you who I am?"

"A man without a face," Davey answered. "Gwendolyn Kingman made a deal with him to get the information. Now, please. Save him."

Domet gave a dramatic groan, turned on his heel, and then waved the children in. He kicked bottles off to the side as Serena and Davey Hollow carried me inside and onto the divan in his foyer. My blood dyed it dark at once. As the others sat next to me, Serena did her best to stanch my wound, but her attempt was desperate, not logical. I was a dead man.

"What happened to the Kingman?" Domet asked as he took a swig from his bottle. He went to his kitchen, returned with his platterfuls of dried fruit and nuts, and then tossed them haphazardly onto the table. Most of it slid onto the floor. "Did he fall out of a tree or something?"

"He opened a door he wasn't meant to," Davey whispered as he clenched his fists in a steady rhythm. "I didn't think the consequences would be so severe. The books *said* it could be done. I just . . . I just . . ."

"Didn't realize the cost? None do until it's too late." Domet motioned Serena away as he put the back of his hand against my mouth. "Still alive. Good start. But not for long. He's too far gone. I could extend his life span but that will do very little. He's deathless now."

"Deathless?" Serena questioned. "What's that?"

"It means he broke the natural order of things and went somewhere he *really* shouldn't have. His head wound isn't lethal, despite how bloody it appears. His death is a divine intervention, since he transgressed on sacred ground." Domet opened my eyelids and exposed my amber eyes. "Still has his eyes. That's good. Maybe he can fight with his ancestors in the realm of monsters. His time in this life is over."

"No," Serena said, standing. "There has to be something we can do."

"There isn't. He's bound to death and nothing short of . . ." Domet suddenly stopped, and his eyes fell on Serena. "How far would you go to save his life? Would you interweave his life with your own? As your ancestors did in the past?"

"What do you mean?"

"Do you know why it's said the Kingman and Hollow families are bound together, not bonded?" Domet began. "It's because 'bonded' implies a two-way symbiotic relationship. 'Bound' implies one serves the other. In the Wolven King War, King Adrian bound the First Kingman to his life to serve as his perfect *unkillable* soldier until the war was over. They won—obviously—but then things changed. The relationship turned parasitic, and King Adrian realized very quickly he had made a mistake. He had chosen the wrong person and created a deathless abomination. One who devoured him for a chance to be something greater. And so all their ancestors swore a vow to repair the mistake King Adrian made. This foolish ideology of service that has been passed down for generations isn't out of duty like you've all been taught—it's out of guilt."

"Wanderer have mercy," Davey muttered. "It's all lies. Everything we've been taught has been a lie. How could this have happened?"

"Villains aren't born but created. Remember that. No doubt in your time as Royals you will make bad decisions that you thought were correct at the time. Every decision has a consequence," Domet explained. "So, dear, sweet princess . . . will you bind your Kingman to your life at the risk of him becoming a monster that cannot die?"

Davey interrupted before Serena could speak. "If he becomes a monster, how do we kill him?"

Domet made a finger gun at my younger self. "You don't." And then he turned to Serena. "But *she'll* be able to. His heart will beat in sync with hers, and if she chooses to . . . the connection can be severed. If she kills him herself. But if *she* dies before him . . . then Michael will become a true immortal. One potentially incapable of ever dying. In theory. Only one other person has been bound to another, and they took a different path."

"I'll do it," Serena said without hesitation. "Bind his life to mine." She looked at me, smiling softly. "He's my Kingman. Forget fate. He won't become a villain no matter what happens. I believe in him. I always will."

"And you, little prince?" Domet asked. "Do you believe in him that much?"

"Can you bind his life to me instead?" Davey asked. "Michael isn't my Kingman. I'll be more levelheaded about him than she will. Besides, it was my fault he was harmed. Let me bear this burden."

"Davey," Serena whined. "I can handle it. I can—"

"Decide on your own." Domet took a seat across from me. "Flip a coin for all I care."

Davey pulled out a coin from his pocket, placed it over his thumb, and then said, "Heads it's me. Crown it's you."

Serena agreed to the terms and Davey flipped the coin, which twirled and spun and then slowly fell before stopping in midair. The scene stopped completely and the Davey I had seen multiple times in my mind appeared out of the nothingness. His hands were in his pockets and his face was solemn. His boyish charm seemed hard and mature for the first time.

"Heads or crown, Michael? Are you an immortal who can never die or one who can only be killed by the one you love?"

"Why was this moment behind the door to my desires?" I countered. "What is here that I desire more than anything else?"

"Isn't it obvious?" he said. "You want to die. To be a martyr. Your issue was never about living up to your ancestor's legacy. Your issue was with living. And here you are again . . . too scared to live, but hungry to sacrifice yourself and let others burden the pain of life."

"So?" I barked. "So what if I am? I've never felt at ease. Or comforted. Or loved, except when I tried to meet the expectations set by my stupid family name. So I became obsessed with it. It was the only way I felt validated. Am I a monster for finding a path in life and following it? Or must I be some mythical man who takes on fate to seize what can never be mine?"

Davey paced in front of me. "And what would that be, Michael? What can never be yours?"

"Peace," I whispered, a lifetime of regret and lies unfurling in my mind. The man who I had tried to be finally succumbing to the man I was. "It's all I've ever wanted. I never understood why everyone wanted to be remembered, but I said the right words because that's what I was taught. Be a Kingman. Be a hero. Be someone who the world remembers. I'd sacrifice it all for a lifetime in a quiet home with Serena, my family, and my friends."

"And now you see death as that peace, don't you? That while you may not get it in life . . . you hope to achieve it in death."

"Yes," I said proudly. "Is that so wrong? Who wants to fight for the rest of their life?"

Davey snapped his fingers and the scene resumed. The coin clattered to the ground and I looked down, wondering if death would ever claim me or if I'd be an immortal monster for eternity. The crown symbol was as clear as glimmering gold in the bright light. My life was tied to Serena's. I could die after all.

"My life it is," Serena stated proudly. "Do what you must, Domet. Bind his life—"

Domet brought his hand around her head as if plucking a coin from behind her ear and Serena fell into his arms, eyes glazed over as strings of thin woven darkness protruded from the crown of her head. Domet moved his fingers across them as if playing the harp, gently examining each one before moving on.

"I'm taking precautions," Domet said before the boy prince could shout his outrage. "Binding their lives together is dangerous enough, but excuse me if I don't want a Royal child to know their Kingman is immortal. I don't like the potential consequences of that."

"But you're fine with me knowing?" Davey countered.

"Of course," Domet said, continuing to mess with those dark strings. "But only because you're going to die tomorrow. Assassinated. Likely painless, but I can't guarantee that."

Davey's lips were pursed together, and his breath turned frantic and shallow. His fists were balled up, knuckles stark white. And I knew how much it must've hurt to croak out, "What?"

"You're going to be assassinated tomorrow," Domet said.

"By you?"

The immortal man shook his head. "I'm not sure who'll do it. Just that it'll happen. Immortals are whispering and congregating in Hollow. Usually that foreshadows destruction." He hesitated, separating one of the darkness strings from the others and slowly curling it around his index finger. "I tried to warn—" My ears popped. "—Kingman but I don't know if that'll be enough."

"You're serious," Davey said, confused by his own words. "Can I avoid it? What if I run away? Or hide? Or—"

"It'll be sudden. You likely won't know when it happens. Life will just cease to be. And do you think I would have told you if there was anything you could do to stop it?" He cut the darkness string's connection to Serena and then wafted it into his mouth, slurping it up like a noodle. "Are you sorry I've told you? Do you wish it would have been a surprise?"

"I—" And something in the young prince changed. The regality melted away until only fear and an unflinching desire to live remained. It was something primal that only ever emerged when the unwavering hunter made its presence known. "Can you extend my life like you are Michael's? Or bring me back from the dead afterwards?"

"The price to bring someone back from the dead is too great." Domet placed Serena's body on the ground while my younger self lay conscious but dying on the divan. "Immortality is easier to accomplish, but creating an immortal Royal heir sounds like a recipe for—"

"I'll abdicate. Or run away. Whatever it takes to live."

"I would be creating another monster. I . . . but maybe that's why I can't die. I'm always reliving my regrets." Domet glanced between Serena and me. "They are bound by fate and will always choose each other—duty or love. It makes no difference which. My immortal killers will never be what I need them to be, not so long as another opportunity is present. But"—his eyes fell on Davey again—"I wonder what I could shape, given enough time. You would do whatever it took to live?"

Death was never kind, but also never mean. It did not hunt with a grudge or a desire to gleefully watch the suffering of a family torn apart. It eased some pains and created others. Death was also inevitable. It was the one lesson children learned more quickly than others. That some falls are too high to recover from. That some bumps are too large and cuts too deep for them to heal entirely. Death was our first friend, our first teacher, and for most . . . our greatest fear. That we may be put in a small box of nothingness for all eternity rather than go to some beautiful after-life and be reunited with our loved ones. Davey feared death or maybe craved more time—to learn, love, and fight—and that was all it took for him to say, "I want to live."

Domet placed a hand on his shoulder. "Then I will do whatever it takes to keep you alive. But it will come at a price, as all things do. Will you discard your regality and become my soldier? Would you be willing to wage war against the kings that came before your family?"

"I want to live," he repeated quietly.

"Then let us craft a tale that outsmarts assassin, Kingman, and king." Domet swept back over to me and Serena, towering over us. "These two will be my greatest weapon. My decoys. They will keep our secret away from Gwendolyn and whatever king she now serves. Especially if I show interest in their development as they grow older." Red flowers sprouted, grew, bloomed, and then died over our bodies until the petals fell over us like blankets. Domet twisted those petals into a long strong coil of rope and then wrapped the magical thread around our hearts until it was tight enough to be plucked like a harp string. A note sung out hollow and empty when he did. "Kingman and Hollow bound together by fate. Their deaths and lives are now intertwined for all eternity."

The memory began to break down, walls and furniture crumbling away like ashes being blown into the wind. Domet walked in front of Davey, smiling ear to ear, as he offered him a hand. "Are you ready to fight to live?"

Davey looked up at the immortal. "I'm ready."

I was ejected forcibly from the memory, swirling upward as my body was pulled in all directions. My mind landed back in my real body with a thud, and I jolted upright as I inhaled loudly. Sirash and Naomi scrambled backwards as I placed my hand over my heart, trying to control and calm my rapid heartbeat. It felt as if my heart might burst out of my chest if I . . . well, I guess it didn't matter anymore. I was a deathless immortal, bound to Serena. Death could not claim me. Not unless she willed it.

"Michael?" Naomi asked cautiously. "Did you find it? Do we have the third brother's name?"

"What happened?" Sirash added quickly. There were nine jars filled with my memories at his side and a syringe filled with seven memories to stab Dark with.

"The third's name wasn't in there," I said. I lifted my right hand, seeing Sirash had replaced it with his bony version. It groaned like cracking knuckles whenever I moved it suddenly. "But maybe something more important was." I closed my eyes gently, feeling the sunlight against my skin, and then collapsed against the grass. "I'm an immortal."

They blinked at me. But it was Naomi who spoke. "Are you telling me I saved your worthless life for no reason? I could have let you die, and you would have lived anyway?"

I nodded. "But that's not the worst thing. I think Davey Hollow tricked death. The boy prince might still be alive somewhere, and under Domet's control."

A FEAST OF INSECTS

There was no time for confusion. I had spent the night searching my memories for the third brother's name—discovering my immortality instead—which didn't leave me much time to figure out how to win without revealing what I was. So, I did what I did best and decided to figure it out mid-fight. After all, how hard could it be to convince multiple Mercenary companies to join my cause? At least I had a replacement for my lost hand now.

I strolled over creaky wooden boards strung together by green-dyed ropes. Numerous signs warned me to turn back the closer I got to the shore where my test was taking place. Some spoke of the threat of gunfire from the dozens of ships that circled the island, while others advised not to drink the water, eat the fruit, or touch the bark of most trees lest lethal insects land on your skin and sting to kill. And all it took was one for someone's skin to bubble and pop, gums to rot, and senses to disappear. Death festered here.

At the center of the island—where the earth had been scorched with fire and only ash remained—there was a stone altar with a ceramic jar on it surrounded by bones stripped clean. Worms, spiders, roaches, and insects with more eyes than legs crawled within it and slithered up the sides only to fall before they could push the lid off. Nothing else seemed to be alive around me, but—considering how many ships had been offshore when I had arrived—my guests were here somewhere.

A voice came from the sea amplified by Sound Fabrications. "Apprentice Michael of Orbis Company! Your initiation will begin when you hear cannon fire! Survive until dusk and you will be recognized as a full member of Orbis Company."

My hands were on my hips. I had to do more than win. I needed an army that would fight with me to the very end, which meant I had to *make* Orbis Company submit to my will. Beating a hundred Mercenaries was the easy part. I had to beat the *right* hundred Mercenaries. And none of the ones I needed would be coming to this island. I'd have to go to them.

Cannons salted the earth of the island, blowing up dirt and destroying trees and sand dunes and anything else taller than a person. I didn't move, listening for the screams behind the explosions. They started off distant and then grew closer and closer until snapping twigs and crunching leaves drowned out their voices. I drew my flintlock pistol and shot the first one that emerged in the leg. He landed with a thump and a scream as two more trampled him to get to me. One had a spear made of fire in their hand, while the other wielded a short sword and a flintlock.

The Mercenary shot and missed, shattering the ceramic jar on the altar in a mist of blood and bugs. The other threw the spear of fire at me. I plucked it out of the air, twisted the magic to my desire, and then threw it back, igniting the Mercenaries and their surroundings. As they struggled to put the fire out, I charged forward and delivered an elbow to one of their faces and a foot to the others.

Three down.

I sprinted toward the beach and through the forest, past other Mercenaries. Each one was caught off guard and I was able to disarm, incapacitate, or hit them in their sensitive bits before they had a chance to respond. It wasn't honorable to fight like that, but it got results, and I only had eighty-seven left by the time my feet reached sand. I had to circle the island twice to find the ship I was looking for—the *Freedioso*—after getting distracted by a Mercenary who could manipulate sand and nearly getting swallowed by a thousand specks of pure pain. But after nullifying my surroundings and punching him in the throat, I stared at the ship. I had to get over there. Luckily for me, my Nullification Fabrications could do a lot of things.

I squatted, tapping my heels as I gathered warmth there and focused on creating discs under my feet. Once they were ready, I ran across the water toward the ship, kicking up water in my wake. Maybe they were surprised to see what I was doing, or knew it wasn't going to end well, but they unleashed cannon fire on me as I approached. I dodged easily, slipping and sliding across the water. Once I was close, I launched myself onto the side of the ship, scrambled upward into the ropes, and bowed to my adoring crowd. All the leaders of Machina Company, Orbis Company, the Wolven King, my friends, and a decent number of the top ten pirates were looking up at me like I was a madman. Three nearby ships were filled with Machina Company Mercenaries who were pressed against the railings to take in the spectacle.

"Hello, everyone! We didn't get a chance to talk this morning, and that's such a shame." I leapt onto the deck and was immediately greeted with dozens of weapons pointed my way. After pushing away the tip of an overly eager spear, I continued, "So, after thinking about it, I've decided this whole trial is going to go a little differently."

"Are you mad?" Tai snarled. "You're breaking tradition. Get back to that island and—"

I shushed him. "I'm talking here. Please listen. It'll be worth the insubordination." Titus held Tai back from walloping me over the head with a dagger. "I've decided to change the rules. You all are going to acknowledge me as a Mercenary."

"Or else?" the leader of Machina Company snapped. He was a short muscular Goldani man with a scar that split his lip in two, wide eyes, and thick eyebrows. "Who do you think you are? What gives any man—an apprentice, no less—who leads no troops the right to talk to us like that?"

"You'll listen to me because I'm the man who will become the Mercenary King. I'll unite every company under my banner, force the world to acknowledge me and my strength, and then break the world so I can rebuild it better than before." I twirled in a circle, making sure they all saw my expression. "Is that clear? Or should I repeat myself?"

Cassia rubbed her brow, muttering impolite things as she tried to hide a faint smile. Naomi—more caring and friendly than I ever deserved—was smacking everyone around her to make sure they listened to me. Most of the leadership of Machina and Orbis Companies were scowling at me, likely wondering where this insolence had come from. Only the Wolven King didn't seem fazed. I stopped in front of him.

"I know your name," I said. "I don't know everything about you and I'm not in a position to free my sister from your chains yet, but I will be one day. And when that day comes, I'll make you beg for forgiveness."

"Insolent."

"Imbecilic." I raised my hand toward the sky. "Want me to prove it? Because I know your youngest brother's name. And I know that if I utter it, he will launch a piece of Celona at me, hoping to wipe me out. He'll take all of us out." I looked around. "Acknowledge me as a full-fledged Mercenary and I won't do it. This feast is over, and I have won."

"You don't know it," the Wolven King stated. "No one on Eham knows it and you didn't get it at the Reborn Titan. You're bluffing."

"Are you really willing to test that?"

"Yes," he hissed.

What an imbecile.

But he was right. No one on Eham had it and I hadn't figured it out at the Reborn Titan or in my memories of my youth, but . . . I'd repeated my conversation with Serena over and over and over again in my head until it was seared into my mind like the brand on my neck. And one line didn't make sense to me. Why, when she was sacrificing her life to save me, had she said, "*We were outplayed. We've had everything we needed from the beginning. We just didn't understand it. I'm sorry, Michael.*"

Because it was the answer. I wasn't special. Serena *had* forgotten me. But Ike had told me she did her best to hold on to one memory. A memory she had deemed more important than the rest: the third Wolven King's name. And without ever being aware . . . my parents had named me after one of the worst people who had ever existed.

"Mikel," I shouted toward the sky. "I know you're listening! My name is Michael Kingman. I know your brothers' names, and I know yours! And if you don't stop me I'll break this world. I'll free your brother from the abyss and—"

The air popped as if shattered in half by the flaming blue-tailed piece of Celona barreling toward me. Unlike red- or white-tailed pieces that could destroy buildings or level cities respectively . . . blue-tailed moon-fall were called worldbreakers. If this one hit, everything in sight would be obliterated. There would be a gaping hole in the sea where Eham had once been.

"Acknowledge me as a full-fledged Mercenary and I'll stop it," I said to the leaders of Machina and Orbis Companies. "No one else can help you." I thumbed to the Wolven King. "Especially not him."

"He's insane," Tai whispered, hands behind his head. All the Mercenaries around us were frightened now. "You've doomed us all. You can't stop a piece of Celona."

"Just like you can't control where they fall?" I countered. Tai was suddenly tongue-tied. "Acknowledge me, and we'll all walk away from this unharmed. Don't make me break the world for your pride."

Tai ground his teeth, trying to hide his displeasure. "Fine. Stop it and you'll have my vote to become a full-fledged Mercenary."

"Delightful." I faced the other members of Orbis Company. "And what about you all?"

There was a chorus of affirmation.

"And will you help me stop Dark?"

Another chorus.

"Wonderful." I patted Machina Company's leader on the shoulder. "Sorry you had to get involved in this. But don't worry. We'll survive this mess together."

I leapt over the side of the ship and landed on bouncy water, the nullification discs under my feet keeping me afloat. I walked toward the center of the four ships around me, steadied my breathing, and stared at the blue-tailed moon-fall hurling toward me. Sirash had always joked that, because I didn't take moon-fall seriously, one day I'd get hit by one directly. But right now that's what I was hoping for.

I could catch lightning, so what were the odds that I could catch moon-fall as well?

Enough to risk total annihilation if I failed?

Absolutely.

The moon-fall zipped past the ships, setting most of their sails on fire instantly, and hit me in my nullified hands. The impact had been contained, but the force and speed at which it had arrived shattered the discs I had been floating on and sent me hurtling toward the bottom of the sea. The piece of moon-fall and I tore through the ocean, smashing through everything in our path until eventually, when my ears had popped and exploded multiple times, I hit the bottom of the ocean. My fingers were broken, jutting out at odd angles and turning into weird shapes before my body remembered it was immortal and I began to heal myself. There was nothing but darkness and small underwater volcanoes churning out bubbles down here. Fish with lights hanging from stalks avoided me as the piece of Celona lit the area like a blazing blue-flamed lantern.

A familiar voice wafted out of the rock. "Hello, Michael Kingman. It's an honor to meet you. If you survive, you'll be the first person I've spoken to directly in over a millennium. One day, I hope we'll meet face-to-face. Yours truly, Mikel Wolvenguard, the third Wolven King."

I tried to laugh, but only bubbles came out of my mouth. I left that piece of Celona at the bottom of the ocean and swam back toward the surface. I died a few times due to the changes in pressure on my way up, but after the second time it was only a slight inconvenience. I was getting more used to my immortality with every death, now that I had finally acknowledged it.

When I broke through the waterline, inhaling a deep breath as if it were my first and my last, there was silence on every ship around me. And then, slowly and steadily, people began to chant something.

"Worldbreaker . . ."

"Worldbreaker . . ."

"Worldbreaker . . ."

"Worldbreaker!"

"Worldbreaker!"

"Worldbreaker!"

The chant quickly became deafening as everyone joined in. I nullified discs on my feet again so I could stand on the water and bask in their praise. After a lot of struggle and pain and no idea where I belonged in the world . . . I had finally found my home. I was known as many things— King Killer, Dragonslayer, deathless, imbecile, Kingman, brother, lover, friend, and enemy. But out of all the names I'd earned, Worldbreaker felt the best. As if it was mine. I hadn't achieved my dream of becoming a Mercenary King yet, but right now . . . this felt like a good start. That it might finally be within my reach. That I might write the ending I wanted rather than be a pawn in another's plan.

I am Michael Worldbreaker.

Nice to finally meet you.

THE KING OF STORIES

Symon was halfway through his morning meander across Vargo in the sunshine—mandated by doctors and physicians who held more sway over his access to libraries than he liked—when he was interrupted by a crowd of clan members blocking the quickest route back to the palace. Most were holding baskets filled with flower petals and chatting nonstop. He pulled his wheelchair up to a man with a flat nose and wide eyes whose normal voice would be another's shout.

"—Queen Serena is returning! They've dealt with that king killer Mercenary bastard and we'll never see him again!" the man said quickly. "He was a stain on our city. What a disgrace to the Kingman name."

"Truly," a woman agreed. "If the rumors are true that Gwendolyn Kingman has abandoned her family name as well . . . the Kingman family is no more!"

"I can't wait. Their time will *finally* be over." He sounded gleeful. "Look! Look! They're coming now!"

Symon could just see, when he pushed himself up against his arm-rests. Dozens of Regal Company Mercenaries led the procession as the crowd threw petals at their feet, reduced to crumpled-up pink specks when Jay Prince and Serena Hollow arrived. They walked hand in hand, though it wasn't as romantic as it appeared. Her hand was curled up in his rather than their fingers woven together. Symon knew the truth of the relationship between Michael and Serena . . . It was easy for him to see this was a façade, not the Hollow Queen's preference. Chloe strolled behind the Queen with her head down and short spear drawn, despair hiding in the edges of her expression. She crushed any petal that had been lucky enough to remain whole. And maybe it was just Symon's imagination . . . but her shadow had been replaced by one that seemed more fitting of the Black Death. Was he stalking her? Always present but out of sight?

Once the parade passed and the crowds thinned, Symon began to roll himself back to the palace . . . only to be interrupted by a hooded man putting a foot against his wheels and halting him. Flintlock pistols gently swayed in the holsters strapped to his side. He smelt of fish guts, bad perfume, and sulfur. Hollow born, or had come from there recently.

"Recorder," the man said. "Join me. We have mutual friends we need to talk about."

"As you wish," Symon said as the man began to push him toward an alley. "Just let it be known that mugging a cripple is a one-way ticket to the eternal void."

The hooded man chuckled. "Don't fear. You'll like this news."

They entered a dirty alleyway where water dripped from the gutters and onto the sandstone streets. Broken wooden boxes, discarded fish nets with rancid guts stuck to them, and rusting copper pissing pots were thrown haphazardly against the side of a building. The hooded man revealed himself. It was Treyvon Wiccard, Big Brother, who wanted to change Hollow for the better. Four others were waiting for them in the alleyway—Kyros and Joey Ryder, Lyonardo Kingman, and—most surprising of all—Gwendolyn Kingman. She held something big, oddly shaped, and wrapped in bloody cloth.

"Oh, this is a terrible sight to behold," Symon said with a whistle. "If you're all here and Serena is with Jay . . . this city is about to burn to the ground, isn't it?"

Gwendolyn nodded. "The finale is coming. I can't participate, but all of you will."

"Delightful," Symon said. "Another thing I'll be on the sidelines for. Unless . . ."

Gwendolyn tossed him the wrapped package, and the Recorder unfurled it carefully, trying his best to ignore the lump in his throat. The anticipation and fear that this might not be what he thought it would be. But once the treasure was exposed . . . he smiled, and it was all teeth.

"You don't have to accept it," Gwen said carefully. "But we thought—"

Symon bit into the dragon's heart, tearing it apart piece by piece until the stringy meat could slither down his throat as easily as water. He ate it as if it were his last meal, and in a way . . . it was. He would never be able to go back to mortality after this. A lifetime of stories and recording history would be his once the meat reached his stomach and the transfer of power was complete. But he never hesitated, never faltered, and never considered another option.

Not a morsel of flesh or drop of blood was wasted.

The heart worked swiftly and powerfully, a warmth raging through his body and easing the pain. The Recorder—with Trey and Lyon's help—got to his feet as black smoke began to seep from him. His bones felt stronger than before, and he could once again move as he had before he was thrown out of a window by a Wolven King.

"Oh, yes," Symon said, staring at his hands as his nails began to sharpen and lengthen. His voice grew deeper, his vision sharpened, and his ears could pick up the sounds of sailors shouting at the docks and children whining to their mothers about wanting bluebell fruits rather than boiled crabs. Voices of the previous smoke dragons filled his mind with warnings and tips, telling him how his powers worked, how to take advantage of his newfound immortality, and—most importantly—how to achieve his wildest dreams. "This is going to be fun. I can't wait for Michael to arrive." He looked up at everyone around him. All of them were smiling. "Let's change the world, shall we?"

PART 5:

ACCEPTANCE

5 DAYS UNTIL THE FINAL DEATH OF MICHAEL KINGMAN

"To taunt death, one must not seek immortality,
but instead—to truly spite the unwavering hunter—it is best
to leave something behind they can never claim."

—Unknown

A DEATHLESS EXISTENCE

In my life, three things never changed. The first was that, despite being nowhere near Hollow or the noble court, I was at yet another raucous party that seemed ill timed at best and negligent at worst. After earning the title of Worldbreaker, all the Mercenaries from Orbis and Regal Company—including the ones I'd injured—celebrated my batshit plan to ascending from an apprentice. Some said I was finally living up to my infamous and sometimes unearned reputation, while others said they would join me if I ever formed a company of my own.

The second constant was my friends. Once we were alone, Naomi and Sebastian berated me for a *very* long time until I understood that if I ever threatened to destroy a section of the world again, they didn't want to be in the area. Since no one else had rightfully yelled at me for my stupidity . . . it made me feel good. No matter who I became or what I did, I would always have loved ones to call me on my nonsense. It was a beautiful comfort.

Sirash was gone by the time the party started. Nothing but a note written in his non-dominant hand left with a jovial pirate who had an eye patch to match my own—which he claimed made us brothers for life—and the syringe filled with memories meant for Dark. The note said: *Thank you, Michael. I'll deliver your memories when I can. May we meet again one day.* I stuffed it into my pocket, wondering if we really would.

The last constant was more subtle. As the party continued, all the attendees fell into a deep slumber except me. Naomi slumped against me mid-rant about being separated from Chloe for so long, while Sebastian fell backwards off the log we had been sitting on, snoring.

Alphonse, the Wolven King, strolled through the crowds with a bone goblet overflowing with bright red balls of memories as he plucked more from everyone on the island. It looked as if fireflies had filled the air around him.

Alphonse stopped in front of me. "Come," he said without dramatics. "You fulfilled your part of the deal and now so will I. Don't worry about your friends. They'll wake tomorrow morning with nothing worse than a minor headache . . . now that I've erased their memories of my brother's name, to keep it from being abused."

"You really think others would try that? It's suicide."

"The intelligent wouldn't, but the crafty would. Send a lone soldier into enemy territory to take the area down with him? It would seem a worthwhile sacrifice to many commanders."

"That's a fair point." I took Naomi's head off my shoulder and laid her down on the ground. "So where's my sister?"

The Wolven King sipped from his goblet, ingesting the memories as if they were wine as he signaled for me to follow. We walked through the town of Eham as everything slept around us. Everything had fallen into a deep slumber: rainbow birds, rats, dogs and cats alike. While some had been lucky enough to fall asleep in their homes or on benches, some had fallen asleep in awkward places like on the edges of fountains or with their faces fallen into whatever they had been eating.

"We should make sure no one dies in their sleep. Someone might have been cooking and—"

"Taken care of." He snapped his fingers. Multiple copies of himself, clear as glass, came out of his body and took off throughout the town, helping whoever needed it. "I've been doing this sort of stuff for a millennium, Michael. There's nothing I don't have a plan for. I will leave no trace that I was here . . . no destruction in my wake."

"Somehow I doubt that."

"Doubt I want to avoid destruction?"

I shook my head. "That you've seen everything. Humanity is evolving and one day we'll stop you and your brothers and all the rest of the immortals."

He made a dismissive sound. "You speak as if you won't be among them." When I didn't answer, he chuckled and then said, "Ah. So that's how it is. Is it romantic or familial?"

"Romantic."

"I hope they're worth it," he said quietly. "Do you know what divided my brothers and me the first time?"

We wandered through the sandstone streets, admiring the twinkling starlight and the orange light cast by the dying lanterns. We were on the path headed toward the Ehamian lighthouse that served as a welcome and warning to all those that approached it. I nicked a lime from a vendor as we passed and bit into it to make sure I still had my mortal taste buds. It tasted so painfully sour, I felt human for just a little longer.

After Alphonse's stares became too intense to ignore, I answered his question. "Lady Javi Victoria of Wolvenguard. She was the Lifeweaver's sister, murdered by one of you Wolven Kings. His grief led to a rift with his husband—the third brother—and intensified the war."

"Yes. Her death was a mistake. But grief is a terrible thing. A disease with no cure but time. And yet many think anger or revenge will make it better." His body was present with me, but his mind was somewhere else. Lost to the endless life that had led him here. "Do you know which one of us was responsible?"

"No. But I suspect it was either the second or the third. Your prison was nothing compared to the second's and given that the third is even harder to find . . ." The immortal man seemed deflated. "Was it you?"

"No." He stared at the shattered moon. "But if it's alright . . . I would rather not talk about it. It's the greatest stain on my history. Do you know how many lives could have been saved if she had lived?"

"Hundreds of thousands."

"Millions," he corrected. "Hundreds of thousands died in the war, but millions died when Celona was shattered and magic—" Alphonse stopped as we neared the lighthouse. The path had gone from mani- cured and defined to rough and wild. Thornblood bushes lined the path to make sure no one approached the lighthouse sneakily. They would inflict more cuts than a blind surgeon. "Have you figured it out yet? The magical secrets we're hiding from the world?"

I looked up at the night sky, Celona, and Tenere. My Forgotten self had told me to stop staring upward. Part of me had assumed it was so I could focus on what was in front of me. Reality versus imagination. The man I was versus the man I had to be. But that was a lie. In truth, it was about protecting myself from something I must've figured out long ago, and was destined to forget every time I slept. All the pieces clicked to- gether once again.

Fabricating, Weaving, Spellborn, Insatiable, Alchemist, Patchworker, and Abyss Walker.

Seven magical systems for the seven pieces of Celona in the sky. A perfect fit.

Magic had been fragmented when Celona was shattered, and only the Wolven Kings and possibly Domet still had access to it all. But that wasn't what Alphonse was asking for. He wanted to know if I had fig- ured out Fabricating and how it worked. The Archmage argued that it was all dependent on the bloodline—that a child's specialization could be figured out based on the patterns and what their parents were—and that magic seemed to be evolving. More and more specializations were showing up with each new generation. But there was just one small issue:

that theory didn't work for Serena's or my family. We were all different Fabricators. So how could a bloodline determine it?

Which left me with Domet's theory: that magic hadn't changed. That it all depended on how it was used. That all specializations had always been around, but sometimes the knowledge was lost. But where had they gone? Why had they stopped showing up in people?

Two opposing philosophies of magic, where it seemed only one could be right.

But they were both right.

Fabrications were all about the blood. Every person's blood carried a distinct specialization and when mixed with another would create a different specialization. The assumption was that it was determined at birth—but that didn't make sense. Me, my siblings, and the royal siblings proved that theory wrong. Because it happened *whenever* someone ingested or traded someone else's blood. Blood oaths, blood bindings, and blood hostages all allowed people to gain new specializations or trade specializations. Having accepted blood oaths in the past, my mother was a Fabricator. One who had likely become a Forgotten by using her magic unknowingly, throughout her life. It must've been something without a visual cue, like my nullification specialization. For all I knew, nullification might be her specialization, too.

But if that were true—that she had been a Forgotten, and that ingesting blood could change or create new specializations—then I had figured out how to cure a Forgotten after all. Magic wasn't a gift; it was a drug. One that took more and more away whenever someone used it. Being a Forgotten was akin to a magical overdose: one that needed to be purged with Nullification Fabrications and then cured with Light Fabrications.

If only I had figured it out sooner, Dawn would never have become a Forgotten. She could have kept using her Steel Fabrications to help her walk, every day of her life. If only. I repeated my hypothesis to the Wolven King when I was confident my voice would hold steady.

Alphonse responded with a slow, steady clap. "Congratulations. You figured it—"

I sucker-punched the Wolven King and knocked him to the ground.

In my defense, it seemed like the perfect time to get my frustrations out. He had imprisoned my sister. Did he really think I was going to let that go quietly? While he was recovering, I planted a foot on his chest and pressed down hard. And then—because I'm a dramatic bastard—I put my finger in his face and said, "If you think I'll let you masquerade as a figure of justice when you released magic into the world and hurt so many fucking people, you're mad. Once I get Serena back and stop Angelo and Dark, you're next. Don't forget that."

I took my foot off his chest. The Wolven King sat up, wiped blood from his mouth, and then severed my head from my body with the side of his palm. My head tumbled to the ground and landed at my feet. But I could still move everything as usual. The only difference was that I had a lower point of view. One of the perks of being an immortal. So I responded in kind. I threw my damn head at the Wolven King, nailed him in his faceless forehead with a flying headbutt, and sent him back to the ground.

"Oh, I'm sorry," I shouted as my head wiggled on top of his chest. "Did you think I was going to die or something?"

"Bullshit above," Alphonse muttered as he pushed my head off him. "How did you become an immortal? I would have known if you were a true immortal—I *know* when new ones are created—and I suppose you could be a beast . . . but I doubt you'll die even if I crush your head and eat your heart."

"I'm a deathless."

The Wolven King had his head in his hands. "The Lifeweaver strikes again. As if the first deathless Kingman wasn't already impossible to kill. Now we have another to deal with." He hesitated. "Don't join a war you're not prepared to see through to the end, Michael."

I picked up my head, put it back where it belonged, and felt as if all the muscle, bone, and skin reconnected with itself. "Consider my words written into my skin like promises I show the world. I will not falter, and I will free my sister from her debt."

"I'll believe it when I see it."

"Don't fear. You will."

"You Kingman have lied to me in the past. I doubt this will be any different." He spat out blood to his side. "She's in the lighthouse. Talk as long as you want, but when you're done . . . you won't see her again. Our story is just beginning, and I won't let you interrupt my plans."

I gave him the single-finger salute and trudged toward the lighthouse. Our conversation was over. He was an immortal who sought to control the world from behind the scenes, and I was a worldbreaker. We would never see eye to eye. There was no point in trying to hide that.

Gwen was waiting for me in front of the lighthouse, arms open, with a smile on her face. "Hi, Michael. Miss me?"

I sprinted toward her, embracing her tightly. "I missed you so much."

Tears started falling down my face, hot and painful, and I never felt more human than in that moment. I longed to be home. To be with those I loved. And not to be walking toward my death in a few days.

CHASING SUNRISES

Gwen and I talked throughout the night, enjoying the peace and each other's company until the stars began to retreat and Alphonse returned to take Gwen away. I hugged her tightly, making sure I never forgot this moment of love and anger. I would find a way to bring her home. She returned my hug with a strong one of her own as she did her best to hold the tears back. When we separated, I said, "We'll see each other again."

"We will," she said with a painted-on smile. The Wolven King opened a tear to New Dracon City—the capital's famous gear-and-bell–inspired architecture and color scheme unmistakable—and stepped through it. Gwen glanced back at me one last time as she said, "Don't go dying on me, alright?"

I smiled true. "Do you really think I'd leave you behind like that?"

"I know you won't."

Then Gwen stepped through the tear, and I watched as it snapped shut, bits of rusted metal falling like rain around me as I lingered where my sister had once been, hoping we'd see each other again. After it was clear she wasn't returning, I watched the sunrise from the beach, amazed by the beauty of this world. Naomi crept up to sit by my side. She rested her head against my shoulder.

"Did you see Gwen?"

I nodded. "Left with Alphonse. Gave me as much information and help as she could, though."

"Is it enough to stop Angelo and Dark?"

"No," I admitted. "They likely know everything I do."

"Are we just giving up, then?"

I grabbed a fistful of sand with my fleshy hand and held it tightly. But even then, some slipped through the cracks. "I think I have a plan to stop them. It's complicated but it might give us a chance."

"Sounds delightful. Is death guaranteed?"

"Only for me," I said with a smile.

Naomi jabbed me in the side. "Prick. So what's the plan?"

I pointed toward the abyss. "First, we have to get to Vargo. It's too far to get there by sea if we're going to stop the wedding, so we'll use Abyss Walking. The second Wolven King will help us with that."

"The price won't be cheap."

"It never is." I exhaled. "Then comes the easy part: we invade Vargo, fight an army of Mercenaries, save Serena, and then stop Angelo and Dark."

"I'm still waiting to hear how."

"Angelo and Dark combined know everything about me. They'll be prepared for anything I can come up with . . . so . . . I'm going to make them fight someone less predictable." I smiled. "Someone they've likely forgotten about."

"Serena," Naomi breathed.

"Exactly."

Naomi took her head off me. "There's more to your plan, isn't there?"

"Yes." I hesitated. "It's not that I don't trust you. It's because—"

"Because you're going to let them kill you. Make them think they've won and get complacent. Just like what happened with King Isaac. It's the only time Angelo was vulnerable."

"I expected more yelling."

She glared at me. "I'm only holding back because the second part of your plan must be to have Serena go through the door, beat Angelo and Dark, and do whatever they were going to do to bring you back, right?"

"Realistically," I said, drawing a square in the sand, "we know defying death means going from reality to the afterlife"—I drew a triangle to represent it—"and back. Angelo's goal is to get to the church between life and death"—a circle represented that—"so he can steal Katherine back to life."

I cleared my throat. "My plan is to go from the afterlife to the church. So, in case I can't defy death . . . I'll delay and maybe help Serena stop Angelo and Dark."

"Insane," Naomi stated. "Either you die and come back, die and die for real, or die and try to trespass back to the church to help Serena bring you back to life."

"Pretty much."

"Have I told you how stupid you are? Why does every decision lead to you being a martyr? Is your brain permanently broken?"

"Do you have any other solution? I don't have the confidence we can beat Dark fairly. Let alone all of Regal Company, Papa Noble, Jay Prince, Adreann, and Emelia."

Naomi inched even closer to me as the first rays of sunlight emerged from the horizon and the stars faded. "What if it doesn't work? What if Serena can't bring you back?"

"Then I'll greet you in the afterlife when it's your time."

"It shouldn't have to be like this."

"I know. But it is."

"I'm happy I met you, Michael. You're my best friend."

I put my arm around her. "You're my best friend. Can you believe you almost shot me?"

"You say that as if I don't still want to on a daily basis."

"Well . . . some things are better when they remain the same."

We sat in the silence together, taking everything in. But eventually, when my skin began to warm, she asked, "Do we have to go soon?"

"No, we can stay for as long as we want. One final day of peace."

"Good." She curled closer. "To a night that never ends."

"And a morning that never comes."

THE MADNESS OF DESPAIR

I abandoned my humanity to learn more about how Fabrications worked in four days than any other had in a lifetime.

Death and I would reunite soon, so I worked knowing every word I wrote might be my last. Naomi tried to make me more rational. Less certain that I would die when we returned to Vargo. But as a man who had grown up in Hollow, I knew a lie when I heard one. At least hers had been for a cause. She was kind like that.

This immortal body of mine—now that I had acknowledged and embraced it—allowed me to accomplish the impossible. Eating and drinking water became nuisances, so unless necessary, I focused on bloodletting, experimenting, and studying magic. Sleeping was forgone as well, but only so I wouldn't lose any of my memories. I didn't have the time to play the immortal's game, so I changed it. I couldn't lose memories if I didn't sleep.

Unsurprisingly, even immortality had its limitations, especially around how quickly I could heal. Losing too much blood left me with a pounding headache and slight nausea until I ate something sickeningly sweet like melted sugar sticks or something soaked in brown butter sauce. My missing eye and arm showed that limbs wouldn't regrow—but they would reattach themselves if the two separated ends were brought back together. My left pinky toe had been the noble warrior to confirm my hypothesis.

Mixing blood to create certain Fabrications was an exercise in anger and love. Thanks to Orbis and Machina Companies, I had access to all the basic specializations. I created about a hundred new Fabricators in a few days, mixing blood until I found a power that could stop Dark and Angelo. Some of my favorites included:

Fire and fire created light.

Fire and smoke created poison.

Darkness and a non-Fabricator's blood created nullification.

Light and darkness created either light or darkness.

Ice and fire created water.

Wind and wind created lightning.

There were hundreds of other possibilities I discovered over those four days. The combination of darkness and nullification was the one I finally picked to defeat Angelo and Dark. There were only three vials with that combination—the lucky Mercenary who had received my initial test suddenly found himself a group captain of other Mercenaries in Machina Company—and Naomi and I held on to one each. Because after I died . . . one of these vials had to be delivered to Serena. Otherwise my plan stood no chance.

I did as much as I could with the other forms of magic. But, fundamentally, the Archmage had been telling the truth. Everything revolved around how they used it. Fabricators created their specialization. Weavers manipulated their specialization. Spellborns had the powers of Fabricators and Weavers along with the ability to transform into their specialization. Abyss Walkers could move substances. Insatiables could destroy substances. Patchworkers altered or extracted substances. And Alchemy could contain substances within something else.

The seven different types of magic, matching the seven major pieces of the moon. My previous letter to myself had told me to stop staring at the moon. Three guesses as to what I must've figured out by stargazing one night. I still didn't understand how I had initially learned it, or why I had forgotten it—maybe in the missing memories that explained why I had been on death's door and brought to Domet's house to be healed—but those details didn't matter anymore. I was out of time to find all the truths. Others would have to carry on without me.

I told Naomi I would sleep on the voyage to the abyss, but instead I wrote. As fast and as much as I could. I was taking this age of ignorance about magic down with me. Never again would there be a boy on the East Side who had to test his limitations at the cost of his memories because there wasn't a magical school. This knowledge would be accessible to everyone. And maybe that would be enough to atone for all the bad I had done.

My time was up as Cassia dropped anchor and Naomi came looking for me. Her words were sweet and careful.

"We're here," she said. "It's time to see if you can cross the abyss and get us to Vargo."

ABYSSWALKER

I walked across the thin strip of land that hovered over the abyss as Sebastian and Orbis Company waited for me to succeed or to disappear forever. The black wind that had pushed me back last time was nothing more than a gentle breeze today. But the mist was so thick the further I went toward the other side, the more I was forced to use my skeleton hand to push it out of my face like smoke. And once I waded into it, I lost sight of the *Freedioso*. Wherever I was going . . . I was going there alone.

My path slowly began to twist and descend into the abyss like a spiral around the edges. Water spat at me from the waterfalls to the sides as the path went from rocky to overgrown, with weeds and grass up to my thighs. I walked and walked until my feet ached, my body was covered in sweat, and sunlight had long since abandoned me. Only strange green crystals like the ones I had seen in Hollow illuminated my path and guided me to a massive iron door.

I pushed against it with all my strength until there was a big enough opening for me to sneak through. And once I was inside, it closed as if pulled by an unknown force. The black walls were covered in bright red webs that looked like veins, while the floor was an unstained white with golden glyphs etched in it. Broken iron chains hung from the ceiling like icicles that rattled whenever I took a step forward, even if I didn't touch them.

"Welcome, Omari Torda," a deep voice rumbled from further in. "I have waited a long time for you to grace these halls. I hope you enjoy it here." It laughed. "Because we are trapped."

I took a deep breath to steel myself and then pressed on.

The hallway led into an amphitheater with thousands of seats. Each one was occupied by an obsidian skeleton that looked brittle enough to fall apart at a touch. The floor was glass, exposing that we were surrounded with water. Three monstrous sea creatures swam in circles underneath us. Things bigger than islands, with more teeth, tentacles, and eyes than anything I had ever seen before. The behemoths. The final group of beast immortals. Were they here as allies or wardens?

I walked down the main set of stairs toward the imposing throne at the bottom. It was covered in enough chains to not move if a crack in the earth opened beneath it. But it made sense. Prisons were meant to be secure. And this one was built for a Wolven King.

The man sitting in the throne was older than time itself. His clothes were tatters, his skin was wrinkly and sun spotted, his muscles had wasted away, and a long grey beard wrapped around him like a knitted scarf. Yet his eyes were bright and golden and his voice imposing as thunder. When he spoke, the whole room shook.

"You're not Omari Torda," the man began. "Who are you?"

I stood straight. "Don't recognize my voice? I'm Michael Kingman."

"A King's man?" The man scowled. "Your ancestors stole my throne and helped lock me up down here. Do you know who I am?"

"You're a Wolven King," I said.

"Yes. Do you know which one?"

It was Zarack, but it seemed better not to let his ego get any bigger, so I shook my head, feigning ignorance. He clearly didn't remember me from our conversations through Omari. Did he have memory issues along with his physical limitations? Maybe he was the one that killed Domet's sister. His prison did seem worse than Alphonse's had been.

"Have our names been erased from history?"

"Nothing about your rule remains except the scars you left on this land." I stared him in the eyes. "And even they will heal in time."

"Doubtful," he said. "But let me enlighten you. I am Zarack, the second brother and rightful king of this world. I was called many things— the god of war, the king of blood and iron, the emperor of salt, the great one, the—"

"Do I look like I care?" I interrupted. "You may have been all those things, but now you're chained up and held in captivity. You were beaten and nothing you say will make me think of you as anything other than a complete and utter loser."

Zarack howled with laughter and all the obsidian skeletons around us joined in like a macabre orchestra. His skeleton army stood and danced on top of their seats and made obscene gestures at me. They stopped only when the Wolven King did. And when they sat again, I noticed that most of them had weapons in their hands, ready to fight at a moment's notice.

"You remind me of—" His words were nothing but movements of his lips. "Ah, how rude of me. You can't hear their name. What a shame."

"Who are you talking about?" I asked without thinking.

"The one who gave you those eyes."

"The First Kingman?"

"Is that what you call them?" Zarack chuckled. "How fascinating. Even without their name or identity left in this world . . . their legacy has lived on. But I suppose ours has as well? Tell me. Do you tell stories of the usurper peasant who stole my throne?"

"Adrian?" Zarack's face fell at the name. "Yes, we do. We call him the liberator. If it wasn't for him, every trace of you would be gone. You're just a footnote in our history."

"For now." He drummed his thin fingers with freakishly long nails against the throne. "But history has a way of repeating itself. And if you are here, then my time of imprisonment draws to a close."

"Do you think I'm stupid enough to release you?"

"No," he admitted. "But if you're here, then you likely traded places with Omari in order to save him." He shook one of the chains binding him. "Because of my predicament, I have been forced to try sneakier methods than I am accustomed to. Yet I still build an army in preparation for my freedom. I'll free you if you want . . . but my price will not be cheap." He held up two fingers. "Or my brothers have returned, and you require my aid to fight them."

"It's amazing to see someone so old be so pompous. You'd think you'd learn some humility after a thousand years. Surprisingly: neither reason."

Zarack huffed at me like a self-important cat. "Then why are you here?"

"I need you to send me and my ship to Vargo via Abyss Walking."

"That's it?"

"That's it."

"How boring," Zarack said. "You are in the presence of true royalty, and all you want is to cross? I could help you conquer the world."

"I don't want the world," I said.

"Then what do you want?"

To save Serena. But instead of the truth, I said, "Revenge. There's a man out there I owe a debt to, and I plan on repaying it with blood."

Zarack leaned as far forward as he could with his chains. "Revenge and blood are my instruments. I can reduce your enemies to ash if you free me from—"

"Not a chance."

"Good for me you don't have a choice in the matter," Zarack declared. The chains rattled on his throne. "Do you know why there's no account of people leaving this place? It's because leaving comes with a price. One all must pay, but luckily . . . you have two to choose from. One is to free me—"

"Still not happening."

"—and the other is to be erased from the world."

Shivers rippled through my body. "What?"

Zarack pointed to a large crack to his left. "That's the exit. But this place is cursed. My brothers were determined there should be no trace of me, and they knew people would stumble upon me eventually, so this was their solution. Anyone who meets me is erased from the world. Their mothers and fathers and brothers and sisters and lovers will forget them. Their names will vanish from the history books as if they had never been born."

"Ah," I said.

"'Ah'? Is that all you have to say? I suppose it must be a shock. But like I said, you have a choice. Release me. Break my chains and set me free and you will not be erased. I will make sure all those who oppose you—"

I muttered something.

"What did you say?"

"Forget my legacy," I repeated louder.

"What? You're a King's man! You have a legacy to uphold! You wouldn't want to let your ancestors down, would you?"

"Fuck my ancestors! They're dead and I'm alive! I don't care what they think of me." I raised my head and finally felt content with my place in the world. "Take my name and strip away my place in my family. Make me a nobody and force me to wander the world without a home. I've found something more important." I smiled at the Wolven King. "I'm in love with a beautiful woman. I have true friends who will call me out when I'm dumb, not abandon me. I have slain dragons, broken cities, and climbed the Reborn Titan to restore my lover's memories. I am Michael Kingman, but I am also Michael Orbis. My last name does not define me and I will not set you free out of fear of losing my place in the world. Because as long as those I love are in it . . . I will always have a place at their side."

"How touching," Zarack said. "But I have waited so long for this op-portunity." He snapped his fingers. "If you won't do it willingly, then I'll make you."

I let my warmth cover my body as the skeleton army dashed toward me, heckling and waving weapons. It was too risky to nullify the entire room in case his chains were magically bound. But I remembered the sea urchins I had fished up during our voyage, with their spiky backsides, and replicated one in my mind with my nullification warmth. Then I extended the thorns on my back outward, impaling any skeleton that came near me. His army crumbled before him in a symphony of clattering bones against stone. Then it was just me and this Wolven King.

"The world will not remember you," the Wolven King cursed. "You will be forgotten. Are you sure this is the path you want to take?"

I put my hands in my pockets and stepped over the remains of his army, walking toward the crack in the wall. "Michael Kingman had a good life, but everyone dies eventually."

"So be it." The Wolven King raised his hand, and a concentrated ball of red light began to form in his palm. When it was perfectly round, Zarack put it against his chest. "Person by person, as the world sleeps you will be erased from history. When you awake, there will be no trace of you. Your name will be ash in the wind, and when those you love look upon you, all they will see is a stranger. You had the chance to be someone, and now you will be *nothing*."

"Don't you understand?" I asked. "I've always been nobody, but just this once, I can be the man I want to be. And the man I want to be is at his lover's side."

"She will forget you, too."

"I know she will. But we're bound together. Whether it takes a day, or a year, or a century, we'll find a way back to each other. Even if I have a new name or a new face or a new personality, she will always be the love of my life." Quieter, I added, "I just hope I have the chance to be hers."

"Goodbye, Michael Kingman. You will not be remembered."

And for the first time in my life, those words felt like a blessing rather than a curse.

Light shimmered around me, heating my body as if it were ablaze, and then I found myself back on the deck of the *Freedioso*. The Reborn Titan was no longer on the horizon, and I knew—

"Michael!" Cassia screamed, slamming me against the nearby railing. Everyone was frantic and the wind howled as if we were in the middle of a typhoon. "What did you do?"

I craned my neck to look over the side of the ship. There was a lurching feeling in my stomach when I saw that I was seeing it from the sky. We were plummeting toward Vargo. The Wolven King must've dropped us above the city rather than into the bay.

I really needed to be more specific sometimes.

THE DAY OF MICHAEL KINGMAN'S FINAL DEATH

We fell out of the sky above Vargo, boards from the bottom of the ship cracking and flying upward around us. The sails and masts snapped and flew away, landing somewhere in the city like pieces of Celona. The crew below deck ran topside with handfuls of weapons, scaro, and a laugh or two. Our ship wouldn't survive the fall, but we might if we were lucky. Cassia was trying to throttle me. It wasn't as if she could *actually* kill me, but telling her that would probably only make her angrier.

"You insufferable piece of shit!" Cassia screamed, hands around my neck. Titus and Alexis were trying to yank her off. Naomi was cackling on her back like an asylum's lifetime guest. After the Heartbreaker and our journey to the Reborn Titan, I doubted anything fazed her anymore. "Do you realize what you've done? You ruined my ship and killed us all!"

Speaking wasn't possible with so much pressure on my throat, and I hoped she'd show me mercy. I hadn't known the Wolven King was going to drop us above Vargo, but I probably should have been clearer about the terms before I betrayed him. Nothing to do but live and learn for next time.

"Cassia! Stop!" Alexis pleaded. She was wrapped around Cassia, trying to heave her off. "We need to figure out how to survive this fall! Hurt him after!"

"First he suffers," she said. "He killed my ship! And blood will be paid in blood."

Tai descended from the upper deck, indifferent to the fact we were plummeting to our deaths. "Cassia, let him go. Alexis is right. Hurt him after we survive this fall. I'll even help you partially drown him if you want."

"Fine!" She shoved me away, and Titus, Alexis, and I fell to the deck together. "How do we survive this?"

"I'll handle it," Otto said, taking his gaze off the rapidly approaching ground. "It would be safe to assume anything in the lower decks will be destroyed. Does everyone have their weapons and valuables?"

All the Mercenaries around me nodded, as did Cassia's crew. Some were holding weapons of various styles and conditions—rusted longswords, gemstone-laden axes, broken spears, and more exotic weapons I could barely describe, much less know the proper names of. Nonna had a sickle and chain with a weight attached to one end, while Jade wore metal gauntlets with blades like a tiger's claws. Titus was unarmed except for his recently used meat cleaver and a well-sized knife that could be used to cut anything. Gael had a sash of gunpowder vials around his chest, Tai had a cutlass in one hand and a double-barreled flintlock pistol in the other, Imani had her broken spears, Alexis had her pistols, and Cassia had so many explosive gems on her person, it could make a jeweler salivate. Naomi held up a stolen sword from the boat at one point like a Thebian about to yell a war cry, while Sebastian debated which of his remaining fingers to break to command all the stone statues in Vargo to do his bidding.

Otto moved to the middle of the deck, used his hands as if mimicking a breath, and then very softly said, "No one interrupt me. Except for you, Naomi. If you need to correct me, do so at your discretion. Only those of us who ride the wind will understand the difference between flying and splatting."

Naomi lowered her sword, slightly taken aback that a Mercenary she had barely talked to had such confidence in her, but gave an affirmative nod anyway.

Otto exhaled and then created a cyclone beneath the ship. There was a sudden jolt, most of us lost balance and seized the closest thing we could find—ropes, wooden railings, whatever seemed sturdy—and held on as Otto moved his hands in the air like a martial artist trying to control the sea. The cyclone slowly shrunk as we got closer to the ground, reducing our speed and cradling us into the town. Right before we dropped onto two buildings and obliterated them into nothing more than foundations. As we all struggled to reorient ourselves, screams rose around us as people fled from the destruction as if we were worse than all the other pieces of moon or dragons that had wrecked Vargo before our arrival. Nothing of the ship below the main deck remained intact.

Regal Company surrounded us on all sides as we recovered. We were maybe fifty strong—Mercenaries and Cassia's crew included—while Regal Company easily had over a thousand. If not more. Only Sebastian's stone statues would even the odds.

Papa Noble emerged from the roof nearest our landing spot, so he was able to look down on us. His purple eyes shone in the morning sunlight. None of the noble siblings were at his side, faceless and irrelevant Mercenaries flanking him. But even if they didn't carry the reputations of his children, they were all nightmares made sentient.

"Tai!" Papa Noble bellowed. "How unfortunate to be meeting like this."

The leader of Orbis Company returned his opponent's gaze. "Is it really? You know me. I always like a good fight. It's the only thing that entertains me these days."

"Given up on traveling to the outer sea and finding your family?"

"Oh, no, I haven't. I'll still do that one day. But first it looks like we have a fight to finish." Tai motioned for one of the crew to let him take a swig from their scaro. They gave it up willingly, but it wasn't a single glug but a long-sustained chug. He burped and then threw the empty bottle aside. "We don't have to do this if you don't want to. I won't feel bad about walking away peacefully. Our companies know going to war would be bad for business."

"The only way this ends peacefully is if you back down and walk away," Papa said. "If any of you take a single step toward the palace, these streets will run red."

"The Worldeaters will be mad at us if we fight."

"Their notion of peace between companies is idealistic." Papa looked toward Nonna. "Historian, when did two of the top five Mercenary companies last fight each other?"

The elderly woman who never blinked rattled off the answer as if she were reading from an ancient scroll. "Regal Company and Thousand Knives fought in the Battle of the Poisoned Lake in the year 716 after shattering. Regal Company was the victor, but the butcher's bill reached forty-three thousand. Thirty thousand of those were civilians. None of Thousand Knives survived, and the two towns on the lake never recovered. Papa Noble's great-great-grandmother was the leader of Regal Company at the time. She was remembered as the Rotten Tongued."

Papa Noble paced along the lip of the roof. "It seems history is on my side, Tai. Are you sure you want to do this? I foresee another disaster if you do."

Tai cracked his knuckles.

"I'll make you a deal, Tai. Give me the Kingman and we'll walk away. History will not remember this day and associate it with your company, weakness, shame, or total annihilation."

"Oh, so close," Tai mocked. He pointed his cutlass at Papa Noble. "The little shit is ours. Just recently voted a full Mercenary with rights and the opportunity to take our name if he so desires. He's family—whether we like his choices or not."

"You'd die for someone you barely know?"

"No, but I'd kill for him."

"How shameful." Papa Noble raised his hand, lightning striking his palm as thunder boomed around it. It formed into a two-handed battle-ax that crackled in his hands. Papa Noble must be a Lightning Weaver. "War it is."

"War it is," Tai repeated. "Have you begun to evacuate the city in preparation?"

Papa Noble nodded. "Most of this quarter has been abandoned and my Mercenaries are helping evacuate the rest of the city. The path to the palace is empty, but we'd best avoid the docks if possible. Some crews stayed in port."

"Don't they know how devastating a Mercenary could be?" And then softly Tai added, "Michael, Naomi, and Alexis. All three of you need to leave when this begins. We'll handle Papa Noble and Regal Company on our own. But look out for Ciara and Liam. Neither are here and no doubt waiting somewhere to catch any of us if we sneak through."

"You want us to run?" I asked.

"Yes," Tai said. "I'm sorry I can't send more of Orbis Company with you to deal with Dark, but it'll take everything we have to repel this many. I don't know how long we'll last, but fear not—none of us will die here. We're too stubborn to go down easily."

"Tai . . . I . . ."

"Don't get emotional on me, Kingman. We're family and Orbis Company looks after family." Tai cracked his neck, looked to all the Orbis Company members, raised his weapons, and then shouted, "Orbis Company! Show them what you've got!"

Titus shoved my and Naomi's heads down instantly, saving both our lives as hundreds of arrows flew past us, riddling the deck with holes. Otto whipped up dozens of mini-cyclones, decimating the lines of archers as they were propelled upward. Jade and Haru leapt into the crowds of Mercenaries—maiming, stabbing, slashing, and slicing anyone in their path until they were surrounded by our opponents. Gael launched vials of gunpowder at Regal Company, most of them exploding on contact with their target and filling the area with pungent white smoke and a smell that I had experienced a great many times in my nightmares. Tai and Imani clashed with Papa Noble. The force of their impact blew up smoke and ash, blasting anyone in a small radius away from them as if nothing but those three could survive in that area.

Tai and Imani fought in perfect synchronization, constantly ducking, and striking as the other repositioned themselves in their bloody dance. But Papa Noble held them both at bay and even pushed them back. Lightning struck the ground all around them, making sure no one else intervened. Titus pushed Naomi and me toward Alexis, who hauled us away from the battle zone as four Mercenaries assaulted Titus. The big man shouted at us to run as he tried to repel anyone who might pursue us.

There was no time to argue, so the three of us sped away from the war zone as fast as we could. Sebastian opened us a narrow path through the crowds with two nearby statues as Alexis picked off anyone who got close enough for a face full of iron and smoke. We didn't stop running until the city streets were filled with nothing more than stone statues that slowly trudged toward the battle between two Mercenary companies.

Or so we thought. Until Ciara Noble emerged from the shadows with her arms crossed. She made a feral cat look calm.

"Papa said you'd get past them," she said, cracking her knuckles without pause or care that they would no longer pop. "Why are you so adept at being the biggest, longest, and sharpest thorn in our ass?"

"That skill was handcrafted over a decade," I said, trying to catch my breath. "If you think I'm bad now, you should have seen me during the Endless Waltz." I paused to take a deep breath, hoping it would slow my heartbeat. "I wasn't just a thorn in the ass, I was the *entire* ass. I made a donkey look well behaved."

Her expression grew grim. "I hate you, Michael Kingman." She drew her claws. "So, will you fight me yourself?" Ciara snickered. "I promise you I won't—"

Alexis shot her in the left leg between her hip and kneecap. Ciara screamed a curse that could make most sailors blush and then tried to stanch her bleeding. Alexis drew two fresh pistols from her sash and then said, "You paid attention to the wrong Mercenary."

Ciara took the sleeves off her shirt, tore them into strips, and then wrapped them around her wound. She looked even crazier when she had finished. "My mistake, little rose. But if you think this wound will be the end of me . . . you're sorely mistaken."

"Go," Alexis ordered, taking aim at Ciara as both paced. "Stop Dark, Michael. Do what you must, but . . . try to save him if you can. Make him see he went down the wrong path. Zahra wouldn't have wanted him to become a monster."

"I'll do my best, Alexis." I hesitated. "Stay alive, alright?"

We took off down a separate alleyway away from Alexis and Ciara. The clash of gunfire and metal on metal echoed off the walls as we ran toward the palace. Neither of us said anything until it was in sight—on the main straightaway—and our final obstacle came into view: Liam Noble. There was a Weaver-made fence of knotty wood behind him as he sat on a kicked-over stone statue. He was shirtless, back covered in fresh cuts from a lashing. Like Ciara, he looked on the verge of a complete mental breakdown.

"I knew you'd get here," he giggled. "I told them you would get to the palace. Only Papa believed me. But he's always so cautious that it was less of a confirmation of my thought process and more of a condemnation that I couldn't stop you at the titan." Liam went to his feet, long scythe in hand. He waved it manically as he laughed. His madness wasn't an act. Whatever had kept him sane was long gone. What had happened? "This time you'll have to kill me, Michael. I won't fail my papa again!"

He reeked of desperation. And rather than rage, only pity filled me. "Liam. You couldn't stop me before. What makes you think this time will be any different?"

"Because this time . . . there is no difference between failure and death." Liam smiled wider and dropped his scythe. He raised his arms to the sky. "Papa. Are you proud of me now?"

The nearby tree's limbs impaled his body and hoisted him up in the air as the nearby roots burst through the street. The dark wood encased Liam's body and twisted him into a gnarly man-made tree that propelled itself toward the sky and blocked out the sun. Tenere was closer to eclipsing it with every passing heartbeat. A dome of wood sprouted up from the sides of the lake and covered the palace.

"What the . . ." I trailed off, still uncertain as to what I was seeing. Liam had covered the entire palace in a wooden dome. We wouldn't be able to carve out a doorway. As long as Liam was alive, he would be able to fix whatever damage we did. Assuming he was still alive, of course. He couldn't be . . . could he?

"Michael." Naomi touched my arm. "Can you nullify that?"

"I don't think so."

"What are we supposed to do?"

I put my hands behind my head and stared after Liam. If he was still alive, he was somewhere near the top of the tree. And, oh, man, it would be a long climb. One I didn't have the time to make if I was going to stop Angelo and Dark.

"Naomi! Michael!"

Both of us whipped our heads in the direction of the voice. Chloe was running toward us, armor clanking as she did. The tip of her spear was covered in blood. As was her face and neck. The only thing that looked normal was her frizzy black hair. Naomi sprinted toward her girlfriend and then kissed her as if it could be their first and last.

When they separated, Chloe smiled softly and then said, "We've been apart a week."

"A week too long." Naomi stole another kiss, then took Chloe's hand. "Why aren't you in the palace with Serena?"

"They threw me out when reports of your arrival reached Papa Noble," Chloe explained. "I fought as best I could to stay, but . . ."

"Are the other Ravens with Serena?" I asked.

Chloe nodded. "Along with Adreann and Emelia. Karin isn't hiding her displeasure about the situation, but she's showing it less openly than I am. She'll protect her for as long as she can."

"How long do we have?" I paced back and forth in front of Liam's tree. "Do we have the time to climb the tree, kill Liam, destroy his wooden barrier, and then save Serena? Or should we try something more drastic?"

"Unsure."

"We need to decide," Naomi stated. The sounds of the Mercenary clash were growing closer. "We can't afford to fight too many people. Not when the palace will still be filled with guards, Mercenaries, and whatever else Angelo and Dark are going to throw at us."

"Thankfully, we have reinforcements."

Naomi and I looked at her with confusion. "Orbis Company and Sebastian are tied up with Regal Company. They won't be able to help us—"

An ear-piercing shout rang above us and a blur flew past. The tree ignited as a bright red dragon with veiny wings blew fire onto it. The tree caught quickly and burned brightly, wood turning to ash quicker than water to steam. Liam never screamed as his tree crumbled, but the Wood Weaver stumbled out of the trunk before it was gone, ablaze from head to toe. He wore no smile this time, skin nearly burned black.

I nullified my body and stepped toward the Mercenary. He fell into my arms and I lowered him to the ground. Friend or foe, no one deserved to die alone and hated. Compassion was all I could offer him, and I hoped it would be enough.

The burning man's hand touched my face and yet the heat didn't reach my skin. "Even in this . . . I was useless. What a miserable life." Liam coughed up a weird mixture of blood and ash. "If you beat them, I'll applaud you in the afterlife. But . . ." He grabbed the back of my head and held me close. ". . . give me a warrior's death?"

I nodded, motioned for Naomi to give me her knife, and then stuck it into Liam's chest. His coughs were wet and heavy, and he seemed to be chuckling despite all the blood in his mouth. "Don't forget the conqueror's will. My death will have repercussions whether you're around to see them or . . ."

And then Liam Noble went limp and the fire consumed what remained of his body. I set him down on the stone and watched as the dragon burned the wooden dome to the ground. While it slowly turned to ash, the dragon landed in front of us, and four people hopped off it. Three I recognized immediately.

"Gwen said you might need a little help," Kai said as we embraced. I slid my magic analysis documents into his pockets without him noticing. Because if I could pick pockets silently, I could put stuff into them as well. "She said she couldn't help herself, but we could. Joey tagged along, too." We separated as the dragon roared. "He's still learning how to use his powers, but we weren't about to turn down a friend in need. We're family, after all."

"It helps that it's hard to turn down an invitation when a tear in reality opens in front of you," Trey added. I hugged my friend tight. "Besides, Emelia is in there, isn't she? We have some unfinished business."

"Unfortunately for me, my target isn't here," Symon said, smoke wafting off his body as it had with Rian. He was walking unaided. So that's where Rian's heart had gone. "I'll just have to settle for testing out these new abilities." His eyes flashed red for a moment. "And your story. I still have one question for you. You haven't forgotten our deal, have you, Michael?"

"Never," I said with a smile.

The fourth man said nothing until he was directly in front of me, seemingly too tentative for such an imposing person. His black hair was messy, his belly slightly protruded from his well-fitting noble clothes, his eyes were a hazy brown, tattooed names covered all his visible flesh, and he held a serrated longsword in his right hand. "I came because Gwen asked me to."

"Who . . . who are you?" I asked, something . . . wrong lodged in my throat.

The tattooed man closed his eyes for longer than a standard blink and then opened them as he smiled. "In Hollow I am known as the dog of the nobility for executing nobles at King Isaac's whims."

"I'm sorry," I said. "I've never heard of you before. Are you Blackwell? Gwen's friend? Is that why you're here? A favor for a favor?"

"That's correct. My name is Blackwell. But I'm not here to repay a favor. I'm here to right a wrong," he explained. "I had a brother once and we argued about everything—the weather, our food, our morals, and politics. I loved him, but I never knew how to talk to him. How to sympathize with how he saw the world." Blackwell gulped audibly. "Gwen told me a lot about you, and you remind me of him. Consider this my chance at repentance."

The man's words made no sense to me. He was going to attack Mercenaries, Angelo Shade, and Dark in a misguided attempt to right a wrong with his brother? It was stupid, but I wasn't going to argue with him. Gwen trusted him and that was all that mattered.

"The more the merrier," I said. "Can you fight? Are you a Fabricator?"

Blackwell craned his neck. "I'm a Blood Fabricator. I'll hold my own."

I smiled as the last of the wooden dome turned to ash. There was a horde of clan guards with spears drawn waiting for us at the entrance. Were they going to fight against us on Erica's orders or someone else's? Had Adreann seized control of Vargo? Did he have Hollow as well? None of it mattered. We'd destroy anyone who got in our way.

"Alright, everyone," I said as I drew my guns. The others did the same with their own weapons. "Let's take back the palace!"

ONE YEAR GIVEN

Kai and Joey set fire to half the palace from the sky and really ruined the whole climatic charge to save Serena that I had envisioned in my mind. Blackwell handled any of the bold stragglers who chose not to flee, binding them with chains of crystallized blood. Naomi contained the fire with her Fabrications, making sure it didn't get too out of control, while Symon gathered the smoke into himself, weaving it into armor. We wanted to make it easy for those who could choose to flee while making sure our targets couldn't escape unnoticed.

Before we knew it, we had reached the shrine of the lockless door. No one was outside waiting for us, but we could hear those inside talking openly. There would be no going back once we went in. This was where my story ended. My desire to tell those around me how much I cared for them was strong, but for some reason the words came out garbled. Yet they all understood what I was trying to say, nodding and smiling in return.

I put my hand on the doorknob, took a deep breath, and then pushed the door open.

Serena was sitting in a chair in front of the lockless door, gagged and unconscious. She was in a wedding dress, a lacy blue design that fell to her glittering white shoes. Her gloves went past her elbows—as was tradition in Hollow—and a golden veil adorned her head and brought out the auburn in her hair.

Angelo stood behind her, hands on the back of her chair. Dark and Jay Prince were in front of the faceless statue, while Adreann and Emelia were near the ever-burning cannister. Erica Vargo sat alone in the frontmost pew with her legs crossed, cuffed with magic nullification bracelets. All the High Nobles that had come to Vargo for the royal wedding were in the pews, chained and bound. For such an arrogant group of people, all the nobles had ever shown me was how weak they truly were.

The ceiling had been cut out, a perfect view to the sky above. The bright sun, which was slowly getting eclipsed by Tenere, shrouded the city in a fading orange glow. It wouldn't be much longer before the moment arrived. Dozens of Mercenaries from Regal Company boxed us into the shrine as soon as we entered. There was no escape now.

"Welcome all," Angelo said, walking around Serena. A smile grew on his face. "I see we have some unexpected guests. Blackwell! Don't you have a child to take care of?"

"Family looks after family," the dog of the nobility declared, sword raised.

"What a shame," Angelo drawled. "I knew you would return, Michael. You see martyrdom as your destiny." He put his hands on the back of Serena's chair. "So did you resign yourself to fate?" Angelo continued to smile. "Are you here to trade your life for hers? Or will we fight? If we do, I'll be forced to shatter Tenere."

"Death is inevitable. A truth we can't ignore." I took off my jacket and tossed it over one of the pews. Then I rolled up my sleeves to my elbows and unbuttoned my top buttons to make sure I could breathe freely. My bony fingers didn't have the same dexterity as my real ones, but I got it done. "And what have I ever been but a fool chasing the truth? I'm grateful that I've been able to see my death coming and to relish life for as long as I could."

"How mature of you." There was a hunger in his tone. A desire to be applauded. To be admired. An insecurity born of the decades of hiding his true self. "Do you know why I'm not worried about you or any of your friends? Why I've never cared if you figured out a few secrets? Or why I left you that memory?"

I shook my head. Feigned ignorance was my greatest weapon. It was the perfect tool to lure him into complacency.

"It's because I am guaranteed to win." Angelo swept two of his fingers across the High Nobles and my friends. All of them fell to their knees as an invisible force pressed down on them. He released his hold on them quickly, sticking his hands in his pockets as everyone recovered. "I've stolen her powers. And if you try to do anything but die here . . . I will escape and use Serena's Fabrications to shatter Tenere and open the door." Angelo took a step closer, loving the moment. "Celona was shattered a millennium ago in a desperate attempt to force these doors open. The destruction of a moon contained power to bypass the measures initially put in place to keep mortals out. So, if you don't die, I'll destroy everything: thousands of pieces of Tenere will rain down on this world and scar it forever. Then I'll stand in the ruins with my beloved and finally be at peace."

"That's why you called our love apocalyptic," I muttered. "Because if either of us couldn't go through with what had to be done . . . you'd bring about the end of the world."

A smile was the only answer he gave me. "Will you do what you must, Michael? Die for peace? Once I get Katherine back, I'll walk away. As will Dark with Zahra. Is that so wrong?"

So much for not dying a martyr.

"And them?" Trey shouted. "What do Adreann and Emelia get out of this?"

"I'm king," Adreann said with a wicked grin. There was a gem-laden golden crown hidden in his auburn hair. "My dear sweet sister finally did the smart thing and abdicated. She's a Forgotten. And Forgotten cannot rule. Wonderful, isn't it?"

"You're not fit to be king," I sneered.

"But now I am." Adreann cracked his neck and the pop echoed through the small shrine. "And with my newfound position, my beloved wife gets to continue her war against the immortals. We seek to wipe them out so a new generation can be free of their chains. Serena would never be able to do it, so she had to be replaced. Hollow cannot survive without radical change. And, thanks to your traitorous father, I'm the only one who can take her place."

The pressure from Chloe's gaze at the back of my head felt like a heavy slap. I could stop Adreann from taking the throne. By law, Chloe was the rightful heir, but . . . could I really damn her to a royal life she never wanted? She had the love she had longed for, but, Ravens or not, would either of them remain in Hollow if Adreann was in charge? Or would they seek to change Raven tradition, as Efyra had, and become a family? There was a belief that only by confronting and overcoming hardships could someone grow. But I had always been in awe of those that were confident in who they were and remained on the path they had chosen. If Chloe didn't want the throne, we'd do it another way.

And maybe because of guilt or pride or whatever else had been stewing in her head for a decade, Erica went to her feet and confronted her monstrous son. "Adreann," she began. "Enough. If you're angry, take it out on me. Not Hollow. I'm to blame for what you became."

"What I became?" he asked, slightly taken aback. "What would that be, Mother? Am I something more to you than your son?"

"It wasn't your fault you grew up how you did," Erica said, advancing toward him. "It was mine. I didn't show you love as much as I should have. I was so lost and angry at the world. But you don't have to stay that way. You can change. You can learn how to lo—"

Adreann clamped one hand over his mother's mouth as his other grabbed a fistful of her hair. "Change? Mother . . . what gave you any indication that I don't like who I am? I am the strongest and most influential man under the sun! Hollow will grow under my rule as we dispose of the immortals that have tormented us for generations. And unfortunately for you . . . while I've grown . . . I'm still the monster you were right to fear."

The Corrupt Prince twisted his mother's neck like someone spinning a top. She hit the floor with a thud that made everyone gasp. Chloe gagged at the sight of limbs folded on top of each other like those of a discarded puppet. Serena didn't awaken, likely under the effects of Night's End.

"Angelo," I muttered, eyeing the clan leader's twisted body lying at Adreann's feet. "I'm ready for this to end. No one else needs to die."

"With pleasure." The pressure forced everyone in the room but me to their knees as Tenere moved in front of the sun. Darkness descended and the time of the solar eclipse was here. "Will you do the honors? Say the names, reveal the lock, and then activate the key."

"Alphonse!" I bellowed. "Zarack! Mikel!"

A dusty bronze lock unveiled itself on the door, shimmering into existence as if had been there the entire time.

Angelo was all smiles and Dark was a nervous wreck. Both had come so far and were so close to getting what they wanted again. Everyone screamed at me to nullify the area so they could fight, but I ignored their pleas and knelt in front of Trey.

"I need your light."

"Bastard," he grumbled. "What are you doing? Don't give up like this."

"Please, Trey. Trust me."

Trey grunted and extended his hand as far as he could. A ball of light materialized in his hand, and I took it from him when it reached the size of a fist. And then I twisted my father's ring off my middle finger and slid it onto his own. It was a perfect fit.

"Your turn," I whispered with an apologetic smile.

His eyes bulged and his hand instinctively sunk under the weight of the puny thing. He had no chance to retort. To demand I take it back. To argue that he wasn't the best man for that kind of responsibility. Yet . . .

none of us were. All broken by a city that lied to us before we could talk and made us participants in a dance that could have only three beats: complacency, tradition, and unwieldy expectations. But he was the *right* man for Hollow. And we both knew it.

Trey could be the hero I had always dreamed of being.

Everyone watched as I freed Serena from her chains. I pressed the ball of light against the side of her head and then shook her awake. Her eyes fluttered open as if in the middle of a pleasant dream.

"Michael?" she questioned, still half-asleep. "What are you doing here? What—" I cut her off with a kiss and then let my warmth nullify her body. Unlike the last time, the effects of Forgotten reversal were immediate. She grabbed the back of my head and kissed me harder.

"Asshole," she whispered when she had enough. "You ignored my command. Why?"

"Because this is what I was raised to do," I responded softly. "I've always been selfish. Did you really think I'd let you suffer when I could instead?"

"Stop it," she commanded, tears beginning to fall. "I won't let it end like this. We can find an alternative."

"Shhh," I whispered, kneeling in front of her. I pushed some of the strands of her hair behind her ears and wiped away some tears. "Don't cry. I'm not scared to die. As sad as it is, I've been preparing for this moment all my life. Heroic sacrifices are the only thing I'm good at."

"It shouldn't have happened like this. We could have found—"

"No," I interrupted. "We've been at a disadvantage from the beginning. And Angelo was right . . . there was no alternative. All we could change was the cost. Maybe if we had been smarter, or maybe if we hadn't been obsessed with fighting each other, we could have prevented this. But we didn't. And so the cards have been set."

"Tell me you have a plan," she pleaded. "Tell me this isn't the end. Please."

"My plan is for you to live. This is the end of me, but it's not the end of you."

Her sobbing intensified, but I held her close. Partially to comfort her and partially to comfort myself. I'd said the right words to ease her heart, but the fear of having to go through with it still made my body tremble. I was a fool for love, but having to face a final death made me more scared than anything else. And this was to be my end . . . I wanted her to know everything.

"I wish we had more time. We'll never get married or have children or grow old together, but this brief time we've spent together is better than a lifetime apart. Know that I love you and always will . . . and I have to ask you a favor."

Her response was nonsensical, but I pressed on.

"You are the love of my life, but please don't let me be the love of yours."

"Stop it," she said, clutching me tighter. "Please don't do this." I held her for a long time, ignoring the many eyes on us.

"Tell me you have another plan," Serena whispered. "Tell me that if I kill you, it won't be the end. Tell me you'll return immortal. Promise me you'll defy death."

My own tears made my words whimpers. "Would you believe me even if I said yes?"

She cried harder, as did I, and neither of us looked dignified . . . but who really cared at this point? Dignity was no use in the afterlife.

"It's time for me to go, Serena," I said, standing. She latched onto me like constricting vines and I extricated myself as best I could, put the revolver in her shaking hands, hugged her again, and took a few steps back. "I'm sorry you have to do this."

"Then don't make me."

"There's no other way. We can't win, but I can save everyone else."

"Don't you deserve to live?" she shouted, rage overtaking her sadness. "Why do you have to be the martyr? Why can't it be me or Gwen or Adreann? Why is it always you?"

"Because I love you all," I said. "A man will lay down his life for others with a smile, knowing he did everything he could. And it won't be easy for you all to live with what I've done. But . . . fortunately you won't have to. You won't remember me."

Her eyes went wide. "What did you do, Michael?"

"I traded the world's memories of me away." There were murmurs throughout the crowd. Even Angelo seemed caught off guard. So even a mastermind like him couldn't foresee everything. That alone made me feel a little better. "It was a steep price, but without paying it, I wouldn't be here."

"It's not enough to die, but you have to take my memories, too?" She waved the revolver at me. "Why would you do this to me?"

"I'm sorry."

It wouldn't change anything, but it was the only thing I could say.

"Fuck you," she spat. "I refuse to forget you. I swear it. And if you die and don't come back, I'll find you. I'll go to the afterlife and drag you back. We will be wed in a field of flowers, we will have beautiful auburn-haired and amber-eyed children, and we will grow old together. Do you understand, Michael? I will not let this be the end. No matter what I have to do."

I smiled appreciatively. "I understand."

Serena raised the revolver at me, wiping her tears away on her dress. "Any last words?"

I pointed a finger at Angelo. "Remember that you are mortal." Then at Dark. "Remember that you will die." Then at both. "Remember your death. I speak these words to you not as a warning or a curse but because we will meet again. You cannot run from the unwavering hunter forever. In that, we are all equal."

They stayed silent with arms crossed. Uncaring, unfazed, eager. Wolves waiting for their prey to collapse so they could feast. My words meant nothing to them. A dying fool's fallacy. And yet . . . I closed my eyes, tilted my head back, and took a deep breath. I didn't want to appear frantic or scared in these last moments. I wanted them to think I was content. At ease. At peace. Even if it was all a lie. Did she know how I was feeling right now? That it was all an act? That I was terrified for what would happen next?

What was it like to die for real? What came next? Would it hurt?

"I love you, Serena Hollow." Another deep breath. "What a wonderful life this has been."

We all have a misguided belief when we're young that we are the center of existence. That everything will cease to be when we're gone. But, in reality, life continues without us. Some grieve. Some rejoice. Some remember what we were and who we could have been. But the only thing death creates is a singular absence. As if a lone street lantern was extinguished, leaving the light from the others nearby to keep the area illuminated. And, in a way, it was comforting to know that my family and friends would continue without me.

I hadn't expected it to end like this, but endings are rarely as perfect as they are in stories.

"I love you, Michael Kingman," she said. The girl was gone, and only the dutiful queen remained. Hopefully she'd be able to open herself up to love again when I was gone.

But no matter what we wished . . . this story only ever had one ending. I had always known it was a tragedy. People like me didn't get happy endings. Or deserve them. Serena's final words eased the last of my tension. It was time to greet death. The pressure on my shoulders finally lifted.

Ah, so this really was—

ONE MOMENT EARNED

Serena heard nothing as Michael Kingman's body hit the ground, a red flower blossoming over his heart. The white smoke that blew over her face was odorless and everything seemed duller as she dropped the revolver and scrambled to his side. She cradled his cooling body, pressed her face to his chest, and pleaded for him to return. For him to defy death. But . . . nothing happened. Michael Kingman died with a smile on his face. And she supposed that was the measure of his life: that he had gone with no regrets.

A bright red ball of light came out of Michael's chest, hovering above it for a few heartbeats before whizzing toward the lockless door and slamming itself against the bronze lock. The door crept open and a soft humming, almost like a singer warming up for a performance, filled the small shrine. When the door was fully open, a dull red mist obscured the other side.

The Corrupt Prince howled with laughter to see it. He made his way over to Michael's body and then kicked it in the side. It barely moved.

Serena tried to wave him away, but her brother didn't back down. His eyes were wild. Uncontrollable. Full of hate fostered, unrestrained.

"I win!" he exclaimed. Another kick to Michael's side. "I told you I'd see your death, Kingman! No one beats me twice! You should have stayed away." The brute continued cackling, growing more manic with every passing heartbeat. "You would have lived if you had stayed away. Only one had to—" Confusion calmed him down as if he were finally seeing the scene painted in front of him. "Wait. If both Dark and Angelo are bringing someone back . . . how would it have worked if Michael . . ." Horror flashed across his face as he turned sharply. "Oh, shit—"

Jay Prince blew half of Adreann's head away with a flintlock pistol barely a finger length away from him. His brains and skull and blood splattered against the near wall. The giant's body hit the ground with a mighty thud, lying on its side as if he had fallen asleep clutching a pillow. One of his eyes was locked onto Serena, while the other was forever lost to a small piece of metal that had spiraled through his head until it had come out the other side flat and hot.

Serena reached out to check if her baby brother was still alive. Maybe he had done something to prevent the bullet from killing him. But she couldn't deny his fate when she turned his head over and found a massive hole in the back where a headful of red hair had been turned into a slick, sticky mess. Faster than an echo disappearing down a hallway— a Kingman, Hollow, and the Vargo clan leader had been murdered. And Serena's dream of sitting at a table surrounded by her family died with them. She was alone. Completely, utterly, painfully alone.

"God, I've been waiting *weeks* to do that," Jay said, blowing the smoke away from the tip of his gun. "In what world was he going to get the throne? He was worse than all the others!"

"Pride is a terrible disease," Emelia cooed. "It makes the wisest men blind. But it was his lack of experience with love that killed him. He couldn't see what was real and what wasn't." She turned to the High Nobles still sitting in the pews, curtsying to them all. "Don't fear, my High

Nobles. I'll be a pleasant queen. You're going to *love* the kingdom I'll turn Hollow into."

Another red ball rose from Adreann's chest as the High Nobles struggled to free themselves, the ball flying upward before slamming against the door as well.

Angelo and Dark finally let their guard down, embracing each other.

"Angelo. Dark," Serena muttered, still clutching Michael's body as she ran her left hand over Adreann's hair. She met their eyes. "I'm going to kill you both. Is that clear?"

The father and son separated, expressions growing colder. "Try it, Serena." Angelo gestured to Emelia and Jay. "But I think these two will keep you busy while we do what we must. Dark?"

"Let's bring them home," the Mercenary declared.

"We should get rid of her as well," Angelo said, nudging his head toward Serena. "Make sure no one can follow us."

Dark nodded. "Jay, do the honors, will you?"

Jay sighed dramatically as he reloaded his flintlock pistol. "Who's going to be the third?"

"My daughter," Angelo whispered. "Maybe there's hope for our family after all."

"What a wonderful dream." Jay pressed the gun's barrel against Serena's forehead. It was still warm and made some of Michael's blood slither down her face, over her nose, before stopping above her lip. "Any last words, my Queen?"

She licked her top lip, ingesting Michael's blood. The effect was almost instantaneous, warmth welling in her core. She focused on it, fanning the flame until it was bright and hot and *powerful*.

"Which is stronger?" Serena asked, unflinching. "Grief, love, or duty?"

"Who cares?" Jay said. "And I thought you'd be more—"

Serena belted out a note in the highest pitch she could reach as she expelled the warmth from her body. The pressure on everyone's shoulders lifted.

Lyon and Chloe flew toward Serena simultaneously, one with trails of crystallized blood behind them and the other with streaks of chirping lightning. Lyon's war cry was nothing tangible, but the cowardly Kingman rammed his shoulder into Jay Prince and slammed the Skeleton into the nearby wall. He hit it with a sickening crack, but he hopped to his feet again as trails of blood trickled down his forehead and made his hair shiny and slick.

Chloe's attack was less precise, lightning bolts raining down on Emelia from above like a thousand concentrated strikes. Emelia batted them away with her bare hands, her body healing quicker than Chloe could strike. When the attack ended, the immortal stood triumphant.

Trey, Kai, and Joey made an about-face and began to hold back the swarm of Mercenaries with their Light, Sound, and Fire Fabrications. The Mercenaries were like an army of ants, some gleefully sacrificing their lives to try and break through the barrier. The ones at the back climbed over the bodies, unrelenting in their attack.

Symon fought a war on two fronts. With his newfound Spellborn powers, he created smoke constructs around him that began to free the High Nobles while his main body created a giant fist of hardened smoke that pounded at any enemy who drew close.

The moon was slowly moving out of sight, the sun reemerging, and the time to enter the lockless doors closing. Amidst the chaos, Dark and Angelo left through the lockless door. It slammed closed behind them. Not even the lock remained.

Naomi slid next to Serena and tried to yank her up. "Serena! You have to get up!"

The Queen stayed where she was, her tears drying. She was too tired to move. Too angry to retreat. Too blind to see anything but the door and the red mist behind it. She would have her revenge and it would be *glorious*. Carefully, she laid Michael's body down, closed her brother's eyes, muttered an apology to her mother, and then got to her feet. Her dress was stained beyond repair, and blood covered her gloves and chest. The days of her being a regal queen were over. Only grief remained.

"I'm going after them." She picked up the revolver, spun its chamber, and counted two bullets. It would be enough. All she had to do was wait for Dark and Angelo to exit the door. "Don't try to stop me."

"Just wait a minute before doing anything!" the blue-eyed woman said. "You need to know—"

"He didn't defy death," Serena stated. "He can't come back. Not unless . . ." Serena didn't let herself finish the sentence. If she did what she wanted to . . . would she be as bad as Dark and Angelo? Did she care? Everyone in her family was dead. Could anyone fault her for taking one of them back?

"No, he didn't," Naomi confirmed, eyeing the horde of Mercenaries that Symon was trying to hold back. Most of the High Nobles remained in their pews, too helpless to do anything but watch. "But Michael knew he wouldn't. That's why we came up with an alternative plan."

"He's dead! Whatever he had planned doesn't—"

Naomi gripped the sides of her head, "Shut up. Michael is waiting for them on the other side! He knew we couldn't beat them here, so he realized the only way to beat them was to give them what they wanted and then strike when they thought they had won. We have to get you through that door!"

"How? There's no way to open it! I'd have to kill a—" Serena stopped, eyes falling on Jay Prince. He still had Michael's arm and one of his amber eyes. If that had been enough to fulfill the Kingman part in killing a Hollow, who was to say it wasn't also enough to make him a Kingman, if she killed him? "I'm going to smash his head against the wall."

"Now you get it. Stab Dark with this when you get the chance." She handed over to Serena a syringe filled with fluttering red balls and a vial of blood. There was only a sip in it. Enough to fill a thimble. "The blood is for you. We weren't able to try every combination, but this should be the one you need, along with Michael's nullification, to stand the best chance."

Serena uncorked it and knocked back the blood. It slithered down her throat like a liquefied coin, catching on the sides of her throat. She forced it down, waiting until the warmth made it to her core.

"What magic is this?" she asked.

"Blood."

Serena made a clicking noise with her tongue as she focused on the blood on her body, the blood in between the cracks in the tiles, and the blood on the walls and ceiling. She imagined it swirling around her, turning into armor and jagged and thorny weapons. And so the blood obeyed, attaching itself to her however she wanted.

"I lost loved ones to the city I had grown up in. Sacrificed my happiness to appease the nobles and made deals to improve the lives of those who suffered in silence," she said, turning to the High Nobles confined to the pews. She raised her hand as if holding a goblet and watched as blood flew out of their mouths and around her arm until it was wrapped in chains of blood from the shoulder to the tips of her fingers. She extracted as much as she safely could. "I'm taking what I'm owed. Be thankful it's not more."

One of the High Nobles screamed something about her and her deceased family. That they were better off without them. That the Hollow Royal Family was over. That Michael Kingman should have died on the steps of the Church of the Wanderer. If she had been a bad person, she would have cut their throat and then extracted every lost drop from them . . . but she didn't. She didn't care about them anymore. They had chosen another queen to lead. Her time in Hollow was over.

"Jay," she cooed, spinning droplets of blood as if it were a top. Lyon and Jay were locked in a stalemate, a blood sword clashing against folded steel. Jay was laughing and enjoying showing off his amber eye to the Cowardly Kingman, who was an incarnation of rage. Serena swept her hand to the side, a wave of blood smashing both against the nearby walls. Threads and chains of blood locked them into the wall. "I'm going to make this hurt."

Jay kept laughing despite his position. "You think I give—"

"Silence." Serena placed the bottom of her palm against his upper teeth, gripped his lower jaw with her other hand, and then yanked them apart until she heard something crack. "I'm going to take everything back you stole from Michael." She ran her index finger around Michael's amber eye and then along the scars around his elbow. "And then I'm going to reach down your throat and pull out your heart."

Serena kept her promise, meticulous and careful in performing her makeshift surgery until it was done and Jay Prince's heart was in her hand. Then she smashed it under the heel of her boot, dropped her blood restraints, and watched his body collapse to the ground like a fallen puppet. Another red ball rose from his back, fluttered upward, and then smashed against the lockless door. It swung open once again.

She heard screams behind her, but it was all nonsense. Serena strolled toward the lockless door, touching the tip of the syringe Naomi had given her as she hummed a lullaby. With nothing to lose, Serena took a breath to steady her heartbeat and stepped through the door. It felt as if her body were being pulled apart from the inside out, muscles tearing and cracking before being smashed back together like bread dough. One part of her face went toward the sun while the other crashed to the ground. She screamed in pain but never felt relief or heard her own voice. When it was over, she fell to her knees and struggled to breathe, clawing at the cool tile she found her face pressed against.

She was in a church, and it was beautiful, albeit corrupted and dirty. The white tile and stone walls had red veins pulsating through them like the Corruption had through people back in Hollow. The wooden pews were chipped and rough, the floor seemed covered in a thin layer of dust that kicked up black ichor whenever she took a step, an endless bell tolled around her like a signal of impending doom, and the place shone brilliantly clear in a dark light that defied everything Serena had ever thought she knew about visibility. How could darkness be a source of light?

The doors at the end of the church were large and forbidding. One giant of iron towered over the others, colored blue, black, and red. Angelo and Dark walked down the center aisle toward the doors and a set of stone statues at the frontmost pew. They were already in mid-conversation.

"I expected this place to look different," Dark said. "Cleaner."

"We're transgressing on hollow ground," Angelo explained. "Us monsters do not get the preferred treatment. Just the one meant for outsiders." He stopped and kicked at the red veins in the tile. "But what a surprise to see the Corruption was not Goldani made but instead a curse from God. Else it would not be in this place."

"Useless details," Dark hissed. "How do we bring them back?"

A red ball of light—identical to the one that had come out of Michael—fluttered around Angelo like a firefly. He plucked it out of the air and then squeezed it in his palm, black ichor seeping out of it like lumpy blood. Pain shot through Serena's chest as if it were her own heart. She couldn't help but yelp and writhe on the ground and bring attention to herself. Angelo smiled to see her, while Dark muttered something unpleasant.

"It seems the Queen is another fool for love," Angelo taunted. "Who would have guessed?"

Dark rolled his eyes, sunk his hands into his pockets, and then strolled toward the Queen. He yanked Serena to her feet and then dragged her to the pew with the stone statues in it. She landed with a plop next to them, and Dark drew his hatchet and pressed it against the side of her neck. But Serena didn't fear death. She stabbed Dark in the shoulder with the syringe Naomi had given her, making sure whatever the contents were made it inside him.

"Fuck," Dark yelped, yanking the syringe out of his shoulder. "Did she just stab me with a syringe full of memories?"

"I think so," Angelo said, eyes still on the statues. "It must've been Michael's final plan, but whatever he left behind for you . . . it won't stop us from accomplishing our goals."

"No, it won't." The Mercenary returned his attention to the iron door in front of them. "Zahra first. Katherine isn't going anywhere."

"No," Angelo whispered, running his free hand over the two stone statues next to Serena. "She isn't. Remain still, Serena." Angelo slid two fingers through the air and put an extreme pressure on her shoulders, giving her a taste of her own powers.

All she could do was watch as Dark and Angelo approached the iron door. The shadows around Dark were fluttering like thousands of flies. Two shadowy arms shot out of his back, gripped the inside of the iron door, and then pulled it apart. Black light shot through from the other side.

"I'm coming, Zahra," Dark shouted. "Soon we'll be—"

The door burst open as if the hinges had fallen off. Something flew through the door at a high speed. It collided with Dark's face and sent him skipping back into the nearby pew.

"C'mon, boys, you didn't think it would be that easy to kill me, did you?"

Serena felt her heart fall into her stomach. It couldn't be . . .

But it was.

Michael Kingman stood in front of the iron door, just as he had been right before his death. Before a bullet had torn through his chest and obliterated his heart, splintering it into bits of fat and muscle. The smile on his face was identical to the one permanently etched onto his corpse.

"Just this once. Just for one moment"—Michael thumped his fist against his chest—"I get to be the hero."

WHAT LIES BEYOND

Death was an ocean.

I never heard the gun go off. Nor felt the bullet pierce my heart or head or whatever it hit to kill me instantly. I awoke on a beach of pitch-black sand, facing an ocean of varying shades of grey as if the rainbow had been corrupted. Mist settled over the water, hiding anything that might be lurking below the surface. A lighthouse towered to my left, flickering over the dark ocean with a gaze that seemed to suck all the light out of the area rather than illuminate it. There were shadowy visages shuffling toward one of the four ships in the nearby docks, trading amber for safe passage. Any who didn't have the price were directed to walk over a stone bridge that led over the sea, disappearing into mist and nothingness on the horizon.

As I sat up, I let the rough sand fall through my fingers. If this was another hallucination or dream like the field of light or the white church had been . . . my psyche had developed a wonderful way of fucking with me. But something felt different about this place. No intake of breath could break the spell and send me back to Vargo.

Death had finally claimed me, the elusive target that evaded it for eleven years.

The only question was whether someone would guide me to whatever waited beyond life. And whether Serena would ever forgive me for throwing away the gift she had given up her life for. A small boy with messy brown hair and amber eyes materialized in front of me. He asked the question before I could. "Will they remember us?"

I knelt in front of my younger self, put a hand on his shoulder, and smiled. "No. We're going to be forgotten by the world."

My younger self pursed his lips and looked away from me. "Why? Didn't we do enough to be remembered?"

"We did," I explained. "But our legacy is unimportant compared to how much we were loved. We had friends who followed us into the abyss and back, we loved Serena deeply and richly, and we broke cycles of violence our enemies thought we'd be doomed to repeat. We did so well. You should be proud."

"Are you?"

"Am I what?"

"Proud of yourself?"

I sat down on the sandy beach, one elbow resting on my leg. "You know what? I am. I'd do it all again. Even knowing this ending. Because this journey was worth all the pain." I hesitated. "So, is this it? Death?"

The boy nodded. "Yes, this is the sorting area for the recently deceased." He gestured toward the four ships. "Each one of those will take you to a different afterlife. Most go to the virtue-based afterlife—a place to be rewarded or punished based on whether you were good or bad. When they board the ship, they have no idea which one they'll end up in. Some choose to be reincarnated, hoping to make up for mistakes in their previous life, others choose to return as animals, and more than you'd think opt to end their journey and go into the endless void to become one with reality."

"What's that bridge for?"

"It's for those who haven't met the requirements to go to their final destination. And thus are required to live another life in this realm of

death." At my horror, the boy added, "It's not so bad. Some find it calming to journey through these lands forever. More families have been reunited that way than you could possibly imagine."

"Have I met the requirements for passage on one of those ships?"

His face grew grim and sad. "You did well, Michael Kingman. And,
luckily for you, you died while most of the world remembered you as a
Kingman. But there's always a cost for power and position . . . and your
family must repay decisions the First Kingman made over a millennium
ago." The boy made a sweeping gesture with his hand. The sea parted
and revealed a stone staircase headed downward. "There are others like
you. People who cannot join the other worlds of the afterlife. If it's any
comfort, know that your ancestors await you. They're waiting to hear your
stories and for you to take your rightful place by their side."

I stared at the staircase, water dripping from the sides of the elevated
sea and down into the darkness. "Is that . . ." I swallowed my fear and
hesitation. ". . . that place a punishment for what we've done? How we
messed up the natural order of the world?"

The boy looked away from me. "It is where all Kingman go. Your
brother, mother, and sister will all join you in due time. It's the way of
death that Kingman continue their war against God for all eternity."

Every decision had a consequence . . . and I knew our war against
God would have one as well. But to be surrounded by my ancestors—to
feel validation that I was a fraction as heroic as they were—was all I had
ever wanted.

"When Serena Hollow dies, where will she go?"

"Wherever she wants to," the boy said. "But not to *that* place. It's only
for Kingman."

"So I'll never see her again," I whispered.

"I'm sorry, Michael. There is an ending for everything, and sadly . . .
there is one for your love as well."

"No, that's not true," I stated clearly. "I need to get to the church. I
need to stop Angelo and Dark. Serena will be waiting for me."

"You didn't defy death," the boy said. "You can't go the normal way and if you don't enter that room now . . . You'll become a parasite in this realm. Without your name or essence, all the afterlives except the void will close for you." The boy looked serious. "Don't do this, Michael. Your fight is over. Let this be your ending."

I looked at my hands, trying to stop them from shaking. "Can you tell me where two people went before I decide? Katherine Shade—born Katherine Naverre—and Zahra of Azil."

A heavy leather-bound book appeared in the boy's hands. He rapidly flipped through it and then stopped with his finger under a name. "Zahra of Azil willingly chose to walk to the end of the road, hoping another adventure would find her on the way."

That sounded right, from what I knew about Zahra. I wondered how she would feel about Dark trying to bring her back to life. Romantic . . . or pathetic? Only time would tell.

The boy flipped through the book again. "Katherine Naverre chose to return to the church between death and life to wait for her beloved. Only the void will await her when she returns, if she is not given another chance to atone for her decisions."

"What? Why did she do that? She really risked everything just for Angelo?"

"Love is love . . . and it's quite . . . how did that man describe it . . . catastrophic?"

"How'd Katherine return to the church?"

"Michael . . ." The boy gently closed his book. "Think about this. The price is too steep, and it won't be easy, you know."

"I'm aware." I stood straight. "It never is. But has that made me give up before?"

Memory bubbles floated through the sea and upward to the sky, filled with moving paintings of my life. From my first meeting Trey to my first kiss with Serena to the day I learned what Angelo Shade had done to my father. It was a lifetime of memories and yet—considering how much I had suffered and loved and lived each and every one of them—there didn't seem to be enough. Was my life so easily condensed?

"You won't be able to return to your life if you go down this path, but you can return to the church at the cost of all your memories. And if you do not find a way to return to life from there and must return here . . . only the void awaits you." He pointed upward and revealed a great iron door in the ceiling. It was barely open, but a blinding light was pouring out of it, illuminating the dark sea we were in. The way back to the church.

"It was naïve of me to think the world forgetting me would be the only price I'd pay. If I mess this up . . . I'll be erased completely. No second chances or reunions with my loved ones."

"Choose wisely."

As if there was any option. Us fools for love had our reputations to uphold. "How do I get up there?"

A thin silver thread fell from the door, stopping just above the breaking waves, swaying whenever it was touched. The pathway to the Kingman staircase was covered by the bleak water again. No turning back now.

"Some bonds even death can't break. Thank them when you get the chance," the boy said before fluttering away like flakes of ash in the wind. The ships and shadowy visages did as well, leaving me alone in this strange dark place. "Best of luck, Michael."

"It's not going to be that simple, is it?" I muttered to myself.

My answer came quickly as a figure crept out of the ocean on all fours. When the waves stopped crashing at their feet, they rose up so I could see their face. The man slicked his messy brown hair back with the salt water, revealing his bright amber eyes. It was the first color I had seen here. And it made sense my father would be the one to welcome me when I died. Maybe choosing not to board a ship had been the right decision.

"Hey, Da," I said softly. "It's been a while."

My father didn't leave any footprints in the sand as he walked toward me. His lips were cracked, his skin was pale, and seaweed hung from the holes in his ratty clothes. Maybe death wasn't all the warmth and grapes it had been for Dawn in the white church. That made sense. Dawn had been a good person, and I was anything but. I deserved to face punishment for everything I had done.

"Are you here to talk?" I asked.

My father said nothing, lurching toward me.

I cursed as I went to my feet. "You're not here to talk, are you?"

My father gave a primal scream and attacked me. His hands gripped my shoulders and pushed me down to the ground. He sunk his teeth into my forearm, drawing blood, as I tried to shake him off like a rabid dog. I punched my father in the temple, knocking him off me, climbed on top of him, and punched him in the face repeatedly as he cried and screamed until his body was perfectly still.

I rolled off him and onto my back, knuckles slick with grey blood. My father's body was gone by the time I looked over, swallowed by the sand as if eaten by a monster. Two more bodies crawled out of the dark ocean as I tried to collect myself. Like the last, they wore the faces of those I loved: Dawn and Sirash. Both had weapons. A war hammer and a jagged knife.

Dawn stormed toward me, her footsteps heavy enough to split the ground in two. She waved her war hammer like it was nothing. Sirash crept behind her, knife held against his wrist and forearm, waiting for a perfect opportunity to put it through my heart. They attacked in tandem. Dawn swung wide as Sirash tried to jab me in the stomach. I tried to dodge but lost my footing and fell onto my back, sand flying up into the air. Dawn was quick to follow up, taking the war hammer in both hands and bringing it down on me. Rolling to the side saved me, but Sirash was quick to stab me in the shoulder.

I yanked the knife out of my shoulder, grey blood falling to the sand and clumping it up, and planted the knife in Sirash's chest. He exploded into a black mist. There was no time to celebrate my victory before Dawn's war hammer struck my left shin. Whatever bone had been there shattered into a million pieces, and I fell. Dawn stood over me, ready to deliver the final blow.

"I'm sorry," I said through gritted teeth. "You shouldn't have died for someone as worthless as me."

Dawn gently rested one end of the hammer against my chest.

"And I'm sorry I have to kill you again."

With my good leg, I kicked her in the chest. Like Sirash, she exploded into nothingness, and I was left alone with only the calming sounds of the ocean to keep me company. I hobbled to my feet and dragged my bad leg behind me until I reached the spot where the sand and ocean met. There was nowhere to go but forward. Cliffs surrounded this little beach I had found myself on, and unless I wanted to wait for more guests to find and kill me, it was time to make my exit.

I crawled into the water. The waves crashed down on me as soon as I did, forcing my breath away, and I floated for a few heartbeats, wondering if it would be easier to give up. Then I continued anyway, like a lovestruck fool. I had once said I would do whatever it took to remain at Serena's side . . . It was time to put that resolve to the test.

I swam forward through the dark ocean until I reached the thread, gripping it tightly. Every muscle in my body was tight and screaming at me to stop. To give up. The shadows below and above pulled at me. Some wanted me to return to the surface, while others wanted me to plunge into the darkness below. There was no warmth in my body, and no warmth came to me no matter how I tried to muster it from my core. My Fabrications had abandoned me, and yet I climbed that thread regardless.

Nothing was going to stop me from returning to her. Not even for a moment.

There were over a hundred shadowy figures crawling up the thread behind me, doing their best to escape this place as well. They pulled me down, shouting as they did their best to break my will alongside my body, and their words hurt more than any wound.

"He doesn't deserve the praise."

"He's as intelligent as a sack of rocks."

"Loser. Utter loser. Anyone would be more interesting than him."

"I'd rather cut my eyes out than read about Michael Kingboy."

"He had such potential."

"I was a better hero than him!"

"You'll never amount to anything!"

"Disgrace!"

"What a disappointment."

"Worthless."

I wanted to fall into the water, to succumb to the void rather than continue fighting . . . but I didn't. I couldn't give up. No matter the cost. I threw my memory bubbles at them to delay their climb, and while it worked, it took everything I had. But next time I slept . . . I would be a Forgotten. When the door was finally in reach, I let go of the thread, launching myself toward it. I caught hold of the circular iron knocker and hung from it as the thread snapped and my pursuers plummeted back to the dark sea.

It seemed simple enough to pull myself up, over, and then onto the door itself before I crawled through and into the blinding light. I flung myself through it feet-first like the bullet in a gun, emerging into a too-bright church without any windows. Dark was standing right where I was about to land, so I aimed for his face with the heel of my boot. There wasn't enough time for him to dodge, so the Black Death took the blow and skittered back like a stone across water. Blood dripped from his nose when he rose again, and he let it fall, snarling at me. His hands turned to a dragon's talons, and black membrane wings with streaks of white, silver, and grey shot out of his back.

Angelo was kneeling in front of two stone statues. Serena was next to him on the pews, struggling as if she were being held down by her own Fabrications. All were wide-eyed as they saw me emerge from the doorway. It slammed closed and the shock made the entire church vibrate. I cracked my neck dramatically.

"C'mon, boys, you didn't think it would be that easy to kill me, did you?" I stood proudly. "Just this once. Just for this moment"— I thumped my fist against my chest and nullified my entire body—"I get to be the hero."

LIKE THE SUN

Serena hurled herself toward me, scrambling on all fours under the pressure and then enfolding me in a tight hug. "Found you."

"Found you," I replied, running my fingers down her face. It was the first warmth I had felt since dying. "Sorry I was so dramatic."

She didn't answer me, taking my hand and turning to face our enemies. She was right. There were more important things to deal with. We had reached this place together and made the fight two against two. But it was far from over.

"I should have predicted this," Angelo sneered. "A persistent imbecile like him would find a way to cheat death."

"It doesn't matter," Dark said. He wiped the blood away and went to his feet. "I'll take them both down with—"

Bells rung out around us, heavy and close, as if we were inside one. The church began to come apart, the walls, floor, and ceiling slowly separating from one another. Each tile in the floor became a platform in and of itself as the walls, roof, and pews slowly turned into a half-formed and crumbling stairway to an unknown destination. The two stone statues that had been in the pews upon my arrival were lingering in the air next to Angelo as the ocean of death appeared below us and the shadows that had tried to claim me began to make a ladder out of one another to try and reach us. Memories floated up from below as well, most of them shining and translucent, but a few were sickly, with red veins protruding from them like parasites gorging on rotten flesh.

The three red balls that had been flickering around Angelo, Dark, and Serena spiraled upward until they smashed together and formed a bouquet of three shimmering golden Moon's Tears that drew in the light. It hovered in midair at the end of the stairway.

"Those who wish to defy the unwavering hunter," a high-pitched voice sang. "Three lives have been sacrificed, and so three can return. Prove your worth, claim your prize, and speak the name of the one you wish to reclaim. But know that if the death claims you"—the shadows below screamed primally, shuffling and frantically gaining ground toward us in the church—"the dead will not be forgiving."

The four of us stared at one another, unblinking. But it was Dark who moved first, a hand against his face as he doubled over, laughing. "Fine, Death. I won't disrespect you. I won't disrespect you, either, Michael." A red eye burned through the gaps between his fingers. "Father, start climbing. Take Katherine, Zahra, and my sister."

Angelo opened his mouth to protest, but when Dark snarled at him with a mouthful of pointy teeth, the proud man moved toward the prize. But each level of ascent was a struggle as the pathway buckled and swayed when any weight was put on it. Serena and I tried to cut him off, but walls of moving darkness blocked our path.

"You two are staying with me," Dark said. "I'll crush you with everything I am." His appearance began to change. "Look upon me and understand you never had a chance."

His body grew larger, expanding outward as twelve wings sprouted out of his back. Half of them were black and veiny like a bat's, while the others were thick, fluffy, and white like an eagle's. His skin turned to various shades of scales folded over themselves until they were thicker than plate mail. His nails and teeth grew long, sharp, and pointy. Four dragon heads sprouted out of his neck while his own face turned more reptilian with every heartbeat. Each head differed from the others. The one to the farthest left was translucent like ice and showed the veins of blue blood flowing through it clearly. The next one was purple and hazy, with half-formed memory bubbles stuck to it like clay waiting to be cut off from the main sculpture. The middle head was pitch-black and swirled like a vortex of mist. The next was reflective as if made of mirrors. Screams of terror shot from it periodically as if the dying were contained in its stomach. The final head was the color of an approaching storm, with white flashes visible beneath the skin.

A five-headed dragon floated above me, and—rather than run in terror or wail for pity at the unsurmountable odds—I found myself smiling ear to ear. Maybe this was how it felt like to be a hero. To have fear and hold it gently in my heart but not let it consume me. To know this wouldn't be the end of me.

"Come," Dark said, voice rumbling as if echoing off walls. "Try and kill a nightmare."

"I need blood," Serena said quietly. "Lots of it."

"You became a Blood Fabricator, as I hoped?"

She nodded.

"Good." I grabbed a nearby piece of crumbly stone in the sky and then slashed it across my left wrist. Blood flowed freely. "Take as much of mine as you need."

My blood began to harden around her, twisting into armor and a slender sword that could find the nooks and crannies in any suit of armor. Or, if things got truly desperate, would be perfect for stabbing a monster in the eyes. She handed me my revolver as her armor neared completion. "I may need more than you can give."

"Everything I am is yours." I opened the cylinder, glanced inside, and saw two bullets. Just enough. "Don't hesitate with me. We'll do this together."

"I'll distract Dark. You get Angelo." She took a breath. "Ready?" she asked. The five-headed dragon in front of us was preparing to unleash some kind of unforeseeable torment.

"Always."

Serena launched herself upward on crystallized blood, twisting and weaving through blasts of darkness and ice from Dark's mouths. I nullified my body, projected a shield in front of me, and dropped to one knee as I took the full force of Dark's attack. When it ceased, I leapt to the next platform, following Angelo as fast as I could. He was already halfway there.

Dark and Serena twisted through the air and around each other like two nobles waltzing in an endless loop. Neither was able to get the advantage over the other, but they continued shooting blasts of ice, darkness, and blood at each other, hoping they would be the one to clip the other's wings first. The shadows from the ocean were halfway to the church now, consuming everything in their path like a horde of locusts.

"You shouldn't have brought her here, Michael!" Angelo screamed as he climbed a ladder made of roof tiles. "We were going to let her live!"

"Fuck off, you lying sack of shit!" I shouted back. "Do you think I'm daft? You wanted three lives restored. Which means three had to die. Me, Serena, and Jay after he took my eye!"

Angelo looked down at me, wobbling as he balanced on half of a wooden pew. "We killed Adreann! Jay shot him in the head when he wasn't looking. Serena didn't have to die! But now . . ." He gestured toward the ocean of death below. ". . . now she will."

"Adreann's dead?" I muttered to myself. With Erica gone as well, Serena must've been . . . but I shook my head and focused on the present. There was time for her to grieve when all this was over. "I liked it better when you and Dark opposed each other!"

Angelo skipped across five tiles like a flat rock over water. Halfway across, Dark and Serena zoomed past him, destabilizing them so much, he was forced to kneel and grab the edges.

"Scared to talk, Angelo?" I continued. I had nearly caught up to him.

"Tell me why so many had to die just so your wife could live? What makes her so special? You killed thousands to bring her back! If you succeed here, carrying the weight of those lives will cripple her! She'll never be what she was."

"I don't care!" He stood proudly. "If she can't handle what I've done to restore her life, I'll manipulate her memories until she can. The politics, philosophy, morals of it—they don't matter to me. Nothing matters except her. Does that make me mad?" He looked away as if contemplating his actions. "Better to be mad and in love than alone and proud."

"Coward."

Angelo reached the final platform, the bouquet of twisted Moon's Tears in front of him. I wasn't going to make it in time. I was still too far away, and Serena was doing the best she could to hold off Dark. I pulled myself closer to the final goal. But I was too far away to take a shot. Especially when I had so few bullets.

Angelo was going to win.

"I have always been a broken man," he said, reaching for the flowers. "But with her . . . I felt whole. If only for a lingering moment. Return to me." He snapped one of the flowers off at the stem, a sticky red liquid gushing out of it. It set his hand aflame, nearly consuming everything down to the bone. But he didn't flinch or show pain, just smiled like a man who had accomplished his ultimate goal. "Katherine Naverre. Return to me."

The shadows howled as a plane of light crashed from above onto the stone statue Angelo had been standing in front of when I had arrived. Stone slowly crumbled away as soft skin emerged from the cracks. Her black hair became unbound and fell downward as parts of her body began to twitch and move and she went from a statue to a human being once again. Her eyes were the last thing to emerge. Bright blue shone through the stone.

She yawned, stretched as if waking from a long slumber, and then lifted her head to take in everything around her. Her eyes fell on Angelo as if drawn to him. "Angelo? What's going on? Where are we? What—"

Mortals couldn't dwell in this realm for long. Before she could finish her sentence, she flew toward the red door near the giant iron one and was swallowed whole by it. The door slammed closed and the echo of it rang in our ears.

"Two lives remain," the high-pitched voice from nowhere sang.

Angelo slumped against the altar, the remaining two flowers floating above him. He was clutching the wound he had received by taking one . . . No flesh or muscle remained. Just stark white bone. I took the remaining steps toward him and then stood over my former foster father, revolver aimed at his head.

"I win," he gloated. "She's back."

"I could kill you right now and you'd never see her again," I said. "How is that a victory? You wanted to remain at her side, didn't you?"

"Better to have her live than not have her in the world." He shifted slightly, still cradling his bone hand. "We both know how this is going to end. Get on with it, Michael?"

I shot Angelo in the chest, a red flower blooming between his pecs. He stanched it as best he could, blood flowing freely through his fingers, before he gave a pained wet cough and slumped over, very still.

Killing never felt good. No matter how much pain they had brought to my life. It was so wasteful. How could people do this? Did the faces and names become numbers in their mind? Or did they—

Dark blew through the floor the altar was erected on, showering me in stone and rubble as the two remaining flowers and Angelo's body fell to another platform, halfway down the stairway, both right on the edge as the shadows from the ocean crept toward them. I free-fell toward the ocean, clawing and reaching for anything to grab hold of. Luckily for me, Serena slammed into my side. We tumbled onto a platform together, both breathing heavily.

Dark in his five-headed-dragon form towered over us like the sun itself.

"You cannot beat me," Dark growled. "My father was just a man. I am something more. Give up and maybe I'll let you live. Maybe I'll forgive you for this insolence."

Serena tried to stand—to remain defiant—but fell to one knee as her blood armor melted away. She was covered in scrapes, burns, and slashes. "I don't know how we can beat him."

"We can't win a fair fight," I said. "He's too strong. Always has been."

Memory bubbles floated past us, up and away. Some showed my life and others showed Serena's . . . and some showed Dark's. An idea about how to beat him began forming in my head as I searched the area for the corrupted memory bubbles I had seen. If my suspicions were correct and some of them belonged to Dark . . . then we had a way to win. I had never stood a chance against Dark physically—our fight at the Reborn Titan had proved that—but I could outsmart him. Or, better yet . . . I could destroy the monster and take away his will to fight.

It was time for Dark to remember what Zahra would have truly wanted for him.

"I need to nullify the corrupted memory bubbles," I said, forcing myself to stand.

"How many are there?" she asked, immediately accepting my plan.

I helped her to her feet. The shadows from below were launching them-selves at Dark now, but the dragon knocked them away with blasts of magic from one of its many mouths. I could see only a lone corrupted memory nearby. Was that all it had taken for Dark to lie to himself about what Zahra wanted? Was that all it had taken for a monster to replace the man?

"Only one," I answered. "I'll get to it as fast as I can. Don't get con-sumed by the shadows."

Serena smiled softly at me. "Never. We're leaving this place together." She put a hand on my shoulder, taking more blood from my body and turning it into chains that seemed thicker than steel. They launched out of her body and chained Dark tightly. The shadows continued their as-sault on him, slashing and forcing their way into one of his mouths. "I'll contain him. Go. Hurry! We have a life to live once this is done."

I kissed her quickly and then leapt off the platform and onto a nearby memory bubble. It popped under my weight and Trey's voice shot out of it: *"Are we good people, Michael?"*

I jumped to another, and Naomi's voice rang out: *"Don't pity me. Don't feel bad for me. Don't see me differently because of this."*

Two more popped and two more voices rang out around me. The first was Gwen's: *"After what I've seen him do, only a fool would bet against him."* The second was my mother's: *"Get the fuck away from my son!"*

My friends and family gave me the final push I needed.

"Besides, wouldn't it be funny if a blind man solved one of the world's greatest mysteries? I bet the Archivists would pull their hair out."

"No matter the cost. That's the beauty of life. We all have the right to choose what we want to do with what little time we have."

"My father was a fisherman. Not a drop of magic in his blood. Sadly, not all men are created equal."

"So, Dragonslayer, do you think you're still worthy of that title, or will you renounce it in shame?"

I shouted as I leapt toward the corrupted memory with my body nullified. I slammed my hand against it and a blinding light exploded out of it, consuming everything around us. Nothing remained but the endless white of a broken mind. A small quiet memory sprouted up around me. Zahra sat at a small wooden table reading a thin brown leather book. Dark crept up behind her, put his arms around the love of his life, and kissed her on the cheek. She smiled yet pushed him away, gesturing for him to join her at the table.

"What do you think happens when we die?" Zahra asked nonchalantly.

"Does it matter?" Dark responded. "We're alive. Who cares what happens after?"

"You're not curious?"

"Not really." He shifted in his seat. "Thinking about the after is a distraction from what happens in the now."

"That's good." Zahra gently put her book down on the table, eyes growing stern. "If something happens to me . . ." Shadows twisted around her, covering her mouth, and refusing to let her speak. Another voice took over. ". . . never forget me. Remember me forever and ever."

"That's not how it happened," I said quietly. I walked over to Zahra, put my hand on her shoulder, and let my warmth scare away Dark's shadows. I stared at the memory of my Mercenary mentor. "Let her speak, Dark."

Zahra smiled at me as the shadows that had bound her melted away. Then she looked at Dark. "If something happens to me, live on without me. Don't become obsessed with my memory. Find something else that makes you happy. I don't want the man I love to be consumed by the past."

Dark grabbed the sides of his head and screamed until the whiteness shattered around us like glass falling to the ground as I returned to the distorted church. Dark was still chained up with blood but screamed as loud as his memory-self had, writhing and wiggling to be free as the shadows tried to consume him. Dark reverted back to his human form and fell to his knees in front of me.

"So, did you figure it out, Michael?" he asked quietly. "Is it you? Is it me? Is it both of us? Who is the monster of this story?"

I stood firm. "We're all selfish monsters. Some of us are just more honest about it than others."

"So you *did* remember what I said that night," he huffed. "I'm so . . . tired, Michael. I can't go on without her. Enjoy the rest of your life. You've earned it. Will you do the honors?"

I raised the revolver, aiming the barrel at his head. "Nervous?"

Dark closed his eyes. "No. Is dying really that scary to you?"

I pulled the trigger, heard the shot, and felt the heat of the gun flow through the tips of my fingers as the bullet tore through Dark's forehead, brains and skull showering the moving floors of swirling darkness nearby. And then Dark fell backwards into the dark ocean and the shadows devoured him, tearing flesh away like a pack of animals. I had no doubt that his last thoughts had been of Zahra.

Serena landed next to me silently. "Michael. Where are the flowers? The shadows are getting closer. We need to bring you—"

A beam of light struck the area where I had last seen Dark's body, slowly lifting it out of the shadows like a puppet held up by strings. My Mercenary mentor met my gaze—alive again, but defeated and tired—muttered something I didn't understand, and then flew toward the door his mother had left through. The door slammed closed again with an endless echo.

"One life remains."

We glanced toward the flowers. Angelo had crawled his way to them—defying death like a cockroach—and claimed another flower, and now both his hands were burned to bone. The shadows were about to consume him and the last flower, but the madman cackled loudly. "I won't let my beloved be alone, so if I cannot be with her . . . Dark will have to suffice. Do you think she'll be a better parent than I was?"

The shadows tore him apart and left nothing behind but blood splatter and chips of bone. His freakishly white smile was the last thing that was visible before the shadows spat out his clothes . . . and the last flower sunk into the darkness, disappearing completely.

"We lost," Serena muttered. "How did we—"

I kissed her, interrupting her pleas. When we broke apart, I said, "Go toward the door the others left through. I'll be right behind you. I'm getting that last flower one way or another." And then, because I didn't want to leave her, I added, "I love you. I always will."

"I love you, too. Please come back to me."

I took a deep breath, gave her another kiss, and then ran to the edge of the platform and dove into the shadows where I had last seen the flower. The shadows tore at my body the moment we connected. I was just able to make out its glimmering light amidst the darkness. They stripped my flesh off me in long thin strips as I swam through them for the fallen flower. My muscles deteriorated, my exposed bones were gnawed on, and pain radiated through my body as I continued. There was no way this could end any other way. My persistence was the only thing I was truly proud of, and so I continued . . . a defiant fool until the very bitter end.

I reached out with my bony hand, taking the flower between my index and middle fingers. The flower set my entire body aflame, banishing the shadows around me and restoring my body to how it had been as I slowly rose back upward toward the church. I twisted the flower between my fingers, admiring it for as long as I could as I weighed the name of the one I wanted to bring back in my mouth. It should have been easy, but of course it never would be.

I have always been a selfish person. A man who tried his best but always came up short. But in that moment I wanted to be a hero. To be recognized as something more than a sad, lonely boy. I was lucky enough to have the privilege of power and opportunity growing up. I had access to magic, and that alone gave me more opportunities than others could ever dream of. Let alone all the benefits of having the Kingman last name—even when we were in semi-exile. But there was one person I had never forgotten, who had never been given that chance to learn and grow and find his own place in the world.

I am Michael Kingman, known by many names. Hated by some but loved by others. This was *my* story, but, in the end . . . it was *ours* as well. It was not my name I said out loud to return to life . . . it was *his*.

"Jamal Wiccard!"

The final beam of light blew open the iron door and brought out a small boy with short black hair. He was wearing the clothes he had died in and carried a replica of the stuffed dragon that had been dyed red with his own blood. He landed in my arms and I carried him to the door where Serena was waiting as the shadows retreated down into the sea and the church returned to its original form.

"I hate you," she said quietly, taking Jamal from me. "You were supposed to come back with me. This isn't how it was supposed to end."

"Why do I deserve to live more than him?" I asked. "There was no reason that would have justified my choice. So I made the one that felt right." I ruffled his hair. "I'm sorry I lied to you. That we won't get our happily ever after."

"We will," she said passionately. "You don't get to walk away from me and our life together. I'll find a way to bring you back to life. One where no one dies and destruction isn't left in my wake." She stared at me as tears began to form. "Do you understand, Michael? I'll find you again. No matter what I have to do."

"I know you will." I kissed her again, softly and slowly, lingering on her lips before we separated. I didn't know how long I'd be waiting here for her, so I enjoyed it while I could. "I love you, Serena. I'll see you again soon."

"You will," she promised. Then she turned her back to me and carried Jamal through the red door and back to life. She looked over her shoulder, shouted something I couldn't make out, and then disappeared in a shimmer of dying fireflies.

The door closed behind her silently.

I rubbed the back of my neck, stifled a yawn, and then walked to the nearest pew and took a seat. I was so tired. I had fought for so long, endured so much, that nothing seemed more appealing than taking a quick nap. Serena would find me again. I knew she would. We were bound by fate and had chosen each other anyway. She would go to the edge of the world and back to find a way for me to return to her side.

This life had been beautiful. Filled with ups and downs. Anger and love. But it had been all mine. Ah. The time of youth. The time of stupid decisions, lasting friendships, and moments I would never forget. The world would continue without me. And that made me happy . . .

My eyelids grew heavier, and I had to use all my strength to stifle another yawn. My head rested against the back of the pew as if it were a pillow. My body tightened as if all my skin was being taken over by stone.

I would never forget my friends and family. Or that moment when I had been a hero. Maybe . . . just this once . . . I had lived up to the idealistic fantasy that had filled my mind as a kid.

I'd just take a small nap while I waited . . .

I couldn't wait to see them all again . . .

My memories might not be there . . .

No, I would be fine . . .

It wouldn't hurt . . .

To just close . . .

My eye . . .

Gwe . . .

Ma . . .

S . . .

And so a nameless boy fell asleep in the pews of a place between life and death, waiting for his beloved to find him again.

PART 6:

FLOWERS LEFT BEHIND

"Did you do good? Did you do bad? Did you make mistakes?
Did you learn? Did you cry? Did you smile? Yes?
Then you have lived a beautiful life."

—King Isaac Hollow

A LEGACY OBTAINED

Serena Hollow stumbled through the lockless door and back to reality. Her grace and poise were left wanting as her muscles admitted they had nothing left to give. She hit the cool tile with a thud as the lock on the door shimmered out of existence. The boy she had been carrying fell from her arms, awakening suddenly with a series of groans. Her time in that afterlife was over, and without another way . . . she would never see Michael again.

Naomi and Chloe were at her side quickly, pulling her up and moving her to the nearest pew. The shrine was abandoned except for those who claimed Michael as family: Naomi, Chloe, Trey, Lyon, Symon, Sebastian, Kai, and Joey. They all waited for Serena to speak. To answer the questions none of them could utter: Was it over? Had they won?

"Michael isn't returning," she said quietly. "We beat Angelo, and Dark, and Michael had complete control of the situation . . . He was able to return, but he gave it to another." She remembered his smile. How bright and warm and sad it had been. Then she gestured to the boy she had been carrying. "At the end, he chose to be a hero."

"Jamal?" Trey asked, voice wavering. His whole body was shaking, and he dropped his gun to the ground with a clatter. Trey fell to his knees, crawling toward the boy as if scared he would vanish if he approached too suddenly. "Is that you?"

"Trey?" the boy said, slowly rising. He rubbed the sleep out of his eyes. "What's going on? Where are we? I was in the graveyard with Michael. I don't—"

Trey tackled the boy to the ground, hugging him and sobbing. The boy didn't understand what was happening and tried to free himself, but Trey held on to him, refusing to let him. "Thank you, Michael. Thank you. Thank you. Thank you. Thank you."

As the brothers reunited, Lyon asked the next question: "What about Angelo?"

"He gave up his life to bring Katherine back."

"And the third life?"

"We killed Dark," Serena said. "But Angelo brought him back almost immediately."

Lyon cursed in frustration. "So the bastard knew how to be a good father after all."

"Delightful," Kai huffed. "From one member of the Shade family to another. Will Katherine come for us as well?"

"I don't know," Serena said. "All I know is Michael isn't coming back and we'll soon forget everything about him." Her eyes began to prickle with pain and tears. "This wasn't how it was supposed to end. We were supposed to be *happy*."

Silence permeated the group. Naomi skulked away and found the bottle of liquor prepared for the wedding and all the glasses that accompanied it. She handed out glasses, poured for everyone, and said, "Then we need to do this quickly before any of us sleep, pass out, or die as we find out if we're on the right side of that Mercenary war out there."

"So this is his legacy. I wonder if he would have liked it," Trey said quietly, looking around the room and then to the familiar ring on his middle finger. Jamal sat on his lap, still confused. The brothers sniffed the drink and had the same painful reaction. "What is this? It smells rotten."

"It's scaro," Sebastian said with a wide smile. "It'll put some hair on your chest and make a man of you, East Sider."

"Who *are* you?" Trey asked.

Sebastian bowed dramatically. "Captain Sebastian of the I-don't-got-a-ship-yet. I'm the twenty-seventh-most-feared pirate on the Sea of Statues."

"Is that supposed to impress me?"

"Obviously! I'm kind of a big—"

"He's Dawn's brother," Kai interrupted.

Trey nodded solemnly, muttered apologies, and then looked toward Michael's body in the corner of the room. It was covered as modestly as possible, but they could still see he had died with a smile on his face. Adreann's body was beside it. Erica's body was already gone, taken to the crypts by some of the clan guards who had refused to abandon their home even in the face of insurmountable odds. "Naomi, we'll need to deal with his body before we sleep. We promised Michael we would."

"I know," she said, pouring the dregs of the bottle of scaro into her own glass. "Let's find the biggest tree in the area and bury him under there. He would have liked that."

"Make sure you take care of it," Serena pleaded. "Even if we forget about him, I want him to know he was loved." Her throat felt as if it was closing up. "All he ever wanted was to belong."

"What should we do with Adreann?" Naomi asked softly. "I hate him, but we shouldn't just leave him here for carrion birds to pick at."

"I'll have Archivists collect it and take him to the Royal Crypts in Hollow. They'll be able to move without politics influencing them. Hopefully," Serena said as tears began to fall. "Wanderer's mercy, this wasn't how it was supposed to go. My family is gone. It was meant to be *me*. Why did this happen?"

None answered, but one by one each raised their glass toward Michael's body.

"At times we all hated him, but here we are . . . remembering a man who did his best. And that is all we can hope to achieve in our short lives," Symon began. "To the King of the Imbeciles."

"To the worst brother I ever had," Lyon added.

"To the King Killer," Chloe said.

"To my best friend," Naomi said with a smile, arm around Chloe's waist.

"To the Dragonslayer," Kai said, and then instructed Joey not to drink the liquid he had been given.

"To the man who pushed me to be better," Trey said.

"To the friend who never forgot me," Jamal said.

Serena got to her feet, wiped her tears away, pointed her glass toward the lockless door, and then said, "To Michael Kingman. This is not the end of us. I promise you that."

And despite the grief or the concern any of them might have felt at her words, everyone drank their scaro in a single gulp. Only Trey and Kai made faces afterward, the others already used to the pain. They crushed their glasses beneath their boots, gathered their thoughts and belongings, and then prepared for another fight.

There was some discussion on where everyone would go now. Trey, Jamal, and Lyon would return to Hollow with Kai and Joey before they went back to the Institute of Amalgamation. Trey still wanted to change Hollow from the inside out so the unjust system would never harm another family, and Lyon just wanted to be with his wife and child. Chloe and Naomi were headed west to lands where they were nobodies rather than the Ravens they spent their lives fighting to become. Sebastian was returning to the Sea of Statues to continue his legend and maybe finally get a ship of his own. But it was Symon's answer that shocked Serena most of all.

Symon put a hand on her shoulder as they stared at the lockless door together. "I'll stay awake for as long as I can to record his story. Without him to correct me . . . some things won't ring true to those that knew him. The world will see his hate while we'll know his love. If they even read it." The Recorder paused again. "After that, I'll go over the knowledge I have about the Wolven Kings. I may not be able to free Gwen as he wanted to . . . but I'll do my best. One of us must remain on top of them. Their war may be halted, but it's far from over."

"If I continue to fight," she whispered, "will I be throwing away the life he gave me?"

Symon forced a smile. "It's only a wasted life if you forget to appreciate what's around you. A life focused on the past will bring regret, just as a life focused on the future will create anxiety. We are in control of nothing but the now. If you want to continue fighting, do it for yourself. Not Michael."

That wasn't the answer Serena was looking for. She needed guidance. Or a sign. Or a person to run away with. Or . . . something that would give her direction. She wasn't a queen anymore. She didn't have her Kingman. All of those around her had chosen their new paths. So who did she want to be now? Where would she go? Would she reclaim her throne from Emelia, or would she choose another path? Could she even be something other than a queen?

The walk out of the palace felt long and desolate, burn marks and fallen weapons littering the path back to the city. The others told her things that were important for Serena to know: Jay Prince—*another* version of him; it was complicated—and Emelia had escaped and were likely going to regroup in Hollow now that they had the throne. She didn't care. It was just a stupid stone chair. It held no importance for her. Not while Michael was gone. Not while she couldn't choose her ending.

And so, for all the fools for love there had ever been, the one that was created during their walk to Vargo was the scariest of them all. She would find a way to bring Michael back. No matter what it cost her. No matter the price. No matter where she had to go. This would not be the end to their story.

"Who did it?" Alexis screamed, sprinting toward them. Her hair stuck to her skin like wet clothes, her face was flushed, and the tips of her fingers were stained with gunpowder. She held a flintlock pistol in her left hand. "Who killed Michael? Which one of you is responsible?"

"Me," Serena said, stepping forward before one of the others could claim Michael's death as their doing. "Whatever consequences there are, I will bear them myself."

Alexis went pale but spoke as best she could. "Wanderer's mercy. What did he do? Did he know? No . . . he couldn't have, but—"

"Know what?" Serena snapped.

Alexis motioned for Serena to step through the entrance gate.

A horde of Mercenaries were outside. At least a quarter of Regal Company. Maybe more. And at the sight of Serena, they fell to one knee like a wave slowly retreating out to sea. It spanned the entire road down to the docks. Thousands of Mercenaries bowed to her and her alone. Orbis Company was off to the side, eyeing the controllable force of nature and Serena as if they carried the same amount of power.

"Michael killed Liam, and then you killed Michael," Alexis explained. "And Mercenaries have a code: the conqueror's will is absolute." She gulped. "They're yours to command."

Serena laughed hysterically until the others started to look at her with concern, wondering if she had finally snapped. If the loss of Michael had been too much to bear. But once she collected herself, she smiled and then said, "Don't you all get the joke? I inherited his dream. I'm the Mercenary Queen."

EPILOGUE

THE MANY LEGACIES
OF A FORGOTTEN BOY

Dark was reborn in a holy place surrounded by flowers, alone and sense-less. He woke with a start, as if falling from a great height, and then began to slam at the ceiling that was right in front of his nose. He hit it with the palm of his hand, slowly and steadily, and then faster and stronger as his breath became more ragged. With a great scream, his fist burst through the wood he was being contained in, tearing open an exit. The Black Death tumbled out of his coffin with a curse.

"I see you've finally woke up. Good," a nearby man said. "Now we can begin."

Dark looked up and saw four people sitting around a table. It was filled with fine delicacies on golden plates and wine poured into crystal goblets. A portrait of his father in his military uniform hung on the far wall above an old, bloodstained divan. The man to the left was some-one Dark could never forget—High Noble Charles Domet. He twirled a slender knife in a small circle as the tip was pressed against the wood. A young man sat next to the immortal. He had his auburn hair cut short and tight, a birthmark on his left temple, and the build of a Thebian Berserker with a war hammer across his lap. There were more scars on his body than streaks of paint on a masterpiece. Dark's mother, Katherine Naverre, as young as she had been when she died, sat across from the immortal and his soldier. Her arms were folded, and she wore a threadbare yellow dress. The one she had been buried in for over a decade.

"Davis," Katherine began. "Domet told me what happened. How your father tried to bring me back to life and how you tried to bring Zahra back. I'm sorry you weren't successful." She crossed her legs and took a sip of wine, her expression souring as she swallowed. "I've decided we're going to work with Domet to bring your father and Zahra back to life. Just as your father should have done from the beginning. His pride blinded him and I'm to blame for that. Usually I keep him in check, but no matter. Our family will be reunited soon enough."

Dark's voice was raw, but he croaked out, "What's going on?"

"We've made a deal," Domet answered. "You're going to help me kill the Wolven Kings so I can finally die in peace. And I'm going to help you open one of the other lockless doors to the afterlife." He huffed. "Maybe this time you won't be thwarted by a Hollow who didn't even have a Kingman to guide her."

Dark didn't respond, finally focusing on the fourth person at the table. It was a man a few years younger than himself. With messy brown hair, deep-amber eyes, a crown brand on the side of his neck, and a smile that he wanted to beat out of existence. The man left his seat, rounded the table, and then stopped in front of Dark as he remained on the ground. Why was he so happy? What reason did he have to be so . . . content?

"Hey, Dark, you didn't think the Reborn Titan would be the end of our relationship, did you?" The man made a flourish toward the others at the table. "And don't bother mentioning me to them. Only you can see me. You didn't want me to leave your side and now I never will."

"Who are you?" Dark muttered, forcing himself to stand. He didn't know why, but he couldn't appear weak in front of this boy. "*What* are you?"

"I'm you, but better." The boy met his eyes and smiled broadly. Amber into a greyish red. "What? Still don't get it? Fine. I'll be clearer: I'm an infection in your mind. A disease you can't cure. A madness you can't ignore. A parting gift from your favorite person in the whole world. And a legacy that can't be erased. My name is—"

ONE NAP LATER . . .

A boy awakens in a too-bright church that hurts his eyes and blurs his vision. He stumbles trying to stand, knees turning weak and inward, and he crashes back down into the wooden pews. His throat is dry and his stomach growls, a twisty knotty pain substituting for the food he craves. There's nothing on his mind. He can't remember his name, his home, his family, his beliefs, or anything about how he ended up here. Only that he did, and that punishment seems fitting enough.

Only when his head stops throbbing does he realize there's a crumpled piece of paper in his right hand, lodged there as if stuffed in a stone statue's closed hand. He unfurls it and reads.

I remember you. And I'll find you again. No matter where you are.
Just wait a little longer. You will come home.
I promise that.
With all my heart,

The sender's name is nothing but scratches.

Regardless, the boy doesn't recognize the handwriting nor understand the letter's meaning. Who's looking for him? And why? This place is his home. It's all he's ever known. And yet . . .

There are doors in the distance. One towering monster of iron that looks as if it would take a dozen men simply to budge it open. Three smaller doors are next to it. One red, one blue, and one black. He checks the door handle on the red one first. It doesn't budge. Nor does the blue one. But the black one creeps open at his touch, with nothingness behind it. The boy doesn't flinch or hesitate, curiosity leading him forward.

His skin feels as if it's being pulled in all directions, stretched out past the point of snapping. And then the pain stops, his feet and hands collide with the ground, and the boy has arrived in a strange new place. Bits of rock float around him, singing strange songs like a child's one-sided conversation. The ground is grey, lumpy, and craters stretch out to the horizon like an endless sea. Everything has a slight bluish tint from the massive thing in the sky, and the ground is unstable. Six huge pieces of rock, excluding the one he's standing on currently, float around him like a broken plane of glass.

There is a man a slight distance away from him. His clothes are in tatters, his hair is long and unkempt, and his skin is paler than that of the dead. A giant beast lies behind him, snoring contentedly. Its wings are attached to its front limbs. It's a Wyvern—not a dragon—and for some reason the boy is more certain of that than of anything else since he awoke.

The man scoops up rocks around him, whispers to them, and then hurls them at the massive round thing in the sky. They flash a bright red, blue, or white before disappearing from view. The boy wonders where these rocks are going and if the messages the man speaks into them will ever be heard by others. He doubts it. There is nothing here but stone and dust. And the massive thing in the sky is probably no different. Is there even anyone else in the world but these two?

As the boy stands, crunching a rock beneath his boots, the man turns to him. There's a symbol of a crying wolf head on his lapel, barely visible, almost withered away by time.

"Who are you?" the man asks.

"Who cares who I am," the boy snaps back. "Who are *you*?"

Rocks tumble out of the man's hands. "I am Mikel of the Wolves, third son of the man who was unrivaled under the sun. Some call me a Wolven King, while others called me the Wanderer." The man stifles a laugh. "Some consider me a prophet. But all I truly am is my husband's prisoner in this forsaken place, doomed to spend my life shouting warnings to those below me." The Wolven King approaches the boy, but the boy does not cower, standing straight and still. He feels stupidly brave and maybe, for a moment, that is all he ever was. "You have the arm that denotes my brother's servants. And you have an amber eye. Are you—"

The boy doesn't hear the man's next words, so he smiles and shakes his head. "I'm nobody."

"Nobody," the man repeats, turning away from the boy. He reaches down, grabs a lumpy rock, and then hands it to him. It shines a dull blue. "Speak into it and then hurl it at the planet in front of us. If you are truly nobody, nothing you can say will cause any trouble."

The boy takes the rock from the man. "And if I'm not nobody?"

"Are you lying to me?"

He shakes his head. "If I was somebody . . . I'm not anymore. I don't remember anything about my life."

"You're a Forgotten, then," the man mumbles. "But how did you end up . . . It doesn't matter. There's only one way to find out, isn't there?"

The boy cradles the rock in his hands, twisting it around like a toy. "I can say anything to it?"

"Anything you want. As long as it's the truth."

The boy raises the rock to his lips, closes his eyes, and then whispers his reply to the letter he found tucked into his hands when he woke:

There's a boy on the moon waiting to be found. Whoever you are, will you remember me?

ACKNOWLEDGMENTS

The idea of Michael Kingman was created in 2010 in my high school AP English class when I was trying to figure out how I was going to come up with a way to get out of writing an essay on *The Grapes of Wrath*. I hadn't read it, and really didn't have any intention to. Obviously, I wasn't the best student, and truthfully, nothing of that version of Michael Kingman remains in the current iteration. Broken down and rewritten too many times for me to count. Except for the core idea of Michael's character: What is a legacy? How is it created? And how does it transform into something new once someone's gone?

Twelve years later, I've done what that sixteen-year-old version of me hoped to do. To take a broken boy with the weight of the world on his shoulders and turn him into someone worth remembering. His legacy was written—all the sharp and pointy bits left intact—and hopefully you've all enjoyed reading about Michael Kingman and his messy memory problems. But after so many years, there are so many people to thank for helping me get to the point where Michael's story exists in print.

570   ACKNOWLEDGMENTS

First, my thanks to my agent, Joshua Bilmes. He was the first person outside of my immediate family to believe in the story I was attempting to create. His friendship and belief in me have made all the hard times easier, and I cannot thank him enough for everything he's done. My thanks also extend to John Berlyn and all those at JABberwocky Literary Agency. They go above and beyond and are the absolute best people to work with.

Next, my sincerest thanks to my editors, Joe Monti and Gillian Red-fearn. Joe's compassion, willingness to listen, and ability to home in on what I was struggling with made many issues I would have had non-existent, and for that I will always be thankful. Gillian's attention to detail and just general awesomeness made the book better after edits than when I began writing it. Without them, the books wouldn't be a fraction of what they are today.

In the U.S., thank you to Jennifer Long, Lexy Alemao, Jela Lewter, Allison Green, Emily Arzeno, Caroline Pallotta, Steve Breslin, and Kayleigh Webb for everything they've done on the book.

In the UK, thank you to Will O'Mullane, Aine Feeny, Claire Ormsby-Potter, and everyone else at Gollancz for their hard work on the series.

I'd be remiss without mentioning Benjamin Carré and Richard Anderson for their killer art. Thanks for creating the absolute coolest covers for a book series. These are the covers I would have looked to for inspiration when I was younger, and now they're about my book! Insane. And thank you especially to all the fantastic writers and members of the book community who have helped me grow over these past few years, including Brandon Sanderson, James Islington, Tamora Pierce, Jeremy Szal, and many others I've had the pleasure of getting to know better over the years.

Thank you to all those outside of publishing that I call my friends and family. You've kept me sane over the years and probably went slightly insane listening to me talk about Michael for so long. To my mother and father, grandmother, my family, the Church of the Overlord, Bots Ambassadors and their plus-ones, Kyle VanLark, Penny, and Erin McKeown. And thank you to my grandfather for all his support over the years. He passed a day after I handed *Voyage* in. I miss him so much every day.

Last, thank you to the readers, reviewers, and booksellers who have stuck by me and Michael. This book was a labor of love, and I hope you've enjoyed it. Here's to many more stories to be told.